GW00703080

Hatred, persecution, fear, terrorism·
around the world. This book takes ⌐
side, to the hope for peace. I highly recommend it for peace ⌐⌐⌐⌐
everywhere.

—U.S. Congressman Mark Siljander (ret.)
Founder, Trac5
Author, *A Deadly Misunderstanding*

SHTD will make you squirm, cry, and smile. You will squirm as
you realize that we are all fraught with stereotypes about Christians and Muslims. You will be confronted with the hypocrisy of
your own faith, regardless of what side of the chasm you find yourself. You will cry as you are confronted with the ugliness of hate
and the gentle power of self-sacrifice. You will smile because love is
stronger than hate, and evil doesn't have to win.

—Erik Lincoln, Peace Activist
Author of the best-selling series, "Peace Generation"

It's easy to demonize those different from us. It's a bit harder to
research facts in order to understand them. It's even more of a
stretch to step into their world and to walk in their shoes. But Jim
Baton has gone one step further: he's told their story. The story is
about conflicts between Christians and Muslims in Indonesia, a
country where Baton has lived for many years, but it is more than
that. It's also a story about us, whether Christian or Muslim. It
challenges us to look at the truths about ourselves, about the preju-
dices, ignorance and anger that are in each of us, and that, if left
untouched by God's love, can spill out to ravage nations, communi-
ties and families. Yet there is hope. God can and does change hearts,
as Baton so beautifully testifies to in this warm and uplifting story.

—Dr. Rick Love
President, Peace Catalyst International
Consultant for Christian-Muslim Relations

SOMEONE
HAS TO DIE

JIM BATON

CREATION
HOUSE

SOMEONE HAS TO DIE by Jim Baton
Published by Creation House
A Charisma Media Company
600 Rinehart Road
Lake Mary, Florida 32746
www.charismamedia.com

Unless otherwise noted, all Scripture quotations are from *The Message: The Bible in Contemporary English*, copyright © 1993, 1994, 1995, 1996, 2000, 2001, 2002. Used by permission of NavPress Publishing Group.

The poem in chapter 95 is "The International" from *Selected Poems*, by Goenawan Mohamad (Katakita, 2004).

Design Director: Bill Johnson
Cover design by Nathan Morgan

Visit the author's website: www.jimbaton.com

Library of Congress Cataloging in Publication Data: 2011931526
International Standard Book Number: 978-1-61638-922-2
E-book International Standard Book Number: 978-1-61638-923-9

While the author has made every effort to provide accurate telephone numbers and Internet addresses at the time of publication, neither the publisher nor the author assumes any responsibility for errors or for changes that occur after publication.

First edition

12 13 14 15 16 — 9 8 7 6 5 4 3 2 1
Printed in Canada

Acknowledgments

Thank you, Katherena Higashi, for understanding the message of this book and telling me I needed to write it! Erik Lincoln, thanks for believing in this project and for your whole family's insights. Thanks, Maren Mauvais, for your medical expertise. Jaci Miller and April Frazier, your editing and mentoring were invaluable. Mark Siljander and Rick Love, your lives are an inspiration.

And special thanks to my wife, whose dream-life with God continues to take me places I never imagined I'd go.

❧ Prologue ❧

June

Washington, DC

IT WASN'T THE first Presidential Prayer Breakfast Louis Staunton had attended, but it was by far the most interesting. The third-term congressman from Michigan had been intrigued when the DC gossip mill had "exposed the secret" that the president had invited a Muslim cleric to open the meeting in prayer. What was it his esteemed colleague from Alabama had commented? "It'll be a cold day in hell before I share my bacon and grits with Akmad Jihad!" Louis couldn't help smiling at the image of the imam explaining politely to the senator from Bama that he couldn't touch the bacon since it wasn't halal.

It turned out to be a perfect day to announce summer's arrival, with both sun and a light, cool breeze welcoming everyone to the outdoor spread elegantly fitted for a breakfast. The cherry blossoms cheerily responded to the sunshine and ignored the cold shoulders of many senators and representatives, faithful attendees in previous years who were conspicuously absent this year. And yet a couple of the more right-wing representatives who ran in the pack of alpha-wolf Pastor Tim Thompson, head of the Christian Conservative Alliance, pleasantly surprised Louis by coming early. He was planning to thank them for their gesture of support after the breakfast. However, when Imam Khalil Jailani was introduced, Pastor Tim stood from the table, dramatically shuffled his feet as though wiping off the dust of this travesty, and marched out with posse in tow. Imam Jailani seemed less bothered than the president, whose stony face matched the color of the strawberry parfait set before him.

Louis felt bad for them both but felt no ill-will toward the dissidents; he had once been in their shoes, and many of his constituency still were. Most Americans had no problems with the Muslim world—as long as they stayed far away and used their bombs on themselves. But with the growing number of Muslim immigrants seeking a new start in America, even in freezing Michigan, Louis knew it was better that people like himself and the president become their first friends in America before the Islamophobes or terrorist recruiters came knocking at their doors.

Imam Jailani's brief remarks were excellent bridge-builders, as Louis knew they would be. He had met Jailani years ago at the dedication ceremony of the Islamic Center of America, the largest mosque in the US, built in Dearborn, Michigan. They had stayed in touch over the years, and as Michigan's Muslim population grew to sixth largest amongst the fifty states, Louis had relied more and more on advice from friends like Jailani on how to represent them effectively.

Louis had heard Jailani pray publicly before and liked the simplicity and sincerity with which he addressed the Almighty. Today was no different. Other than opening his prayer with the Arabic phrase, *"Bismillah ir-Rahman ir-Rohim,"* "In the name of God the Most Merciful, Most Compassionate," the imam had prayed in English, as Louis had recommended. He had stuck his neck out suggesting this idea and this man to the president, but he knew the imam would come through. Khalil radiated the same passion for peacemaking that Louis did and was willing to face some rock-throwing to make an enemy into a friend. Finding same-hearted Muslims used to be Louis's hobby. Now it consumed more and more of his time. Men like Khalil held the keys to world peace. Islam needed a reformation, and Louis believed new leadership from within would be a thousand times more effective than wiping out the Taliban or removing a dictator.

But any disappointment at the anemic turnout was wiped away by what happened after the breakfast ended. Louis had stayed behind to watch the US Secret Service whisk Imam Jailani safely away, avoiding the angry demonstration at the main entrance to the White House. He thought the president had also disappeared when a USSS agent tapped him on the shoulder. "The president is hoping you have a few minutes to chat."

The president had the tall and lanky body of a basketball player, a good four or five inches taller than Staunton. The man's chiseled jaw and steely gaze could be on motivational posters titled "Determination."

Louis was working on a double chin inherited from his mama, who deep-fried everything, and his eyes were more soft than steely. His dark, bald head brought back images of Louis Armstrong, though he was named after Joe Louis the boxer. Yes, Louis was still standing in his namesake's ring, but facing opponents far more difficult to knock down, much less knock out—prejudice, religious radicalism, hatred. Yet, Louis was as determined a man as the president in his own peace-loving way.

"Mr. President, I appreciate what you did today. I'm sorry about my colleagues' inappropriate reactions."

The president waved his hand in dismissal and smiled, "Don't worry Louis. I know what we're getting into here. I'm in this for the end game—for my children, not my polls. Right now we need every friend in the Muslim world we can get."

"Yes, sir. Khalil can open doors for us. He's connecting me with several key leaders around the world right now."

"Actually, Louis, that's what I asked you here to talk about. I've been informed you're planning a trip to Indonesia in October to meet a presidential candidate."

"Yes, sir. We just set this up two weeks ago. You've got good intel."

"The best." The president smiled again and drew closer to Staunton's ear. "You know I like you, Louis, and I'm behind what you're doing. That's why I'm asking Secret Service to send six agents to watch your back; I can't afford to lose an ally like you in this fight."

"Thank you, sir. That's very kind."

"But here's the deal: the current president of Indonesia may be more of a man of war than of peace, but right now he's at war with terrorists and doing a bang-up job flushing them out. This candidate you're meeting, from what I hear, is a sweet-talker, but I don't know if he'll carry a big enough stick. You know what I mean?"

"Yes, sir, you want me to stick to peacemaking and stay out of politics." The president nodded ever so slightly and added nothing else, so Louis guessed this meeting was over.

"Honestly, sir, I'm looking forward to the day when that's exactly and only what I'll be doing."

Camp Hudaibiyah, Moro, Southern Philippines

A fist like a hammer pummeled Saifullah square on the jaw. His martial arts skills had mostly kept the younger man at bay, but his own punches and kicks felt like they were connecting with a rock wall. *I can't afford another mistake like that one. Come on, focus! Find his weakness!*

Saifullah licked the blood from his split lip as if it were coconut milk. He locked eyes with his opponent and stretched his lips in a wide grin, exacerbating the bleeding on purpose. He circled with cautious steps, feeling the loose rocks with his bare feet for slippery ground he might lure the larger man onto. A patch of larger stones felt more tenuous than the smaller pebbles around it, and without breaking his stare, he curled his two fingers, calling the man forward while himself inching backward.

"Where did you learn to fight, little brother? From some *kafir* woman in a brothel? Did she leave you in as much pain as I'm going to?"

The giant grunted and lunged at Saifullah, who didn't sidestep but waited till he knew the man's foot was in his trap. Then he suddenly dropped under the flying right aimed at his head to a crouch on his left leg. He swung his right leg out away from the man, then in a circle brought it back with a thud behind the giant's right knee. The man's forward right leg lost its footing, extending forward violently, leaving his left leg far behind in a cheerleader's splits. The sound of ripping pants and the sight of the burly man grabbing for his crotch sent a howl up from the crowd.

Saifullah raised his hands in victory just for a moment to remind them all who he was. Then he offered his hand to his groaning comrade, who was not yet ready to stand.

"It's not about size, strength or speed," Saifullah spoke loud enough for all the new recruits to hear. "Keep your focus, control your emotions. Anger, fear, these are just as much our enemies as the cursed Americans. Don't attack until you find your enemy's weakness. If you die, die for glory, not because you were stupid."

"*Isy kariman au mut syahidan!*" The martyr's cry rose from the crowd. They might have all broken out in spontaneous sparring right there if Umar hadn't strode into the clearing. War cries turned to silent salutes, and when Umar lifted his chin toward the barracks everyone hustled off.

Saifullah barely had time to grab the arm of his defeated foe and whisper, "Don't forget you owe me a pack of clove cigarettes!"

When only the two of them were left, Umar and Saifullah sat on a log at the edge of the clearing. The evening breeze rustled the palm trees, cooling this humid paradise for a few hours. A foot-long lizard paused to stare at them. Neither man paid it any attention.

Umar began. "What do you think of this new boatload of Indonesian recruits?"

Saifullah's eyes had that faraway look. "I miss the old days."

"What do you mean?"

"Remember back in '98 when Noordin was here? We'd spend all day memorizing the *Duras* Afghan training manual, learning guerilla tactics, bomb-making, and we always had enough energy for simulations at night. We had *passion*. These new recruits come in hardly knowing the principles of *Mausu'ah Jihad Afghan*. Sure they're bigger and stronger, but they give up too easily. For the last week I've whipped the butts of these kids half my age for cigarettes and not a one has come back the next night wanting to fight me again. Not a one! Noordin would have fought me every night till he won or died trying."

"Yes, it's true. Most of these recruits will never become like Noordin, or a hero of any kind. But we still need foot soldiers in this army. And who knows? Maybe hidden in this pile of rubble is a diamond in the rough."

"Have you heard what these kids talk about at night before they sleep? They talk about mosquitoes, sore muscles, Filipino girls. Is that all they care about? Remember the debates Nasir Abbas would challenge us with? Hambali arguing we should bomb churches, Zulkarnaen countering that the Prophet never attacked a house of worship. I never agreed with Hambali when he carried out those Christmas Eve church attacks in Jakarta, and I know Zulkarnaen never forgave him, because he set us back maybe ten years. But aren't those the kind of discussions you want to hear? I'd take one Hambali over one hundred of these spineless whiners any day."

Umar said nothing. Saifullah wondered if he'd gone too far bringing up Hambali, knowing how close Umar was to Zulkarnaen, a leader of mythic proportions in Jemaah Islamiyah (JI)—the visionary who supported the attacks on the Jakarta Stock Exchange, Bali Bomb I, Marriott Bomb I, and the Australian Embassy. Though in deep hiding, Zulkarnaen was more active today than he had been from '99–'04, when Indonesia first received their calling to holy war. But soon the hiding would be over. And Saifullah was destined to lead JI to even greater glory.

Umar pulled a water bottle out of his camouflage vest pocket and took a swig. Saifullah thought how in the old days they would have passed the bottle around. But now Umar was careful and shared his water with no one. Umar was also still alive—Noordin, Dulmatin, most of his brothers were not.

Umar wiped his mouth on his sleeve and met Saifullah's eyes. "It's time."

"It's time for what?" Saifullah asked cautiously.

"It's time for redemption."

Could it really be? After over a year of hiding in Moro, hiding from his failure, could his day of redemption finally be here? No one at the camp but Umar knew. But he knew.

"Talk to me."

"In four months' time there will be an event in Jakarta. An American congressman, a Christian, will be meeting with that swine traitor Ramadani. Other foreign diplomats are likely to be present. And hear this—the event will be held in the very building of your previous...disappointment."

Failure. Just say it, Umar. My previous failure.

"Am I in charge of the operation?"

"Yes, we have a sleeper in place, and a safe house with all the...necessities. All you have to do is coordinate the mission and recruit the 'bride.'"

"This isn't much time."

"I know, but because of the location this is too good a chance for you to miss. We just got word on this today, and I've already arranged a pump boat to stand by for you in South Mindanao. Fifteen hours to Sangihe, on to North Sulawesi, and by the end of this week you'll be recruiting a 'bride' already. My suggestion is you recruit in Sulawesi—Java is too hot right now. Densus 88 has spies everywhere. Bring in someone from outside Java, and they'll attract less suspicion. Of course all this I've arranged assuming you'll say yes."

"Thanks, Umar. I've waited a long time for this."

"Redemption, my friend."

"Redemption."

"Al-jihad sabiluna."

"Al-jihad sabiluna."

❧ Chapter 1 ❧

July
Banjarmasin, South Kalimantan Province, Indonesia

*H*E'S SITTING AT *a table with his family eating meatball soup at Bakso Mawar, his wife Siti's favorite restaurant. His boys Iqbal and Syukran are smiling. Everybody's happy.*

Until the waiter comes with the bill. He recognizes the waiter's face. An old comrade from Afghan. He tries to hide his face, but the waiter recognizes him. "Hey, aren't you—" But before the waiter can say his name he jumps up, knocking his chair back, pulls his wife and kids out of there, yelling, "Get out! Get out!"

Outside a group of men run by carrying machine guns. A bomb explodes. He considers pushing his family back in the restaurant to be safe, but fears the waiter will talk about him, so he pushes them into the ditch. Siti screams. He looks down to see that he pushed her onto the corpses of dead bodies. "Stay down!" he orders, and he runs, and runs and runs. His legs start to feel like lead. His sandal breaks, and its flop flop against the asphalt is drowned out by his pounding heart. He feels the hot breath of his pursuers. He even thinks he hears them calling his name, but he's too terrified to look back. He sees a wall ahead and knows he'll be safe on the other side, but he's slowing down. He'll never get there.

At the foot of the wall they catch him. They start beating him mercilessly. Suddenly he's a baby, dressed all in white, powerless, and he knows he's going to die. He sees the first red blotch splash on his clothes, the red of his own blood. He cries out for the last time...

1

Abdullah sat up in bed, his chest pounding, his eyes wide open. The dreams were getting worse. He looked at the clock. Four a.m. Soon he'd hear the call to prayer from the neighborhood *musholla* and be up anyway.

He leaned over to whisper into Siti's ear: "I'm going to *sholat* at the *musholla*." No response. Abdullah dragged his forty-year-old body out of bed and put on some blue running shorts and a white tank top. He wasn't really going to morning prayers like the other neighborhood men his age, but his wife preferred that fantasy to what Abdullah did most mornings.

He downed a glass of water and grabbed his running shoes off the shoe rack by the door. He'd need the hydration. Banjarmasin could get down to the low seventies each morning, but the high humidity meant you sweated buckets no matter what time of day you exercised. He stretched his back and legs briefly, and then he was off.

Abdullah always started with half-length strides at a slow pace till his muscles warmed up. At this speed he had more time to look around as he turned right out of his tiny front yard and headed up the alley toward the main street, Kelayan B. Later he'd lengthen his stride and might see nothing while he ran except the ghosts of his past.

Only Pak Zaini's light was on between Abdullah's house and the *musholla*. He was probably getting ready to open the *musholla* up for morning prayers. Most people preferred to pray there in their own neighborhood. Only Friday worship drew them to the larger mosque.

He looked for the night watchman the neighborhood had hired, who sometimes sat on a bench in front of Pak Fachmi's house, but the bench was empty. *Probably sleeping off his booze on someone's porch. But at least he has a job.*

As he turned right on Kelayan B heading toward the intersection with Gerilya Street he remembered the *Banjarmasin Post* stating that Kelayan's unemployment was over 40 percent, and he believed it. This southern region of Banjarmasin was nicknamed "Texas" because of the high crime and rough-and-tough mentality of the men here. In a city where buying and selling alcohol was illegal, liquor was a staple of Kelayan life. Gambling, thievery, prostitution, murder—many of the cases around the province traced back to Kelayan. The police were very careful how they handled themselves here. *Thank Allah for small favors.*

He kept his slow pace traveling south, picking his way in the dark carefully around the road construction. Kelayan B Street was barely wide enough for two cars, but one-third of the street was torn up to fix a leaking water pipe. The people on the left side of the street didn't need a water pipe. Their homes were built on stilts four feet over the river, which functioned as their bathing facility, dishwashing water, and with neighborhood outhouses built on a short platform out over the river, their sewage system. But the people on the right side of the street had been clamoring for years for water piped into their homes so they wouldn't have to bathe or carry their laundry across the street every day, and a couple years ago the city government actually put pipes in. Of course, every so often muddy water would come out of the faucet, and a construction crew would have to tear up the street to find where the leaky pipe was letting swamp water mix with the city water. *But that's what happens when you build a city on a swamp.*

It was 4:15 when he reached Gerilya Street peeling off to the right. Today he decided to stay with the river and continue south through Teluk Kubur, or "Grave Cove." The Japanese had brought hundreds of suspected Indonesian resistance fighters here, made them kneel, then shot them through the back of the head and pushed them into the river. Abdullah tried to block that image from his mind, afraid of where it might lead.

More people were up now. He could see them taking their morning *mandi* in the river. Men squatted on small platforms behind their river houses scooping water over their underwear-clad bodies. Women did the same, side-by-side with the men, but covered with a sarong stretching from armpits to ankles. Some children jumped into the river playfully; others screamed as parents poured scoops of frigid water over their naked bodies. Though the water color was more chocolate than blue, a city ruled by river life exhibited its own unique charm.

Abdullah never tired of the scene. He had not grown up here on Borneo, Indonesia's largest island, but in the hills of Java. He had played in a little stream as a boy but hadn't learned to swim till he went to boarding school in Malaysia for a year at age fifteen. His little village wasn't as densely populated as Kelayan, and he liked the crowds. Crowds meant anonymity.

He felt his feet pick up their pace naturally. His strides lengthened, more befitting a six-footer. His shaved head began to glisten with sweat. His breathing was calm and steady, for he was in nearly as good a shape now as he had been in Afghanistan. Of course, then he was running for a different reason.

Stop it! Block it out! Run!

He focused on his breathing, letting it come in through his nose and out through his mouth. The sound was soothing, relaxing. He'd learned this from a counselor: regulate your breathing to calm yourself. That's about all he'd learned. Four years of chronic fatigue and depression and nightmares had been conquered by running in the mornings and returning to his *silat* exercises, teaching the Indonesian martial arts form to his *pesantren* students on Saturdays. Well, he was doing much better, except for the nightmares.

He crossed a footbridge over the river and turned left, now heading back north up Kelayan A Street. This area was quieter in the early morning than Kelayan B. Famous for being the stolen-motorbike center of Banjarmasin, most men went to bed after midnight and slept through their morning prayers. Both Kelayan A and B were practically 100 percent Muslim neighborhoods, but that didn't mean everybody would faithfully do their five *sholat* prayers each day; it just meant you'd better not insult the Prophet Muhammad, or you'd have a knife stuck up your gullet.

He rarely felt afraid here. Everyone knew him as a *pesantren* teacher. And Kelayan guys, no matter how violent or drunk they were, they took care of their own. He wasn't a Banjar; he was Javanese, yet these were his people now. His old life was over.

He jogged toward a group of men headed for the *Subuh* prayers at their neighborhood *musholla*. He thought he recognized a man who had sold him a goat last year, and he raised his hand to wave, then suddenly put it down and, ducking his head, crossed to the other side of the street. *Who was that other guy with the bin Laden beard? Where have I seen him before? Was he in JI? Was he in Afghan? Did he recognize me?*

Abdullah took the next bridge back over the river to Kelayan B and headed home, breathing much faster now. The sound of his lungs sucking air nearly drowned out the *klotok* chug-chugging under the bridge, bringing its fruits and vegetables to market. *Get a hold of yourself! Maybe you saw him a few years ago at a wedding. It's probably nothing.*

As he turned the corner of his alley, named Gang Hanyar, he could hear the imam's voice leading the prayers in his *musholla*: "*Subhanallah. Alhamdulillah. Allahu Akbar.*" He saw maybe seven or eight men kneeling on their prayer rugs repeating the phrases. As the largest Muslim nation in the world, there were millions of his countrymen repeating those exact phrases at exactly that time all across the country. They would repeat these phrases thirty-three times each. Abdullah felt grateful to be part of a religion that found unity in expressing its worship to God. He repeated the phrases to himself as he slowed to a cool-down walk. He caught himself thinking, *But what I really need is an Arabic phrase for "Help me, Allah!"*

As he entered through the unpainted wooden gate to his small front yard of reclaimed swampland, he took a deep breath before opening his front door. If only he could just run all day long. But unfortunately there was this business of *living* to attend to.

❦ Chapter 2 ❦

PAK ZAINI GOT drafted for garden duty. His wife Aaminah's hip was acting up, so she sat in a white plastic chair on the porch and tossed out orders laced with social commentary. But Pak Zaini was an agreeable slave. He was in his first year of retirement from PLN, the national electric company, and enjoying having nothing to do. The last few years had given him an ulcer, trying to handle the complaints of an entire province when the ancient turbines they still used at the hydro-electric plant took turns breaking down. They could never seem to produce enough power to keep everybody's lights on at the same time. It was definitely a form of relaxation to limit all the complaints he would hear that day to just one person's.

"Don't forget the orchid the school gave me. Do you think it's getting too much sunlight there? I'm worried it's getting too much sunlight."

Zaini moved the orchid slightly, though it was already in the shade of the early morning sun, and he figured it had been fine where it was. Aaminah was obsessively particular about her plants, but she had the right instincts for it. He'd never seen a plant die under her care. He, on the other hand, had the green thumb of an exterminator. Taking orders was all right by him.

"It was so nice of them to honor me like that. They didn't have to, you know. I wonder who paid for it."

"Well, they should honor you. How many years have you been teaching at the street kids' school for no pay? Maybe they're trying to tell you to retire and let some younger teacher take over."

"It's only once a week now. I'm sure I can do it for ten more years at least. And it's not like the young folk are clamoring to take non-paying jobs helping scavenger kids get an education. If I have my way I'll be with those precious kids till I pass on to the next life. If by God's mercy I make it to heaven, *Insha'Allah*, that's most likely who we'll find there anyway. Give a little more water to my gardenias, dear. Did you notice Ibu Mibah has a new motorbike? I wonder how they could afford that."

6

"Just tell me she didn't come borrow the money from you when I was taking a nap."

"Of course not, dear. I would have told you if she had." Zaini doubted that but let it pass. Everyone in the neighborhood and apparently several people he'd never even laid eyes on knew Aaminah was a soft touch for a handout. Well, he had a decent pension, but if his wife needed hip surgery, and if anything happened to him…better to have money in the bank than to call in loans from the poor, Zaini thought. *I have to talk to my wife about this. But how?*

"Do you think it's time to repaint our fence this year, dear? It would be nice to have it done before the Ramadan fasting month. Maybe one of Pak Abdullah's sons would like the extra work. Teenagers with too much time on their hands can slip down that slippery slope into mischief, don't you think?"

"OK, I'll talk to Pak Abdullah next time I see him." *Which wasn't likely to be at the* musholla. *A father who didn't set an example in keeping the morning sholat with the neighbors couldn't expect his sons to become role models.*

Aaminah shifted her position in the chair. She wore her usual house-dress: light cotton baggy pants and a matching, long-sleeved cotton top long enough to cover her rear. Zaini always appreciated his wife's modest dress. When she was younger, she'd never gone in for tight clothes or low necklines. If she left her yard she'd throw a head covering on, the true sign of submission for a Muslim woman. He noticed her tugging at her long, white hair. A tell-tale sign. What are you up to now, Aaminah?

"You didn't give enough water to my bougainvillea cutting! That's better. And can you pick up the fallen *jambu* fruits on the street? They make such a mess. Do ask our neighbor to let the scavenger boys pick from the tree next time they come. There's far too many for us and all the neighbors on this street to eat. Why is it you're doing all the work, dear, yet I feel so tired, and the day's hardly started?"

Zaini didn't know why his wife needed another bougainvillea. They already had planted a deep purple one when they moved into this house five years ago, and it was now taking over the eastern corner of the yard as high as their roof. And the *jambu* tree actually belonged to their neighbor, but the bright pink rose-apples dropped from branches extending over his yard and section of the street, so he got to deal with the mess. He hesitated before making his next foray, but couldn't help himself. "Maybe you need to not stay up so late reading. I don't know why you want to read a Christian book anyway." Zaini greatly admired his wife's intellect, but sometimes she didn't know where to draw the line.

"You mean Mother Teresa's biography? What, you think the only great people in the world are Muslims? What about all the hospitals and schools started by Christians? The scientific breakthroughs? Who wins the Nobel Prizes every year? If we can't compete, let's at least be grateful to God for them and humble enough to learn from them."

"Next thing you'll be telling me you want to become the Mother Teresa of Banjar. If I'd let you, you'd fill our house with dirty street kids."

"Don't be silly, dear. I don't want to be her. I get to be me. I have my own struggle against injustice right here in our neighborhood."

Here it comes…

"Now what are you thinking? You're not going to get me in trouble with the neighbors again are you?" Several memories flashed by of crazy stunts his wife had pulled, meetings he'd been called to by the RT—the neighborhood chief—in this neighborhood and several before it, and some long and bitter arguments with his wife. Somehow they'd survived it all and stuck together, but one thing was clear: Minah hadn't learned a thing.

"You know, I think our rain gutter is clogged again. Could you borrow Pak Fachmi's ladder today and clean it out? The porch ceiling looks like it's about to cave in again."

"Minah, tell me what's cooking in that lovely head of yours."

"Nothing much. Just an observation and maybe a thought. Have you noticed that one of our neighbors has been sharing her dinner with Ibu Dina from time to time?"

"You mean the beggar lady at the end of the alley?"

"Yes, Ibu Dina, Nina's mom. You remember Nina don't you? She dropped out of school last year to help her mother. Well, sometimes they come home at *Mahgrib* with not much to show for their labor, and one of our neighbors takes notice. Isn't that marvelous?"

Zaini knew he was getting set up. "Which neighbor?"

"Ibu Kris."

"Minah, I don't know what you're thinking, but I know already that I don't like it. I don't know how the neighborhood agreed to letting that Batak Christian woman live here, but it sounds like Christianizing to me. Stay away from her! And warn Dina to do the same!"

"Well, it sounds like compassion to me, and I've decided it's time to get to know Ibu Kris better." Aaminah had that look in her eye like Pak RT starting a chess match. And Pak RT always won at chess.

Zaini couldn't resist one last barb. "Just you watch. Soon she'll be taking the beggars to church, where they'll remove their head coverings and get new Western clothes. Next thing you know the church will be holding pork and alcohol parties right here in our Muslim neighborhood! Just see if I defend you *this* time, woman!"

"If you're worried that such a terrible thing could happen, dear, maybe it's best I get closer to Ibu Kris so I can keep an eye on her." Minah's eyes twinkled as she awkwardly stood. "And while I do that, you can keep an eye on our rain gutter."

❧ Chapter 3 ❧

ABDULLAH HAD FINISHED taking his *mandi* and was dressed in beige slacks and the white Muslim button-down cotton long-sleeved shirt accepted as uniform for teachers at the *Al-Mustaqiim Pesantren*. This was his fourteenth new school year, and the principal had unexpectedly broken with precedent to kick things off with a sports competition. *Syukran should do well*, Abdullah thought. *He seems to have grown even taller over the summer and is developing into quite an athlete. Another year and he'll be as tall as me. If I'm not careful, Syukran will overtake me in silat sparring soon.*

Iqbal, the older son, went to a government high school, since he seemed to be blessed with the brains in the family. He was a bit shorter than Syukran, but well proportioned, and had bangs that parted in the center and flopped just above each eye, and a happy-go-lucky smile.

Siti's shrill voice called her men to the breakfast table. The normal rice and fried eggs were complemented today with a large fried patin fish. Abdullah's eyebrows jumped. The boys cried, "Fish!" and "Nice!" and using their hands, efficiently ripped off chunks of meat while avoiding the bones. Add a little homemade chili paste called *sambal*, and it felt like a feast.

Siti looked much younger than her thirty-seven years. She kept a close eye on her petite figure, and most days, like today, already had her hair and makeup done before breakfast. She wore a red apron to keep the cooking oil from splashing on her glittering sequined black Muslim shirt and her fake Calvin Klein jeans. As soon as her boys were off to school, she'd head to the outdoor market, and wanted to look her best.

"I thought you boys would like a special breakfast to start the new school year." Siti loved seeing her boys eating happily. "*Alhamdulillah, ya Allah*, today we could be the picture of a truly *saleh* family."

The men were too busy eating to respond.

"But you know what would even be better? Did you notice, honey, that this morning's *sholat* had a different voice doing the call to prayer?"

Abdullah grunted. Siti continued. "I heard this morning from Ibu Mia that Pak Haji What's-His-Name who usually does the *adzan* had a stroke last night. So I thought this was a perfect opportunity for Syukran to volunteer to do it."

"Why does it have to be me?" Syukran complained.

"Well, aren't you learning to lead the *sholat* and a hundred other Arabic prayers in your *pesantren*? Don't you think it's time to take your responsibilities as a Muslim man in our neighborhood seriously?" Siti glanced sideways at Abdullah, who kept focused on his fish.

"Why don't you want Bali to do it? He's older."

"Iqbal has to focus on his studies so he can become a lawyer and *someone* in this family can finally make enough money to get us a decent house." Another sideways glance. Abdullah finished his coffee without looking at his spouse.

"Yeah, Syuk, I'm expecting a lot of hard nights studying my senior year, so I doubt I'll be able to get up for morning *sholat* like you." Iqbal winked at his younger brother.

"At least the sleeping in part is true," Syukran countered, his disapproval evident.

"Son, are you ready for the obstacle course?" Abdullah asked Syukran. All his *silat* students had trained on it over the summer when there was nothing else to do.

"Yes, sir. But what's the point of making it a race? Everyone knows Hafiz will win."

"You never know what life might throw at you. Let's go." Abdullah and Syukran got up and headed for their bicycles, stored in a lean-to beside the house.

"Dad, wait." Iqbal put on his worried face. He did have a knack for drama sometimes. "I'm running late, and the motorbike's out of gas. You've seen the lines at the gas station. Can I have some extra cash to fill it up on the street?" A great, legal small business in Kelayan was displaying a roadside rack of one-liter bottles of gasoline filled up early in the morning from the gas station and then sold at a twenty percent profit.

"Iqbal, Iqbal," Siti called from the sink where she was washing dishes. "You know we don't have extra money lying around. What with your father's low-paying job and me selling kerosene, we're doing the best that we can, and we don't need you begging for money when you could just as well be out looking for a job; in fact, I heard it through the grapevine that Pak Fachmi may be planning to put in a brick walkway to his house, and if you asked him I'm sure he would..."

Abdullah had already slipped a 5,000 rupiah note into his son's hand, and there was no one left in the kitchen to hear Siti's lecture on fiscal propriety and gainful employment.

❧ Chapter 4 ☙

SITI WAS SWEEPING her front porch when Kris walked by on her way to the *pasar. Oh, I wish I still had my figure like Ibu Siti does*, she thought. Kris had kept the delicate face of her youth, but at forty she'd given up the battle to fit into the clothes she wanted and tried to "go with the overflow." She nodded and smiled, but Siti pretended not to see her. *I am the invisible woman. Most of my own neighbors seem to not even know I exist.*

She nodded to Ibu Mibah who politely nodded back while getting on her new motorbike. She seemed in too much of a hurry to talk, but it wasn't like Kris could think of anything to say to her anyway.

She nodded again to Ibu Aaminah's husband, who was sitting on the front porch reading the *Banjarmasin Post*. Perhaps his wife had already left for the market. The man met her eyes, then paused before giving her a slight nod and returning to his reading.

Kris knew most of the women's names on Gang Hanyar. Only a few were referred to simply as "Ibu Hajjah" because they'd been on pilgrimage to Mecca, fulfilling the last of the five pillars of Islam. *I wonder how many of these women know* my *real name.* It had ceased to bother her that the neighbors here called her Kris, as though to highlight her despised Christian faith. When her parents were still alive everyone had called her Yana, since her full name was Kristyana. A name like Yana could blend in; apparently her neighbors wanted her Indonesian Christian minority status to wave like a red flag, warning everyone to keep their distance.

But Kristyana was used to living in her own world—just her and her teenage daughter, Mayangsari. By the time she reached the *musholla* at the end of the alley and turned left onto Kelayan B Street, she was enjoying the early morning bustle of kids headed to school, mothers going shopping to the outdoor market, and the few lucky fathers who had a job, making sure they didn't lose it. There were still patches of high, wispy clouds in the sky keeping the sun from scorching everything yet, and a light breeze from the river to her right made the walk downright refreshing. It was July, the middle of dry season, so she didn't have to worry about getting caught in the rain.

Sari had offered to drop her at the *pasar* as she left for school on the motorbike, but Kris had insisted on walking. Sari kept telling her she had to get over her fear of motorbikes, but Kris didn't ride one unless she had to. During her first year of university, her parents had been killed in a coal-truck-versus-their-motorbike collision. She had waited until Sari entered high school before she broke down and bought one, and she prayed every morning when Sari left that God's angels would keep her safe.

Speaking of angels, she had to thank God for her daughter. This morning Sari had opened up to her that she was nervous about starting her senior year and what would come after that. Kris had listened as she brushed Sari's long, silky black hair and had told her to just pray on her motorbike as she went to school. Kris's soothing encouragement and kiss on Sari's cheek was usually all she needed. *If she only knew how nervous I am! Sari has the striking face and attractive body of a model. How will I keep the boys off her? And she has no father to protect her.*

Pasar Baimbai was the largest open market at the south end of Kelayan B and offered virtually everything: from clothing and makeup, to dishes and tools, to dry goods and fresh groceries. There were even pirated movies and CDs and toys for the kids. Of course, the selection wasn't as good as the larger Pasar Baru downtown, but it was convenient, and nearly all the women of southern Kelayan B knew it well.

Kris started first on the list of supplies for the small kiosk she had in front of her house—her main source of income for the last few years. She would pick up staples like soap and laundry detergent, toothpaste, soy sauce, matches and cigarette lighters, bottled water and sodas, and various snacks and treats for the kids. She could sell them to neighbors too busy or lazy to make the trip to the market at a slight markup to cover her daily food costs. While she sat in the three-foot by four-foot stall waiting for customers, she also made wallets. If she sold just one wallet it would cover Sari's motorbike gas for two to three weeks. No one in the neighborhood had bought one yet, but some of her church friends had.

Extra work cleaning the church covered *pulsa* for her and Sari's cell phones and other emergencies. She owned the house free and clear—it was left to her by her aunt when she died. And though the motorbike was old and cranky, she owned it too. Living simply, under the burden of no monthly payments, was how Kris liked it. After getting her supplies into several plastic bags, which she left under the watchful eye of the kind chicken-seller everyone called *Bibi Ayam*, or "Auntie Chicken," Kris thought about splurging on some breakfast of yellow rice and *haruan* fish but decided against it. She should really get groceries for her and Sari and get back to open the kiosk. She headed for the fresh vegetables.

The spinach looked extra fresh today, and there was quite a crowd gathered there, so she headed for the carrots first. Some women were champion bargainers. Whatever price the seller offered they could come up with brilliant, irrefutable reasons why the actual price should only be half of that. Kris had never been a good bargainer. Once in a while she'd try a pathetic sounding, "Could you please lower that price a bit?" But if the seller refused, she'd buy it at whatever price he started with anyway. Sari was a much better bargainer and often did the kiosk supply run with her to save them money. She was proud of how strong Sari had become, not at all like her mom.

After buying carrots, tomatoes, cucumbers, long green beans, shallots, tofu and tempeh, fresh chili peppers, and finally the spinach, Kris decided to buy chicken this week instead of fish. She returned with a new armload of bags to *Bibi Ayam* and was surprised to see three women from her neighborhood gathered there: Ibu Mia, Mama Rizky, and Ibu Aaminah. She wanted to turn away, but she had nothing else to buy, and she couldn't go home without getting her bags out from behind *Bibi Ayam's* chicken counter. She tried to quietly slip past the group into the stall but couldn't quite squeeze through and found herself standing there stupidly listening to them gossip.

"…came home drunk Saturday night last. That's how I got this!" Ibu Mia rolled up her sleeve, showing a nasty bruise.

"You poor thing!" commented Mama Rizky, hoisting her baby son up higher on her hip. "Why do you stay with him?"

"Well, he's hardly a bother during the week when he's at his first wife's house. He always brings me a thick envelope of cash when he comes. And that's not the only thing 'thick' about him." Ibu Mia let out a little growl in the back of her throat. Mama Rizky cackled.

"Good morning, Ibu Kris! How are you?" Apparently Ibu Aaminah decided it was time to redirect the conversation.

"Fine thanks. How are you, Ibu Mia? Mama Rizky?"

"Fine," they answered.

Now what?

"Your daughter Sari just gets lovelier every day. Is she a senior this year?" Kris nodded. Ibu Aaminah smiled warmly and kept eye contact. "She must be a very hard-working student to be second-ranked in her class last year." *How could she know that? We never told a soul.*

"Yes, she is, and thank you. It's kind of you to notice us." *That sounded stupid.*

"Well, to tell you the truth, my dear, I have been noticing you." Ibu Aaminah paused and smiled again. "You seem to keep to yourself a little too much, my dear, and I was wondering if you would like to join our ladies' *arisan* meeting on Monday afternoons. We'd love to have you come and get to know you a bit better."

Kris couldn't help but notice the little gasp from Mama Rizky and Ibu Mia's open-mouthed shock. She was probably more shocked than they were. "Wow, I'm honored. But I'm afraid I'm not too good with reading Arabic." *In other words, Isn't this meeting only for Muslims?*

"You must be thinking of our ladies' *pengajian*, which we moved to Sunday morning. On Monday afternoon we just have a short prayer, then we gather everyone's contribution of Rp.10,000 and pull a name out of a bottle to see who gets the *arisan* savings for that week. Then we eat together and talk about the issues that are important to us. You've been a good member of our community for a long time, and I'd like to hear your thoughts about our women's issues too. So if you're not busy this Monday, the next *arisan* just happens to be at my house right after *Ashar* prayers, about 4:30. Please do come, dear." And Ibu Aaminah was off, posse in train bouncing exclamations off her like moths off a light bulb.

Kris was so deeply puzzled that she gathered up all her bags and headed for a *becak* guy to pedal her home in his pedicab. She forgot to buy any chicken for dinner.

❧ Chapter 5 ❧

A L-MUSTAQIIM PESANTREN WAS about a ten-minute bike ride for Abdullah and Syukran down Komplek 10 toward the rubber factory, just about one hundred yards inland from the large Martapura River. The rubber factory had its own slums for employees, mostly Javanese and mostly women, but Abdullah and the other teachers made sure their students kept their distance from the factory workers. The school itself was the opposite—all male, from the teachers down to the sixty boys from grades seven to twelve.

Abdullah was the last of the four teachers to arrive. The principal, Hasan Amman, known as "Pak Ustad" to his students, was greeting the handful of parents who had come to watch their sons compete. The other two teachers, Budi and Irfan, were taking roll in the small courtyard between two classroom buildings on each side, reclaimed swampland where the *silat* team practiced.

Every year Abdullah was amazed to see how many students were enrolled. With so many better schools available, he knew that parents sent their boys to this school for basically one of two reasons: they wanted their sons to get better religious training than the regular schools offered (and didn't care that in all other subjects their sons would lag behind their peers), or they couldn't afford the regular schools. At *Al-Mustaqiim* student fees could be paid for in bags of rice or other farm produce.

Abdullah and the *silat* club had marked out the rigorous obstacle course a month ago at the beginning of summer vacation. Only twelve students were ambitious enough to try it, all but one of them from the *silat* club. Most of the younger boys chose climbing the flagpole, doing push-ups or sit-ups, or running a road race down to the rubber factory and back.

He grabbed his whistle from his P.E. bag and headed for the flagpole, where Pak Ustad was calling the students to line up. After reciting a prayer for God's protection over the day's activities, Pak Ustad motivated the contestants by quoting this Qur'anic verse from Surah Al Ma'idah in both Arabic and Indonesian:

> To thee We sent the Scripture in truth, confirming the scripture that came before it, and guarding it in safety: so judge between them by what Allah hath revealed, and follow not their vain desires, diverging from the Truth that hath come to thee. To each among you have we prescribed a law and an open way. If Allah had so willed, He would have made you a single people, but (His plan is) to test you in what He hath given you: so strive as in a race in all virtues.

Pak Ustad smiled warmly at his students. "Today you'll be competing against each other in races. But I want you boys to remember there is a higher competition you're all entered in—the competition for doing virtuous deeds. In fact, the Qur'an tells us in this verse that God could have made the Christians one people with us, but He chose not to in order that we both would strive in our own ways to outdo each other in good deeds. Just like your competitors today are your friends, not your enemies, remember that those of other religions are also not your enemies. At *Al-Mustaqiim* we believe that the best way to do *jihad* for Allah is to attract people to our message by shining the brightest in our good deeds.

"Now go out there and do your best. May Allah grant you success."

Syukran was lined up between Juki and Hafiz for the final event of the morning, the obstacle course. Abdullah could see Hafiz saying something to Syukran, who was trying to ignore him. Probably a taunt or put-down. Hafiz was the best fighter in the *silat* club, the fastest runner every year, and let everyone know it. But the fact that he was leaning on trash talking for a mental edge just exposed what Abdullah suspected— Syukran was getting close to dethroning Hafiz. Abdullah was proud of his son but unsure of what defeating Hafiz might do to his character.

"Ready, set, *brrrrrrrrtttt!*" Abdullah blew the whistle, and the boys were off. Hafiz made it to the tires first, Syukran right on his heels, then they headed between the buildings for a four-by-six-inch beam that stretched thirty feet over the swamp behind the school to a knoll of dry land in the center. The watching boys cheered wildly when Juki and Udin both slipped off the beam and splashed gloriously into the swamp.

Abdullah smiled and remembered why he loved this old *pesantren* so much—it was so terrifically unremarkable at anything. The *pesantren* he'd been to as a teenager in Malaysia produced successful businessmen, teachers, political leaders, imams, and especially terrorists. This *pesantren* had so far turned out no geniuses, prodigies, famous athletes, or otherwise. The closest they'd ever gotten was a student who took the regional prize in MTQ, Qur'anic recitation. Abdullah hoped the school turned out good people, that was all.

And being unremarkable meant being relatively unknown. That's why he had come here in the first place. He needed a job where people wouldn't ask questions about his past, a place where neither police nor old JI comrades would drop by. Nobody dropped by *Al-Mustaqiim*.

The boys had crawled through the knoll of rocky land covered by a twenty-by-twenty-foot blue tarp suspended eighteen inches off the ground, and he could see Syukran and Hafiz grab the two climbing ropes at the bottom of the ten-foot rock wall almost simultaneously. Hafiz scrambled over the top first and leaped out of Abdullah's sight on the other side of the wall. As Syukran scrambled over the top Abdullah heard a cry of pain. Was it his son? *Please, Allah, not my son!* He strained to see, but Syukran had leaped off the wall, and both boys were out of sight for a few seconds. Two other boys were starting up the ropes. Unconsciously, Abdullah held his breath waiting for Syukran to come around the corner wading through the waist-deep swamp, the last leg of the race.

There he was! Syukran's lighter skin than many of the other boys showed he was now in the lead. Abdullah's clinched fists relaxed. But where was Hafiz?

Abdullah strode between the classrooms to the edge of the swamp even as Syukran was crossing the finish line at the flagpole, unnoticed by his father. No one cheered. All eyes were on the rocky knoll.

"What's happening over there, boys?" Abdullah called.

Udin popped his head around the wall to yell back. "It's Hafiz, sir. I think he broke his leg. He can't stand up."

Abdullah turned back to Syukran, "Son, ask Pak Ustad if he has a large roll of tape. And take the water bottles out of that box and bring the tape and the box for me out to the knoll. *Ayo*, quickly!"

Abdullah trotted across the four-by-six beam as easily as his wife crossed the street. Training at the Mujahidin Military Academy in Afghanistan had its ironic advantages. Abdullah probably could have done this training course in half the time the boys did, at night, in monsoon rains, with twenty pounds on his back. But the kids didn't need to know that.

He skirted the wall rather than climb over it and found Hafiz conscious but moaning, holding his left calf.

"Show me where it hurts, Hafiz."

Hafiz pointed to his ankle. Abdullah squatted with the foot between his legs and gripped it firmly, twisting it slightly in a circle. Hafiz cried out in pain.

"Did you turn your ankle when you landed?" Hafiz nodded. "Like this?" Abdullah stretched out his hand and rolled it from palm-down to palm-up. Hafiz nodded again. He was barefoot, like all the boys, and the swelling was already starting.

Just then Syukran showed up with the tape and cardboard. "Turns out we don't need it, son. His leg's not broken; just a sprained ankle. Hustle back over there and ask Pak Ustad to send someone for some ice." Syukran turned without a word and went back across the beam.

"Let's go." Abdullah asked two boys to help Hafiz stand on his one good leg, then he bent forward, grasped Hafiz around the waist, and hauled him up over his shoulder like a sack of rice. He had to step ankle-deep in the swamp to get around the wall this time, but soon he was crossing the beam confidently back to the schoolyard. The other boys followed, Udin slipping and falling in for the second time that morning, lightening everyone's mood.

One of the parents drove up with ice in a plastic bag purchased from a *warung* just down the road. Abdullah taped it around Hafiz's ankle, and the parent agreed to drive Hafiz home on his motorbike.

When all the commotion finally subsided and the teachers gathered to prepare the awards for the event winners, Syukran sidled up to his father. "Hey, Dad, did you clock my time on the obstacle course?"

Abdullah stared at him for a moment, blinked twice, and answered, "No, I forgot."

"But Dad!"

"You should have stayed to help Hafiz. I don't care if he is a jerk to you. He's your schoolmate, your *silat* club mate, and your friend. People are more important than winning a race."

Syukran's jaw clenched, and his neck muscles tightened, but he said nothing. An awkward silence passed. Then he turned and walked away.

❧ Chapter 6 ❧

MAYANGSARI CRUISED DOWN Kelayan B Street on her way home, her eight-year-old Yamaha Vega weaving through the narrow street, avoiding the potholes, road construction, bicycles, *becak* pedicabs, and pedestrians. Fortunately, not many cars or trucks braved this always-crowded street, but she also had to watch out for young hotshots zipping past on their newer, higher-horsepowered bikes. Her motorbike's zipping days were long gone.

Sari saw a pothole at the last second and swerved, nearly hitting an old grandpa walking in the street instead of beside it. He shook his cane at her. She hoped he couldn't recognize her with her helmet on. Some young men sitting on a bench noticed this exchange and started whistling. "Hey, *cewek*, stop here for a while!" She didn't honor them with even a glance; just kept her focus on getting safely to her alley turnoff.

Gang Hanyar—"New Alley"—but nothing new ever happens here. I don't have to read the B-Post *to know what's "new" in Kelayan: Knife fights in Peace Alley. Drunks beating their wives and kids in Family Alley. Unemployment soaring in Fortune Alley. As soon as I finish high school, I've got to get out of here.*

And as usual, Sari's mom was waiting for her at the kiosk with a kiss for each cheek and the ritual question: "How was school?"

"Actually, it was great, Mom! And I have a special announcement to make, but first let me get changed." Sari walked past her mother into their little two-bedroom wood house, already removing her motorbike gloves and unbuttoning her white school-uniform blouse.

Kris followed her in. "What is it, honey? Tell me!"

Sari gently closed her bedroom door and took off her navy blue pleated school skirt, calling, "Just be patient, Mom. I'll be out in a minute." She dropped her school clothes on her twin bed with the same Sleeping Beauty sheet she'd had since she was eight. With barely room to turn around she slipped into some pencil-jeans with a colorful butterfly embroidered on the left hip pocket and a white t-shirt that said "Eat, Pray, Love" after the

Julia Roberts movie filmed in Indonesia. She released her hairclip and shook out her long black tresses. She smiled into her mirror and tossed her hair like a movie star. God had given her perfect teeth, bright, lively eyes, and a face that had no need for makeup, so she rarely used it. In the mirror it looked like her right hand was the perfect one. The left one was in her pocket. If only it were true. Her smile slipped a bit as she waved a playful good-bye with her left hand to herself and left the room.

Sari went straight to the kitchen in search of her favorite fruit—a *pisang muli*, a local banana only four to five inches long and sweeter than their larger cousins. Kris did her best to wait patiently for Sari to speak. Sari sat at the kitchen table opposite her mom and started peeling the banana.

"Guess who my class voted in as class secretary?" Sari teased.

"You?"

"Yes, me! My teacher suggested my name to the class, and no one objected. The students came up with two other candidates, but they chose me! I never thought they'd choose a Christian for class leadership. There are only two Christians in my class, and we never get picked, only *picked on*. I never imagined my teacher would even suggest my name."

"That's wonderful, honey! I'm so excited for you!"

"Not only that, guess who they voted in as class president? Our neighbor, Bali! Can you believe it? Two students from Kelayan leading the senior class of one of the top high schools in Banjar. We're the only two students from Kelayan in the entire class, and they want us to be their leaders! I just can't believe it!"

"Were any of your other friends chosen?"

"No, actually, I don't know the other leaders that well. At least I know Bali. He wasn't always nice to me when we were kids, but we get along OK now."

"Does he like you?" Kris emphasized the word *like* and raised her eyebrows.

Sari rolled her eyes. "No, Mom! I think he likes Putri. Well, at least Putri thinks he likes her. I don't know who he likes. It's not like we hang out or anything."

"Any other boys chase you today?"

"Mom! Give me a break! Like they're really going to want to date *me*!"

"I'm sure they'll be lined up outside our door soon, honey. I just hope you take your time and choose wisely. One mistake with a boy can affect your whole life."

Sari tried to be patient with her mother's daily warnings, because she knew how much her mother had suffered. But her mom's constant worrying could suck all the life right out of her if she wasn't careful. *It's not like any guys would want to date me anyway. Holding hands…* Sari shuddered. *Time to change the subject.*

"How was your day, Mom? Anyone interesting come visit our kiosk?" *As if!*

"No, nothing unusual. Except—" Kris's brow furrowed, and her fingers involuntarily twisted her shoulder-length black hair.

"Except what, Mom?" *I hope no one was mean to her again. She doesn't deserve that.*

"Well, I guess I have a surprise announcement to make too. I was at the *pasar* and bumped into Ibu Aaminah. She invited me to join the ladies' *arisan* on Monday!"

Sari's eyes nearly popped out. "They *invited* you? They've never invited us to anything."

"I know. I don't think the two women with her were expecting that, or very thrilled about it, but there it is. What do you think?" Kris bit her lower lip and arched her eyebrows.

Sari stood and stretched her hands toward the plywood ceiling, as though trying to hold back the leaks that would start come rainy season. Then she began pacing with eyes narrowed and lips protruding. Sari was thinking.

"Well, Mom," Sari began her argument, "you've always taught me to see people as individuals, not to put them in a box, that someone can be surprisingly better or worse than the attributes of their group if you take time to get to know them. So, if you think that Ibu Aaminah is sincere, I think you should try it. Who knows? Maybe she'll turn out to be a kindred spirit. And you know how I'm always pushing you to look for new friends. What if there's a new friend waiting for you right here in our neighborhood? Of course, some of the other women probably won't like it, but we're used to that, right? Anyway, do you *want* to do it? It's really up to you."

"Honestly, I'm afraid. I think Ibu Aaminah *is* sincere, but I'm afraid of what the other women might say or do. I don't really enjoy rejection, you know."

Sari grinned as she reached for her second banana. "Come on, Mom. Try it! What's the worst that could happen?"

❧ Chapter 7 ❧

IQBAL BOWED REGALLY when he announced he'd been chosen senior class president.

"*Astaghfirullah al-adzim!*" his mother screamed. She took Iqbal's cheeks in her hands and kissed him on the forehead. "I've got to share this good news with someone!" Siti's words drifted behind her as she raced out the door.

"We're very proud of you, son," Abdullah added, with a bit more restraint.

"Cool," chimed in Syukran. He forced a smile, then abruptly coughed and left the room.

"I was up against that loser Dhani, who was the top ranked student last year but has the personality of a squid. He didn't stand a chance. I'm way more popular than he is. What a sweet way to finish my high school career!"

"Who else got chosen with you?" Abdullah asked.

"I don't remember; just some other kids. Our first meeting is tomorrow after school, so I'll be home a bit late. No problem, right?"

"No problem. So what is a class president supposed to do?"

"How should I know? I've never been one before. But the teacher said he'll tell us all about it tomorrow. I think this could be my favorite year of school, Dad! This'll look good on my university application, too, right?"

Iqbal high-fived his dad as he jogged to his bedroom to change out of his school uniform and start his homework.

Syukran found his gang of friends on Hafiz's porch, smoking and trying to cheer up their crippled friend by poking fun at him. Syukran asked for a cigarette and a light, then sat pensively on the edge of the porch watching the traffic turn from Kelayan B Street to Gerilya Street. Nobody mentioned his winning the obstacle course.

"So…you guys want to go to the night market again tonight?" Udin asked.

"Maybe we should stay here and keep an eye on Hafiz," Juki countered. "Make sure his girlfriend doesn't come over to massage his ankle." Everybody laughed.

"I guarantee that if she came over, she wouldn't waste her time fondling my ankle," Hafiz bragged.

"Huuuuuu! Aren't you the confident Romeo!" teased Udin. "Anyway, we know she's not coming over to visit some crippled loser. I think maybe Syukran should go to her house to check on her." More laughter. Syukran almost smiled at Hafiz's discomfort but knew better than to agree out loud and make him angry.

"What's the point of going to the night market anyway? We never buy anything," offered Fani, the youngest of the group.

"Fani, Fani, when are you going to grow up and become a man?" Hafiz put his arm around Udin. "The reason we go to the night market is so Udin can grope the girls, since not even a blind one would go to bed with him."

"Hey, if we *don't* go the girls will miss me, not like your two-timing girlfriend who'll be happy to have a night free from you!" Chuckles rose again. Udin rarely lost a battle of insults.

Syukran finally spoke: "There's more to life than groping girls, you idiots."

"Yeah, there's sex!" joked Fani. They busted up again at thirteen-year-old Fani acting like he knew anything about sex.

"Don't talk about what you don't even dream about yet, little brother," Udin rebuked the boy. "Let us men keep the ladies happy, and you just make sure you keep us happy."

Syukran growled. "You stupid-heads, quit your gutter talk and turn on your brains for a minute. I'm talking about *jihad*."

Hafiz surprisingly backed him up. "Yeah, I'm with Syuk. When are we gonna quit playing around with *silat* and start doing something to fight the infidels and take back this country? I read in *Sabili* magazine about this teenager in Java who bombed a church because he heard they brought three giant pigs into the city for some kind of feast. *Gila!* If someone brought pigs into our city we'd have to do something equally intense to teach them a lesson."

Hafiz stole my rightful attention this morning at school; now he's stealing my thunder on jihad.

Syukran took a long drag on his cigarette, then dropped his voice like he was telling them a secret. "That's nothing. When my dad was young and went to Afghanistan, he said one day Mullah Omar sent him out with a grenade and a knife and told him that the Christians from this particular church had ripped up a Qur'an and needed to be taught a lesson. My dad snuck up to a window near the front of the church where the leader teaches from. He threw the grenade right on the platform, blowing the leader and the first few rows of people to smithereens. Then he ran around to the big doors at the back, and as people came pouring out he cut the throats of fifty-seven people, piling them up on the left and right of the doors, before they even realized the danger. One of the guys he sliced was carrying a Bible. My dad sliced it in half and laid one half on each of the piles of dead bodies before he disappeared."

It was deathly silent. Finally Juki cleared his throat and asked, "Why doesn't your dad tell any cool stories like that in class?"

"My dad's way too modest to brag like some people." Syukran caught Hafiz's eye for a second, then looked away. "He made me promise not to tell all his stories, but he probably wouldn't mind if I just told one." Syukran could feel everyone's respect for him rising like mercury in a thermometer on a hot Banjar day.

Fani's eyes were tracking two men walking past across the street, one carrying a bottle of homemade liquor. Syukran noticed and watched them, too. Fani mumbled, "I wish my dad was as cool as yours. He don't do nothing but drink and beat on us." Everyone knew Fani's dad was a violent drunk. Even though they picked on him, they all protected him like their own brother, at least when he was outside his own home.

"Syuk, are you going to Afghan like your dad?"

"Maybe someday. My dad won't hook me up, though. I'll have to find my own way."

Juki tossed his cigarette butt in the ditch. "Maybe that JI recruiter we saw last year will come back."

"What I want to know is how come all the JI studs are Javanese? You know, the Bali Bombers, Noordin M. Top; those guys are all from Java. How come there's no Banjar *kafir*-killers?"

Hafiz held up both hands as if to quiet the crowd. "I've been saving this announcement for the proper moment. Let me introduce you to the future first *amir* from Banjar." He bowed his head slightly as though expecting applause.

Udin couldn't resist. "Yes, everyone, our one and only *Amir Cacat*—the

'Crippled Leader.' On his way to assassinate the American president he shot himself in the foot." Udin cackled hysterically, and the rest joined in, slapping Hafiz on the arm and hooting.

Hafiz had to defend himself. "Hey, me and Syuk are the only decent athletes here. You think they take fat boys like Kiki?" Kiki was the fattest boy in the *silat* club and tried to stay in the background to avoid his friends' merciless teasing. "Or punks like Udin, whose biggest muscle is his mouth?"

"At least my mouth wasn't parading around on a motorbike this morning with a plastic bag tied around it! You looked like a grandma who got her foot stuck in her grocery bags!" At this Fani laughed so hard he rolled sideways and fell off the edge of the porch, prompting even greater howls. A few passersby on their motorbikes glared at them, but people in Kelayan Dalam were so used to seeing drunks any time of day, no one stopped to hush them.

Juki continued the theme: "It's true. They want to recruit athletes. Remember that bombing in 2009 at the Marriott Hotel in Jakarta? I read that the bomber was a high school guy about our age named Dani. He was a basketball star, and a smart kid, too, from a good school, not like ours."

"Well, if he can do it, why not us?" Syukran challenged everyone.

"Yeah, why not me?" Hafiz added.

"Yeah, why not me, too?" Udin agreed. "You better take me along, 'cause if we get to be martyrs and meet those seventy virgins in heaven, I'll be the only one who knows what to do with them."

❧ Chapter 8 ❧

RIDAY, AFTER THE noon worship, Syukran and Iqbal came home from the Grand Mosque in the center of the city together on the motorbike. Abdullah had done his *sholat* at a mosque within walking distance of home, while Siti had stayed home and cooked lunch.

Iqbal could smell the *sambal* chili paste the moment he came through the front door. His mom liked to make it herself, buying the chilis fresh and mixing them with garlic, shallots, tomatoes, and shrimp paste in an aluminum wok over her kerosene burner. Even the neighbors could catch the wafting smell of the shrimp paste permeating the whole house. Added to this chili mixture were smaller chilis, sugar, and salt, ground in a stone mortar using a pestle made from the core of a palm tree. Siti always used lots of small chilis, because Abdullah liked it hot. It could certainly spice up an otherwise boring spread of rice, tofu, spinach, and dried salty minnows.

Iqbal was grinning from ear to ear. "Hey, Dad! I made Rp.20,000 today watching the motorbikes at the mosque. That's twice as much as usual! Three of the regular guys didn't show up."

"Syukran, did you help out your brother? Please tell me you made some money too," Siti begged.

"No, Mom, you know I'd rather give myself fully to worshiping Allah than chasing after *fulus*."

"Well, someone in this family needs to learn how to make more money than just Rp.20,000 a week! Here we are struggling financially, and I don't see you healthy young men contributing to our grocery bill. God knows you eat a lot!"

"Hey, as long as I make enough to pay for my cell phone *pulsa*, I'm happy." Iqbal dug into his rice with his right hand and dipped it with the tofu into the *sambal* he'd scooped onto the edge of his plate.

"I'm worried that you won't only not make enough money, you won't know what to do with it when you get it," Siti continued her mother-logic.

"Do you even listen to the sermons while you're outside watching the parking lot?"

"Hey, I always hear the sermons," Iqbal protested, his mouth full of food.

"Oh yeah?" Syukran challenged. "What did the imam preach about today?"

Iqbal answered without missing a beat. "He taught us to leave behind what is bad and take a hold of what is good."

Siti leaned toward him, "So how are you planning to do that?"

Iqbal winked at Dad. "I already did. I left behind my bad pair of sandals on the rack outside the mosque and brought home a pair that is good." He noticed his dad start to smile but quickly look down to avoid being noticed by Siti or Syukran, neither of whom saw much humor in religion.

Mom looked shocked. *"Astaghfirallah al-adzim!"*

"I'm just joking, Mom! I'm doing my best to be a *taqwa* person, especially now that I have to set a good example as the class president. Which reminds me"—*Better be careful how I ask this*—"tomorrow night one of my high school classmates has invited me and a few other close friends to a *haulan* at his house in Pekauman after 'Isha prayers. I think it's the fortieth day commemoration of his father's death. He's pretty well off—I think his dad was a judge or something. Anyway, I thought it was a good opportunity at the beginning of being class president to make a statement of support for our students who go through difficult times, don't you think?"

Iqbal paused, giving his parents time to digest this presentation, hoping it sounded plausible. It was mostly true. Change the *haulan* commemoration to a birthday party, and add that the student was a Christian, and it was almost the same. But he knew they'd never agree to him eating at a Christian home where there could be pork and alcohol. Lying was his only option. He fought the urge to hold his breath and tried to look sincere.

Iqbal watched his mom look to her husband. He was the imam of the home and had to make such decisions. "I guess so. Home by eleven, OK?" his dad acquiesced.

"Thanks, Dad! Well, better get to my homework!" Iqbal timed it perfectly to have finished his food right at the end of the conversation so he could make his escape before any more doubts or questions arose. *If only girls were as easy to handle as parents...*

❧ Chapter 9 ❧

SATURDAY NIGHT SYUKRAN was watching Iqbal carefully. He knew his brother well enough to know he was hiding something. When Iqbal headed off on the motorbike, Syukran raced over to his friend Adi's to borrow his motorbike for a few minutes.

The only clue Syukran had to his brother's destination was Pekauman—the neighboring district to Kelayan to the north, nearer the Martapura River. *There's no way I'll ever find him, but I've got to try. What is my brother up to?*

Syukran drove slowly down the main street looking left and right for his brother's motorbike. Fortunately, his brother had a fairly distinctive bike, a blue Kharisma with a bright red Gigi sticker above a Tasmanian devil sticker on the rear flap. Syukran only saw one blue Kharisma parked on the main street, and it had no stickers.

He decided to start with the smaller streets near the river first, then work his way back inland. Along the waterfront were mostly warehouses accessible for boats delivering cargo and other large buildings. No sign of the bike there.

Syukran was on maybe his seventh or eighth alley—he'd lost count—when he passed a large, two-story bright green home with about thirty motorbikes filling the front yard and spilling onto the street. He cocked his head to listen. He'd never been to a *haulan* where they didn't have a microphone and a portable speaker broadcasting the reciting of the *Yasin* prayers for the dead for the whole neighborhood to hear. But all he could hear was a distant thumping of rock music. *This ain't no haulan, that's for sure.* He parked out front and walked cautiously toward the door, checking out the motorbikes along the way.

There it was! Iqbal's bike was parked inside the yard. If Iqbal decided to leave early, he'd have to pick it up over his head and carry it out of that parking mess.

He thought about trying to climb up on something and peek through the windows but was afraid if someone saw him and cried, *"Maling!"* he could be caught and beaten to death as a thief before he had a chance to explain. He'd seen a guy brutally killed by a mob in Kelayan for stealing a chicken before. No, he'd better walk in the front door like a regular guest and hope for the best.

Syukran swallowed nervously on the doorstep and reached up to smooth down his hair when he realized he was still wearing his white *kopiah*. He took it off and scrunched the religious cap into his front pocket, slicked down his hair, and cracked open the door.

The music hit him like a wave, not rock, but house music. The lights were dim. He could see some people dancing, others standing holding small plates of food and drinks. No one paid him any attention. He tried to look confident and invisible at the same time, slowly moving down the front hall to where he could peek into the living room.

All the furniture had been removed, and the room was packed with teenagers. Syukran didn't see an adult anywhere. He scanned the crowd for his brother, praying under his breath that Bali wouldn't see him first. He decided to stay near the front hallway in case he needed to make a quick exit.

He felt someone touch his arm and he turned, then froze. A girl was touching him. She had curly hair and darker skin—definitely not Banjar. Her eyelids were covered in heavy blue makeup, and her bright red lipstick enhanced a very pretty smile. She was wearing a spaghetti strap top that showed her entire shoulders and a miniskirt that showed almost her entire thighs. Syukran could feel a heat rising inside him that was surely the fires of hell. He wondered if his face radiated the furnace within him.

"You must be one of Kevin's friends. I'm his cousin, Julia. What's your name?"

Ya Allah! These people were Christians! He needed a Christian name, fast!

"Hi, I'm, uh…Glenn." He almost said, "Glenn Fredly." The first Christian to pop into his head was Glenn Fredly, the famous musician who had married the Muslim vocalist Dewi Sandra amidst much controversy.

"Well, Glenn, would you like something to eat?" Julia still had her hand on his arm and was steering him toward the buffet table, then she was holding out a plate to him.

"What is it?" he asked without accepting the plate.

"Oh, fried chicken, fried noodles, meatball soup, beef *rendang*, barbecued RW, and some chocolate rum cake over there by the cocktail fruit and drinks."

The term *RW* threw him. He wasn't completely sure what it meant, but alarms were going off in his head. "I'm not hungry. Maybe just a drink. Do you have any soda?"

"Sure, right over there in the cooler. Help yourself, and have fun!" Julia finally returned his arm to him and went off to seduce some other poor guest. Syukran walked toward the cooler in case she was still watching and opened it.

Even though it was dark, he could recognize the brands of Coke and Sprite and Fanta, but there were a couple brands he didn't recognize— Green Sands and Heineken. But his alarms went off again, and he knew what it was. He had to get out of there. He glanced left and right, hoping no one was watching him as he started for the front hallway.

Bali! His brother was directly in front of him, holding a plate of food and talking to a girl, facing the front hallway! Bali would see him for sure! He wanted to run for the nearest window and throw himself crashing through, anything to get out of the devil's playground.

The thought hit him like a slap to the face—his cell phone! He grabbed it out of his pocket and raised it to his ear and began an imaginary conversation, "Hello? Hello? I can't hear you."

With his left hand holding the cell phone to his ear, partly covering his face, and his right hand massaging his forehead as if he were in a stressful conversation, Syukran pushed his way into the front hall and out the front door. More people were coming up the steps to join the party.

"Don't worry, I'll be right there! It's no problem," he promised loudly to no one on the other side, as he climbed through the motorbikes in the yard to where he'd parked his on the street. He fired it up and was back at Adi's house faster than you could recite the *Al-Fatiha*.

Adi's text messaging brought Hafiz, Juki, Udin, and Kiki over within minutes. Adi decided not to invite Fani in case the conversation got too "adult" for him. They sat on Adi's porch and listened to Syukran's story with a mixture of gleeful curiosity and religious horror. When Syukran told them about RW, he paused to see if anyone knew for sure what it was.

"They're cannibals!" offered Udin. The term *RW* is commonly used for a district chief one level higher than the RT.

"That's impossible," countered Hafiz. "Maybe out in the jungle but not here in the city. Not in our city!"

Kiki contributed a rare remark. "No, I know what RW is. My mom dragged me to a Christian wedding once when I was a kid in Palangkaraya. It's dog meat."

"No way!" Everyone was aghast. Dog meat was about as *halal* as pork for a Muslim.

"Was your brother eating it?" Hafiz asked.

"No! Well, I'm sure he wouldn't. I couldn't really see what he was eating, but he had a plate of something."

"Even if he didn't, it's still *haram* to eat food off the same table as dog meat. A fly could have touched the dog meat and then touched the fried noodles, and they'd be contaminated. Even just being cooked in the same kitchen contaminates everything."

Everyone knew Hafiz was right. Learning the difference between *halal* and *haram* was a significant part of their religious education at the *pesantren*.

"Did they have alcohol?" Udin asked. It's not like Kelayan wasn't full of alcohol on the streets, but somehow it was different if Christians were serving it at a party to their Muslim brother.

"Yeah, looked like imported beer to me."

"Was Bali drinking it?"

"I didn't see him drinking anything. I'm sure he wouldn't."

"How can you be sure? He was there, wasn't he? And he lied to your parents to go there? If he tells you he didn't drink it, how do you know he's not lying to you too?" Hafiz's logic had Iqbal condemned already.

"What were the other girls wearing?" Udin asked. "Was anyone making out?"

Syukran ignored him as he slapped at a mosquito biting his arm. "What are we going to do? We can't let these *kafir* corrupt my brother!"

"Let's get a mob together right now and go break up the party," Udin suggested. "We should teach those girls a lesson, maybe rip off their seductive clothes and make them run home in their underwear!"

"Shut up, Udin. Syukran's right. We have to do something. But not something for your perverted pleasure. Something that will really teach these *kafir* a lesson. They got no business bringing their hedonism into our city, especially not to Pekauman—that's practically our backyard!

No, we need a way to kick the cursed Christians out of south Banjar, or out of Banjar all together!"

They all sat and thought for a bit. Juki passed around some cigarettes to stimulate their brains. With the first few puffs of smoke the ever-present mosquitoes flew off to find dinner elsewhere.

A sneer crept onto Hafiz's face. "You guys find me the right target. I know what we're gonna do."

❧ Chapter 10 ❧

SUNDAY MORNING WELCOMED Sari with a bright blue sky and a bird singing outside her window. If there was a reason Sari looked forward to Sundays, it was the worship part of her church service, the singing and dancing to the Lord. When Sari danced she could feel God's pleasure upon her, deformed hand and all. Sometimes she felt her heart bursting with worship before she even walked in the church doors, and today was one of those days.

She hummed as she picked out a knee-length lavender dress with tiny, deep purple violets cinched tightly around her waist. She wore the amethyst earrings her mom had bought her for her last birthday—her birthstone. Her mom said she looked beautiful in purple, and who was she to argue?

Sari's dress had no pockets, but she didn't mind. Sunday was the one day when the disfigured skin on her right hand didn't matter. At school she tried to hide it; at church she was going to meet God, who loved her just the way she was.

Sari and Kris had arrived on time at 9:00 a.m. to the remodeled warehouse right on the river they used for church. They joined nearly eighty adults and over twenty kids in the sanctuary, which boasted a six-foot-high wooden cross behind the pulpit, a cherished Christian symbol the leaders chose to put inside the building rather than outside in sensitivity to the Muslim neighborhood all around them. The padded pews were enough to hold two hundred people, but that only happened at Christmas and Easter.

After the singing, offering, and Pastor Susanna's sermon, the children and teenagers left the sanctuary for Sunday school: children went to the kitchen, Sari and four other teens headed for the pastor's office. Usually only five or six teens came to their church, all from different minority ethnic groups.

Youth Pastor David reviewed the pastor's chosen text from the Gospel of Luke 23:34, where Jesus, dying on the cross at the hands of evil men, prayed, "Father, forgive them, they don't know what they're doing." David asked the teens, "Is there anyone who has hurt you that you need to forgive? If God forgives you, wouldn't you like to extend that forgiveness to others? Let's take a few moments to listen to God's Holy Spirit tell us who we need to forgive."

Sari closed her eyes to pray and knew there was only one person who had hurt her so deeply that she found it almost impossible to forgive him: her father. Seventeen years, and she'd still never seen him, never had a phone call or letter from him. Did he even know she was alive? Could she really say with Jesus, "Forgive him. He didn't know what he was doing to me"? *God, I'll say the words if You'll help me to mean it from my heart.*

After Sunday school, Sari found her mom with Pastor Susanna.

"How *are* you, Ibu Kris?" Pastor Susanna asked, somewhat dramatically for Sari's taste. *Maybe she's still in preaching mode.*

"Fine, thank you. It was a lovely sermon. Thank you so much."

"Praise the Lord. It was just burning inside me and needed to come out. I'm glad it spoke to your heart. And don't worry about *anything*, Ibu Kris. I'll be checking the poor, widows, and orphans fund this week to see if we have any extra money to help you out. We do want to take care of our widows! If there is anything we can do for you, anything at all, please let me know." Pastor Susana nodded to Sari and moved on to receive her reward from the next satisfied parishioner.

Sari grabbed her mom's hand and led her toward the parking lot, slipping on her motorbike gloves as she walked. She again wondered if the pastor's loud voice showed her passion for helping the destitute or was meant for others to notice. They certainly hadn't received any gifts from the poor, widows, and orphans fund for the last two months. But she rebuked herself for that uncharitable thought. Hadn't they received gifts from the church before that really helped them out in desperate times? Pastor Susanna may be overdramatic, but the church was still the church, and if you couldn't count on your community of faith when you were in trouble, whom could you count on in this world?

Note to self: Ask Mom how she handles forgiving Dad every day.

Chapter 11

"COME IN, COME in! So glad you decided to join us!" Ibu Aaminah welcomed Kris to their Monday afternoon *arisan*. Kris looked around the room for a spot to sit on the floor. All Ibu Aaminah's furniture had been moved out of her living room for this event, and the floor was now covered with Persian carpets. Nearly all the women in her neighborhood, thirty-two in all, were already seated around the walls of the room, and there was hardly any space between them. No one moved to open a space either, so Kris wound up sitting with her back to the open front door. She hoped no one came in late and tripped over her.

Most of the gossiping stopped when Kris walked in. Some women stared at her; others stared at Ibu Aaminah, as if surely there had been some mistake and Ibu would realize it. A few whispered their comments in a nearby ear. In the awkward silence Kris felt like an accused criminal being brought before the jury. She checked her clothes—long, baggy black polyester slacks, a peach blouse covering neck and wrists well, a peach-and-gray paisley square cloth folded in a triangle and wrapped around her head like a *kerudung*. Ibu Dina had shown her how to fasten it under her chin when she'd attended Dina's husband's funeral. So unless she had a soy sauce stain on her shirt, surely they weren't talking about her clothes.

It's because I'm a Christian. They think I don't belong here. Maybe I don't. Maybe this was a terrible idea. Maybe I should leave early. Or would that only make things worse? Oh, God, I should never have come! Kris tried to look everyone in the eye and smile, ignoring the sweat beads forming on her upper lip and under her hair. She hoped desperately that someone would smile back. A couple women did, but she wasn't sure whether they were sincere or just acting polite.

When her eyes met Ibu Aaminah's, she knew the smile was genuine. It reminded her of her mother's smile that said, "Relax, everything's going to be all right." She decided to keep her eyes on the beautiful carpet, the walls, and Ibu Aaminah's friendly face.

"*Assalamu alaikum Warahmatullahi Wabarakatuh.*" Ibu Aaminah welcomed everyone. She was the *bendahara* of the group, the one who organized things and kept the money. Only a very trusted woman could have this role, and Aaminah was one woman everyone trusted completely. *Except in her choice of guests,* Kris thought.

Ibu Aaminah passed around the small booklets containing the *Yasin* prayer taken from the Qur'an and a few other selected prayers. Every week the women recited this prayer as a way of remembering that life here is temporal and that they must be ready to face death and stand before God. Once all the books were passed around and opened, Ibu Hajjah started the Arabic recitation, and the other ladies all joined in.

Kris had politely accepted a booklet, but she found it was all in Arabic script with no Indonesian translation, so she couldn't join the chanting. She sat quietly, watching the others. She'd heard that hardly anyone in Banjarmasin could actually speak Arabic, although most Muslims were taught to read the sounds from the time they were children. Some women struggled to read the Arabic as fast as Ibu Hajjah; others closed their eyes and rocked meditatively back and forth as they recited words they'd heard since they were small girls—familiar, cherished words, an unchanging anchor in the ever-changing storm of life. Not all of the women understood the words they were reciting, but they all knew it was something about the afterlife and that chanting this *Surah* was pleasing to God.

After a few minutes Kristina decided she'd study the walls and find out what she could learn about Ibu Aaminah. The largest wall decoration was a family portrait of Pak Zaini, Ibu Aaminah, and their three children as young adults. She wondered where Ibu's son and two daughters were now. Were they married? Did they ever visit? She had no idea about the family lives of her neighbors beyond what she learned from her little kiosk every day. *My window on the world is too small. I wish I knew my neighbors better.*

Just to the right of the family portrait was a photo of her son's university graduation. She couldn't see it clearly, but it looked like the fine print said "Gajah Mada University, Yogyakarta." *If her son went to Gajah Mada in Yogya, he must be pretty smart. I hope Sari can make it to a good university like that. But do I really want her to go to Java to study? I don't think I could stand it to live here without her! Maybe she'll want to go to a local university like UNLAM. But whatever is best for her, I have to be ready to let her go . . .*

Her attention drifted over to the next wall, where there was a photo of Pak Zaini with some big-boss-looking types outside an electric plant. Then one of Ibu Aaminah with Megawati, the fifth president of Indonesia, but both women looked much younger than now; maybe the photo was taken before Megawati became president. *There's more to Ibu Aaminah than meets the eye.*

The prayers seemed to change rhythm for a bit, then suddenly they were over. The ladies were passing the booklets over to Ibu Aaminah, who put them in a box, presumably for next week. The chattering started to return, and Kris went back on alert mode, wondering what was coming next.

Someone started passing around glasses of tea. Next came plates of yellow rice and a duck egg topped with fried onions and a red sauce, then small bowls to rinse your right hand in before digging in, the preferred Banjar way to eat, with no utensils. Kris loved yellow rice and was glad to eat a dish she never cooked at home. No one talked to her as she ate, and she racked her brain for questions to ask the ladies sitting near her but came up blank. At least having a full mouth took away some of the pressure to speak. *I better prepare some questions to ask people next week. If I'm invited back.*

She tried to eavesdrop on some of the other women's conversations. Ibu Siti, Ibu Mia, and Mama Rizky were not too far away discussing how to keep a husband faithful.

Mia seemed the most animated. "This witchdoctor I went to totally has the answers. He told me to"—she covered her mouth with her hand as though telling a secret—"and if I added that to my husband's food he'd always come back to me."

"Food *is* important!" Siti agreed. "Everyone knows a man judges his wife first by her figure and second by the dinner she serves him. I feed my husband whatever he likes—fried food, spicy food, anything—as long as he's happy."

"But don't you have an ulcer? How can you eat that food?" wondered Mama Rizky.

"I can't. But I'm so scared he's going to take a second wife sometimes I forget to eat anyway," Siti explained.

Mama Rizky put her hand on Siti's arm and glanced at her trim waist. "No wonder your figure is so nice! But your husband works in a *pesantren* with all men, not like my husband, who works in an office with younger women wearing short skirts. My husband's more likely to have an affair or take a second wife than yours."

"All men are looking for a younger woman," Mia took charge again. "That's why I go to the witchdoctor. But I have another secret too—kinky sex. Have you ever tried—" again Mia covered her mouth with her hand and lowered her voice. Kris saw Mama Rizky's mouth drop open and Ibu Siti's face turn red. *Maybe it's time I eavesdrop on some other conversation.*

But then the meal was over. Kris took a slice of watermelon off a plate in the center of the room and quickly polished it off even while she was handing her plate down the line to be cleared away for the main event— the actual *arisan.*

The *arisan* was the poor woman's savings system. Every woman contributed a sum of money to the "pot"; then they drew names for the lucky winner to collect the money. The winner's name was removed so that next time a new woman would get the money. Many women planned ahead to save for something too expensive for their monthly salary to afford by paying into the *arisan* until their name was drawn; then they could buy it.

For this *arisan*, Ibu Aaminah had dropped by the kiosk earlier to remind Kris to bring Rp.10,000 every week. This was doable for her, and she was already imagining what she might do with the winnings when her name was drawn. The winnings totaled nearly Rp.500,000 because some of the richer ladies like Ibu Aaminah put in Rp.10,000 for herself, another Rp.10,000 in her first daughter's name, and another Rp.10,000 in her second daughter's name. When their names came up, she might use the money to go visit them or buy a special gift for them.

Kris handed over her Rp.10,000 bill to Ibu Aaminah, who wrote down Kris's name and the amount in her booklet. The booklet was so that in case anyone was absent, Ibu Aaminah could go to their house and collect the money owed, then pass it on to the proper winner.

Since this was the first meeting of a new cycle, everyone's names were written on small papers, which were then rolled up and slid into straws that had been cut into 1-inch lengths. These straws were dropped into an empty plastic Aqua bottle. When everyone's name had been dropped in, Ibu Aaminah asked Ibu Mibah to shake the bottle. To Kris, it sounded like the small boxes of rock candies she'd had as a kid. *This is kind of exciting! What if my name gets drawn today?*

Ibu Mibah then poured one straw out of the bottle into Ibu Hajjah's palm. She slid out the rolled-up paper and read loudly, "Noorminah." There were oohs and ahs and a cry of delight from Ibu Noorminah, who shook hands with Ibu Aaminah and took the envelope of cash.

"Before everyone leaves," Ibu Aaminah said loudly, "we have a few announcements. First of all, next week we'll be signing everyone up to take a turn preparing the fast-breaking food for the neighborhood men to break the fast every day at the mosque. If you will be traveling during fasting month or can't afford to provide food and just want to help one of the other women with cooking, please tell me or Ibu Fina sometime during the week. Then we can give a completed schedule to you next week.

"Also, I want to welcome a newcomer to our *arisan*, though not a new-comer to our neighborhood. Ibu Kris has been a fine member of our community for many years now, and we're very happy to receive her into our *arisan*. Ibu Kris, would you like to say anything?"

Like a lamb to the slaughter...

Kris smiled her warmest, friendliest smile. "Well...I'd just like to say thank you for allowing me to show honor to the women of this community by joining the ladies' *arisan*. I hope I can get to know all of you better."

A few women smiled back and nodded their heads; other sat still as statues. No one told her she had to leave, that she was unwanted there.

Then someone stood with an, "*Assalamu alaikum*," and the event was over. Kris realized she'd been holding her breath and gasped for air. Then she stood, too, and moved to thank her hostess before heading for the door. She walked next to Ibu Noorminah on the way home, asking her how she planned to spend the money. Noorminah was so excited it seemed she was happy to bubble over on anyone, even on a Christian.

The dawn of a new hope tugged at Kris's heart—hope that her years of rejection and isolation might be coming to an end at last.

❧ Chapter 12 ❧

LOUIS STAUNTON SURVEYED the damage. The Detroit mosque's front door was covered with blood. But this wasn't a homicide scene. The two victims' dead bodies lying on the doorstep were not human, but pigs. Their heads were decapitated, their entrails spilled onto the sidewalk. Louis didn't know which he hated worse—the stench of hate or of death.

Next to him were seven people Louis's staff had invited as soon as they'd heard about this hate crime. They were the pastors of the seven churches geographically closest to this mosque. Louis wanted them to see, touch, and smell, not hear about it on the evening news.

"Lord have mercy!" Pastor Johnson kept repeating. Five other pastors stood in horrified silence. Pastor number seven was puking in the bushes.

Imam Muhammad Noor, the leader of the mosque, stood quietly with them staring at the carnage, having said no more than, "Thank you for coming."

Louis turned to look the pastors in the eye. "This morning the worshipers could not enter the mosque to pray, as touching the blood of a pig would make them unclean, much like Moses's Law in the Old Testament. Until the blood is thoroughly washed away, this mosque will be empty.

"In many countries of the world, our Christian brothers and sisters face similar persecution. Well, I'm sad to say that America has its problems with persecuting religious minorities, too. The question is, Will the Christian majority here do something about it?

"I invited you all here today because you are this mosque's neighbors. It's time to do what Christ taught us, to 'love your neighbor as yourself.' I'd like to ask you to call some members of your church staff or congregation to bring their buckets, soap, and scrub brushes, and make sure our neighbors here will be able to open their doors for tonight's evening prayers. Will you do that?"

All the pastors nodded. Soon they were all talking on their cell phones.

Louis put his arm around Imam Noor. "I'm so sorry. I'm sure the delinquents who did this do not represent the majority of the good folks of Detroit, the folks who maybe never knew your mosque was even here, but now they will. Let's turn this into an opportunity to meet the neighbors. What do you say?"

Imam Noor smiled through his obvious pain. "My people already feel isolated. I'm concerned this may drive some of them to paranoia. But I agree with you. I will tell them it is time to meet the neighbors."

Louis admired the man's courage. "The key to a future of peace lies not in the hands of politicians and religious leaders like you and me but in the hands of regular folks. Every day, somewhere in the world, even in the places most filled with hate, ordinary people can become extraordinary peacemakers. When your mosque members and those pastors' church members start eating in each others' homes, carpooling their kids to soccer practice together, going to see a Pistons game together, it won't stop the hate crimes, but our community will stand as one."

Louis started rolling up his sleeves. "Got any water and soap? I want to be the first one to wash this hate away."

❧ Chapter 13 ❧

KRIS CONTINUED TO pray every day for God to open her heart to the Muslim women of her neighborhood. Her second visit to the *arisan* was not as nerve-racking since she now knew what to expect. She had prepared a few questions to ask those sitting next to her, about their children mostly, and this week there were fewer suspicious glares.

Two nights later she had a dream. She'd received several dreams over the years that she thought were God trying to tell her something. So she got out her journal and wrote everything she could remember, including drawing a couple pictures of what she'd seen.

July 28

I had a dream that I was having an affair with a married man. In the first scene, we were eating together in an elegant restaurant. I was young and beautiful. I knew he was rich and handsome, but I couldn't see his face clearly. (Could it be Hendri?) He gave me a single red rose. I knew I had totally fallen for him.

In the next scene we were holding hands walking toward his home, where I knew we were going to spend the night together. I was trembling with the thrill of his love. It was a lovely starry night with a full moon. He pulled me to him and kissed me, and I closed my eyes and melted in his arms.

When I opened my eyes I was alone. I panicked, looking around for my lover, but he was gone. At the end of the street was a glorious mansion that I knew had to be his home, so I started running toward it, and as I ran it started to rain. It rained harder and harder until I wasn't sure I'd make it, but I knew if I could just reach that house my lover would take me inside, and I could feel the thrill of his touch again.

Finally I reached the front steps with a great sigh of relief and scanned the windows for his face. Only one window upstairs wasn't covered by curtains, and there was a woman looking out of it. Her eyes were filled with hate, so much that she scared me. I froze, not sure what to do. Maybe I had the wrong house, I thought.

Suddenly the door opened, and there he was! My lover stepped outside and held out his hand. He was handing me an envelope. I reached out my hand and took it as I looked at his face to know what this meant, but I still couldn't see his face clearly. I could only make out that he wasn't smiling. I felt a chill settle over me from head to toe.

He closed the door and left me standing on the steps in the rain with the envelope in my hand. I stood there for a long time weeping and weeping, not knowing where to go or what to do. After what seemed an eternity, my tears began to wane, and I turned my attention to the envelope. Should I open it? I wrestled in my heart. It was probably a letter from my lover. If the letter told me to go away because he never loved me, I've deceived myself and I've been used. If the letter told me that he still loved me, why would he close his door to me and break my heart?

I decided to never open the letter so I'd never have to face the pain of what it said. Then I woke up.

Kris was still thinking about the dream that afternoon as she went outside to retrieve the pillows she'd hung out that morning to soak up some sunshine and fresh air. *I wonder if the dream is about me and my husband. Or about the letter I keep in my Bible? Please, God, you told people like Joseph and Daniel the meanings of dreams. Help me to understand what this dream is saying to me.*

It was already six o'clock. Dinner was on the table; they were just waiting for Sari to get her bath. Many of the neighbors chose to walk down the alley and across Kelayan B street to the river for their baths, but ever since Sari had become a teenager Kris had decided to protect her from perverted comments by paying a man with a wooden cart to bring them twelve gallons of city water each week for baths and dishwashing and, after they boiled it, for drinking. Kris still took her laundry to the river to wash it each morning.

The alley was almost empty, with most people getting ready for the *Mahgrib* prayers and dinner, but it wasn't completely empty. Kris noticed two figures plodding toward her. It was Ibu Dina and her younger daughter, Rini. Kris threw the pillows inside the front door and returned to check on them.

"Hi, Ibu Dina! Hi, Rini! You both look tired! Did you walk really far today?" Since her husband's death, Dina had resorted to begging as a way to pay the bills. Kris wondered where Nina was. Nina was Sari's age, and after her father died she had dropped out of school to help her mom make a living.

"Ibu, I'm so tired. I don't know what to do anymore. We started at the Jati Street traffic light, but the police chased us out of the intersection again. So we walked to Bun Yamin Street, where some really nice houses are, but half the homes were locked up. The other half were so stingy! All we got today is Rp.12,000. How are we going to live on Rp.12,000?"

"You poor thing! That must be six kilometers from here! Wait right here. I want to tell Sari something." Kris called through her open front door to Sari, who appeared with a towel around her hair, then disappeared again. Kris returned to Dina and Rini.

"Sari's just going to package up some leftovers if you can wait a minute. Where's Nina?"

"I don't know. She hasn't helped us at all the last two days. We'd have made more if she'd been there. Last night she didn't even come home. I don't know where she is."

"You must be worried sick!"

"No, she's probably staying with a friend to get a good meal in her stomach and cool off. She was pretty upset a couple days ago."

"Why? Did she get groped on the street again?"

"No, that kind of thing doesn't seem to upset her as much. You remember that pair of Sari's sandals you gave her last week? The broken ones? She stayed out late one night begging until she got the extra Rp.3,000 she needed to fix them, and she loved them so much. Then just two days ago they got stolen from our front porch while we were washing our laundry and only Rini was home. Nina only got to wear them for four days! She was devastated."

"Oh, that poor girl! Sari will be upset to hear it too. Remember that time when they were about eight years old and the tide was so high the river spilled over and the swamp water rose up and our street and most of our yards were underwater, and Nina and Sari went swimming in the street? They were having such a fun time splashing and laughing; then Nina lost a little bracelet that Sari had made for her. They searched for hours in the brown water until we made them come inside. I remember

Sari cried that night for Nina and wouldn't go to bed until she'd made another bracelet for her best friend."

Kris smiled at Dina, hoping to relieve some of her heaviness with a happy memory, but it didn't seem to be working. Dina was staring dejectedly at her own filthy feet.

"Well, I'll ask Sari if she's heard anything from Nina. Oh, here she is now!" Sari came down the steps with a plastic bag holding two containers.

"Where's Nina?"

Kris touched her daughter affectionately on the elbow. "We were hoping you might have heard something. Nina didn't come home last night."

Sari's neck jerked back in surprise. "Huh! I haven't heard anything. Where do you think she is?" she asked Ibu Dina.

"She's probably with a friend. I'm not going to worry about her. She's a big girl. It's me and Rini I worry about." Dina took the plastic bag with a nod to Kris. "Well, thank you, Ibu, for sharing your dinner with us. We need to get home and sit down."

"All right. Get some rest, and keep your chin up!" Kris sent them off with a wave good-bye. Then she and Sari went back inside for a dinner that was half as nourishing as they had expected it to be. And the small, empty place left in their stomachs now filled with worry for Sari's friend Nina.

❧ Chapter 14 ❧

Pak Zaini returned home from playing chess with the RT that night red-faced, and not because he lost the chess match. *This time my wife has gone too far.*

Zaini cleared his throat. "Minah, the men have been discussing this crazy idea of yours, inviting a Christian woman to join the *arisan*."

Aaminah barely glanced up from her book. "How wonderful, dear! That's better than them discussing how sexy Pak Syaif's twenty-two-year-old second wife is, which is what they always seem to be doing whenever I walk by!"

"I'm serious. Some of the men are outraged. This has never been done before!"

Aaminah finally looked up. "Don't you remember the time, dear, when a Christian group was passing through Mecca and had no place for their worship? The Prophet offered them the use of his mosque. If Nabi Muhammad could invite Christians into the mosque, how much more should we be willing to invite them into a little ladies' meeting?"

"Most of the men are more upset with you than they are with Ibu Kris. They're saying you should know better. One of them even said something about you that I refuse to repeat out loud. It bothers me when people say such things about my wife!" Zaini raised his right arm and bent it backwards to massage his tense neck.

"If I were you I'd worry less about what men say and more about what God says about us."

"Please, as your husband, I'm begging you: put a stop to this nonsense! I supported your marching against polygamy and all your other causes. I support you helping the street kids' school. Can you at least leave this neighborhood alone? I always get stuck cleaning up your messes, you know!"

Aaminah closed her book and smiled sincerely. "Yes, dear, you've always been wonderful at cleaning up my messes. I wouldn't be courageous enough to make them if I didn't have you! And you should be proud of me. I'm just finishing reading another biography. This one is about a Muslim: Benazir Bhutto of Pakistan." She showed him the cover of the book, then picked up a little note card that she'd written on. Zaini had seen hundreds of these scattered around the house over the years with Aaminah's favorite sayings.

"Listen to this quote from the end of Bhutto's biography, where she quotes Martin Luther King Jr.: 'Our lives begin to end the day we remain silent on things that matter.' *Insha' Allah* that will *not* be said of me!"

"You're not going to listen to me, are you?"

"Of course. I always listen to you, dear! And when you say something that makes my heart rise up in passionate agreement, I'll do whatever it was you said."

Zaini grimaced. He knew he was defeated once again. Over the years he'd learned to revise his ambition from being the wise leader of his wife to just preventing riots in the city and keeping his wife out of jail. What did he have to show for it? Three headstrong kids who wouldn't listen to their parents. A reputation among the men as the neighborhood *wuss*. He'd accepted it as his fate. At least he'd die of stress rather than boredom.

Aaminah put down her book and reached for her husband's hand. He took it, still frowning. "Loving the street kids isn't easy, you know. They stink. They're unruly. They're disrespectful. Loving Ibu Kris isn't easy either, but I want a different world, and I'm prepared to pay the price. Just like you have to pay, dear, for loving me. Is it easy for you?"

"Not today it isn't. But it's usually worth it," he admitted grudgingly.

Aaminah smiled at her husband. Then she lay back in her chair and closed her eyes before continuing. "I'm exhausted. Would you be a dear and finish washing the dishes for me, then?"

"Mark my words, Minah, no good will come of this. For once in your life you're going to regret you didn't listen to your husband!"

Zaini's sharp gaze was wasted as he waited for an answer, since Aaminah refused to reengage. Eventually the wisdom of experience whispered that he'd better focus his smoldering anger at his deaf wife on the dirty dishes.

❦ Chapter 15 ❦

O̲N JULY TWENTY-NINTH, Saifullah reached Banjarmasin.
He spent his first morning sleeping in till noon. He was still
behind on sleep from the exhausting trip to Makassar. He had started
looking for a "bride" there, but it was too hot. Maybe it was all the
university student demonstrations and the recent vandalism at the
McDonalds—there were police everywhere, and a lot of them weren't in
uniform. Saifullah could usually spot them by the type of questions they
asked and the way they carried themselves. But he couldn't afford to get
nabbed in some random sweep; he had more important things to do. So
he had taken the boat across to Borneo Island, landing in Balikpapan,
then taking the twelve-hour overnight bus to Banjarmasin.

Saifullah had never been to Banjarmasin before, but he'd heard that it
was one of the five most conservative Muslim areas of Indonesia. Most of
the *jihad* network in Indonesia was made up of recruits from Java, many
connected by bloodline with other recruits, and Saifullah had always
thought these outlying regions underrepresented. JI had tried to establish some training camps in these areas that the Densus 88 police weren't
watching as closely as in Java. He'd heard that there used to be some
training camps northeast of Banjarmasin in the jungle but didn't know
if they were still active. Anyway, it would be too risky to ask questions
locally about those camps. He'd have a better chance of going undetected
alone.

Poor Dulmatin! It seemed like only yesterday he'd left the Philippines
to take charge after Noordin M. Top's death, and the first thing he did
was set up a *jihad* training camp in the remote jungles of Aceh for the
fifty new recruits the network had signed up. He'd started the rookies on
gun and knife fighting, guerilla warfare, bomb making, and the tactics
of *fa'i*—stealing from non-Muslims, using violence if necessary, for the
greater good of funding *jihad*. The recruits had practiced by attacking
banks and foreign non-governmental organizations (NGOs) still there
rebuilding infrastructure after the tsunami.

The Americans had put a $10 million bounty on his head, and soon the camp was discovered and Dulmatin gunned down in a public Internet access facility.

Not this time! Soon I'll be valued by those kafir *Americans at more than $10 million. They will not forget the name Saifullah!*

After ordering room service for lunch, Saifullah checked out at one o'clock, paying cash. He laid his backpack on one of the fraying vinyl chairs in the lobby and leaned against the counter. It was time to get oriented to his new haystack, for he had to find the perfect needle, and he didn't have much time to do it. The hotel clerk seemed friendly and supremely bored, ripe for dispensing information.

"Seems pretty quiet here in the hotel. Isn't this the height of the tourist season?"

"We don't get many tourists here. Sometimes they come in for a night, then they're off trekking to the interior to see the orangutans or up to Martapura to see the diamond mines. There's not much to see in Banjar."

"Martapura. I've heard of it before. Tell me more about it." Saifullah had seen a police report state that the second Bali bomb had been planned in Martapura, although he greatly doubted its accuracy. The police were always lying to the press. But it might be wiser not to mention to the hotel clerk anything with the word *bomb* in it. Wouldn't want him passing on such a conversation to the authorities.

"Oh, it's a great place to buy souvenirs—wicker products, gemstones, traditional swords. A lot of people go out there for *ziarah* to the grave of Al Banjari, the guy who brought true Islam to this region. There's a lot of *pesantrens* out there, too. Kind of fanatical city, you might say. You know how they call Aceh 'Mecca's Porch'? Well, they call Martapura 'Medina's Porch.'"

Sounds like an excellent place to go courting a "bride."

"Interesting! I do need to pick up some souvenirs for my trip home, so maybe I'll do some shopping there tomorrow."

"I should tell you, they close all their stores on Fridays from about 11:00 a.m. to 2:00 p.m. for worship. Better to go early or late."

"Thanks, I'll remember that. Are there any mosques you'd recommend here in the city for worship? Maybe one with a real interesting teacher?"

"Well, people used to leave Banjarmasin for the Friday *sholat* in Martapura at Guru Ijai's place. He was the most famous teacher we've ever had here. But he died a few years ago, and nobody's really replaced him. For a while Guru Bakrie was a popular speaker at the Grand

Mosque here in Banjar, but then he went to jail for illegal logging. Can't say there's anyone really special anymore."

Better change the subject.

"Any tourist locations nearby?"

"The most famous tourist site here is the floating market out on the Barito River, but you probably already know about that."

"Of course, but I haven't seen it yet. How do I get there?"

"You have to leave about five in the morning to arrive there when it's busiest. I can reserve a *klotok* to pick you up by the river near our hotel here, and it takes them about an hour to wind through the city's river network out to the big river, where the wholesalers from up river gather to sell their produce to the city folks. Besides all the fruits and vegetables, there are floating restaurant boats you can get breakfast from. The whole trip takes about two hours, three if you go down river to visit Monkey Island. But you've already checked out—where are you going to be tonight?"

"I'm planning to stay in a bigger hotel with a nightclub just for one night. I think I'll do that and skip getting up so early in the morning for the floating market. Maybe on my next trip."

"Sure, I can recommend Hotel Banjarmasin International. They have probably the biggest nightclub in the city. I'm not really into the night life myself."

Neither am I, kid. If you only knew . . . My last visit to a nightclub I was nineteen years old and delivering a smoke bomb.

"Thanks for your advice. I hope this city will have just what I'm looking for."

❧ Chapter 16 ❧

SAIFULLAH THREW HIS backpack over his shoulders and headed out to survey the streets around him. He had no intention of going to nightclubs or souvenir shopping—he was hunting for treasure of a much more valuable kind. And he needed to find a crowded area where young men were hanging out doing nothing.

How to woo a "bride"... Saifullah had never excelled at this part of the job. His Afghan instructor's words still convicted him: "I see in everyone I meet a future jihadist. They just need the proper motivation." Noordin and Dulmatin were masters at getting into a mosque or *pesantren* and very persuasively turning the conversations to religious-oriented conflicts like Palestine, Ambon, or Poso and the encroaching darkness of the West. Sometimes they'd bring out the *Mausu'ah Jihad Afghan* book or look for students they could offer free *silat* training to, often without the knowledge of the boys' parents. Or there was Syaefuddin's way. He'd find a boy with no father and take him into his home and over a few months have him ready to do anything in the defense of Islam. Or there was the more direct way: Hambali would just drive around in a van looking for groups of angry young men, university activists, or small-time criminal gangs and ask, "Who wants to go to heaven?"

Saifullah needed his own method. And he had an idea. Marginalized people often made great recruits, and surely young Javanese men as a minority here might feel marginalized. And he had a trick up his sleeve to help him find such men in a crowd.

Saifullah himself had been recruited one day at a *silat* tournament he took part in. His *silat* club was called *Pintu Surga*, or "Heaven's Door." There are many such clubs in Java, almost like secret societies. Since many Javanese had spread all over the Indonesian archipelago, he figured there was a good chance he'd find a former Pintu Surga member somewhere in Banjar who could help him.

Pintu Surga had its own oath, code, secret book of rules and prayers, burial cloth, and secret signs. There were special prayers to pray while facing the four directions of earth—north, east, south, and west—to receive either knowledge, authority, influence, or raw power. There were special techniques for breathing in, focusing your power, and breathing out as you released that power against your opponent, often knocking him backward or off his feet without even touching him.

Pintu Surga possessed a secret sign: both pointer fingers pointing upward, just left and right of the face, then brought together before the nose as the person closed his eyes, symbolizing a closing of the door to this world to see what is in the next. Any member of the club seeing this was required by oath to assist in whatever way needed, whether providing food, loaning a small amount of money, providing escape from the police, or defending the gesturer against a rival gang.

Saifullah had once used this sign to call for help when he was surrounded in the street by seven bullies about to tear him apart. An old man he'd never met walked into the circle of bullies and told them they'd better think twice about messing with his son, or he'd have a whole martial arts school tear certain extremities from their bodies. When he had turned to thank the old man, he got a lecture to stay out of trouble, because there might not always be someone from Pintu Surga to bail him out.

Saifullah's idea was to flash that sign a few times in a few different places around the city and see what he turned up.

Several hours later, Saifullah found himself wandering around a large shopping plaza called Ramayana after the national chain department store that took up most of the plaza. He wasn't interested in shopping but in the groups of men hovering outside the building.

Since Saifullah still hadn't had any luck with his Pintu Surga sign, he decided on a new tack. A group of young men were perched on the bricks of a planter in the courtyard between the department store and the Agung Mosque. He walked over to them, three of whom were wearing the white skullcaps common to *pesantren* students, and started with a question.

"*Assalamu alaikum.* Hey, I'm new in town, and want to know where the 'real' Muslim's *sholat* on Friday is."

"*Wa alaikum assalam.* My name's Hafiz. What do you mean?"

"Are you guys *pesantren* grads? Where did you go to school?"

"We're still in *pesantren*, not graduated yet," Hafiz responded.

"Oh, you guys looked older. What kind of school is it? Traditional or modern? Liberal or orthodox?"

"I'd say it's pretty traditional. We mostly learn the Qur'an and the *Hadith*, but we do get to learn some math, science, history, and English."

"Do you guys have a *silat* club?"

"Yeah!" Hafiz brightened at a topic more interesting than school. "Syukran's dad teaches us." He nodded toward Syukran. Hafiz glanced at Saifullah's chiseled body evident even through his brown, long-sleeved *batik* shirt and khaki pants. "Are you like a pro *silat* guy or something?"

"Something like that. Maybe I can meet your dad sometime. So back to my original question—which mosque would you recommend for someone who wants to worship with the 'real' Muslims?"

A smile came over Hafiz's face. "I get it. You're talking about the kind of mosque a martial arts expert would go to. Islam with teeth in it."

"That's right, son. Islam with teeth in it."

Hafiz turned to the guys who murmured back and forth for a bit. Finally Hafiz was ready with their recommendation.

"Most of us go to the Grand Mosque in the center of town every Friday 'cause that's where our friends go, but we wouldn't recommend it for you. The imam mostly talks about donations for building projects, the importance of education and stuff like that. But there is a mosque in Kelayan that we attend once in a while where they talk about taking action against society's evils. They signed up volunteers for *jihad* in Palestine a couple months ago. I signed up, but they still haven't called me to go," Hafiz added proudly.

"That sounds more my style," Saifullah grinned. "Any of you want to take me there tomorrow?"

"I will," Syukran offered quickly. "It's near my house." The other boys stared at Syukran, then back at Hafiz.

"Can you pick me up here before *sholat*?"

"Uh, yeah, I think I can. Right here?"

"Yes, right here. Is the mosque far?"

"No, only about ten minutes," Syukran answered.

"Hey, guys, let's all go!" Hafiz decided. "Let's get Juki and Fani, too." Hafiz seemed to be in control again. He turned back to Saifullah. "Are you a recruiter for JI?"

Saifullah cast him a disarming smile. "Why, are you hoping to meet one?"

"Actually, yes. Me and the boys here have been talking, and we think it's high time we struck a blow for the good guys, but we don't know where to start. What do you think we should do?"

"I think you guys are already demonstrating your good hearts by offering to take a Muslim brother to the mosque to worship with the real *umat* tomorrow. Let's continue this conversation tomorrow, shall we? I need to be going. *Assalamu alaikum.*"

"*Wa alaikum assalam.*"

As Saifullah walked away, he argued with himself. *Be careful what you reveal till you're sure. I may only have one chance to do this right. If I choose the wrong "bride," it'll be like the Marriott bombing all over again. I can't fail again. This is the time for my redemption.*

This is the time for my glory!

❧ Chapter 17 ❧

FRIDAY MORNING AT 11:30 a.m., Saifullah stepped off a yellow mini-bus at the Ramayana terminal. He figured he had a few minutes before meeting the *pesantren* boys. Better scope out the situation. He took the escalator up to the second floor of the plaza and walked around the northern outer ring of small shops till he found the perfect vantage point. From here he could see the boys approach, with the taxis on his right and the mosque on his left, as well as the police post across the intersection from the mosque. If he saw anything fishy he'd have to find another means of contact.

The boys were right on time, turning their motorbikes into the parking lot at about 11:45. There were two on one bike, the third riding alone but with an extra helmet dangling below the steering column. They parked and walked toward the designated meeting place, the planter. They were looking around in all directions watching for him. Well, he'd let them wait just a bit longer.

Two uniformed traffic policemen were headed across the intersection from their police post, presumably to join the Friday worship. *Go on into the mosque like good little cops.*

He could see the policemen stop outside to do their *wudlu*, their ceremonial washings, before entering the mosque. The boys were now standing on the planter looking around dramatically. They were drawing too much attention to themselves. He saw a plainclothes security guard from the mosque watching them. Without taking his eyes off the boys, the guard sidled over to have a word with one of the policemen who had just finished his *wudlu*. Now the policeman was looking at the boys too.

Last night at a different hotel, a very cheap one that didn't require his ID upon check-in, he'd had an enlightening chat with a traveling religious teacher who wore a full-length white Arab robe and a white turban on his head. The man's long white beard reminded him how every hardline Muslim teacher wants to look like Osama bin Laden. The teacher was explaining how he had been trying to get into various mosques and *mushollas* in the city to correct their passivistic, anemic faith, and had been run out of most neighborhoods after just one or two sermons. Even though the Banjar were conservative by nature, he had said, the men aren't strong enough in the faith to make their wives and daughters dress modestly and cover their whole bodies in public. The women are so weak in faith they pray only once a day facing toward Mecca and spend ten times as much of their time watching soap operas, facing toward America! Be warned, he had said, many mosques now had security guards, not to guard against infiltrating Christians but to guard against the true Muslims! Saifullah had listened sympathetically and taken the guy's namecard, pretending to have lost his own, figuring if this teacher eventually found a mosque ready to hear his message maybe Saifullah could find a "bride" there.

The policemen left their sandals out on the steps and entered the mosque. The security guard stayed outside and watched, giving special attention to the boys, who seemed to be arguing among themselves.

Sorry, boys. I'll have to find you another way. Where did they say they were from? Kelayan. Looks like another stop on my tour of the city. I'd best find another mosque for my prayers today, then maybe I'll spend a few days checking out Martapura. See you boys when I get back. Have patience.

Saifullah headed back through the row of shops closing for worship and melted into the crowd.

❧ Chapter 18 ☙

AT THE *AL-MUSTAQIIM Pesantren*, students only did half-day studies during Ramadan and took off the final week of fasting completely. Abdullah's English class, like all the other non-religion classes, was thus cut to twenty-five minutes in length rather than the usual fifty minutes. Today he had taught the Ramadan story in English—the story of Muhammad's receiving from the angel *Jibra'il* the supreme gift of God, the revelations later written down as the Qur'an, revelations which transformed Muhammad from an ardent seeker of God into a prophet and a messenger. He'd taught them the English vocabulary for Ramadan words like "fasting," "abstain," "revelation," and so on. It was time to wrap up the class. Abdullah started copying some words from a book Iqbal had procured for him onto the chalkboard and told the students to copy these words into their notebooks. Abdullah waited for everyone to finish before explaining.

"One of the purposes of fasting during Ramadan is learning to deny our own comforts to reach for something greater. It's learning to hunger for not what we want but what Allah wants.

"Throughout history there have been heroes who have lived their whole lives like this. They were willing to sacrifice their own lives to bring this confused world back into the light of what Allah wants it to be. We're going to be learning a little about one such hero through a speech that he made. You see the title here?" Abdullah pointed to the board: *I Have a Dream*. "Does anyone know who made this speech?"

Silence.

"It was an American named Martin Luther King Jr." As Abdullah said the word *American*, several eyebrows went up. "As a black man living in the America of fifty years ago, Mr. King saw that the white citizens were treating the black citizens unfairly. He knew that God wanted something better for them. So he gave this speech about his dream for a better world. Then he was killed for it."

Reza raised his hand.

"Yes?"

"Excuse me, Pak Guru, was Martin Luther King a Muslim?"

"No, he was actually a Christian pastor. What does that have to do with anything?"

"Well Pak Guru, if we're going to learn about a hero, don't you think someone who does *jihad* against the Americans would be a more appropriate hero?"

"Yeah," Hafiz cut in. "We'd like to hear about someone who, like, bombed a church in Afghanistan and cut the throats of those *kafir* dogs as they came out the doors. That's a real hero!"

Abdullah stared at Hafiz for several seconds, the words caught in his throat. Finally he spoke in a choked whisper. "What are you talking about?"

"Come on, sir, we all know, but we can keep a secret. You're a much better hero than some black *kafir* American. Why don't you tell us some of *your* stories?"

"Did someone tell you I bombed a church in Afghanistan? Who?"

Silence.

Abdullah spoke each word slowly and forcefully. "I never want to hear another crazy lie about my past, got it? You think bombing people takes guts? Any gutless worm can do that! A real hero is someone who takes the beating, even to the death, to change the hearts of the violent fools who are ruining our world, like Martin Luther King did. I'm certainly no hero, nor will I ever be!"

The boys cowered at this rare display of temper from their teacher. Abdullah glared from face to face. Reza shifted uncomfortably in his wooden chair. Hafiz stared confusedly at his *guru*. Syukran avoided Abdullah's gaze.

Then the moment passed. Abdullah turned back to the board and pointed halfway down the text. "Those of you in the front three rows will work together to translate the first half of the speech, back three rows translate the second half. Make sure each group has a dictionary. The first group may borrow the school's English dictionary tonight through Sunday night, then bring it Monday morning for the second group, unless one of you students can borrow a second dictionary somewhere. Your group must have your section completely translated by next Thursday, and be prepared to talk through the themes Martin Luther King presents. Got it? Class dismissed."

School finished at 11:00, but some of Syukran's classmates seemed in no hurry to head home. With no lunch waiting for them it seemed more important to discuss the bomb dropped in today's English class.

"Syuk, I don't get it," Hafiz started. "Did your dad deny it or not?"

"Sounded to me like he denied it. But it also sounded to me like he was lying," guessed Udin.

Hafiz glared at Syukran. "Well, at least one of you is lying."

Syukran didn't know what to say. Fortunately, he was saved by Reza's sincere confusion.

"But how can Pak Guru pick a hero who is a black American Christian? He's even a pastor! Those guys hate Muslims! Christians are killing our brothers in Ambon! This is wrong, wrong, wrong! We've got to do something about it! Maybe we should tell Pak Ustad."

"No, you don't need to do that," Syukran begged. "Let me talk to my dad. I'm sure if I talk to him he'll straighten everything out."

Udin had a cheerful thought. "Can you talk to him tonight? Maybe you can get us out of this homework assignment!"

"Yeah, I'll talk to him tonight. Don't worry about it, guys. Chill out."

Syukran headed for his bicycle. *What if Dad suspects I made up that story? This is not going to go well, is it? Unless this is the kick in the butt Dad needs to open up about his past and finally tell us the truth.*

❧ Chapter 19 ☙

THAT NIGHT ABDULLAH'S family was gathered at the dinner table early, waiting for the end of the fast. It had been a hot and dry day, and Syukran's tongue felt like a cotton ball in his mouth. He gazed longingly at the pitcher of tea in front of him, hoping that taking a mental drink would soothe his parched throat. Siti had already set out tiny plates for each person with a date and a slice of green layered cake called *kue lapis*, a traditional Banjar cake she'd picked up at the market earlier that afternoon. It was a simple snack for breaking the fast; no fruit cocktail drinks or expensive cakes from the Ramadan cake fair like many others in the city would be eating, but fourteen hours without food or drink could make anything look like a feast.

Siti had just paused in a long lecture about the boys not helping wash the dishes after the pre-dawn meal, and Syukran saw his chance. He turned to face his father.

"Dad, what happened at school today, well, some of the boys are confused about your past and what you really did. What should I tell them?"

Abdullah continued meditating on his snack plate. "Nothing. It's none of their business."

Syukran hesitated. *Should I tell him they're going to protest to the principal?*

Iqbal's curiosity was piqued. "Dad, did you tell your students about your past? You've never even told us about it. What did you tell them?" Then he directed to Syukran, "What did he tell you?"

"Nothing! I told them nothing! But some *fool* has been spreading lies about me killing people in Afghanistan. And that better never happen again!"

He knows it's me. He'll never forgive me.

"Come on, Dad! What is so bad that you can't tell your own kids about? We just want to know who our father is. So what if you went to Afghanistan? What's the big deal? Why can't you just tell us?" Iqbal, even more than Syukran, had always wanted to know about his father's past.

Abdullah's voice rose to a dangerous pitch. "There are good *reasons* why I don't talk about my past! There are things I'm not proud of. There are things I've done that if someone blabs to the wrong people it could attract a deadly kind of attention. That life is buried in the grave, and I'm *not* digging it back up to satisfy some empty-headed fools who can't tell the difference between heroism and lunacy. So drop it!"

Their normally calm and disinterested father had disappeared; this angry father had clearly ended the conversation. But Iqbal wasn't satisfied.

"Well, I don't care what you're afraid of. I'm your son, and I have the right to know. So tell me."

Abdullah glared at his son. "No!"

"Fine!" Bali retorted. Syukran had never heard his brother raise his voice to Dad like this before.

Abdullah stood up, his white knuckles gripping the table between him and Iqbal so hard he might crush it. His arms were trembling. He spat his words out as though a bug had just accidentally flown into his mouth.

"Because I don't talk about my past I am alive for my kids today. Are you telling me you don't want that? You want to be raised without a father because I threw my life away for some idiot ideology? If that's the kind of father you want, go find someone else!"

Abdullah stormed out of the house, slamming the front door behind him. Iqbal was shaking, half angry, half terrified. Syukran realized he hadn't taken a breath during the entire conversation and started sucking air loudly. Siti was sniffing back tears but took charge now to comfort and correct her boys.

"Don't feel bad, boys. He'll cool down, and everything will be all right. He's usually not angry like this. Iqbal, you shouldn't have raised your voice to your father. Your father used to be a great man and deserves your respect. He risked his life in the defense of the faith. It's just this horrible city that's made him paralyzed by fear. If we could only move back to Java someday, you'd see; everything would turn out fine."

Iqbal rolled his eyes. "You're not making any sense, Mom. I just don't see why Dad is so afraid to tell us who he really is."

"Who he is, *is* your father, and you need to respect him! Now I want you to apologize to him when he comes back in, and we'll pretend this never happened."

"That's not good enough for me, Mom. I have to work this out on my own." Iqbal poured himself a cup of tea, grabbed the plate of snacks, and carried them into his bedroom and slammed the door.

Syukran was alone with his mother when the siren from the mosque went off, announcing it was sundown and time to break the fast. He took a long sip of the tea, then popped the sweet date into his mouth, stripped the meat off with his teeth, and spit the pit back onto his plate. He noticed his mom wasn't eating or drinking. She just sat very still staring at her lap, a tear falling from her eye.

"Mom, you OK?"

"Why can't things be the way they used to be? My husband walks out on me. My son walks out on me. Syukran, please tell me you'll never leave me." She looked at her youngest pleadingly.

Syukran didn't know what to say. He took a bite of his cake to gain a few seconds to think.

"Don't worry, Mom. They'll be back."

Siti heard what her son said. More importantly, she heard what he *didn't* say. She blinked at him twice, then suddenly burst into tears and ran into her bedroom. Just a moment ago the kitchen had been charged with emotional electricity; now it felt like a graveyard.

Happy fasting month, Syukran! How'd you like to celebrate the first day's fast-breaking all alone?

❧ Chapter 20 ☙

O<small>N</small> F<small>RIDAY, AFTER</small> the students had all gone home, Ustad Hasan Amman called Abdullah into his classroom for a chat.

"How's your fast going today? Energy still good?"

"Yes, no problems so far."

They both knew Abdullah wasn't there to discuss fasting. He waited quietly for his boss to state his case. Ustad Hasan Amman pulled at his wispy white beard and, glancing heavenward, mouthed a silent *Bismillah*.

"Pak Abdullah, one of the parents called me last night. He said something about your English homework that I'm sure isn't true, but I thought I'd check with you. According to this parent, you assigned his son to study a speech made by a Christian pastor, who quotes the Bible in his speech. Please tell me this isn't true."

"Actually, I did assign a speech made by a famous human rights activist who also happened to be a Christian pastor. If he quoted the Bible in the speech I wasn't aware of it. I've never even seen a Bible, so how would I recognize a quote from it? And I'm curious how this parent recognized a quote from it too."

"Hmmm. My guess would be the parent used to be a Christian but, praise God, has now repented and doesn't want his son exposed to the same lies he used to live under."

"I understand the parent's concern, Pak. But quote or no quote, the speech is brilliant, inspiring, much like your favorite song or painting or movie. We don't turn off the radio every time a pop song written or sung by a Christian artist comes on, do we? We don't boycott the movie theater because they're playing some film directed by Steven Spielberg, a Jew, do we? Why can't we appreciate this speech for the amazing work of art that it is?"

"And my question to you is, Surely there are Muslim speeches better than this—why can't you choose one of those?"

"This is English class, not Arabic. Where do you expect me to find speeches from famous Muslims in English?"

"Just find them. Or stick to your English 900 textbook. If the parent calls again, I'll tell him that you didn't realize the speech included a quote from the Bible and that by the next class all the students will be informed that you've chosen a new homework assignment for them."

For the first time in the conversation Ustad Hasan Amman looked directly into Abdullah's eyes. "Abdullah, we've been friends for a long time. I've never known you to rock the boat. You've always done everything by the book. What's going on? If there's anything you need to talk about, I'm always here for you."

Abdullah sighed and looked down at his twice-mended sandals. How could I tell this man about my nightmares? If he knew about my past he might fire me. Maybe it's because of the nightmares that I'm drawn to Martin Luther King's words about having a dream. But the nightmares are screaming so loudly they're drowning out my dreams, and I don't even know what my dreams are anymore.

"I'm sorry, Pak Hasan. It won't happen again."

☙ Chapter 21 ❧

"PLEASE, HEAVENLY FATHER, speak to me. I so want to understand. What does my dream mean? Why does my heart hurt so much whenever I think of it? Has my heart never really healed from Hendri? What are you trying to tell me?"

It was three in the morning, but Kris wasn't sleepy. She had taken her sheet, her pillow, her journal, and her Bible out of her bedroom to the living room floor. Whenever she felt like this she knew God was about to do something new and was preparing her for it. He was opening up her heart. Somewhere she had blocked out His love, and He wasn't patient for her to live without it any longer.

She sat silently for a long time, trying to listen for His gentle whisper to her heart. Nothing. She could feel His presence but could hear nothing. And then a nudge, almost like a breath of air, and she felt she was supposed to open her Bible and read. She touched the worn black leather cover affectionately.

"What do you want me to read, Lord?"

She felt the words drop into her spirit: "Genesis 16."

Kris quickly flipped through the first book of the Bible to chapter sixteen, the air around her charged with anticipation. *God's going to show me something! Thank you, Lord!*

> It was a story about the great patriarch Abraham, from whom three religions trace their beginnings: Jews, Christians, and Muslims. But it wasn't a flattering story of Abraham's great faith; on the contrary, it was a story about his lack of faith. As she read it she wrote a condensed version in her journal.

> God had already promised Abraham children as many as the stars in the sky in chapter fifteen. But time went by, and his wife Sarah still couldn't get pregnant. So Sarah suggested that her husband take her maid, Hagar, as his second wife, and her child

could be Sarah's child, too. Abraham agreed, married Hagar, slept with her, and she gave birth to a son. The plan worked perfectly.

Except for one thing. Neither woman liked sharing a husband, much less a son.

The animosity between them finally reached boiling point, and Sarah demanded her husband choose between them. He replied that Hagar was Sarah's maid, so Sarah could do what she wanted with her. Sarah abused Hagar until she couldn't take it anymore and ran away.

An angel met Hagar and gave her a promise from God for her son. Then he sent her back to Sarah, telling her to endure the abuse. And Hagar gave birth in Abraham's house to a son that he named Ishmael. Thus began the line of the Arab race.

Kris pondered the story and wondered if there were any more. She continued reading and found that in Genesis 21 Hagar and Ishmael appeared again.

By this time Isaac, the miracle child God had promised, was born. The older Ishmael was teasing his younger half-brother and made Sarah angry. Once again she wanted to throw Hagar and her son out.

This time Abraham felt a deep anguish over the matter. He had come to love Ishmael as his own son. But God told him to send Ishmael away and that God Himself would take care of him and make him into a great nation. So Abraham sent them away, but this time with supplies. When the supplies ran out, the angel appeared again to Hagar to comfort her and to show her a life-saving spring of water. And God took special care of Ishmael.

Kris read the words over and over again, as if she were trying to absorb them into her spirit like a sponge absorbs water.

The third time she read it she noticed something she'd missed the first two times—Hagar became Abraham's *wife*. Hagar was a second wife, just like Kris! Suddenly Kris saw herself in the story. Of course, when Hendri had proposed to her she didn't know he already had a wife. But she was so in love, would she have cared? She might have married him anyway.

And it's always the second wife who gets sent away. A tear slipped down Kris's cheek even before the thought struck her: *I am Hagar!* Another tear fell, then another, and then the dam burst. Her chest heaved to draw in enough breath to match the unrhythmic sobbing, facedown on her pillow so as to not wake Sari. Over and over in her mind those words echoed: *I am Hagar! I am Hagar!*

After about twenty minutes and at least as many tissues later, Kris sat upright, feeling somewhat like a ghost trapped between the living and the dead. She went back to reading and felt the comfort of God wrap around her from the words of the angel to Hagar. Hagar was not alone; God cared about her. And God promised to take care of her child. Yes, she had often told God that He had to be Sari's Father since she had none on earth, and He had agreed. She stayed in God's comfort, feeling His embrace of love, until she could smile again.

It was nearly 5:00 a.m. Kris laid her hand on her Bible to close it when she felt in her spirit His voice again. "I'm not finished yet."

She held her Bible open and asked God to speak more, wondering where else He wanted to lead her. She was quiet for several moments. Then a picture appeared in her imagination. It was her friend Ibu Dina. She was saying something. Kris focused in, then she could hear it: *I am Hagar!*

Kris was taken aback. She thought Dina was a first wife, not a second wife. *I don't understand, Lord! What are you saying?*

He whispered back, "Listen."

She quieted her heart again. There was Mama Rizky's image, and she was saying, *I am Hagar!*

Suddenly all the women in her *arisan* group were there in her mind, chanting together in Arabic, but she could understand them. They were all chanting over and over, *I am Hagar! I am Hagar!*

Then the picture was gone. The sweet presence of God's Spirit also lifted, and she was alone to face the mystery.

"But I don't understand yet, God! Please speak to me more! Don't draw back from me yet!"

She tried desperately to wrap her mind around the images, but the more she tried the more she felt overwhelmed with her own dullness.

"Mom, you OK?" Sari asked. "You've been quiet all day." It was evening now, and the two were sitting together at the kitchen table, as they often did before heading for bed. Sari knew something was going on in her mom's heart and that she'd share when she was ready.

"I'm sorry, darling. I guess I have a lot on my mind." Kris reached across the corner of the table and caressed Sari's cheek with her fingers. "Did you get all your homework done?"

"Yeah, Mom, yesterday, remember?"

"I'm sorry. You're right. Did you enjoy church today?"

"About as much as usual. The music was great. I didn't really get Pastor Susanna's sermon though. That verse about Jesus being the 'firstborn of many brothers.' I think it makes more sense literally, like He was the firstborn of Joseph and Mary, but pastor said it means, like, He is our older brother, and we're all born into God's family after Him. But then what about the guys before Jesus was born, like Adam and Abraham and David? How is Jesus 'firstborn' before them?"

Sari looked at her mom for an explanation, but Kris seemed to be in another world. She muttered the word *firstborn* a couple times, then abruptly spun around to face Sari.

"I need to go pray."

Kris headed for her favorite prayer spot on the living room floor. Sari shrugged and went to bed.

Ishmael was the firstborn son. But Isaac got the inheritance. Even today their children are fighting over their father's inheritance-land in Palestine. The firstborn should have the rights of inheritance. But Ishmael was the child of the second wife. The child of the first wife always gets the inheritance.

God, what are you saying to me? Why do I feel this pain in my heart over these two boys? And why did I see all the *arisan* women chanting, "I am Hagar?"

Once again Kris fell asleep on the floor. And this time she dreamed.

Her lover kissed her on the mouth. She could taste his passion. She grabbed him tightly. She would never let him go. But then he was moving away from her, toward the bedroom door. She vaguely heard him say, "I'll be back soon." Then he was gone. She was alone in the bedroom with a heavy weight of dread hanging over her.

"He'll be back soon," she repeated as though to convince herself. There was nothing of interest to her in that room without him. So she moved to the window to watch for his return.

The window was high up, high enough to see far down the street. At first she saw no one, but then a solitary figure appeared walking on the street. As the figure came closer, she could see it was a young woman, but it wasn't anyone she knew. She scanned from right to left for her lover. He was nowhere to be found.

She turned her attention back to the young woman. She was getting closer. Kris could see that she was quite pretty. The woman paused in front of her house! She even started up the first step before pausing again. Was this stranger coming to see her?

It started to rain.

Suddenly it hit her like a bolt of lightning. She knew where the woman had come from—from a restaurant. She had been given a single red rose. She had held hands with, she had kissed Kris's lover!

Kris had never felt such hatred in her life. She glared down at the woman as if to say, "One more step, and it will be your last!" Then the woman's face transformed before her eyes. It was Ibu Dina! No, now it was Mama Rizky! No, it changed again—it was Ibu Siti.

And it was Kris's face full of hatred in the window.

Kris awoke with a start. Her breath came in quick gasps. *It was my face in the window!*

She grabbed her journal and started writing the dream down while it was fresh in her mind. This was what God had been trying to tell her. She was Hagar, yes. But she was also Sarah. Could this be the root of the animosity between her Christian friends and her Muslim neighbors? Could it really go back to Abraham, to a struggle between two wives, neither of whom could accept their husband loving the other one? To a struggle between two wives over whose child should be considered the firstborn and get the inheritance?

Kris understood in a unique way both sides. Her life was Hagar's life, for she was a second wife, loved for a moment then tossed out with yesterday's trash. She felt the injustice, the rejection, the consequences for her and her daughter every day of her life.

But she was also Sarah, a Christian tracing her spiritual heritage through Isaac, struggling to love her Muslim neighbors who treated her with contempt, believing they were the holy children of Abraham and she was a *kafir* dog. And she resented them for it. Christians were the rightful heirs in God's kingdom, not them!

That's it! That's what God's been trying to show me! I've resented these women, who are really just like me!

Kris spent some time confessing her sins to God and asking Him to cleanse her evil heart.

Then she asked God, "Now what do You want me to do about this?"

❦ Chapter 22 ❦

WHEN KRIS ENTERED Ibu Hajjah's house for her third visit to the ladies' *arisan*, she noticed fewer glares, fewer dropped conversations. It seemed like the women were beginning to accept her presence there.

Enjoy it, Kris! This could be your last arisan.

She felt her hands tremble as she passed along the *Yasin* booklets. She would wait until after they ate, during the announcement time, if she didn't pass out before then of fright.

Oh, God! Is there another way? I'm so scared!

The prayers were over, and she expected to see the tea and food passed around, but nothing came. In her consternation she had forgotten everyone was fasting.

Ibu Noorminah was talking to her. She tried to reply intelligently, but it was hard to listen to Noorminah while rehearsing in her mind what she wanted to say.

Mama Shafa's name came out of the plastic bottle as this week's winner. Ibu Hajjah was asking for announcements. Ibu Aaminah was thanking and reminding women about their dates for preparing fast-breaking food for the neighborhood men at the *musholla*. Everyone looked a little lethargic from fasting all day, so no one brought any new issues to discuss. Ibu Hajjah was about to close the meeting when Kris held up her hand.

"Yes, Ibu Kris, do you have something you'd like to say?"

Kris nodded dumbly, hoping the words were on their way out. Everyone stared at her. She had only a vague idea of what she wanted to say, no idea how to start, or, for that matter, how to end.

She closed her eyes and spoke, "I am a second wife." She heard a couple surprised gasps from the crowd. *Just keep talking, Kris!*

"My husband ran off and left me when I was pregnant with my daughter. I've never seen him since. I've struggled with resentment toward him for many years. Every single day I pray for God to give me forgiveness in my heart for him. But this week I discovered he wasn't the only person I resented.

"I was reading the story of, let me see if I can say this right, Nabi Ibrahim. His first wife, Siti Sarah, couldn't have a child. So he took a second wife, Siti Hajar, who gave him a son named Ishmael. But Sarah grew jealous and threw Hajar and Ishmael out. Later her son Ishak received the inheritance, not Ishmael.

"When I read this story, at first I felt like Siti Hajar. I've been treated unfairly and abandoned by my husband. My child had to grow up with no father. I hated Sarah for what she did.

"Then I read the story again, and realized that we Christians trace our heritage through Sarah, and you Muslims trace yours through Siti Hajar. We have such a difficult time getting along. Like two wives competing for their husband's favor, we claim to God that we are right and wish He'd give us preference over the other. I've done this. I've been a hateful Sarah, resenting you all, and I just want to say I'm sorry."

Kris paused. There was more in her heart to say, but no more words came.

Once again she felt like in her first *arisan* visit, that she was standing in the dock waiting for the jury's verdict. For a few seconds no one spoke. Then Ibu Hajjah cleared her throat.

"Ibu Kris, thank you for sharing. But I think you don't really understand yet the purpose of the *arisan*—it's about praying the *Yasin*, saving money, eating together, discussing women's issues, and gossip. It's *not* about pushing religious ideas. There are other events where we invite a teacher, a Muslim teacher, if we want to discuss religion. I'll thank you not to bring your Christian ideas into this gathering ever again. This meeting is adjourned! *Assalamu alaikum Warahmatullahi Wabarakatuh.*"

"*Wa alaikum assalam.*" The women stood quietly and filed out. Kris joined the exit line, tears building behind her eyelids. She had to hold it in till she got home, so she focused on the rocks in the road before her and kept walking.

As soon as she pushed open the door and looked at Sari, she collapsed in tears on the floor. Sari rushed to close the door, then knelt beside her mother and held her.

"What is it, Mom? Are you hurt? Sick? Did something happen at the *arisan*? Mom, talk to me!"

But Kris couldn't talk, not for quite some time. She just wept the bitter tears of the rejected.

Eventually Sari coaxed her mom to eat a little tofu and rice for dinner. Then she washed the dishes while Kris just sat at the table watching a gecko slowly creep along the wall sneaking up on an unsuspecting mosquito. When Sari had finished cleaning, she sat across the corner of the table from her mother and tried again.

"Please, Mom, tell me what happened!"

Kris knew Sari could never understand her feelings at the *arisan* without knowing the dreams, so she asked Sari to fetch her journal and, starting with the first dream, told her the whole story.

"...and they didn't want to hear it! Outwardly they're smiling, but inwardly they still see me as the enemy. When Ibu Hajjah said they don't want my Christian religious talk, I felt so, so belittled. I don't think they want me to come back. Why now, when I just started to hope, do I have to face rejection again?"

"Mom, you weren't sharing religion; you were sharing your heart! They have no right to reject you for that! Who do they think they are?"

"They think they're the rightful wife. What am I going to do? Should I withdraw from the *arisan* so they can go back to normal?"

Sari mulled it over. "Hmmm...Remember how the angel told Hagar to go back to Sarah and take the abuse? Maybe God's giving you a chance to stop the bad blood between Sarah and Hagar by staying in the house as a peacemaker."

"I don't want to be abused." Kris's voice was barely audible.

The two of them held hands as Sari prayed for courage for her mom and for the *arisan* women to open their hearts to her.

Chapter 23

MAMA SHAFA AND her three-year-old dropped by Kris's kiosk on Tuesday morning.

"Hi, little Shafa! You look so pretty today in your pink jumper! Are you helping your mom shop?" Kris asked the girl.

Shafa smiled and pointed to a bag of Chicki cheese balls. "Chicki, Ma!"

"OK, 'Fa, let me count my money first." Mama Shafa took some coins out of her purse. "I think there's enough. I need a packet of Rinso detergent and a bag of Chickis, please."

"Certainly." Kris put the Rinso pack in a small black plastic bag and handed the cheese balls to Shafa. "Here you go!"

Shafa smiled and hugged them to her chest as if to say, "All mine!"

Mama Shafa didn't leave. In fact, she came around the side of the kiosk and sat down in the little side doorway. Kris had never had another woman sit down at her kiosk before except Ibu Dina, when she was too tired from walking all day.

Mama Shafa sighed, looking up into the sky. "I hate Ramadan."

Kris was shocked to hear a Muslim say that. "But why? Does the fasting make you sick?"

"No, it's not that. I'm not really fasting anyway. I keep a bottle of water in my bedroom to drink during the day. Don't tell anyone that though!"

"No, of course not."

"It's all the family events. My husband doesn't like going to visit my family, and I don't like going to visit his family."

"Why not?"

"Well, my family wasn't happy about the marriage in the first place. When they found out I was going to be a second wife, they didn't trust my husband. They still don't. They wanted to arrange a marriage for me with someone who had never married, but I was hard-headed and wouldn't listen. I wonder now if I would be happier if I had listened."

"What about your husband's family? Did they approve of the wedding?"

"No, they didn't even know about it until after we were married. He told me he was avoiding conflict. I never realized he was hiding me from them until after we were married. He told me that his first wife gave him permission, but he lied. She never knew till afterward. And she hates me. Just like that story you told about Siti Hajar. That's me."

Kris reached out and put her hand on Mama Shafa's knee. "I know how you feel."

Mama Shafa kept going. "My husband drags me to his family's house. They all tease him that since I'm more than ten years younger than his first wife he must have married me for sex. That's all they talk about! They'll ask him right in front of me if I'm enough of a sexual goddess to keep him satisfied. It's so humiliating! His mom treats me like a naughty teenager and makes me work like a slave to punish me. I hate his family!"

Kris murmured soft encouragements and kept stroking Mama Shafa's knee.

"Then on Idul Fitri I have to face the first wife! My husband makes us shake hands and ask forgiveness for all the sins we've committed over the year. As if that's going to wash all the pain from my heart! His first wife hates me and tells me to my face how much she hates me for stealing her husband. I didn't steal him. He pursued me! If he'd told me the truth that his first wife didn't approve I wouldn't have married him! She's like that Siti Sarah to me. If she could, she'd throw me out. But since we live in separate houses and my husband doesn't want to lose me, she can do nothing but try to make my life miserable."

"At least your husband seems to love you."

"Yes, I think he still loves me. But when I was pregnant with Shafa and couldn't have sex for several weeks I started to get terrified that he was going to look for bride number three to take my place! I had to force myself to eat for the baby's sake, I was so afraid. So far he hasn't done that, as far as I know. Maybe he's already married a third woman and just hasn't told me."

"I'm sure you're a great mom to little Shafa."

They both paused and watched Shafa. She had a stick in her hand and was dragging it through the water in the narrow ditch that ran down the side of the alley and out to the river.

"My family wants me to leave him, but how can I provide for Shafa? My parents want to take us in, but they're getting older. Shafa and I can't live off their pension. And I don't really want to be a widow with a child—no one would marry me then. I feel trapped."

"Maybe we could pray together?" Kris offered.

"Please pray for me later. You're a very kind person." Mama Shafa wiped a damp eye and smiled at Kris. "Well, I have to get back to my housework. Shafa, you ready to go home? Get your Chickis!"

Shafa toddled over to pick up her Chickis from where she'd dropped them, took her mother's hand, and walked away.

"See you later."

Kris sat in her kiosk lost in thought. *I had no idea she was a second wife! She seemed to have such a happy family. Poor thing! It must be brutal to face the relatives during Ramadan. That's one trial I managed to avoid, never meeting Hendri's family and he never meeting mine.*

She was so caught up in memory land that when someone leaned into the kiosk with an "Excuse me!" she jumped.

"Ibu Aaminah!"

"Good morning."

"I'm so glad to see you! I feel I owe you an apology for using the *arisan* to share my own struggles."

"Nonsense, my dear! I'm here precisely to thank you for what you shared. That took great courage. This issue of Christians and Muslims competing with each other is one we've avoided for generations by ignoring each other. But it's time we changed. And the image you presented of Sarah and Hajar has kept me up at night thinking. I've often wondered why we so strongly resent people we don't even know. This resentment has a history; it has roots. Ibu Kris, I think that what you shared is the most thought-provoking thing I've heard in this neighborhood in many years! I thank you. And please keep coming to the *arisan*! Our ladies need you."

"Oh, well, thank you, Ibu Aaminah. You're too kind. Did you want to buy anything today?"

"Not really, but just so my husband doesn't think I'm only here to gossip—" Ibu Aaminah winked—"why don't you give me a box of matches. Together, you and I are going to light a lantern and show these ladies a new way."

❧ Chapter 24 ❧

S ITI WAS SITTING on the couch watching a Ramadan soap opera when she heard someone call from her front yard, "*Assalamu alaikum!*" Probably someone wanting to buy her kerosene. She got up slowly and headed toward the door with her eyes still glued to the TV set. Finally she turned to face the interrupter.

"Ibu Aaminah! I'm surprised to see you walking about! I heard your hip keeps you mostly at home these days."

"I'm happy to say that my hip is not as bad as all the rumors. May I come in?"

"Of course, come in!" Siti opened the door and showed Ibu Aaminah to a green vinyl couch in the narrow sitting room. Aaminah sat down gingerly, glancing around the room at what Siti hoped would be considered an immaculately clean home.

"How's your family?" Ibu Aaminah started.

"Oh, wonderful! My husband is away teaching today, of course. Syukran has half-day school, and Iqbal only goes in for some special sermons or other extracurricular activities in the mornings. They're both doing well in school, of course. Couldn't be better."

"They seem like fine young men! Would they like to earn some extra money? Our old fence needs to be repainted. They could do it during their free time this month."

Siti nearly clapped her hands with joy. "Of course! Of course! They'd love to do it! You just tell me when you want them, and they'll be there!"

"Well, since they're fasting, I was thinking they could paint for two or three hours a day in the late afternoon when it starts to cool off, right before breaking the fast. They can work slowly; that's no problem, as long as they finish before the Idul Fitri holiday. I'd be happy to pay them Rp.300,000 for the whole job, and they can split it depending on who works more or if they do the whole job together."

"Wonderful! Thank you so much! I'm sure they'll be excited to make some money and, of course, help their neighbor."

"Good. Well, that's settled. Now, can I ask your thoughts on what happened at our *arisan* yesterday?"

Perhaps Siti's excitement over the job for her boys caused her to pour out her heart a bit too freely without anticipating her guest's reaction, a mistake she rarely made. She edged forward on her chair and waved her arms expressively as she spoke.

"Oh, wasn't it too *awful*! I knew from the beginning that it was a mistake to invite that Christian woman, and look! It's only been three weeks, and she's already preaching to us! Thank God Ibu Hajjah put her in her place. I expect she won't come back and that will be the end of it. I don't know what possessed someone to invite her in the first place! I could have told the poor soul that inviting a Christian to a Muslim ladies' group would never work. Don't you agree?"

"Actually, I am the poor soul who invited Ibu Kris, and no, I don't agree. I think integrating our *arisan* is working splendidly. In fact, I was just down at Ibu Kris's kiosk a few minutes ago thanking her for sharing her thoughts with us. And believe it or not, before I arrived one of the other women was sitting there at the kiosk thanking Ibu Kris too."

"Who was it?" Siti interrupted.

"Oh, I'm sure you'll find out soon enough. But I'd be surprised if, by the time you find out who it was, there's only been one person stop by her kiosk. I think Ibu Kris has touched a sensitive place in the hearts of our neighborhood. It will be a challenge for us to build on what she shared about mutual understanding, releasing resentment and extending forgiveness, but I believe it's a solid foundation to start with. In fact, yesterday was the most fun I've had at an *arisan* meeting in a long time." She paused and slowly rose to her feet. "Well, dear, as they say, 'I'm having so much fun, how will I get all my work done?' I'd best be going. Send your boys on over this afternoon if they're ready."

"Oh, yes, of course. Thank you!" Siti's face looked like she had more to say, but her engine had stalled. Had she just been insulted? She wasn't sure. She opened the door for Ibu Aaminah and a thought whistled past her mind of giving the old busybody a helpful push off the porch. But when Ibu Aaminah took her leave with a cheery, "*Assalamu alaikum*," she managed a "*Wa alaikum assalam*."

Then she remembered her soap opera and hurried back to the TV.

❧ Chapter 25 ❧

O**N SUNDAY MORNING** Sari needed to go to the church early to rehearse with the worship dance team one last time before the service. Kris was planning to watch her daughter rehearse, as usual, but when she saw Pastor Susanna walk by on the way to her office she decided to follow and share with her pastor how for the first time she was getting to know her Muslim neighbors.

Kris was bubbling with excitement as she sat in front of Susanna's giant desk. The pastor had her Bible and notes on the desk but did her best to ignore them for the moment and give her attention to her parishioner.

Kris told about her prayer, about the dreams, about the *arisan*, and about the women dropping by her kiosk all week. "One woman has come twice! She's a second wife. And another woman who is a fourth wife came by and cried on my shoulder. I offered to pray with them. They're too shy to pray right there, but both asked me to pray for them later. Maybe if I visit their homes I can pray with them! I really feel my heart being stretched to feel their pain and love them. It's like my whole neighborhood has come alive to me now! Isn't that wonderful?"

Pastor Susanna smiled and leaned forward, "Yes, of course. Are you saying that you think they're ready to repent of their sins and come to church? If so, I'd be happy to arrange a day to do visitation with you."

"No, that's not what I meant at all. They don't want to come to church. They just want someone to talk to who understands them. And for the first time in my life I understand them! It's not about *them* repenting; it's me! In fact, I was thinking...maybe we should stop inviting them to come to church, and we should go to them. Why don't we offer to cook food for their fast-breaking and take it to the mosque and serve them?"

"Oh my! I'm sure...you don't think...." Susanna looked at her watch. "Well, I really must get ready for the service. If you'll excuse me." She stood up. Kris stood up too.

"Of course. Thank you for listening."

Pastor Susanna bustled past Kris into the sanctuary.

Kris sat in her pew at the end of the singing and worship dance overwhelmed by the beauty and love of God. Her eyes were closed, her cheeks wet with tears. She didn't want to leave this holy place but felt Sari squeeze in next to her. She opened her eyes and hugged her daughter, thanking her for ministering so beautifully through her dance.

Pastor Susanna took the pulpit.

"*Shalom*. Praise the Lord!

"I'd like to welcome any visitors to our service this morning. Would you please stand up and introduce yourselves?" She waited, scanning the audience. No one stood up.

"Well, if you are new here but feeling shy this morning, that's OK. Please come and introduce yourself to me at the end of the service.

"Today I'll be preaching on freedom in Christ as we prepare ourselves for our national Independence Day coming up on Tuesday. And let me remind everyone to please come to the church at five o'clock in the afternoon for our Love Feast, where we'll also be taking up a special love offering for the poor in our midst.

"But before I begin, I need to give this congregation an important reminder. It has come to my attention that one of our church members has joined in a Muslim women's group that chants the Koran in Arabic and has even started covering her head in an effort to be accepted by these people. Now, I'm sure her heart is right, but since this could be a temptation to any one of us, I want to address it publicly."

Kris felt her entire body go limp as a dishrag. She felt Sari's hand tighten around her arm.

"The Bible teaches us in Second Corinthians 6:14–15, 'Don't become partners with those who reject God. How can you make a partnership out of right and wrong? That's not partnership; that's war. Is light best friends with dark? Does Christ go strolling with the Devil?' And in another passage, 'Come out from among them and be separate.'

"Listen to me closely. This church already reaches out in love to our neighbors. Every Christmas we pass out packets of basic food items to hundreds of Muslim families living around the church, and we always invite them to join us for our Christmas worship service. That is kindness, and that is prudence. But joining in their religious groups where they're chanting a book inspired by demons—I can see only two possible outcomes of such foolishness.

"Number one, you could slip away from the safety of the church and find yourself tempted to join their religion and lose your salvation.

"Number two, you could offend someone and bring down the wrath of the community leaders against us. How many of you remember when the Muslims closed down our church three years ago, and it took us weeks to get the city government and the police to help us open our doors again? We had to move to this location and start over. Do we want to go through that again?

"No, we don't! So I implore you all, leave well enough alone! Let us do our part to be a good neighbor and keep our church out of trouble, for the sake of us all. Amen?"

And all the people, well, almost all the people, echoed, "Amen."

Kris and Sari skipped the Sunday school class and headed home early. As they headed for the parking lot neither one spoke. Sari did her best to squelch her anger. She held her mother's arm, propelling her through the maze of motorbikes. Since they had come early it was blocked in by at least a dozen others. The parking attendant came over to help.

"Why you guys leaving so early?" he asked.

Sari tried to smile but didn't quite succeed. "My mother's not feeling well."

"Oh, that's too bad. You should ask the pastor to pray for her. Last month my mother had the flu, and pastor prayed and she was healed that very day!"

"Thanks. Maybe later. We'll just wait over there."

Sari knew she couldn't hold it in much longer, so she dragged her mom back through the motorbikes to wait near the street, farther away from Mr. Nosy Chatterbox parking man.

Across the street the *becak* drivers were beginning to gather, lining up their pedicabs to take people home from church. Sari didn't always understand what the *becak* guys said to each other since they were almost all Madurese and Muslim, but she figured they were probably joking about how much they loved church; it was their best chance in the week to have some beautiful girls wearing makeup and miniskirts ride in their *becak*.

One called across the street to Sari, "Hey, sweetie! Leave your bike there, and I'll take you home." Sari looked the other way and could hear the *becak* guys laugh. She would have happily punched one in the mood she was in but was afraid if she let go of her mom's arm she might faint.

After what seemed like an eternity her motorbike was ready. She paid the guy Rp.1,000 without saying thank you, convinced Mom to get on the back, and whisked her to the safety of home.

Sari had been angry earlier that week at Ibu Hajjah, who had publicly humiliated her mom. But that was nothing compared to this. How could a Christian pastor do that to her mother? It was unthinkable! Maybe even unforgivable.

I'm sure my mom's backstabbing wounds will heal. But don't put that knife in my hands right now.

⛧ Chapter 26 ⛧

O N MONDAY AFTERNOON Kris skipped the *arisan* meeting to help
Ibu Noorminah prepare the fast-breaking snacks for the men at the
mosque. She imagined Ibu Hajjah smiling triumphantly at her absence.
But something inside her knew she'd give the *arisan* at least one more try.

Sari also helped with the sixty plates of homemade cakes: there was
bingka in a six-petal flower shape, vanilla *agar-agar* with fruit cocktail in
the top layer, and a chocolate *kue lapis*. Accompanying these delicacies
on the plate were a date and a small banana.

Kris wondered, *What would Pastor Susanna say if she saw me now?*

That night Kris and Sari were too tired to cook for themselves. Ibu
Noorminah had sent home a few of the uglier pieces of cake with them,
so they ate cake for dinner. Then they lay on the living room floor staring
at the ceiling and talked.

"Thanks for giving up your afternoon to help me, Sari."

"No problem, Mom. It was kind of fun. I always wanted to learn how
to make *agar-agar*."

"Did you know I suggested to Pastor Susanna that instead of inviting
our Muslim friends to church, the church should cook a fast-breaking
meal and serve it at the mosque?"

"You said that? No wonder she freaked out!"

"Do you think it's a bad idea, too?" Kris looked worried.

"No, Mom, I think it's a great idea! But I don't think our church is
ready for it."

"Apparently not."

"What did she say yesterday: *'We invite them to our Christmas service
every year.'* What a joke! When is the last time we had a Muslim walk
into *our* church?"

"I certainly can't remember it ever happening."

"Me neither."

They were quiet for a while. Sari rolled over on her side and faced her
mother.

"Maybe we should find a new church."

Kris's eyes widened. "Sari! Why would you say that?"

"Because Pastor Susanna is a witch."

"Don't say such things! I think she's probably still not forgiven the men who closed our church down three years ago."

"And she thinks humiliating her own sheep is going to help that? *I'm* having a hard time forgiving *her*!" Sari fluffed the pillow under her elbow aggressively.

"There are no perfect churches. This one is the closest, we have friends there; you have worship dance team."

"I know. But hey, Mom, you remember in the bulletin there was an announcement about the youth retreat? I've decided I'm not going this year."

"Because you're mad at the pastor?" Kris reached over to touch Sari's knee.

"No, Mom, she's not going to be at the retreat, thank God! But they scheduled it the same weekend as Idul Fitri! What were they thinking? I want to go visit all my Muslim friends from school and wish them a happy holiday."

"I think this time last year I wouldn't have understood, but now I do. Sari, I'm so proud of you!" Kris edged closer to Sari and ran her fingers through Sari's long, black hair. "Do you want to do something special tomorrow for Independence Day?"

"Like what? We can't go out to eat. All the restaurants are closed for fasting."

"I don't know. You want to go to the mall?"

"Let me see what my friends are up to first. And there's that Love Feast at church. Can we skip it?"

"I really think we should go."

"No way I'm going! I don't know how you can even stand to sit at the same table and eat with Pastor Susanna after what she did to you."

"Don't be like that. I don't want to go alone," Kris mumbled.

"You do what you want, Mom. I'm not sure I'll ever go back to that church!"

❧ Chapter 27 ❧

ARI SKIPPED THE Love Feast. She was afraid that, surrounded by
not enough *love* in the feast, she'd end up making a scene. So she
grumpily dropped her mom off at the church at four o'clock to help set
up, then picked up her classmate Maya and headed for the Ramadan
cake fair.

Stretched out for over one hundred yards along the western bank of the
Martapura River just north of the Grand Mosque were stall after stall of
the most colorful cakes anywhere in Indonesia. Traditional Banjar cakes
like *bingka* and *kue lapis* shared tables with cakes from other parts of
the country and even from the Middle East. There were dates from several Arab countries and from California. There were dozens of fruit juice
combinations, some with the fruit blended, others with it chopped into
little squares and served with gelatin cubes in coconut milk. Any free
ground was taken by peddlers of cheap toys, junk food, stickers, roasted
corn, or cotton candy.

Sari wasn't fasting. She didn't have money for the expensive cakes
either, so she just tagged along with Maya. Maya's mom wanted her to
find an expensive cake with a cappuccino flavor called *lapis india*. Maya
told her she wasn't fasting either. She had explained to Sari how there
was special dispensation for small children, the sick, those doing heavy
manual labor, travelers, pregnant or nursing women, and women (like
Maya) having their period. But Sari knew they couldn't sample a snack
or drink in public and dishonor those who were fasting.

It took them half an hour to wade through the crowd and find the right
stall. Maya bargained ferociously but still ended up paying Rp.40,000 for
a portion big enough to feed about eight people. Maya's family only had
six, but better to have extra in case someone dropped by.

They were on their way back to the motorbike when they passed a
group of young men hanging out by the cotton candy. One of them whistled and called to them.

"Hey, sexy! Come talk to me, and I'll buy you some cotton candy."

Maya always dressed fashionably and didn't cover her shoulder-length hair. Sari was used to Maya getting most of the attention for her looks. Maya turned around and looked at the boys scornfully. "I doubt you losers could afford it."

"Maya!" Sari hissed without turning around. "What are you doing?"

"I just want to see if he'll really do it."

"Don't! Let's just go!"

"Hang on." Maya let go of Sari's arm and took a step toward the boys. "Show me the money."

"Whoa! Don't you want to talk first?"

"Not if you're lying. Show me the money."

The boy took Rp.5,000 out of his pocket. "Now tell me your name."

"You first."

"I'm Udin. Unfortunately my friends here don't have names, because they don't know how to talk to girls yet. Who are you?"

"I'm Maya. This is my friend, Sari. Now prove to me you're not a big fat liar and buy me some cotton candy."

"If I do, can I have your cell phone number?"

"While you're buying I'll think about it."

Udin paid the seller for a swirling pink cotton candy. Sari could hear the boys whispering and refused to look directly at them.

Udin handed the cotton candy to Maya cheerfully. "So, Maya, how 'bout that phone number?"

"Tell your friend to turn around. We want to see her," one of the boys cut in.

Sari turned just enough to see who had spoken. She didn't know him but immediately recognized Syukran.

"Let's go, Maya," she pleaded.

Udin put his hand on Maya's arm. "You can't go till I get that phone number," he teased.

Without thinking, Sari took her right hand out of her pocket and grabbed Maya's other arm and pulled. Udin noticed the shriveled-up skin on the back of Sari's hand.

"Hey guys! Check out her hand! That's nasty!"

Another boy stood up to see. "Maybe got chewed up by a dog. That's seriously ugly!"

"Let her go, Udin." Syukran spat on the ground. "She's probably a dog-eating *kafir* like her friend."

Maya angrily ripped her arm from Udin's grasp and glared at the boys.

"You jerks!" Then she pushed Sari back into the crowd and away. Sari couldn't keep the tears from slipping down her cheeks.

Sari was ticked off at Maya.

"Why did you have to stop? Guys like that are losers. You shouldn't pay them any attention."

"I just wanted some cotton candy. My little sister loves this stuff. Hey, I'm sorry they treated you like that. What jerks!"

"People like that make me so mad!"

"Yeah, they're major idiots all right! I'm sorry they said those terrible things to you. Let's just forget about them!"

"You don't understand. The people at my church persecute my mom and me because we want to be friends with Muslims. Then the Muslims persecute us because we're Christians. We can't win."

"I don't persecute you. I'll be your friend even if we're different religions. Not all Muslims are like those lame-o's."

"I know. I'm sorry, Maya. It's been a hard week. Thanks for putting up with me."

"No problem." Maya held Sari's left hand as they started to jog across the street to where they'd parked the bike in front of the Grand Mosque. They were halfway across when Sari froze. Tires squealed as a car braked just a few feet from her. Maya waved a sorry to the unhappy driver then pulled Sari across the street.

"What are you doing? You could have been killed!" Maya exclaimed.

"Over there. Near the bridge. There's someone I need to talk to. Can you wait for me?"

"I guess so. Girl, you are on another planet today! I'll wait here, go ahead."

"Thanks, Maya, be right back."

Sari crossed the street again, then jogged down the boardwalk toward Freedom Bridge. She thought she had recognized someone but had to be sure. Something was wrong, very wrong.

As Sari drew closer she examined the girl's outfit—black boots, black criss-crossed hose, a black mini-skirt, an extremely tight white T-shirt, and a half-length short-sleeved black leather jacket. The girl's long black hair was curled into waves, a dark contrast falling over the white T-shirt. But the face...the face was Nina's!

Nina was standing next to a girl about her age wearing exceedingly tight jeans with stiletto heels and a black shirt that swept down from one shoulder across her cleavage, leaving the other shoulder entirely bare. Sari thought both girls were wearing way too much makeup.

When Sari walked up, Nina started to turn away.

"Nina. Hey, it's me, Sari."

Nina turned casually and faced her. "Hey, Sari, what's up?"

"Your mom stopped by again the other day. She said you haven't been home in weeks, and she's worried sick! Where are you living?"

"I'm staying with a friend. A girl friend."

"Nina, what are you doing?"

"Just tell my mom I'm all right, OK? I'd appreciate that. Look, I gotta go."

Nina and her friend started walking away, leaving so many unspoken questions unanswered. Sari started after her for a minute, then changed her mind and went back to Maya.

Maya asked her, "Who was that?"

"A friend in trouble," Sari answered.

Chapter 28

"This cake fair is boring. Let's get out of here," Hafiz decided.

"Why not?" agreed Udin. "I've got three girls' telephone numbers. I'm happy."

Kiki saw Saifullah first. He hit Hafiz. "Wait guys. 'Fiz, look over there."

Everybody looked.

"What, Kiki? That fat girl? You like the fat chick?" Udin joked.

"No, fool! Standing by that tree, kind of in the shadow."

"No way! It's that martial arts dude!"

"No it's not. You guys are imagining things."

"I'm telling you, it is!" Hafiz was sure. "Let's go ask him why he dissed us the other day."

Hafiz got up to hobble across the cake fair walkway toward the riverside. His ankle was healing well, but he wouldn't be running speed races any time soon. Everyone followed.

Saifullah looked delighted to see the boys approach. He waved them over.

"Hey, Pak, how come you didn't meet us at the plaza a couple weeks ago? We waited for you." Hafiz sounded offended.

"Well, hello, my friends! It's good to see you! I apologize about missing my appointment with you. An emergency came up, and I didn't know how to get a hold of you to cancel. Perhaps we can try again?"

"Maybe," Hafiz was unwilling to yield the high ground yet. "Why don't you tell us more about yourself first, and we'll decide."

"Fair enough. My name is Ali. I'm Javanese but raised in South Sulawesi. I am a martial arts trainer. I love Islam, the true Islam, and I love those who fight in the way of Allah everywhere. Now it's your turn. Tell me about what you've already learned in your *silat* training."

"Tell him, 'Din." Hafiz folded his arms over his chest and watched "Ali" like a hawk.

"Yeah. Well, we train every Saturday morning with Syuk's dad. He says that *silat* should only be used in self-defense or to protect the weak, after you've tried every other way to avoid a fight. Is that what all *silat* gurus teach?"

"Every *silat* teacher is worthy of honor. Perhaps your teacher is helping you through the beginning phases. When you get to my level you learn the complete art, both defensive and offensive. If any of you are interested, perhaps I could give you a few pointers."

Hafiz had made up his mind. He pointed his finger right at Saifullah's chest. "You're recruiting for *jihad*, aren't you? I know it. I know it. Are you with JI? Tell me the truth. Tell me now, or I'll announce to the crowd that you're with JI."

"Son, do you think if I were recruiting for *jihad* I'd be passing out cards or using a microphone? Use your head! Don't start things you can't finish." Saifullah seemed to expand his chest muscles, then breathe out, and a chill went down Hafiz's spine.

But Hafiz didn't back down. "Well, if you are recruiting, I want to join. I want to meet the top guy. I want to be his apprentice and take over when he dies."

Saifullah started a half-turn away from them. "You're too young. Go back and find a teacher of manly Islam. Learn all you can, then prove yourself worthy. If you are truly worthy, Allah will find you."

Saifullah walked away. The boys stared after him. Hafiz went to sit his tired leg down by the river. Everyone followed in silence and sat down. He reached for a cigarette out of habit, then remembered he was fasting and would have to wait till sundown to smoke. The boys watched a speedboat rush by, sending a wave toward them that collided with the wooden planks below with a loud smack.

Finally Hafiz spoke, "You heard the man. We've got to prove we're worthy. And we're going to do it. Tonight. The perfect night to strike a blow for freedom from Western immorality corrupting our nation. Syuk, have you forgotten what they did to your brother?" Syukran shook his head. "Remember I told you to find me a target? Anybody got one? How 'bout you, Syuk?"

A holy hush fell as the words tumbled out of Syukran's mouth. "There's a Christian woman in my alley who's been preaching her *kafir* filth at my mom's *arisan*. Mom hates her. I've seen where she goes to church. It's in Pekauman."

"Perfect! Juki, Udin, you know what to bring. Meet at my place at nine. First Bali; now the *arisan*. There can only be one winner in this war, and it's gonna be us!"

❧ Chapter 29 ❧

"WHAT? BURN THE Qur'an? Where is he now?" Louis Staunton stood up abruptly from his chair at the round table.

"He's in the parking lot, Mr. Staunton," the young Arab-looking man whispered. "Please, we need your help."

Louis apologized to the other participants of the Interfaith Roundtable discussion: Pastor John Wilshire from the United Methodist Church; Father Peter O'Reilly from St. Paul's Catholic Church; Rabbi Eli Ben Avraham from the local synagogue; and the host of this event, Imam Yassir Mustafa, spiritual leader of this mosque. He suggested they pause the discussions momentarily to pray together over this situation before he exited.

Outside the mosque, a protest of no more than thirty people had gathered, angry white and black faces, some carrying signs like "Christians 4 a Moslem-free City" and "No more tolerance for terrorists." He would have been surprised to see a TV crew filming this small a group if he hadn't heard about the plan to burn the Qur'an.

The Arab-looking security guard pointed him toward a large white man at the front of the crowd waving a book over his head, then the guard discretely disappeared. Louis ignored the hate-filled remarks in the air and, after taking a deep breath, made a bee-line straight for the book-waving man.

"Afternoon. I'm Congressman Louis Staunton." Louis interrupted the man's speech by getting directly in front of him and offering both his hand and a big smile. "And you are?"

The big man was taken aback but shook Louis's hand. "I'm Pastor Billy Barton."

Louis kept control of the conversation. "And are all these fine folks from your church?" He smiled briefly at the crowd but kept in Billy Barton's face.

"Yes, sir! These here are good Christians every one, and we want our city to stay that way."

"Well, praise the Lord!" Louis agreed, putting his hand on the pastor's sweaty blue dress shirt. "You must be the kind of folks that love to spread the Good News about Jesus. Am I right?"

"Yes, sir. We do street preaching, jail ministry, homeless shelter…and we don't want no Moslems ruining our community with their poison, undoing all the good we done. That's why we're here."

"Pastor Billy, this city is indeed fortunate to have a church like yours that cares for the hurting. Not every city has good folks like yourselves that care for the orphan, widow, and stranger like the Bible teaches. Why, I'm just thinking of the strangers in our land that make up this tiny worship congregation right here." Louis pointed to the mosque behind them, a former restaurant now with a dome on top displaying the crescent moon above. He continued, "Do you know what the chances are of these poor immigrants hearing the gospel of Jesus in their home countries? Some of them almost nil. They're sure lucky God moved them into a loving, Christian community like yours where they can hear about Jesus without getting killed for it."

Pastor Billy looked unsure how to respond. Louis kept up the barrage, his hand still on Billy's shoulder like they were old friends.

"How would you feel if you and I sat side by side at your church tonight and helped the good folks of your congregation plan some creative ways to share the gospel of Jesus with the immigrants God has brought to our city?" Louis's warm smile invited a positive response.

Pastor Billy looked pleased. "That'd be mighty fine by me, Mr. Congressman. We'd love to have you in our church." Louis shook Billy's hand again, his eye on the Qur'an in the other hand.

"Then how about you save that book for tonight, as I've got something in it I want to show your folks. And maybe y'all should break up this event and get the church ready. Just send someone here to pick me up at 6:00."

Billy hesitated. "But we ain't done yet what we came here for." He turned to the crowd. "The Congressman here wants to come visit our church tonight. So let's get this here book-burning over with so we can get back and get ready." Billy waved the Qur'an aloft amid cheers from the crowd. The TV cameraman looked like he was beginning to roll film.

Louis started to panic. He knew exactly what repercussions the burning of an Qur'an in America could have around the world—riots in the streets, burning of American businesses, attacks on American citizens, and even attacks on random minority Christian churches that had nothing to do with America. In the name of world peace he had to stop that book-burning!

"Pastor! Is that a real Qur'an or one of those fake ones?" Billy stared at him. "I better take a look to be sure." Louis reached his hand out toward the Qur'an.

Billy's eyes narrowed suspiciously. "What do you mean?"

Louis continued reaching till his hand touched the book gently. "Usually you can tell by looking…Let's see if I remember…" Now he had his fingers gently opening a page. He took his other hand off Billy's shoulder and reached for the book. "Give me just a second here…"

Billy released the book into Louis's hands. Louis pretended to study it intently. Then he looked up with a warm smile. "Pastor, this is just what I need to prepare for tonight. Let me keep a hold of this for a few hours to prepare my thoughts, and I'll get it back to you this evening." He started to slide the book into his inside sports jacket pocket.

"Now wait just a minute, Mr. Congressman!" Pastor Billy protested, reaching for the Qur'an. "We came here to make a public statement, and we need that book!" He tried to pull it from Louis's grasp, but Louis wasn't about to let go.

"I'm sorry, my friend, but this book has a destiny for peacemaking on it. Burning it would cause people all over the world to react with hate toward Americans. I love my country, as I'm sure you do, and we both gotta make sure those riots don't happen." Louis jerked the book away and put it firmly in his pocket while grabbing Billy's right hand and pumping it up and down in friendship, smiling to the crowd. He noticed the TV cameras were definitely rolling. A scatter of *boos* made known the crowd's disapproval.

Pastor Billy's face turned red. "Give me back my book!"

Louis spoke loudly for the sake of the crowd and cameras. "God bless you, Pastor! God bless you, everyone! Hope to see you all at church tonight!" He waved as he retreated back into the mosque.

As soon as the door closed Louis pulled out his cell phone. He knew he'd better get the police over right away in case Billy and his buddies' anger turned violent.

Louis had no doubt how the TV news would spin his tug-of-war over the Qur'an with a local pastor. The Christian fundamentalists would have a field day with this one. Like he didn't get enough hate mail from them already. If only he could save the world and save his political image at the same time.

Yeah, if only.

❧ Chapter 30 ❧

AFTER EATING DINNER alone Sari heated a pot of water over her kerosene burner, then poured it into a round plastic tub and scooped enough cold water in to make a wonderfully warm bath. She was used to taking cold baths every morning and evening, but tonight she needed to relax and wash off the slime of the day. If she scrunched her legs up she could actually sit in the tub and pour the relaxing water over her body.

First she washed off all the slime from those creepy guys. Then she washed off the yuckiness of finding out that her best friend had become a prostitute. Finally she scrubbed away her anger at Pastor Susanna, and at her mom for even going to the Love Feast. She told God that she couldn't take much more. *Nothing else better go wrong!*

After her bath she was surprised that her mom still wasn't home. Usually when she went to a night event without Sari one of the other ladies dropped her off at the front of the alley. Sari turned on the TV and tried a bit of *Cinta dan Kebaikan,* or *"Love and Goodness,"* one of the many special religious soap operas for Ramadan.

At 10:30 the soap finished and Sari turned off the TV. She picked up her cell phone and noticed a text message waiting for her.

"Sar, staying late to clean up. Pastor promised extra donation from tonight's offering for the poor. Can you pick me up about 10:00? Love, Mom."

Poor Mom! She must be wondering where I am.

Sari hurriedly ripped off her pajamas and put on some jeans, a T-shirt, and a jacket. As she walked to her bike, she quickly text messaged her mom to wait at the church and she'd pick her up in five.

As she put on her helmet, she noticed a faint smell of smoke in the air. *Probably just a neighbor burning trash.*

❧ Chapter 31 ❦

THE GATE TO the church parking lot was conveniently unlocked. There were no vehicles parked inside. The church was obviously empty. And with high walls on the right and left of the lot and a river in the back, there would be no witnesses to see what was about to happen.

Hafiz instructed Udin and Juki to pour the gallons of kerosene all around the base of the church, at least on the three sides away from the river. What kerosene they had left they splashed on the two doors, the walls, and just the lowest edge of the roof. When they were done Hafiz handed the box of matches to Syukran.

"For your brother."

Syukran nodded and struck a match. He stared into the flame, then looked up at the church building. His hand was trembling. The match went out.

"Strike it closer to the kerosene, out of the wind."

Syukran squatted down next to the church wall and took out another match. His hand was shaking even worse than before. He tried to strike it but missed the strip on the box. He tried again and failed.

The other boys were tense, ready to run as soon as Syukran lit the fire. But he kept delaying.

Without warning, Syukran started having a coughing fit. He thrust the matches into Hafiz's hand and stumbled away, coughing violently.

Hafiz mumbled, "Go to hell, Christians." He struck the match and touched it to the kerosene.

The sleepy scene suddenly exploded to life. The roar of the fire and the brilliance of the light scared the boys so much that Kiki actually fell backward on his rear end.

"Let's get out of here!" Udin cried, and they all made a run for the gate, jumped on their motorbikes, and zoomed away.

Kris had finished cleaning everything about ten minutes earlier. Pastor Susanna had told her to take the extra food home with her. Since pastor had apparently forgotten to give her any of the money from the offering for the poor, orphans, and widows, she decided she'd better be grateful for the food.

Unfortunately the plastic bag she'd put the food in had caught on a sharp countertop corner and ripped, spilling food everywhere. It took Kris an extra ten minutes to clean the floor a second time. She was just finishing scrubbing the tiles when she heard a *whoosh* outside. Before she had a chance to open the door and check it out, her cell phone beeped. She read the message from Sari. "Stay put. Coming to get you." *Why is she so late? I hope nothing's wrong.*

Kris threw the plastic bag into the trash, rinsed out the rags she used to clean the floor, and picked up her purse. *I wonder if I should wait out by the gate.* She reached her hand toward the doorknob.

It was then that she noticed the key on the floor near the door. She stooped down to pick it up. It wasn't the size of the doorknob's key, which she carried in her pocket. Where could it come from? She looked around the kitchen for anything that needed a key. A drawer perhaps. Nothing. She decided it might have come from Pastor Susanna's office, and she might as well check it out while she waited for Sari. Leaving her purse behind, she opened the door to the sanctuary.

Smoke filled the room, choking her lungs. Above she could see a shining red glow. *Fire!*

She saw a piece of the red roofing tile crash down onto a pew. Dropping the key, she retreated to the kitchen. She sprinted to the exit and grabbed the doorknob, then screamed in pain.

The doorknob was white hot.

Kris ran to the sink and tried to run water over her burning hand, but that only made it feel worse. She wrapped it in her shirt, crying out in pain. She noticed that she'd forgotten to close the door to the sanctuary, and the smoke was pouring into the kitchen.

There was no way out.

Oh Jesus! Oh Jesus! Help me! Send an angel to protect me! Oh sweet Jesus!

Kris wanted to scream, but the smoke was choking her lungs. She could see the fire burning through the edges of the door now, licking up the wall and curling down from the edge of the roof, as though she were surrounded by the hungry hordes of hell.

The cell phone!

She lunged for the counter where she'd left it, though the smoke was getting so thick she had to feel around with her hands. She found it! Sari had programmed her own cell number as a speed dial, so all she had to do was push "2" and "Call."

She fell to her knees, begging Sari to answer the phone. The deafening roar around her kept her from hearing if the phone was ringing or not. She was coughing so hard, would her daughter even understand her?

"Sari…please…hello?"

A flash of light and the sound of roofing tiles crashing into the sink startled her. She managed one final, weak cry before she dropped her cell phone and fainted.

"Jesus!"

❧ Chapter 32 ☙

E's CAUGHT!
They finally caught him and took him for his punishment back to Afghanistan. What's worse, they brought his whole family, too.

The four of them are marched single file into a tent, then told to stand before a large chair. He's seen this chair before. It has several knife-marks in the wooden arms. Yes, he remembers this chair.

Maybe he could fight his way out! No, his hands are tied behind his back. So are his family's. They wait for the judge. A man walks in and sits on the chair.

Mullah Omar!

The Taliban leader points his AK-47 at Abdullah. "You are a coward. You will die a coward's death."

"Please, just let my family go free."

Mullah Omar turns to Syukran and asks him, "Are you ready to die for Islam?"

Syukran answers proudly, "Yes!"

Mullah Omar swings the AK-47 toward Syukran and puts a burst of bullets into his head.

Abdullah bolted upright, the word "No!" formed on his lips but not yet screamed. He wiped the sweat off his face with his sheet and looked at the clock by his bed. Ten-thirty. He'd barely fallen asleep, and already the dreams were torturing him.

Besides the exercise of running and *silat*, Abdullah had discovered one other release from the ghosts of his past—reading. His wife ridiculed him if she caught him reading anything other than the newspaper or the Qur'an during the day, so he mostly read at night when he couldn't sleep.

He reached under the bed, where he had hidden the latest book Iqbal had checked out for him from the school library, *Three Cups of Tea*. This story fascinated him, not least because he recognized some of the places referred to in the book. An American named Greg Mortenson got lost hiking in the mountains of northern Pakistan. A poor Muslim village nursed him back to health. Greg was so grateful, he wanted to do something to thank the village. He noticed they had no school building. So Greg started a campaign to raise money, then brought the money back to Pakistan to build the school. Greg decided to devote his whole life to building schools in poor villages across mostly Taliban territory in Pakistan and Afghanistan.

The American is building schools because there are no young men in the village to build them. The young Afghan men are all away training to kill the Americans.

Abdullah saw *jihad* in such a different light now. When he was young he'd have been anxious to kill the American too. Now he wished he could join Greg Mortenson and somehow redeem his wasted life.

Abdullah had just gotten comfortable on the couch in the living room when he heard the incessant *ding, ding, ding, ding* of someone banging on the light pole. Everyone in Kelayan knew what that meant: fire!

Abdullah raced back to the bedroom and pulled on his trousers. He was still wearing his white tank top and sandals as he raced down the steps. Not exactly proper attire for the volunteer fire department, but in Kelayan, where wooden houses were built only inches from each other, a cigarette carelessly dropped in one house could mean an entire neighborhood razed to the ground in a few hours.

He reached the front of the alley just in time to see the volunteer fire truck pull up, waiting for him to jump on. Pak Darsuni jumped on first, then gave Abdullah a hand up. They and six men from the neighboring alley filled up the empty spaces of the pickup truck around a water pump, their only fire equipment. Abdullah hoped the fire was near a source of water; then the water pump was invaluable, drawing water out of the river with one hose and spraying it with another.

The air was thick with smoke. The men could see the orange glow in the sky north of them, probably over Pekauman. They tore up the street, siren wailing, shouting at people to jump out of the way or get run over. In the distance they could hear the wail of several other small fire trucks from nearby neighborhoods racing to the inferno. Speed was everything.

Fires were all too common in dry season. Abdullah didn't have the faith tonight to pray for rain. He just prayed that they'd get there before anyone lost their lives.

❧ Chapter 33 ❧

SARI WAS LESS than a hundred yards from the church when she heard her phone ring. Panic was already constricting her breath, hoping against hope that the raging flames lighting up the night sky ahead of her weren't coming from the church. She had to know. She gunned her motorbike and seconds later came screeching to a stop in front of the church gate. It *was* the church!

She ripped at her jeans for the phone, now on its fourth or fifth ring. *Oh God! Let it be my mom telling me she's safe somewhere, anywhere but here.*

"Mom! Mom!" No answer, just noise. Then a crashing sound. Then a distant shriek, "Jesus!" Then a sound like static, but not telephone static, something else. Fire!

"Mooooom!" Sari screamed into the phone. Then she jammed it into her pocket and ran toward the church screaming. She circled toward the side door to the kitchen. It was covered in flames. She couldn't get in, and her mom couldn't get out.

"Oh my God! Oh my God! Somebody help! Please, somebody! Oh God!"

Sari's hysterics brought some of the neighbors, who had begun to gather outside the gate in closer. People of all ages appeared in pajamas or sarongs, wakened from their sleep, concerned about the fire spreading to their homes. Passersby on motorbikes pulled up to the gate, and a few even pulled inside just to watch the spectacle.

Sari screamed at them to help, but most couldn't understand her or even hear her above the fire's roar. A few figured out from her gestures that someone was trapped inside. They passed the news along to the other spectators, who passed it along as well, but no one knew what to do.

A siren blared, and the first fire truck arrived. One of the volunteers jumped off the back of the pickup and opened the gate wider. The pickup raced through and parked as near to the river and the flames as possible. They started unloading their water pump. Sari ran after them screaming that her mother was trapped inside, but they just ignored her.

Sari thought about throwing her own body against the door, but was afraid all she'd accomplish would be burning to death with her mother. *Oh God! Where are you when I need you? I need a miracle!*

She scanned the crowd again for a sympathetic face. Surely there was someone who would help her! But no one would meet her eyes; they all turned their gaze from her back to the raging inferno.

The second fire truck careened through the gate and skidded to a halt next to the first. Sari ran to it, knowing time was running out.

Abdullah jumped over the side of the pickup and was nearly run over by a wild young woman. He grabbed her arm to keep her from falling. When she looked up at him, her eyes were puffy and red, her cheeks wet, her breath coming in gasps.

"Sari?"

"Pak Abdullah? Oh, Bapak, please, you have to help me! My mom is inside the church!"

"What?" Abdullah grabbed her by the shoulders, eyes wide as saucers.

"She was cleaning the kitchen. She called me on the phone. She's trapped inside! Oh Bapak, please, please help me!"

Abdullah took a deep breath. *The woman is probably dead by now. But how could I live with myself knowing I did nothing?*

He leaned closer, right into Sari's face. "Which part of the building do you think she's in?"

Sari pointed to the side door. "There. That's the kitchen door. Please, Pak…" She burst into violent sobs again.

"Darsuni! Focus your hose on that door!"

Abdullah knew he couldn't go in there wearing sandals, slacks, and a tank top. He looked around. A young couple on a motorbike had pulled inside the gate to watch the show. He ran over to them and felt the "command voice" rise up inside him. In Afghan they had trained recruits how to take control of situations, rob banks to fund *jihad*, etc., with the command voice. Abdullah had hoped he'd never have to use it again.

He straddled the front tire of the couple's motorbike blocking their view of the fire and released "the voice."

"Son, I'm going in that fire to save someone's life. It's time for you to be a hero. Give me your jacket, gloves, and helmet, *now!* Daughter, give me your *jilbab*, *now!* Quickly!" The young people obeyed. Abdullah quickly put on the jacket and gloves, then wrapped the head covering around his neck like a scarf. He grabbed the helmet and sprinted to an older man nearby wearing a sarong around his waist. "Father, I need your sarong, *now!*" The man was wearing shorts underneath and gave up his sarong without a word. There was no time to search for proper shoes. He sprinted back to Darsuni manning the water pump hose.

"Spray me down, I'm going in!"

Darsuni looked at Abdullah skeptically but finally turned the hose on him. Abdullah spun around quickly, then held up the sarong and soaked it too.

"Focus all the water on that door!" As he ran toward the building, he pulled the *jilbab* tightly over his mouth and nose, then put the helmet on his head. Ten feet away the heat was already unbearable. He pressed through the pain. He could feel the skin on his feet was already singed before he reached the building.

He stood to the side of the door and reached over for the knob, the sarong wrapped thickly around his hand. He turned it and threw the door open. Dragon-like blasts of fire shot past him, and thick black smoke exploded outward. Like the doorway to hell.

Darsuni aimed the hose through the open doorway. Abdullah stepped in front of the water blast, and it propelled him into the room. He crashed headfirst into a counter about halfway across the room and hit the floor. His head felt fine. But his eyes and feet were burning.

It was too dark to see anything. He decided to crawl along the floor, head out first to meet any fallen debris or solid furniture with the helmet. He went right until he hit something hard, then turned right again. Nothing. Another something solid, another right turn, and he was heading back to the door. Nothing. Now he was in the line of the spraying water. He let it soak over him for just a second, then headed back to the counter he'd originally crashed into and turned left. Another dead end, another left. Still nothing. His exposed feet were in searing agony. He stopped to wrap the sarong around his feet and started pulling himself along with his arms, feet dragging behind him. There was a huge pile of burning debris between him and what should be the outer wall. If she were under there, it was too late anyway. He turned left and headed back toward the door.

Maybe she isn't in here! Maybe she's in another room, a bathroom or something. This is hopeless. I've got to get out of here soon, or I'll be joining her in the afterlife.

Suddenly a light flashed on the floor not more than a meter to his left. He dragged himself toward it. A cell phone! Someone was calling. He extended his hand past the cell phone and felt a body. She was no more than two meters from the door, just slightly to the left of where he'd crashed into the counter; he'd slid right past her. He had no idea if she were dead or alive. It didn't matter now anyway. He was taking her out.

He whipped the sarong off his feet, screaming with anguish as he felt his skin peeling off with it, and wrapped it around Kris's limp body as best as he could. Then he dragged her toward the door, where the force of the water hit them again. The slippery tile made it easier to slide her along. When he reached the doorway he waved his hand. Darsuni must have seen him, because he turned the hose away.

Abdullah slid his hands under Kris's shoulders and thighs and tried to stand. As he did, he let out a cry that Darsuni would later describe as that of a jungle animal caught in a trap. His rubber sandals were melted to the bottom of his feet. He took one excruciating step toward the door, then another. He was through the doorway. He saw Darsuni running toward him. Then he heard a noise like a train wreck above him, and something heavy slammed into the back of his helmet, glancing off onto his shoulder and back, throwing him forward. Then everything went black.

❦ Chapter 34 ❦

Sari watched as Pak Darsuni and two other men dashed toward the place where a part of the wall had crumbled onto Abdullah. Her mom had been thrown forward, clear of the wreckage. The first man scooped her up and carried her away from the extreme heat of the building, yelling at the onlookers, "Somebody get a car in here now! Get this woman to a hospital!" He laid her gently on the grass.

Sari crumpled at her mother's side, desperate to know if she were still alive. Kris reeked of smoke and burnt flesh. Her lovely skin was now a charcoal black. Her hair had kinked up and turned white. Her clothes were basically intact. Only the edges of her shirtsleeves showed a ragged burn line. Mostly she was hot. She radiated so much heat Sari was afraid to touch her. She just sobbed quietly with her mouth near her mother's ear, crying, "Mom, Mom, it's me, Sari. Wake up, Mom." It was hard to tell if her mother was breathing or not. Please, *God, don't let her die. Please let her live.*

Darsuni and the other man were looking at Abdullah lying facedown on the ground, a burning nine-inch wooden beam across his calves. Darsuni called to the man with the hose, "Here! Now!" He blasted the beam with a furious spray. Darsuni then jumped to a straddle position at Abdullah's waist and put his sandal against the beam and pushed. Slowly it rolled over Abdullah's feet and off of him. The two men grabbed Abdullah's arms and dragged him to safety near Kris.

The helmet was hot as a teakettle, but by wrapping his hand in his shirt he managed to get it off his friend's head. Abdullah was breathing. Darsuni had never seen anyone as badly burned as Abdullah's feet were in all his years as a volunteer fireman, but he figured such a tough guy would probably live. *What a fool! He could have died in there. But what a friend to have if I'm ever in trouble.*

One of the neighbors pulled his Toyota Kijang up next to the fire victims. He opened the side door, and they laid Kris across the seat. Sari climbed in after her and sat on the floor between the front seats, facing backward. Then he opened the back door and propped the fold-down seats on each side up against the wall, and they laid Abdullah inside, his six-foot body curled up like a fetus just to fit him in. It wouldn't be a comfortable ride to the hospital. Darsuni figured it was a good thing Abdullah was unconscious.

Darsuni called to one of the other firemen to let his wife know what had happened, then jumped in the front passenger seat. He figured it would take them less than ten minutes this time of night to get to the emergency room at Ulin Hospital. He hoped the woman lived. If she didn't, Abdullah's sacrifice would mean nothing.

Two hours later, the fire was out. No less than fourteen volunteer fire crews had showed up, some from as far away as Kayutangi in the north part of the city. A couple policemen had arrived on motorbike from the Southern Banjar office just down the road and were already interviewing bystanders and firemen, trying to piece together the story.

There was just a shell of a building left. The iron rods in the cement pillars were exposed in several places. The back wall facing the river was completely intact but stained black from the smoke. The other three walls all had significant damage. More than half the roof had collapsed. Anything on the inside of the church would be counted a total loss.

The neighbors all shuffled back to their beds around 1:00 a.m., grateful to God that only one building was destroyed and none of their homes affected. The firemen headed home to a bath and fresh set of clothes to get the stench of smoke off their bodies before climbing back into their beds, thankful that none of them were hurt, hopeful that the two victims would pull through and they could say that no one had died tonight. The policemen motored on back to the night watch at the office, already planning their investigation.

Finally, the church grounds were quiet once again. No one had bothered to close the gate. And the last person to leave paid no attention to the solitary figure in the shadows across the street, a figure who had been standing there like a dark statue for nearly an hour now, watching.

Pastor Susanna had watched her dreams go up in smoke once again.

She didn't want to remember the first time, but as she had stared into the demonic blaze the memory had bullied its way back into her consciousness. Nineteen ninety-seven. She and her husband had built their first church building with sacrificial gifts from their congregation of twenty-nine people, plus every penny she and her husband had. They'd still had to borrow a fair amount, but she was confident God would help them pay off the loan.

Two months later riots swept Banjarmasin as people called for the overthrow of President Suharto.

In one night, Western and Chinese businesses all over the city were torched. Over two hundred people died in the Mitra Plaza fire alone. Every single church of the Christian minorities in Banjarmasin was ravaged, and most, like hers, were burned to the ground.

Her husband blamed God. He decided to walk away from the ministry. She refused to blame God or leave the church. So her husband walked away from her, too.

He was weak in faith. Not like me. I will persevere. Whatever those cursed heathen throw at me, I will not be moved!

No, she would never blame God. God was always good. It was man that was cruel. And she had a good idea on which man, or woman, the blame should fall this time.

✇ Chapter 35 ✇

FAMILY MEMBERS WEREN'T allowed in the emergency room, so Siti, Iqbal, and Syukran paced the concrete outside, anxious for news about Abdullah. All the medical staff would tell them was that he was in critical condition and they were doing all they could. When asked if he were conscious, the staff told them, "Not yet."

Pak Darsuni had told them all he knew of the story, but no one knew exactly how bad Abdullah's burns were yet or the effects of the burning beam falling on his shoulder. Siti had grabbed her health card and jumped on the bike with Iqbal. All the way to the hospital she was cursing Ibu Kris for "murdering" her husband. Syukran took Rp.5,000 from Mom and jumped on a night *ojek* to arrive just after his family.

Iqbal tried to calm his mother down. "Mom, if Dad was strong enough to walk into a burning building and carry someone out, he's strong enough to pull through this! I don't know hardly anyone as tough as Dad. He'll be fine!"

"How could your father do this to us? Doesn't he know we can't afford to lose him? You kids haven't even finished school yet! How am I supposed to take care of you? I'm too young to be a widow!" Siti was barely coherent between her sniffing and whining.

"Mom, it's going to be all right. Give the doctors some time. If Dad's not conscious yet, there's nothing we can do anyway. Why don't you go home and get some rest. Syukran or I can keep an eye on things here, and you can come back when we go to school in the morning."

Syukran wasn't in total agreement. "Why do any of us have to be here? If Dad's unconscious, what's the point of being here?"

"Hey, he's still our dad! When he wakes up, he deserves to know we're here supporting him."

"Suit yourself. I'm not spending the night sleeping on concrete outside the emergency room. Come on, Mom. I'll take you home." Syukran held out his hand for Iqbal to give him the motorbike keys.

"If he wakes up, you call me right away, OK, Iqbal? I'll be back at 6:00 so you can go get ready for school."

"OK, Mom. I'll call you. Get some rest." Iqbal was piqued that he'd been railroaded into spending the first night at the hospital, but maybe Syukran would take the second night. He could catch up on sleep later.

Iqbal looked around for a comfortable spot to sit and found none. Everywhere was hard concrete. The night air was giving him goose bumps. He tried to get his mind off of his suffering by thinking about what his dad was going through. *What possessed Dad to run into a burning church to rescue someone he hardly even knew? I would sure never do that!*

As Iqbal wandered around a corner trying to figure out where to sleep he discovered Sari. At first he didn't recognize her, but on second look his brain kicked in. *Of course! Sari's mom is in the emergency room too!* At least neither of them would be alone tonight.

"Sari?"

Sari wiped her eyes and looked up, surprised to see Bali registering on her face, then understanding.

"Hi, Bali. I'm so sorry about your father."

"I'm sorry about your mother, too."

She wiped her nose on her sleeve and tried to manage a smile. "Thanks. I have to admit, it's nice to see a familiar face. I've never slept outdoors before, and I was kind of nervous about getting bothered by wandering lunatics."

Bali laughed. "I'm wandering, but not quite a lunatic! May I sit down?"

"Sure, anywhere you like." Sari waved her hand around the concrete slab. Iqbal sat leaning against a pillar about two yards away.

"Comfy! Remind me to bring a pillow tomorrow."

"Good idea. Listen, if it's all right with you, can we talk about something not related to our parents? I've cried enough for one day and don't want you to see me start again."

"Sure thing! What should we talk about?"

Sari stared off into the darkness. "How about student council?"

"OK. I have some ideas I was planning to present to the group at the next meeting. Would you like to hear them?"

"I'd love to!"

"Well, it seems like most student councils get too involved with maintenance, you know, keeping things running smoothly at the school, troubleshooting, that kind of stuff. I think we should be more visionary."

"Cool! I agree. So what do you want to do?"

Bali shifted positions, the energy of "visionizing" pumping fresh adrenaline into his system. "Well, you know the new Coke machines that are showing up in special places like the airport? I want our school to be the first one to have a real Coke machine on campus!" He paused for effect. *Let no one say Bali doesn't think big!*

Sari was quiet, too quiet. Finally she asked, "Anything else?"

"Anything else? What, don't tell me you don't like my idea! Some schools don't even have a small refrigerator to sell cold drinks like we do. But that's so yesterday. And we can be the school that leads the way to the future!"

"OK, fine, a Coke machine. But what if we also raised some money to help a worthy cause, like a scholarship for a student with financial hardship or hiring a foreigner to lead a weekly English Conversation Club or buying books for our library that students actually want to read or hosting an inter-school seminar on the issues facing our generation?"

Bali's mouth hung open. His brain was too busy assimilating Sari's ideas to remember to close it. Part of him felt really stupid for being so proud of his Coke machine idea. Another part of him felt really curious to hear more. Sari seemed so quiet at school. He had no idea the class secretary was a creative genius!

He leaned forward. "Tell me more."

"About what?"

"About each one of those ideas. And any others you have. I think your ideas are amazing!"

"You do?" Sari looked surprised.

They were still talking at six when Siti showed up. Iqbal offered to give Sari a ride home so she could make it to school too. He could see that she felt torn. Of course she would want to be there when her mom woke up; so did he. But who knew how long that would be.

"OK, let's go to school."

As Bali said good-bye to his mom, he added. "And don't worry. After school I'll be back and spend the night again."

For the first time in hours Bali actually thought he saw Sari smile.

❧ Chapter 36 ❧

ALI AND SARI rushed straight to the hospital after school. Ibu Siti informed them that both Abdullah and Kris had been moved from the emergency room to the intensive care unit (ICU). She promised that Syukran would bring Iqbal some dinner and a pillow. All this she said without looking even once at Sari. Then she was gone.

Family members weren't allowed in the ICU, so the hospital provided a waiting room just outside. Sari and Bali picked out a corner unused by the other six people also waiting for news about their loved ones and sat down on the hard white tile floor. Both of them were anxious for news and watched the door into the ICU like hawks, hoping a nurse or doctor would come out.

Both Sari and Bali knew Ulin Hospital well since it was the largest hospital in the province, and the busiest. Poor families, like theirs, could be treated there for free, providing they showed the health card given to families who proved their financial inability to pay. The health card didn't cover everything, but without it the costs for say, a Cesarean operation, could cost nearly a year's wages. Sari knew most of her Kelayan neighbors were more likely to take their sick to the significantly cheaper local witchdoctor before trying the hospital.

Sari saw the doctor emerge first while Bali's head was buried in a math book. In his long, white coat covering a pink dress shirt and magenta tie with black slacks, carrying a white clipboard, he looked just like a doctor on TV. His hair was slicked back, and he wore thick, black-rimmed glasses on a prominent Arab nose. His smile showed his perfect teeth. He couldn't be more than thirty years old, Sari thought. She wondered if he were married.

The doctor addressed everyone in the waiting room. "Excuse me, is there anyone here from the families of Pak Abdullah or Ibu Kristyana?" Sari and Bali stood up. He motioned them over to the quietest corner available and asked them to introduce themselves. Then he introduced himself.

"I'm Dr. Santo. Nice to meet you, Iqbal and Sari! I've been assigned your parents' cases. The good news is that both of them are in stable condition, and we have high hopes that they will live through this trauma.

"However, I'm afraid you can't see them for a few days. We have a lot of work to do to get them back to health. Ibu Kris was apparently in the burning building longer than Pak Abdullah, judging by the smoke in her lungs. We'll keep her on a ventilator for a few days while her lungs heal. Part of the healing process involves the lungs sloughing off the top layer of burned skin, and the resulting mucus can plug her airway, so we'll have to keep suctioning it clear. Usually the third day is the worst. If we get through that without pneumonia or other complications, her lungs should be OK.

"As far as the burns on her body, I have to say this is an unusual case. When the ER guys told me the story of what had happened, I expected upwards of 50 percent of her body surface to have third-degree burns. Well, she has partial-thickness burns on her face, hands, and feet, but not nearly as bad as I expected. It's almost as if she was being shielded from the fire. Her skin is red and weepy, and we'll treat it with a cream, keep her on an IV with lactated ringers and keep an eye on her blood pressure, swelling, and urine output. She'll be in the ICU for at least four days and, depending on her progress, may be able to move to a regular room at that point, where you can stay with her. When she's off the ventilator, she'll be able to receive guests. Any questions?"

Sari shook her head. She really didn't understand most of what Dr. Santo said, but it sounded like her mom was going to make it, and that was enough for her.

Dr. Santo turned to Iqbal. "About your father, he's a very tough guy, and we have high hopes that he'll make it through too. He's a bit worse off than Sari's mother. His lungs are relatively clear, and when we cut his burned clothes off we noticed that he had protected most of his body quite well. But his feet, well, there are full-thickness burns on the tops of both feet, partial burns on the soles. They look almost black and feel hard, almost like plastic. This hospital doesn't have a burn unit like where I studied in the US, and I've been told that we don't do skin-grafting operations here. But I'm willing to try one. I studied this at the University of Southern California, and I'm confident that it is vital to your father's recovery. It's not covered by your health card, so they tell me, but if you will sign a release saying that you will not hold me responsible for the results I think I can save your father's feet, and I'm willing to do the operation for free—call it a chance to practice what I learned in school. If we don't operate and graft on new skin, it's possible he could lose his feet to infection and perhaps never walk again.

"Let me explain grafting. Because the skin is damaged so deeply, we need to cut it off and replace it with skin from another part of your father's body. We can slice a thin layer of skin from his thighs or buttocks, sew it over his feet, and it should protect the feet from infection, giving the body time to reproduce its own skin naturally. Speed is important here. The sooner we can get the old, charred skin off and the new skin on, the better chance we'll have at fighting infection. If your family agrees to this surgery, I need your mother to come back before eight tonight and sign the papers, because I've tentatively scheduled the first operation for eight tomorrow morning. If she wants to talk to me before she comes, let me give you my cell phone number right now."

Dr. Santo took out a name card and wrote his personal cell phone number on the back. He handed it to Iqbal.

"Besides the critical issue of his burned feet, your father also sustained a broken collarbone. We've already set it and hope it will heal fine. The significant bruising around the collarbone will keep him in severe pain, as, of course, will his feet, so we've been giving him a sedative in his IV. After the grafting surgery we'll downgrade to some painkillers, and he'll be able to move to a regular room and talk with you. But he'll have to be immobile for a matter of weeks. Any questions?"

Iqbal shook his head. "I'll go talk to my mom right now. Thanks very much, doc."

"You're welcome. God willing, we'll get your dad walking again."

❧ Chapter 37 ❧

HOTEL BATUNG BATULIS was reasonably priced and reasonably quiet. No nightclub music shaking the floor. No swimming pool with rambunctious kids dripping through the lobby. The service wasn't great, but then Saifullah preferred a lackadaisical staff to those hyper-helpful ones who asked too many questions and entered his room too often.

The hotel was just north of the Grand Mosque along a convenient public transport route. Outside the front door was the Ramadan cake fair and the Martapura River. It was his sixth hotel since he'd come to Banjarmasin, and he just might stay here a bit longer than the others.

Every morning Saifullah sat in the lobby perusing the international and national news, then intently examining the local news. He needed a sign from Allah, and he needed it soon. Considering the time it would take to prepare everything and train for the mission, recruiting the "bride" was best done expeditiously.

Today's front-page headline was about Ustad Abu Bakar Ba'asyir's latest accusations from his prison cell. The Americans claimed the founder of Jemaah Islamiyah was Al-Qaeda's representative in Southeast Asia. He'd been arrested several times already before this with accusations of terrorism, but he somehow always wriggled out of serious jail time. Besides, being filmed in jail gave him a nationwide TV audience to hear him bash the Americans. Saifullah figured it was probably Ba'asyir's strategy to tell his *jihad* troops to confess to his vague, unprovable involvement to get them less jail time. Even though he'd have to endure incarceration, they could get back out sooner and get back to work, like his old classmate Soghir—five years in jail for the Australian embassy bombing, and the moment he got out he started working on a car bomb to take out the president. *Too bad he got caught before he could deliver his present!*

On page three a headline grabbed his attention: "House of Worship Burned in Pekauman." Reading between the lines, he figured out this wasn't a mosque but a church. And though the policeman interviewed

115

didn't say he suspected arson, Saifullah did. He memorized the address and decided his afternoon plans had just been made.

During fasting month most Muslims try for an extra-long nap in the hot hours of midday. But around four o'clock the city comes back to life. At 4:30 Saifullah headed to Pekauman.

Across the street from the ruins of the church some pushcart vendors had set up shop expecting to get a lot of curious visitors to the site, and they were right. All afternoon people drove or walked by just to look at the blackened skeleton and offer their thoughts on the tragedy. Saifullah made friends with the Pak Haji who was selling *terang bulan*, a pancake-like snack filled with chocolate or cheese, for people's fast-breaking meal. He grabbed one of the two plastic stools for customers and sat down next to the cart to hear what everyone had to say.

"Is that the place I read about in the *B-Post*?"

"Yeah, Pak," answered Pak Haji. "It used to be a church. Pretty big blaze last night. We could see it from our place in Teluk Tiram." He pointed across the Martapura River.

"What started it? Independence Day fireworks maybe?"

Pak Haji just shrugged. Another customer, a woman with a toddler, picked up the thread. "No, I don't think so. I walked home last night from *tarawih* prayers right by this place around, maybe, 9:30, and the last motorbikes were coming out of the parking lot there heading home. They didn't have any late-night event there, I'm sure."

"Probably an electrical short," Saifullah suggested.

"It was arson." This matter-of-fact statement came from a younger man sitting on a blue tarp next to the *terang bulan* seller surrounded by *bal-ungka batu* melons.

"How do you know that?" Pak Haji challenged.

"My little brother was hanging out just over there last night around 10:30. He says he saw the fire erupt, then three motorbikes came roaring out of that gate over there and took off that direction." The young man was waving his melon-cutting knife different directions as he explained.

The lady chimed in with a suitably shocked voice, "Maybe it was terrorists!"

"Doubt it." The young man shook his head. "My little brother says he thinks he knows one of the guys. Said he's seen that T-shirt, helmet, and bike before. Says he plays soccer with that guy on Saturday mornings over at the Lambung Mangkurat Stadium. A *pesantren* kid. That's what my brother says."

"Now, why would a *pesantren* kid want to burn down a church?" Saifullah wondered aloud.

"I don't believe it," stated Pak Haji. "It wasn't *pesantren* kids. We don't have any schools in Banjar that teach that it's OK to burn down another religion's house of worship. No way! I say it was an accident or ... "

"Or what?"

"If anyone torched that place, it was probably the city government."

Melon-man snorted. The woman took her plastic bag of *terang bulan* from Pak Haji and expressed her disbelief. "That's crazy!"

"You remember that fire a few years ago in Pasar Baru, where everyone sold birds? The guy they arrested for it was a scavenger that used to pick through the trash by my cousin's shop. He just got out of jail a few months ago and came by to ask my cousin for a job. My cousin asked him why he did it. He said two guys wearing city government uniforms paid him to do it—one million rupiah up front and another two million rupiah a month later if he didn't get caught. Well, he got caught."

"Why would the city government want to burn down their own *pasar*?" Saifullah asked.

"Because they wanted to build a parking lot there, over the river. They'd already asked the bird dealers to leave, but the bird dealers refused to go unless the city government found a better location for them. Since they didn't like the alternatives the government offered and refused to budge, the government found another way to get rid of them."

"Why would the city government want this land? I'm telling you, some *pesantren* boys did this!" Melon-man had a new customer, who wondered what everyone was talking about. He was wearing the long white Arab robe of the ultra-conservatives. Saifullah listened while Pak Haji and the melon seller caught him up.

"*Alhamdulillah!* It's Allah's judgment, that's what it is. That church is famous for Christianization. Every year at Christmas they try to lure innocent, uneducated Muslims like a spider lures a fly into her trap, except they use packets of food to prey on the hungry. If anyone burned down this pigsty they should be considered a hero."

"But I heard," cut in another woman in a business suit who had just arrived and ordered a chocolate *terang bulan*, "that someone was trapped in the building and burned alive."

Saifullah raised an eyebrow. The newspaper hadn't mentioned that. "Who was it? Maybe the pastor?"

"I heard it was a woman."

The Arab idolizer bounced with excitement. "Hopefully it *was* the pastor. This church had a woman pastor, an evil woman. We've been looking for something we could use to discredit her for some time. She deserves to die for her foolish war against Islam."

"We—?" Saifullah asked.

But the robed man already had his melon bagged and started pulling his motorbike away.

"What a jerk!" the melon-seller said now that he had no more customers. "That church gave me a packet of rice, sugar, and oil last Christmas, and they didn't try to convert me. I hope whoever did this gets caught and punished. It's not right."

Saifullah could see a pair of uniformed policemen pulling their motorbike over and starting to ask questions to the lady selling Ramadan cakes not far away. But he had to squeeze in one more question before he left: "If it were *pesantren* boys, surely they wouldn't be from any schools around here. Do we even have any *pesantrens* nearby?"

Pak Haji answered, "I only know of two in this area. *Al-Mustaqiim*," he said pointing south, "and *Al-Falaq*." He pointed southwest. "Maybe there are more I don't know about."

"Well, I'd best get this *terang bulan* back to my wife before sundown. Till we meet again." Saifullah casually strolled off in the opposite direction of the police as though he lived just down the street.

Pesantren boys. What would be the chances that I've already met the boys who did this? I've got to find those boys again! If they did do this, one of them just might be ready to take it to the next level.

🎵 Chapter 38 🎵

THE FIRST NIGHT Sari felt uncomfortable sleeping on the floor next to Bali. It just seemed a little too close, too intimate. But she felt even more uncomfortable with the alternatives—leaving her mom alone in the hospital, staying awake all night, or sleeping next to the other people in the waiting room that she didn't know. She kept telling herself that she and Bali were neighbors and had to stick together. And he wasn't so bad. Hopefully his mom and jerk of a brother would keep doing day watch and let Bali keep the night watch.

By the second full night in the hospital she was more relaxed. After they'd studied together, nibbled on some dinner, and studied some more, they both lay their heads on their pillows and began to talk. There was something about this posture that allowed thoughts deep in their subconscious to leak out.

"Bali, I'm so worried about my mom I can hardly eat anything, and all the wondering about her is killing my sleep worse than this hard floor. Do you feel like that too?"

"Yeah, I guess so. I hate waiting. I just want to know what's going on in there." Bali pointed with his chin toward the ICU door. "But being depressed isn't going to help them, you know!"

"I know."

"Maybe we should try to think happy thoughts." Bali flicked one of his bangs out of his eyes with his fingers and grinned at Sari. She tried to smile back.

"OK, I'll try." Sari took a deep breath and pushed her anxiety aside. "Tell me one of your happiest memories."

"Sure! I've got lots, you know." Bali sat up. "One time Syuk and I were just kids, and we were messing around stealing rambutan fruit from some trees down in Teluk Kubur, when a monkey grabbed Syuk's white *pesantren* hat and scampered up a tree. We yelled at him to bring it down, and he wouldn't, so I went up the tree after him."

"No way!"

"Yeah, and when I held out my hand and told that monkey he better surrender the hat or be the first in his family to go home without a tail, he held it out like he was going to give it to me, then dropped it. I reached down for it, and he jumped on my head! Then he screeched at me and leaped away. But hey, Syuk got his hat back!" Bali had enthusiastically acted out the story as he spoke.

Sari laughed. "You made that up!"

"Nope, I swear it's true! Ask Syuk! Although in his version he'll probably claim that *he's* the one who climbed the tree to rescue *my* hat!"

Sari laughed again. "Sounds like you're pretty close with your brother."

"Not so much anymore." Bali frowned. "Around the time I started high school we sort of drifted apart. I started hanging out with school friends and not so much with the neighborhood guys anymore. But he's a good guy. I know he'll be there for me when I need him, just like I'll be there for him."

Bali laid his head back down on the pillow. "Now it's your turn. What's one of your happy memories?"

Sari knew right away which memory was at the top of that list. "You know at Pasar Baru you can go on the roof of the Sudimampir building, and there are some little *warungs* where you can get snacks?"

"No way! I've lived here all my life and didn't know that! How do you get on the roof?"

"You obviously don't like shopping in the *pasar*! Everyone knows that place! You can drive up a ramp that winds around the building onto the roof."

"Cool! I'll have to try it sometime. So what's the memory?"

"When I was really young, maybe around kindergarten age, my mom's uncle actually came to visit. He used to visit more when I was a baby and my mom's aunt lived with us, but I remember this visit because it was his last.

"He took me and Mom up on the roof of Sudimampir at night. He bought me a red Fanta, and we sat on the edge of the roof, about three stories high, watching the boats go by on the Martapura River below. When I finished my drink he asked me if I wanted another, and I said yes quickly before my mom could object—she would never buy me two sodas! I drank them both and listened to my mom and great-uncle talk.

"But the best part was at the end. When we stood up to go home my mom took me by the left hand, my great-uncle by the right hand, and as we walked across the roof I picked up my feet, and they swung me through the air. If I closed my eyes, it felt like…it felt like I had…a father."

Sari's eyes were moist. Neither spoke for a while. Finally Bali broke the uncomfortable silence with a mumbled, "I wish I had a story where I felt loved like that. My parents didn't do much cool stuff like that. They're just kind of average, I guess. Nothing special."

"Bali! 'Nothing special'? I think your father is one of the greatest men I've ever met!"

"What do you mean? I don't think he's so great."

Sari brought her face closer to Bali's. "How can you say that? He saved my mom's life! If it wasn't for him I wouldn't be laying here talking to you right now! I'd be knocking on the door of some orphanage, begging them to let me in. I'm forever indebted to your father."

"Yeah, I guess so."

"Why do you think he did that? Why did he risk his life to save my mom?"

"I don't know. I don't think I would have."

"I don't know if I would have either. Your dad…" Sari paused and shook her head, then continued. "Well, he's a better follower of Jesus than I am."

"What are you talking about?"

"It's rare for someone to be willing to die for their family member or friend, almost unheard of for someone to die for someone they hardly know, even someone from a different race or religion. That's what your dad did, like what Jesus did when He died for us."

Bali protested. "We Muslims don't believe Jesus died. We believe God switched Judas for Jesus so Jesus could be caught up to heaven without suffering such a horrible death."

Sari was quiet for a while, but there was something stirring in her heart that had to come out. She tried to look Bali in the eye, but he seemed to be watching a trail of ants crossing the floor.

"What's the highest expression of love? Isn't it someone giving their life for another? Maybe a mom who risks her own death in childbirth because she wants her baby to live. Or a husband who chooses to fight an armed gang of men threatening to rape his wife because he'd rather die for her than stand by and do nothing. Or people in the tsunami who jumped into the raging flood to save a child they'd never met. Everyone acknowledges that there is no greater love than this. If this is built into the DNA of every human being in every culture, that sacrificing one's own life for another is the highest form of love, where does this come from? Doesn't your faith teach God is the 'Most Compassionate'? Our Book says 'God is love.' How could God communicate to us that His love for us is greater than our love for each other unless He too was willing to somehow sacrifice Himself to save us? If He refuses to do that, our expression of love is greater than His."

Bali wasn't sure. "I never thought of it that way before. But is that kind of love really in everyone's DNA? When I was six I remember playing down by the river, when a kid I knew went to wash off his sandals and fell in. He couldn't swim well and called out for help. All us kids called for help, and two *ojek* guys came. One went to find a rope to throw to him; another went on his bike to call a policeman. The boy kept going under, and we knew he wouldn't last long. The policeman came back with the *ojek* driver, but no one would jump in to save him. I heard the policeman explain something about whirlpools, and the *ojek* guy say it was the crocodile spirits pulling him under. Finally the boy disappeared under the water and drowned. We all watched—us kids, including the boy's twelve-year-old brother, the *ojek* guy, the policeman. No one would risk drowning to save him. How come none of us had the courage to save him?"

Sari's heart was touched. She reached out and let the fingertips of her left hand lightly brush Bali's arm. "I can't imagine how hard it was for you to see that. I know when my mom was trapped in the fire I felt so helpless, so desperate, and there was absolutely nothing I could do but pray and hope for someone to take the risk to save my mom. I'll never forget watching your dad charge into that burning building; hope rushed into me for a miracle. I don't know if I could have lived through it if no one would have tried to rescue my mom. There's something different about your dad compared to the people who watched your friend drown."

"Yeah, but what?"

"I don't know. Maybe your dad understands sacrificial love? My mom always tells me that it doesn't matter what else I do well at in life; as long as I learn to love well, she'll be happy."

Bali rolled onto his back and stared at the water-stained plywood ceiling. "Your mom and mine are so different. I think my mom only loves herself."

"Well, your dad is number one in my book! You're lucky to have a dad like him."

Sari laid back and stared at the ceiling, too. She could almost feel jealous of Bali, but she was too grateful.

❦ Chapter 39 ❧

AFTER FIVE DAYS both patients were moved to a regular hospital room, which they shared with six other beds, five of which were full. Sari and Bali were excited to be able to finally take care of their parents directly, to finally talk to them. There was no curtain separating the beds in this room, which suited both teenagers just fine. In spite of the hard floors, both were increasingly enjoying their long nocturnal chats.

Abdullah's right arm was taped to his side so as to not move his collarbone. He was going to have to do everything left-handed for a while. His feet were still swollen and bandaged, and he wasn't yet allowed to stand on them, so a catheter drained his urine. But the doctor said he believed the grafting would prove successful. Heavy painkillers kept him very groggy.

The nurse told Sari that her mother had awakened a few times but usually went right back to sleep. Her skin was still extremely sensitive. The cream applied to it made her look like she was melting. The nurse had trimmed most of her beautiful hair, which had curled up in an ugly white tangle and smelled of smoke. Sari hardly recognized her. But it was the wheezing and coughing that worried Doctor Santo most. In spite of regularly suctioning her lungs, Kris's airways still weren't completely clearing up. Doctor Santo said she didn't quite have pneumonia, but they were treating her as though she did in hopes of preventing it.

Sari and Bali sat on the floor between Kris's and Pak Abdullah's beds and started their homework. Both could hardly wait for their parents to wake up. Kris woke up first. Sari heard a little cough and a moan, and leaped to her feet.

"Mom! Mom! You're awake! I've been here every evening just waiting for you to wake up. How are you feeling? Are you in a lot of pain?"

Kris's eyelids fluttered open, then closed, then open again as if emerging from a deep slumber.

"Sari? Hold my hand." Her eyes closed again as she attempted a feeble smile. Sari reached for the hand not connected to an IV.

"Mom, I'm so sorry. This is all my fault! I should have gone with you to the church."

"Hush. It's not your fault, sweetie. Are you OK? Are you eating?"

Sari noticed her mom's voice sounded kind of raspy when she talked.

"I'm fine, Mom. We still have money in the shoebox."

Kris's eyes closed, but she coughed weakly once, then spoke again. "If you run out, sell the bike."

"Mom, don't worry. Just focus on getting well."

Kris squeezed her daughter's hand lightly and slipped back into her drug-induced sleep. Sari let go of her mother's hand and sat down next to Bali again.

"Did you hear that?"

Bali nodded.

"I don't want to sell the bike! How am I supposed to get to school?"

"I could give you a ride every day. At least it would save you gas money."

"Thanks. Maybe I'll take you up on that for now. But if I don't sell the bike, she's right, we won't be able to keep buying medicine or pay our electric bill. I guess I can bathe in the river and eat less. I don't know; what do you think I should do, Bali?"

Sari tried to hold back the tears, but they were slipping out and dripping onto her English textbook. Bali gently touched her arm. "Don't sell it yet. Let me see if I can think of something."

Bali's heart went out to Sari. He wanted so badly to step in and save her from her suffering. *Just like my dad did for Sari's mom*, he thought. *Well, almost.* He grabbed his cell phone and walked outside to call his mother.

"Hi, Bali. Is something wrong?" Siti answered.

"No, Mom. Dad's fine. He's still sleeping. I'll call you if he wakes up."

"Do you need Syukran to bring you something?"

"No, listen, Mom. I need to ask you something."

"What is it, honey?"

"Sari's worried that they're not going to have enough money for medicine for her mom. I was wondering if we could loan her a couple million with her motorbike as collateral. Do we have enough to do that?"

"No, we certainly don't! We can't afford to make huge loans like that! Tell her you want to buy the bike. Is it in good condition?"

"Yeah, it's in great condition. She could probably sell it for three or four million. But they need that bike. I know she'd pay back the loan."

"Offer her two million. I'm sure I could borrow that much from my *arisan* friends."

"No, Mom! We're not going to take advantage of her! Forget it!" Bali hung up.

He strode back into the room but didn't sit down. "What's wrong?" Sari asked.

"Nothing. My mom said something stupid. Look, I need to get out of here for a while. Call me if my dad wakes up?"

"Sure."

Bali stomped out of the hospital to hunt for dinner, thinking. *God, I need a solution to help Sari. Help me out here. Should I drop out of school and get a job? Should I sell my blood to the Red Cross? Come on, You're the Most Wise. Give me some help here!*

Bali rarely asked anyone for advice. It had been several years since he had sought his father's counsel. Yet he found himself thinking, What would Dad do?

❧ Chapter 40 ❧

WHEN SARI REACHED the hospital two days later she first checked if Bali was already there. Ibu Siti was still on day watch and turned her back at Sari's entrance. Pak Abdullah seemed to be sleeping. As she looked toward her mom's bed, she was pleasantly surprised to see her mother sitting up.

"Hi, Mom! Look at you! Are you feeling better?"

"I am. My body is feeling a bit better, and my heart is feeling much, much better."

Sari could still hear the wheeze in her mother's voice, but her eyes were shining with life.

"What do you mean?"

"Sari, sit down. You're not going to believe this!" Kris patted a spot on the bed next to her. "This morning Ibu Aaminah, Ibu Noorminah, Mama Shafa, Ibu Fitria, and another woman, I forgot her name, came to visit me! Look! They brought me this fruit basket!" She pointed out a small basket with two red apples, two oranges, two pears, and a bunch of purple grapes. "No one has ever given me a fruit basket before! And that's not all! This envelope has the *arisan* money for the week. The ladies decided I could be the winner this week to help pay for my hospital bill."

"Mom, that's awesome! I thought they didn't want you."

"I guess they do. And that's not all! Ibu Aaminah gave me this smaller envelope as a personal gift. She said she sold one of her gold bracelets that she brought back from Mecca. Get this—she said, 'The gold I wear makes me look beautiful, but what could be more beautiful than giving it away to help someone in need?' Isn't that wonderful?" Kris coughed a couple times.

"Wow! Mom, I had no idea there were people like this in our neighborhood."

"Neither did I. Remember how nervous I was about going to the *arisan* for the first time? I was so sure they would reject me. I never imagined..."

Kris paused for a moment to cough again. "Well, that was my day! How was yours? Anything interesting happen at school?"

"Not really. Pretty boring. The only thing was Bali started telling the student council about my ideas."

"You mean, he was taking credit for them?"

"No, actually, he told everyone they were my ideas, and he thought they were brilliant! It felt really good to have someone talk nicely about me at school for once."

"It sounds like you're getting pretty fond of Bali."

"He's just a friend, Mom. But he's been really kind and helpful here in the hospital. The other day he even brought me some fried noodles for dinner. And he's a good guy. I noticed he doesn't cheat on tests like most of my classmates. It's just...well, he's really popular with the girls. He treats them all nicely, not just me. He's probably already got his eye on one of the pretty girls anyway."

"If he's got his eye on the prettiest girl at school, that means he's looking at you."

"Right, Mom! There are tons of girls prettier than me. When you get out of the hospital he'll probably forget all about me."

"I think it's good if a guy has a crush on you, sweetie! You are lovely, and any boy with half a brain should have a crush on you. But please don't fall into the trap of seriously dating a boy from another religion. You know you can't marry him." Kris started coughing again, several times.

"I know, Mom. I want to marry someone who loves God like I do. Anyway, I wouldn't marry someone you didn't approve of."

"That's my girl!"

Later, Sari opened her history book to start her homework. At the bottom of the page she realized she had no idea what she'd just read. Bali's face, with those adorable bangs bouncing on his forehead and his cocky grin, were fixed before her eyes. His words of praise for her ideas were still ringing in her ears. She couldn't wait to talk to him tonight. *Maybe I can't marry him, but surely we can be good friends, can't we?*

❧ Chapter 41 ❧

SAIFULLAH SCANNED THE hallway, then cracked open the door into his hotel room about two inches, slid his fingers through, and ran them down to about ankle height, where he felt the hair, taut and unbroken, that he'd taped on the inside of the door and on the door-frame when he left. If it were hanging loosely or broken he'd know someone had been or was still in the room.

He entered the room and threw today's newspaper on the twin bed, a creaky old thing with a lumpy mattress and a bright yellow comforter that hardly matched the bare grey walls. There was nothing else in the room but an old lamp missing its shade and a small TV. Not even a mirror, except for a small one above the sink in the dingy bathroom. *This is the path to glory?*

He was starting to despair in his hunt for his needle in the haystack. Several potentials had fallen through. The church fire was the only sign Allah had given him. He hadn't read that the arsonists had been arrested yet, so there was a glimmer of hope, if he could just find the boys! Since all he knew was that they were from Kelayan, he had asked someone where the nearest hotel to Kelayan was located, and they had pointed him here—this dump, right at the head of where the parallel Kelayan streets A and B connected to the rest of the city. What his informant had neglected to mention was that this was the heart of the red light district.

Being the only single guy in the hotel who didn't have a prostitute visiting him was suspicious looking. He thought about hiring one just to keep his cover. He laid back on the bed and played with the idea for a few minutes. Surely he deserved some reward for the sacrifices he was making. But those thoughts didn't take root. He wasn't like Herman, that hedonistic slimebag he'd gotten stuck working with on the mission where he failed. Herman, always bragging about raping Chinese girls during the Jakarta church bombings, always volunteering to stake out nightclubs as potential bombing targets. Herman would compare the "amenities" at this hotel to the seventy virgins in heaven. He never cared about restoring the glory days of Islamic world domination. That's why he wimped out on getting the third bomb out of the Marriott hotel room in time to take out the third target. Saifullah remembered it like it were yesterday.

July 17, 2009. Ibrohim had smuggled four bombs from Moro into the Jakarta Marriott Hotel, Room 1808. There were three teams, three targets. Ibrohim was the "sleeper," a florist on the inside. He was in charge of planning and distributing the bombs. Nana attached the bombs to their detonators in the hotel room. That's when they discovered one of the detonators was faulty. But it didn't matter; they'd planned to have a spare bomb for contingencies such as this. Nana dismantled the faulty bomb, and Ibrohim smuggled out the important parts in his flowerpots for later use. When the three bombs were armed, Nana took the first one in a laptop bag over to the Ritz-Carlton across the street, walked into the Airlangga Restaurant right on schedule, and triggered the detonator. Herman was Saifullah's assigned "bride." He was to pick up the second bomb and deliver it to the Bellagio down the street. But Herman chickened out. When the time was up Dani picked up the third bomb in a small suitcase, went downstairs to the lounge where several foreigners were eating breakfast, and blew himself up. When the police combed the building later, they found in Dani's room the third bomb, armed and ready to blow but left behind like a broken umbrella.

It was Herman's fault, the coward! But it was also his fault. He was the team leader. He knew what a flake Herman was, and he had no backup plan. Oh, he found Herman later all right, at the safe house, and put a bullet through the roof of his mouth. He told Amir Abdilah to clean up the mess and then walked out. Because of that fool Herman he'd had to run all the way to Moro. Nearly everyone who knew of his failure was now in prison or dead. The world never even knew the Bellagio was a target. But what mattered was that he knew. And now he'd been given another chance. This time he'd recruit his own "bride." And this time he'd have a backup plan.

Saifullah knew he'd have to bolt the door to keep out the prostitutes that night. And he would. He wasn't weak like some. No alcohol. No Western music or porn movies for him. He lived his life with a singular focus—the glory of Islam!

Maybe he'd wake up at midnight and do a special *sholat tahajud* asking for favor on his search for a "bride" in Banjarmasin. Time was ticking by. The sooner he found one, the better.

Saifullah could hear the TV blaring in the room next door to him. He wondered if the occupant was waiting until sundown for sex like a good fasting Muslim, or if he was getting it on now. He smiled to himself.

You can have your prostitute. I'm gonna have me a bride.

Chapter 42

"Have the police talked to you yet, Sari?" Bali closed his history book as soon as Sari came through the hospital door, much later than usual.

"About what?"

"About the fire. Mom said they came to the house today looking for Syukran. He wasn't home. They told Mom they want to interview my dad and your mom too, but she told them our parents aren't conscious yet. I'll bet they want to talk with you too."

"It's not like I can tell them anything." Sari looked puzzled. She set down a small plastic bag of what Bali guessed represented dinner on the floor in front of her. "Why did they want to talk to your brother?"

"I'm wondering the same thing. It's not like he saw anything."

"Well, I hope they catch whoever did this. Not just for my mom's sake. For your dad's, for the church's, for our city's sake! Hate crimes against any religion don't belong in our city."

"I'm with you. There has to be a better way to overcome our differences than that, don't you think?"

"Of course!" Sari stopped opening her dinner bag abruptly to stare at her friend. "Bali, did you always think this way, or just since your dad got involved? I mean, if the fire had been a church on the other side of the city that burned and you read about it in the newspaper, would you be saying what you said right now?"

"I don't know. I think so. Maybe... OK, maybe not. So what?"

"I don't understand why my Muslim friends get so angry about injustice done to the Palestinians on the other side of the world, but injustice done to a minority group right here in our own city doesn't seem to bother anybody." Sari started eating her *nasi goreng*.

Bali bit his tongue. *This girl always backs me into a corner! What is it with her?*

"Well, maybe it took my dad's involvement to wake me up. I'm only a high school senior. Is that such a bad age to start thinking about these issues?" Bali hoped he didn't sound childish.

"I'm sorry. You're right. I appreciate your response. I especially appreciate that you let me feel offended without defending those who did this. Actually, you've been wonderful through this whole thing." Sari stopped suddenly, as though shocked at what she'd just said. Then she quickly stuffed her mouth with another bite of the *nasi goreng*.

Bali's offense evaporated instantly. *Sari thinks I'm wonderful!*

"Since we seem to like each other so much—" Bali began. Sari blushed. "There's something I've been wanting to ask you. How come you always try to hide your right hand? What's wrong with it?"

The blood rushed to Sari's face, and Bali could see her willing the words to come out.

"When I was three I wanted to help my mom iron the clothes. When she turned away to answer the door, I kept working. The iron fell on my hand, and I didn't know enough to get it off. I just screamed until my mom came and knocked it off my hand." She took her hand out from where it had been covered by the long sleeve of her sweatshirt and held it out for Bali to see. He stared at the deformed skin, a twisted, convoluted mess covering the back of her hand.

"It's not that bad." Bali tried to think of something positive to say. "Just needs a bracelet or a ring to spice it up."

Sari looked down. Bali was afraid he'd hurt her feelings, so he added, "I'll have to work on that." He smiled at her, and she smiled back. "One more question. Tell me about your father."

He watched her stiffen once again, then breathe out deeply and take the plunge.

"You really go for the killer questions, don't you? I've never met my father. My mom told me that he left us when she was pregnant with me. Growing up, I saw all the other girls with fathers, and I was extremely jealous. I also struggled a lot, wondering what was wrong with me, why my father didn't want me. And sometimes I struggled with hating him for abandoning us.

"My mom has always taught me to forgive him, but for many years I couldn't. Finally something that helped me was when my mom prayed that God would give me a dream, and He did. In my dream I was in the kitchen with my mom and a man that, even though I couldn't see his face clearly, I knew was my dad. My dad had left the door open, and a python came in. Mom and I screamed. Mom told Dad to get rid of it.

But Dad said he was busy and had to go to Jakarta. He packed his bag and left us with the python under our kitchen table. I woke up from the dream and ran crying to my mom's room. I told Mom I didn't want any more dreams.

"But a few weeks later, she convinced me to ask God for dreams again, and that night I had the same dream about the python. But this time in the dream, after Dad left I cried out to God, and a figure dressed in shining white appeared. He stepped on the snake's head, and it disappeared. Then he sat down in Dad's chair and said, 'Let's eat.' After we ate together I felt a new strength inside me, and we all walked outside. There was a beautiful mountain with a steep path leading to glory at the mountaintop. The white figure started walking, and after several steps motioned for us to follow. He smiled.

"I told Mom my dream, and she interpreted it for me. She said that my dad opened the door of our family to bad stuff like bitterness and hatred. Without God's help it would terrorize us all our lives. But when we asked God to help us get rid of that stuff, He would do it, and He would fill the void left by an absent father. He wants to not just free us and help us, though; He wants to lead us to a glorious destiny if we'll follow Him."

"Whoa! That's really cool! Do you often get dreams like that?"

Sari took a last bite and wadded up the brown paper the fried rice had been wrapped in. "Not really. Mom gets a lot more than me. How about you?" She covered her mouth with her hand as she both talked and chewed.

"Never! All my dreams are about sports or fighting bad guys or pretty gir—uh, you know, normal stuff."

"Sorry, I've talked too much. We should get some sleep." Sari yawned.

"Please, just one more question: What kind of guy do you want to date?"

"A very special kind of guy." Sari laid her head down on her pillow and closed her eyes.

"What's that supposed to mean?"

"Why don't you ask God to give you a dream to explain it? Good night, Bali."

Bali laid down next to her wishing he would dream of Sari.

❧ Chapter 43 ❧

THE FOLLOWING EVENING when Bali noticed his father's eyes flickering open and closed and his body squirming to get more comfortable in the bed, he decided to sit next to his father and just talk to him. He wasn't sure how much his father could hear, or if he could respond, but he needed his dad to know he was there for him. He found a plastic chair out in one of the many hospital lobbies and carried it back to his dad's room. Sari wasn't there yet. She'd gone home to wash the laundry and clean the house after school.

"Hey, Dad! Glad to see you're starting to come out of your sleepiness! You've hardly said a word since you've been in the hospital. We all miss you, you know. Mom's here every morning to see you, and Syukran dropped by a couple days ago. I sit here every night hoping you'll wake up. You want to wake up and talk tonight?"

No answer.

"Well, maybe this is a good time to get some things off my chest. First of all, I really wish I knew you better. It would mean a lot to me if you would tell me more about your past. Not just what you did, but how you felt about it then, how you feel about it now. I'd also like to know how you feel about me. Do you really want me to be a lawyer, or is it just Mom? If so, why? I'm not that interested in law, you know." Iqbal rambled on about his various interests, his dad unresponsive.

"Actually, what I'd love to do is study abroad. Maybe I could study political science, or international law. It seems like people in other countries think so differently than here. I'd like to know what they think. Maybe Europe, or America, or even Australia or Singapore, if you wouldn't let me go so far away. I know it's expensive, but I could work hard for a scholarship. I heard about a guy—"

Abdullah's eyes were flickering open and closed again, but what got Iqbal's attention was that his dad *spoke*. Then he was quiet again.

"What, Dad? What did you say?" Iqbal leaned his ear closer to his dad's mouth.

"Study abroad. Don't like it." It came out as a murmur, but clear enough.

"You don't like it? Why not?" Bali was so happy to hear his dad's voice he didn't mind so much that his dad disagreed with him.

"A lot of bad things out there in the world—and getting home can be tough."

At first Bali wanted to protest, but something held him back. *What if Dad's comments aren't about me but about himself?*

"Was it tough for you to get home, Dad?" Bali held his breath, wondering if this was the moment of revelation he'd been hoping for. Silence echoed in the hospital room for so long he thought maybe his father had slipped unconscious again.

Eventually, Abdullah mumbled a reply. "Yes. Can't talk about it."

Iqbal's disappointment was evident on his face if his dad could have kept his eyes open long enough to see it. But then his father went on.

"I only thought of my baby boy, you, waiting for me at home…" It sounded like his dad would say more, but Bali waited and nothing came. The eye flicker stopped. *Dad must be out again*, Iqbal thought.

"Dad? Dad?" There was still more Iqbal wanted to share, so he decided to keep talking anyway.

"I got a question for you, Dad. I've been talking a lot with Sari. She's been teaching me a lot about forgiveness. I realized this is something I've hardly ever heard about in the mosque. She said that when the Jews were torturing the prophet 'Isa, he responded something like, 'Forgive them, God, 'cause they don't know what they're doing.' Is there anything in Islam like that? Seems like we're mostly taught to hate our enemies, especially Christians, Jews, and Americans. I've heard some teachers say that 'the blood of anyone *kafir* is *halal*,' that 'it's OK to steal from or cheat Christians.' This is kind of important to me, Dad, 'cause I don't want to be in a religion that burns down churches. I've been thinking about changing to the Christian religion. It's probably a good thing you're sleeping, or you might have a heart attack hearing this, huh, Dad?" Bali chuckled to himself. He couldn't imagine saying such words directly to his father's face.

Abdullah's eyes suddenly opened, and he answered his son.

"What's this about burning down churches?"

"Dad! Did you hear that? Uh, I hate to tell you this, but there's a rumor going around with the guys in the neighborhood that the arsonists of that church fire are, well, some students from your *pesantren*."

Abdullah's eyes looked wide awake now. "I have to find out the truth! How much longer are they keeping me here?"

"I don't know, Dad. They're worried about infection in your feet and keeping your shoulder still. The police have been wanting to question you too, but Mom told them you weren't conscious yet. And they're looking for Syukran."

"For Syukran? Surely not my *pesantren* boys...After all I've taught them!"

Iqbal could see the pain on his father's face had nothing to do with his body and everything to do with his heart.

"Listen, son," Abdullah looked intensely at Iqbal. "You will always be my son, no matter what you decide, but please, please, I beg you, don't change your religion lightly, since you know it will break up our family. There's no way Mom or Syukran would understand. Plus it will draw a lot of negative attention in our community. Take your time to fast and pray about this. Talk to some moderate scholars, maybe at IAIN University. Ask them if what you're looking for can be found within Islam. And please, tell *no one* that you're even considering such a step until you're absolutely sure there's no other way. Do you hear me?" Abdullah's hands didn't move, but Bali could almost feel his dad's fingers digging into his neck and shoulders, wanting to shake some sense into his son.

"Yes, Dad. I'll do what you said."

"Good." Abdullah closed his eyes again and seemed to be asleep.

Iqbal stayed by his dad silently for several more minutes, too scared to say anything more.

❧ Chapter 44 ❧

Aᴛᴛᴇʀ sᴏᴍᴇ ꜰᴜᴢᴢʏ thinking during the minutes Abdullah could stay awake, he began to suspect that his son's desire to change religions just might be connected to falling in love with a Christian girl. He decided that when the kids weren't around, he'd best get to know Sari's mom a little better and see if the two of them couldn't talk some sense into their children.

The first day they were both awake without the kids around, Kris mostly expressed her thanks, and both of them shared their feelings about the fire and about their hospital stay. On the second day Abdullah found himself asking a personal question. "Ibu Kris, can I ask, how did you come to join the *arisan*?"

"Actually, Ibu Aaminah invited me. I was quite shocked and wanted to refuse. But my daughter encouraged me to give it a try. At first it was difficult. I didn't understand the Arabic prayers. Several of the women threw hostile glances my way. But Ibu Aaminah's kindness gave me the courage to come back. She's an amazing woman!"

"Yes, according to her husband she's a real handful," Abdullah joked.

"But you know, Pak Abdullah, I also had a lack of love in my heart for my neighbors. I knew it and asked God to change my heart, and He did it through a dream."

"Really? Can you tell me about it?"

Kris shared the second-wife dream with him, and what she'd learned about Abraham's wives Sarah and Hagar. Abdullah was fascinated by this and curious to hear more.

"It sounds like you relate to this second-wife dream as though it were your own life experience. I don't mean to pry, but did something like that happen to you?" He was afraid the question might be too personal, so he kept his eyes on the *drip, drip, drip* of Kris's hanging IV bottle rather than meet her gaze.

"Yes, that's exactly what happened to me. I was fresh out of college and got a job at a local bank here. Hendri came to our branch from headquarters in Jakarta for several weeks. We fell in love, but because we were different religions he convinced me to recite the *Shahada*, becoming a Muslim, and to marry by *nikah siri*. I knew this traditional 'marriage' ceremony wasn't recognized by the government, but I didn't care. My parents were dead. I was alone in the world. I would have done anything for him. Within three months I was pregnant, and three months later Hendri was recalled to Jakarta. He told me to stay at work till I finished seven months of pregnancy, and then he'd come get me. I never heard from him again.

"Around the seventh month a woman called me threatening me to stay away from her husband. It wasn't till then I learned that I was a second wife. I took my maternity leave, and with no word from Hendri I was too humiliated to go back to work at the bank. I quit my job and moved in with my aunt in Gang Hanyar. Did you ever meet her? She died and left me the house when Sari was two. When Sari was two she died and left me the house."

Abdullah shook his head. "When we moved into the neighborhood Syukran was already born, and I think your aunt had already died."

"Pak Abdullah, I've told the *arisan* women that I'm a second wife and that my husband abandoned us, but I've never told the whole story to anyone outside my church. Please, I'm trusting you with my story. Even my dream—please only share it with someone who is ready to hear it."

If *Sari is anything like her mother, it's easy to see why my son likes her. Ibu Kris seems so simple, so sincere, yet there's a depth there that makes you want more.*

"What about you? Does God ever talk to you in dreams?" Kris asked.

Abdullah was quiet for several seconds. Kris had just shared her secrets with him. *Do I have the courage to do the same?*

"My dreams...No...I mean...It's my past." He still couldn't meet her eyes, choosing to focus on a nurse passing by the open door.

"Go on."

"I can't really share much about my past. Just that when the kids were small, it was a difficult time for me. I spent some time in...overseas. When I came home it took me about four years before I could sleep through the night. Over time I've rebuilt my life, but one thing I can't get over is my nightmares." Abdullah's muscles had all tightened involuntarily. His heart pounded. Something in this woman was pulling his heart out of a dark pit toward the light. He wanted to tell her the whole story, but it was too dangerous. Instead he closed his eyes and imagined he was telling the story for the first time.

"I was twenty-three. I'd been in the military academy in Afghanistan for two years, and I'd already seen many things I wanted to forget, when I saw the baby.

"We had just returned to our camp not far from Kandishan from a 'judgment' carried out on a village that had helped the Americans. Thirty of us had gone door-to-door through the village with our AK-47s killing everything that moved. No sooner had we arrived than we were told to gather at the soccer field to hear Mullah Omar, who would surely praise us for carrying out Allah's judgments against the infidels.

"It so happened the same day that my friend Ali, a young Afghani about my age, received some special visitors from his hometown—his father, who was old and sick, his wife, and his son, who had been born forty days earlier. Since no women were allowed in the camp, his wife and dad waited outside while Ali showed off his son to everyone in the camp. The baby was wearing a white robe and white cap, like he was a tiny imam. I saw Ali's pride and joy, the life in his eyes, and remembered my son, Iqbal, at home, and suddenly wanted nothing so badly as to see my baby and hold him for the first time.

"Suddenly a missile rocked the camp, then another and another. Everyone ran for shelter. Some grabbed their anti-aircraft guns, but we couldn't see the enemy for the smoke. And just as quickly, it was over.

"Four men were killed, eleven more injured. Fortunately they didn't get Mullah Omar, who was spirited away before he ever got to meet the troops. Unfortunately, a piece of flying debris skimmed the top of Ali's baby boy's head, and in seconds he stopped breathing. Ali screamed for help, but everyone was afraid to move for several minutes, anticipating more missiles. By the time they came out of hiding Ali was running back and forth screaming for help, but his son was already dead.

"I'll never forget seeing that white baby robe covered in blood, the white cap gone, along with the baby's scalp. This was no infidel's baby. It was my friend's precious newborn son. Or was it mine?

"I had never seen a man more hysterical! He held his baby as he screamed at everyone, kicking things, including an M-16, sending people ducking for cover. Finally the general approached. Ali screamed in his impassive face, 'Why do you love war so much? Why do you love death? When will our children have a chance for peace, a chance for life?'

"'Calm down, son,' the general commanded.

"'Don't you tell me to calm down! I want my son back!' Then Ali let out a horrible wail and slumped to the dirt in tears, not five meters away from me, still holding his dead son.

"The general said, 'I can't give you your son back. It's best you go to him.' And as I watched the general pulled out a pistol and shot Ali in the head.

"They made me and another Indonesian carry the bodies back to the father and wife, made us explain that both were killed by American missiles. I've lied many times in my life. That one was by far the hardest.

"The next day I happened to be in Kandishan listening for clues about what the Americans were up to when I saw a funeral procession. I followed at a distance. I saw the gravesite, with a photo of the baby on it and a photo of Ali, whose death was celebrated as a martyr's. But I couldn't bring myself to go any closer, afraid that if I looked at those photos I'd see the faces of myself and my own son."

A tear ran down Abdullah's cheek, but with his eyes still squinted shut he ignored it and continued. He imagined that Kris was nodding sympathetically, helping him to finish the story.

"I was still stationed there three nights later when I heard a platoon of Americans had been spotted just outside the village. I donned a burqa and went to investigate. The Americans had set up a guard outside the cemetery. Then one man went in alone with flowers, and when he came out the group disappeared into the night. I decided to slip into the cemetery to check out why they were there and found that the American soldier had laid the flowers on Ali's baby's grave. I don't know how they knew about the baby's death, but they did.

"The next day a large family was leaving by bus for a wedding at a village nearer the Pakistan border. I took my chance. I told them I was assigned to accompany them for protection, and of course they couldn't say no. I never looked back. It wasn't hard to cross into Waziristan. The rest of the trip was harder, but after six months I found my way home. It was the happiest day of my life to arrive home and see little Iqbal's cute face for the first time. But holding Iqbal reminded me of all the babies I'd killed, of the blood still on my hands. Did they really deserve to die, while I and my son lived?"

Abdullah couldn't open his eyes and face Kris. Maybe if he'd died in the fire it would have been better. Then he could have finally paid for what he did.

🦋 Chapter 45 🦋

ALI WAS SHOPPING for a bracelet for Sari when his mother text-messaged him to come straight home. *What's got her in a tizzy this time? A mouse in the kitchen? Because Syukran and I haven't started painting for Ibu Aaminah yet? Why can't she just let me live my own life?*

But this time Ibu Siti had something much more significant to talk about. She started before Iqbal even made it all the way through the front door.

"The police were just here! They were looking for Syukran again. I told them I didn't know where he was. They said they'd be back at night to arrest him!"

"For what, Mom? He wasn't anywhere near the fire. Wasn't he here sleeping?"

"He sleeps in your room! Was he here or not?"

Iqbal tried to remember the night of the fire. He vaguely remembered hearing the banging on the light pole, but he'd just rolled over and gone back to sleep. *Was Syukran there or not?*

"They told me if we don't want Syukran to go to jail we better have an envelope ready when they come back at night."

"An envelope? You mean a bribe?"

"Yes, what else! They said twenty million! Where are we supposed to get twenty million? I'm not sure we can even afford to pay the hospital bill when your dad gets out in a few days. If we sold everything we own we couldn't raise twenty million! It's not even our fault. My husband tried to stop the fire; doesn't that count for something? It's all the Christians' fault! If that idiot Kris had known enough to get out of the building, Dad wouldn't have gotten burned, and we wouldn't be bankrupt right now, and the police wouldn't even be bothering with us. What do they expect us to do? Twenty million!"

Iqbal could never understand his mom's logic when she was upset. He tried to calm her down.

"Mom, sit down. Let me get you a drink. I'll get changed, and we'll go see Dad. He'll know what to do."

Siti collapsed on the couch, moaning and mumbling incoherently. Iqbal went to the kitchen for a glass of water. He had little patience with his mom's hysterics, but he was concerned about Syukran. *Could my little brother really have been involved in such an evil deed?*

He came back with the water, then went to change his clothes. *If only I could talk to my mom about forgiveness, but she isn't nearly sane enough.*

Iqbal picked up his phone to text message Syukran that he probably shouldn't sleep at home for a while.

Chapter 46

SYUKRAN MET HIS brother at Sports Station in the mall. He moved to a corner where no one would overhear them and pretended to look at soccer shoes.

"But why do the police want to interrogate me? I didn't have anything to do with it!"

"I don't know, Syuk. Makes no sense. Weren't you at home with me sleeping?"

"Duh! Where else? I swear I was nowhere near a burning church!" Syukran dropped the soccer shoes he had been fiddling with like they were burning his hands. "What am I supposed to do, huh? I can't go to jail!"

"There's no way we'll be able to pay the bribe. Maybe you should just sleep elsewhere till it all blows over."

"How long will that be?"

"Who knows? We need to ask Dad what to do. He's more alert now. Why don't you come back with me to the hospital and discuss it with him?"

"What if the police are watching the hospital? No way. Besides, I'd hate to interrupt your sleazy love life with that *kafir* girl."

"Shut up! She's a girl, not a '*kafir* girl.' And you're a jerk." Bali pushed Syukran's shoulder and turned to walk away.

Syukran let it go this time. *If Bali pushes me too hard, though, he'll find out what a mistake it is! My stupid brother is flirting with a stupid Christian, and he's too stupid to even know how stupid that is. He better drop this girl when Dad gets out of the hospital, or I'll have to intervene.*

❦ Chapter 47 ❦

SARI AND BALI were relieved when school closed for the final week of fasting so they could spend more time with their parents in the hospital and more time with each other. Even the police seemed to have their minds on the upcoming holiday and left them alone.

But the first day of vacation Siti ruined their plans. She showed up at the hospital to kidnap Bali to join her and Syukran shopping for new clothes for Idul Fitri. When Bali protested that they needed the money for the hospital bill, his mom would have nothing of it. "We will not celebrate this holiday looking like beggars!" she stated with more than a passing glance at Sari before dragging Bali out.

While Bali was gone, Sari spent the whole day with her mom. First she helped her take a sponge bath in the bathroom with a bucket of water Sari had to fetch from a friend's house not too far walking distance from the hospital, since the poor patients' rooms had no running water. Then she helped her mom get into a clean dress. Doctor Santo had suggested cotton clothes would stick to the healing skin less, so she'd brought a short-sleeved, knee-length red dress with subtle yellow flowers on the shoulders and waist. She brushed her mom's hair. Then she painted her mom's nails a bright red to match her dress. Kris protested that Sari shouldn't make such a fuss over her, but she also said she enjoyed the feeling of Sari's gentle touch on her healing skin.

Pak Abdullah watched the whole thing with amusement, teasing the two of them more than once. Sari wondered if he were wishing for some attention himself.

Finally, Ibu Kris couldn't look any prettier and collapsed back on her pillows.

"My dear daughter! Let me rest for a bit! I can't take any more beautifying!"

"OK, Mom. I'll take a break. We'll do your makeup later."

"Makeup! Goodness! Are we expecting any important visitors you haven't told me about yet?"

"No, Mom! I just miss seeing you looking pretty; that's all."

"If I'm not the one receiving visitors, maybe you should be prettying up your own self! Bali should be here soon, shouldn't he?"

Sari blushed and put her finger to her lips, instructing her mom to not let Pak Abdullah hear any more.

"Mom, check this out." Sari showed off her new bracelet. It was gold colored, although she knew it wasn't real gold, and had two hearts with the word *forever* between them. Kris held it for a minute, then handed it back to her daughter.

"I showed Bali my hand, Mom, because he asked what happened to it. Then he said it just needed a bracelet or a ring to make it pretty. He gave me this the other night and told me I had to wear it on my right hand. Do you know what this means, Mom? It means he accepts me the way I am. Even though I'm deformed, even though I'm a Christian, he's opened his heart to me."

"You know, I've been surprised at Bali's dad too," Kris spoke in a hushed tone so Abdullah wouldn't hear. "He's far more open than I expected. You know how I've taught you the Bible says man looks at the outward appearance, but God looks at the heart? I think we were so sure they were looking at our outward appearance that we did the same to them. It turns out because of this fire, we found their hearts open to us, and we found out their hearts are beautiful. We'd be foolish not to open our hearts a little more too."

"Mom, are you saying I should open my heart to love Bali?"

"What if he asks you to be his girlfriend? What are you going to do?"

"I don't know, Mom. You always told me I couldn't date till I was eighteen, and that I could only date a Christian. Now are you telling me the opposite?"

Kris put her hand on Sari's cheek and looked deep into her brown eyes. "Honestly, my love, I don't know what I'm saying. But I feel different than before, don't you?"

Yeah, Mom, and I'm scared of where my feelings might lead.

❧ Chapter 48 ❧

IDUL FITRI! SYUKRAN loved this, the most important holiday on the calendar. He always took his fasting seriously and believed his sins would be wiped out, making him pure once again.

The only part he didn't like was all the visiting. Everyone dressed so beautifully and acted so forgiving, but he knew to most it was just a show. He knew many of his friends and relatives didn't keep the fast faithfully, and many would keep a grudge no matter what they said on Idul Fitri. Three days' government holiday was nice, and so was eating at every house they visited, if he could stomach the hypocrisy.

Bali had told him the hospital was in chaos. Since Muslim doctors would only come in for extreme emergencies during the three-day holiday and many nurses took time off (with or without permission), the two days before Idul Fitri were a mad rush to get checked out of the hospital. Fortunately his father was cleared to go home at the last minute. Bali related how Dr. Santo had proudly showed off the successful skin grafts on Abdullah's feet to a couple colleagues and a train of nurses, claiming it was a first for Ulin Hospital. Photos were taken and hands were shaken all around—an unusual sight in the ward for the nonpaying patients. Bali brought Dad home on the motorbike, his shoulder still bandaged to restrict his right arm's movement, and his freshly photographed feet rebandaged too thickly to wear sandals or shoes. That night everyone thanked God they could be together as a family for the holiday.

On Idul Fitri morning Syukran watched his mom leave early to walk with some neighbor women to the nearest mosque in Kelayan, and his dad said he would say his prayers in a sitting position at home.

As usual, Syukran and Bali decided to join the worship at the Grand Mosque on the motorbike. With over five thousand worshipers expected there—filling the mosque, the porch, and a city-block's worth of grass encircling the mosque—the boys were sure to bump into some friends.

After the required prayers at the Grand Mosque were finished, many of the men seated on their *sejadah* prayer rugs around Bali and Syukran stood up to go home. Bali started to stand up too, but Syukran pulled him back down.

"I want to hear the sermon."

"Sermons here are boring! I'm going home."

"Would it kill you to actually listen to your own religion being taught at least once a year? Are you a real Muslim or not?"

"Lighten up, Syuk! You can catch a ride home with somebody else." Bali started to stand again.

Syukran snatched his brother's sandals, which had been positioned on the ground just in front of the prayer rug. "You want me to tell Mom you're in love with that Christian girl from the hospital?"

Bali paused, then sat down. "Fine, if you want to be a jerk about it, I'll listen to the sermon. There, you happy?"

Syukran didn't answer, nor did he return his brother's sandals till the end of the sermon. *Sometimes you have to be forceful in the defense of the faith.*

That thought led him down a path of shame. Images flashed in his mind. Gallons of gasoline poured out. The matchbox handed to him. His feeble attempts at striking a match. His coughing fit. Hafiz throwing the match to strike the decisive blow for Islam.

How could I have been so weak? After all, it was my brother we were getting revenge for. My idiot brother who couldn't care less that I'm trying to keep him out of the fires of hell. He's a kafir-*loving fool. But I'm a coward. Just like Dad. I swore I'd never be like him, and look at me. Just like my coward father.*

The imam was preaching about how fasting purifies us and grants us a new start. Syukran wasn't really listening any more than Iqbal was. He was thinking about his own new start. About making up for his act of cowardice.

What could I do to prove to myself that I will fight for my faith? This time I don't want Hafiz to bail me out. This will be something that I do alone.

What about the police investigation? Should I lay low till it's over?

No, they've got nothing, or they would have arrested me by now. It's time to get on with life.

Let the old, timid Syukran die with the fast. It's time for the bold Syukran to live.

He finally thought of an idea, a perfect idea. And he knew when he could unleash this idea without anyone on the streets seeing. Yes, he'd heard about other defenders of the faith who had done this, and now he would carry on the battle in his own time and place.

He glanced sideways at his older brother, as though worried Bali could read his thoughts. But Bali was playing with his cell phone. *Probably writing a message to Sari,* Syukran thought.

I already warned him.

Yes, this idea was perfect.

❧ Chapter 49 ❧

"I HEARD THROUGH THE grapevine that you're planning another trip. Louis, exactly when were you planning to tell me?" Louis didn't answer, so Selena continued. "That's it. I've had it. You have to stop this interfaith stuff. You're killing me."

Louis Staunton stared at his wife, lips pursed. *Where is that waiter? Looks like I need that glass of wine already.* He glanced around the five-star restaurant, one of his wife's favorites, nearly full with the evening crowd of congressmen, lobbyists, and lawyers, and suddenly regretted he'd chosen this place to celebrate twenty-seven years of marriage.

After a long pause, Louis offered, "Happy anniversary to you, too."

"I mean it! I can't take it anymore. I didn't make all those sacrifices to get you in office just to see you throw it all away for—"

"Honey, we both agreed that God gave me this position of influence to do some good in the world. What could possibly be better than peacemaking?"

Selena Staunton clutched at the deep maroon cloth napkin and started dabbing her eyes. "Yeah, but while you're off risking your life in some Arab war zone, you're losing the war at home."

Louis's appetite was rapidly disappearing. He'd better get this anniversary date back on track fast, or things could get ugly. *Why now? This is really not the right place for this, Selena, and you know it.*

"Honey, let's just enjoy our anniversary and talk about this later, OK?" Louis raised his hand to call a waiter over, but the man apparently didn't notice and turned away.

"Later? When? I never see you anymore. You used to ask me before you planned a trip overseas. Now you spend more time with those beloved *Muslims* of yours than with your own family. Do you think I don't worry that one of these trips you'll get kidnapped or killed? Aren't there lots of terrorists in India?" Selena's voice was rising. A couple at the next table scowled at them.

"Indonesia, honey. I know it's your prayers that always keep me safe...Should we try the lobster tonight?" Louis knew it was risky to change the subject. If Selena felt she wasn't being heard, well, she'd always hated that more than anything. *Please, God...*

"Lobster? I don't like lobster. Are you listening to me?"

Uh-oh.

"Louis Henry Staunton, you listen, and you listen good!" Louis met the fire in Selena's eyes with an impassive calm that usually infuriated her more, but what else could he do in a public place? "I'm done praying for you. No one at our church prays for you anymore anyway, except for you to quit wasting your life on *those people* and put family and country first. I'm sick of facing the church prayer group every week alone. I'm sick of defending you defending *those people*. I'm sick of having a husband that most people in the world hate, including me sometimes. So if you insist on leaving me for Indonesia or wherever, don't expect to find me happily praying for you when you come home."

Selena stood abruptly, nearly bumping the waiter, who had finally appeared as she rushed out of the room, sobbing loudly. A flash lit the room. Louis turned as another flash caught him full in the face. *Great, a journalist!* He imagined the morning headline: "Globetrotting Peacemaker Can't Keep the Peace at Home."

Louis apologized to the waiter and followed his wife out. They'd come by separate cars. Maybe he could pick up some flowers to give her time to cool off before he got home.

❧ Chapter 50 ❧

UNFORTUNATELY FOR SARI and Kris, the doctor refused to release Kris before the Idul Fitri holiday. That meant at least three days in the hospital with no visits from doctors and only once daily a nurse popping in to wake her up and tell her to try to get some sleep. Ever since Bali had taken his father home Sari found that she grew increasingly impatient with the nurses. Her mom had no more cough and was eating just fine. Sari couldn't understand why they'd keep her mom on an IV when she seemed ready to go home. Every time the IV ran low Sari would have to hunt all over the ghost town of a hospital to find a nurse willing to change it. They refused to stop the IV until the doctor gave the order. Sometimes Sari wanted to scream at them to just let her mother go home. But she knew without the doctor's cooperation the hospital could decide to charge them instead of the government health program. So she was stuck.

To distract her irritable daughter, Kris suggested Sari go home and visit the neighbors for Idul Fitri, and Sari finally agreed. Since she knew most families would pray at 7:00 a.m. at the mosque, then visit their own families first before visiting friends and neighbors, Sari decided to wait until 10:00 a.m. before heading home. Her mother reminded her to follow the Muslim custom of asking everyone, "Please forgive me for any sins against you in deed or in thought." Yes, she knew she'd judged many of her neighbors too harshly in the past, and she was looking forward to making things right.

The streets were quiet as she drove. No beggars, scavengers, or pushcart vendors. Hardly any traffic. And those who passed her were all dressed in their holiday best—glittery gold *batiks*, or the traditional, colorful, tie-dyed Banjar *batik* called *sasirangan*. Even the smallest children were fancied up with brand new *jilbabs* or *kopiahs* on their heads. Sari had to smile. There were times when she was small that she'd been afraid of Islam. But now her mother was invited to the *arisan*, and she was close friends with Bali. How drastically everything had changed!

She pulled into Gang Hanyar and noticed a group of parents and kids walking from Ibu Mia's house towards Bali's. Maybe she could join a group visiting the neighbors and stand out less. She pulled her bike into her front yard, lifted off her helmet, and shook out her long black hair. She stepped up onto her front porch and kicked off her sandals.

Then she froze and stared at her front door, trembling.

In small red letters, perhaps not clearly visible from the street, was painted a message:

Go to hell Pigs! You and your church don't belong here.

Her hands shook as she fumbled with the door key and finally opened the door. *What if someone was waiting inside to attack her?* She checked the kitchen first and picked up her mom's biggest frying pan. Then she cautiously went from room to room, pushing each door open with the pan raised high, every muscle in her body tensed to do violence before violence was done to her. But the house was empty, just as she'd left it on her last visit two days ago.

Sari returned the pan to the kitchen with a sigh of relief. She decided to search around for some paint but found none. She had to cover that message on the door before anyone else noticed it!

In the living room there was only one decoration on the wall, a cross-stitch her aunt had done many years ago that said simply, "God bless this home." She took it off the wall. But she still needed a hammer and a nail! *Where does Mom keep the hammer? Hurry, Sari, people will be walking by any minute!*

She found the hammer in the kitchen under the sink but no nails. It took her what seemed like forever to pull out the nail the picture used to hang on, and it was slightly bent, but it would have to do. She went outside and closed the door, held the picture up over the red words, then put it down and started driving the nail. *Oh, God, please let no one see me and ask what I'm doing.* She could see the previous group down the street leaving Bali's, headed toward Ibu Aaminah's. *As long as they're going far from here...*

It took about fifty taps of the hammer for the nail to seem strong enough. She hung the picture, and only a tiny bit of red poked out behind it. She had to buy some paint and cover those words before Mom got home! But no stores were open during the holiday. She stepped back inside the house and locked the door behind her.

As she sank to her knees, Sari realized she was still trembling. Her breathing started to quicken. Panic rose up within her like an angry sea wave. It smashed against the sides of her head over and over, making it hard to think. *Who did this? What do they have against us?*

The sea waves grew taller and more violent. *Is it the same people who burned down the church? Will they burn our house down, too?*

Oh, God, I can't take this anymore! Our pastor humiliates us. The Muslims are out to kill us. I feel like I'm going crazy! Please, God, this is the last straw! I can't take it anymore!

Sari's arms wrapped tightly about her knees, and she rocked back and forth sobbing for a long time. She couldn't face visiting any of her neighbors or friends. Later that day she would just have to return to her mother in the hospital and lie to her that she'd had a great Idul Fitri.

❧ Chapter 51 ❧

"I WANTED TO DO a little special something to welcome you home." Sari prepped her mother.

"What?" Kris started up the steps, then stopped. "Oh, how nice! You painted our front door red!"

It was the third day of the Idul Fitri celebrations, and Kris had finally been released from the hospital. Her first stop had been to Pak Abdullah's house to thank him once again for saving her life. As she entered her home, she had a feeling that it wasn't just her door that was new. God was about to make everything new.

That evening, the first neighborhood woman came to visit. It was Ibu Dina, with Nina and Rini.

"Happy holidays! *Minal aidin wal faidzin.*"

Ibu Dina fussed over Kris like a mother hen. "Oh, Ibu, I was so shocked to hear about your accident! I want you to know we prayed for you every single night, didn't we Rini? That you wouldn't die. We know there's no way we could repay you for all your kindnesses to us, but like you always taught us, God hears the prayers of the poor, so we prayed with all our hearts that you'd be OK."

Sari took Nina's hand and pulled her back to her bedroom. She knew this was her best chance to find out what was going on with her lifelong friend. They sat on the bed together, legs curled up underneath them, just like when they were little girls playing dolls.

"Nina, you look so beautiful in that outfit! I've missed you! I'm so glad to finally get out of that hospital!"

"Yeah, I was really sorry to hear about your mom. That fire, that was terrible. I don't know how people can do things like that."

"Me neither." Sari didn't want to talk about that subject right now. "So tell me about you? Are you back home just for the holidays, or for good?"

"Just for the holidays. I have to go back to work this weekend."

"Do you want to tell me about your work? I don't like being so blunt, but is it prostitution?" Sari waited for Nina to answer.

Nina looked down. She played with her toes, her toenails polished bright red. The last time Sari remembered seeing Nina's toenails painted was when they were seven and had used magic markers.

"Sari, you don't understand. You have a perfect life. I'm so tired of being a beggar. One day a couple months ago I was at the stoplight near Capung Cafe begging, and this hot-looking guy rolled down his window. I walked over, my hand held out. He looked at me up and down, at my dirty beggar clothes and my dirty beggar hair and my dirty beggar face, then he rolled his window back up without giving me anything and drove away. It was humiliating! At that moment I knew I was never begging again.

"Now if that same man sees me, you know what he does? He smiles, because he likes what he sees. And I don't have to hold out my hand, because he holds out his. And guess what? His hand doesn't have little Rp.500 coins; his hand has Rp.500,000. At the end of the night I don't go home wondering if I even have enough for a decent meal. I go home with a full stomach, credit in my cell phone, gifts for my mom and sister, and still more cash in my pocket than they bring in. What's wrong with that?"

"Nina! I know I don't understand everything you have to go through, but don't you want to save your body for your husband?"

"What husband? Who's going to marry a beggar? My mom actually talked about selling me in a 'marriage contract' to an old fat man from Taiwan here on a two-year contract with a coal company. Someone told her he was looking for a teenage girl he could 'marry' for two years while he's here, then leave her behind when he went back to his wife in Taiwan. They offered my mom Rp.10 million! When she said that I slapped her. If I have to earn money for my family with my body, I want to choose who I sleep with, and if I don't like how someone treats me I can walk away."

"Please, Nina, there has to be a better life for you than this."

"Well, when you think of one, let me know." Nina's eyes and lips tightened in sarcasm. "In the meantime, I don't want you gossiping about me and ruining my name. If you do, you can kiss our friendship good-bye!"

"I won't, Nina. I promise I won't. Please, let's not lose our friendship. I'll be your friend no matter what."

Sari put her arms around Nina, who didn't respond at first, then finally extended her arms to hug Sari, too. Sari felt her heart breaking for her friend. She wished they could just go back to the old days of brushing their dolls' hair together on the bed, chatting about cute boys and meddling moms. Now everything had changed, definitely for the worse, for the both of them.

Later that night Kris came into Sari's bedroom to say good night. She sat on the bed and stroked Sari's hair, feeling so incredibly happy to be home again.

"How did it go with Nina?"

"Not great. She can't see any other solution to her begging but this. Her life does look pretty hopeless."

"God can still turn her around. Just pray."

"Yeah, Mom." Sari closed her eyes and smiled. Kris imagined her a purring kitten, enjoying the affection. Finally Sari asked, "Have you ever felt like if you could give everything you had, your whole life, to see someone have a chance to climb out of the black pit of death and find a wonderful life, would you do it? I think I'd do it for Nina, but I don't know how."

"The best thing you can do for Nina right now is to love her no matter what happens. Someday she'll want to be free of that life, and she'll know who to go to for help."

"I hope I'll still be able to help when that day comes. So many bad things have happened recently, I'm starting to wonder if I'm not the one who's going to be needing the help."

"What are you talking about? I'm the weak worrier in this family. You've always been the strong warrior."

Sari opened her eyes to gaze at her mother's. Kris thought she noticed a tinge of fear in them, or was it lostness? "I may look strong on the outside, but sometimes I feel like I'm about to snap on the inside. I'm afraid that if one more bad thing happens, I'll completely lose it."

"Oh, my love! Don't think such thoughts! Now that I'm well and home again, I'm sure the worst is past! Just focus on living your own life fully so you have something extra to give to those who need it."

"Thanks, Mom." Sari closed her eyes and smiled once again. She stretched out her right hand and held her mom's while Kris's left hand continued to stroke her hair.

As Kris said a prayer over her daughter, Sari slipped off to dreamland. When she felt her daughter's breathing slow, Kris whispered to her, "Yes, my darling, I understand your desire to give everything for Nina. My whole life is dedicated to making sure you stay out of the black pit of abandonment and rejection your father dropped us in, making sure you get to experience a full and wonderful life."

A tear slid down her cheek into Sari's hair. A silent witness to a mother's sacrificial love.

❧ Chapter 52 ❧

USTAD HASAN AMMAN offered Abdullah to take the first three days back to school off, then join the first full week of school after the Idul Fitri holiday, but Abdullah told him the first two days were dispensation enough. He wanted to meet with his *silat* club on Saturday. One lengthy conversation with a certain visiting police officer over the holidays had caused Abdullah some restless nights, and it was time he did something about it.

At 8:00 a.m. the boys gathered in the schoolyard. By now they all had heard the story of the fire countless times, but only Syukran had visited his father in the hospital, and rumors were rampant that Abdullah looked practically unrecognizable, a freakish Frankenstein, terrifying to behold. Abdullah had actually chuckled at Syukran's retellings of the rumors. But the boys' fears were put to rest when their *guru* rode slowly into the schoolyard on his bicycle, his face and hair (or lack of it) much the same as before, his uniform the same, too. Only the bandages on his shoeless feet and his ginger steps toward them proved that at least some of the stories were true.

"*Assalamu alaikum*. Good morning, boys."

"*Wa alaikum assalam*."

"I'm sure after the long fast your physical conditioning needs to be restored before a full martial arts workout, so I've decided that today we're going to walk down the road past the rubber factory to a dock on the river, and there we'll spend our *silat* class time swimming. You might call it a chance to 'celebrate' the achievements of our fasting month." Abdullah smiled. "Well, you all will walk to the river; I'll ride my bicycle."

A joyful murmur rippled through the group. Having lived on or near rivers all their lives, most of the boys were strong swimmers, and everyone could at least tread water. They jostled and joked as they headed down the street.

The dock was a somewhat private place, with mangrove trees and swamp on the right and left, no houses immediately nearby. Abdullah instructed the boys to put their sandals in one pile, their *silat* uniforms in another pile. They boys happily obeyed, stripping to their underwear and running down the dock to do cannonballs into the refreshingly cool river.

"Dad, you OK?" Syukran asked. Abdullah thought he saw his son wince as Syukran glanced at his bandaged feet. *Feeling guilty, son?*

"I'm fine. I'll just sit here on my bike. You go on and have fun with your friends."

"OK, Dad." Syukran turned slowly, stripped off his uniform and laid it on the pile, then headed for the dock. He was the last student to jump in and was roundly splashed by everyone else for it.

Abdullah looked at his watch. He'd wait a few minutes until they were really having a good time and stopped looking back to check on him.

About twenty minutes later Abdullah opened the plastic bag hanging from his handlebars, the same blue plastic bag in which he always carried his water bottle and a small snack of fruit if they had any. Only today's bottle was not filled with boiled drinking water but kerosene. He nosed his bicycle a little closer to the pile of school uniforms, then using his more mobile left hand, poured the bottle's contents over them, soaking them in the kerosene. Also from the bag he extracted a matchbox. He lit a match and dropped it on the clothes. A flame of fire shot straight up, and he had to slam his foot down on the pedal once to get clear of the blaze. He sat there, about four feet away, his foot throbbing, listening. Soon he heard the boys cry out with alarm, warning, fear, confusion, and he saw them scrambling out of the water and running down the dock toward him.

Abdullah didn't say a word to their shocked queries until every student had gathered around in a circle to watch the final threads of their clothes burn. He knew that it would cost most of their parents three to five days' wages to replace them. But somehow he had a hard time feeling any sympathy.

"I want to thank you boys. This Ramadan as I fasted and prayed for Allah's wisdom, some of you boys showed me a new solution to overcoming my problems. You taught me that when I'm not happy with someone, I should use fire to teach them a lesson. Well, my feet, my shoulder, and my heart are telling me that I'm not happy with some of you. As of today there's only one way to keep me as a teacher in your school, and that is for every single one of you to come back to school on Monday ready to help rebuild a certain burned-down church. Now pick up your sandals and go home. Discuss your decision with your parents and with each other. I expect your answer Monday morning."

Abdullah turned his bicycle around and agonizingly pedaled home.

Chapter 53

O N MONDAY MORNING every single student from the *silat* club was back in school. First period, Pak Abdullah and Pak Ustad held a meeting with the *silat* club in Pak Ustad's classroom. Pak Ustad started with an authoritative voice.

"Thanks to Pak Abdullah here and a long talk with the police, some very distressing news has reached my ears that some of the students of *Al-Mustaqiim* were likely involved in burning down a Christian house of worship. This behavior is intolerable! Islam has nothing to do with hooliganism! I am shocked and angry and have a mind to take a switch and beat the lot of you!"

Pak Ustad stared around the room and saw discomfort, fear, but no one who looked surprised at this news. He noticed beads of sweat form on some foreheads, though it was too early to feel the sun's heat. He lowered his voice but kept it menacing.

"Pak Abdullah and I met with the police again yesterday. At one point in their investigation they were about to take each one of you into the police station and interrogate you. If that had happened you can be sure that all of those who are guilty would have been eventually found out and arrested, and you'd be in jail today. It is also highly probable the police would have shut down our *pesantren*. But yesterday they told us that since the only victim has now been released from the hospital and there is no murder charge, they were willing to negotiate with us on the arson charge. We presented to them an alternative punishment to jail time, and they've agreed.

"We've agreed to provide free labor in the reconstruction of the church. This *silat* club will be rebuilding on the site where you did so much damage."

Now some of the boys looked surprised, though none dared speak.

"Now I know that we have two hours of Qur'anic recitation practice scheduled every afternoon in preparation for the upcoming MTQ competition. I'm sorry, but your participation in the MTQ competition is hereby cancelled. You will all finish your studies by 1:30 as usual, have twenty minutes to eat lunch, then will bicycle or motorbike as a group over to Pekauman, where you will work hard every afternoon under the supervision of Pak Abdullah and one of the pastors of the church. If either of them reports to me that there's a student who is not working wholeheartedly or is causing trouble or is skipping out of work early, that student will be put on suspension. You will be released from this obligation when the church building is completely built and painted inside and out.

"If for some utterly insane reason the whole group of you decides you won't agree to this, or causes any more vandalism to the church's property, I will not only suspend all of you; I will personally contact the police and request that they take you all to jail until the guilty ones confess. Is that understood?"

Pak Ustad emphasized this last question by whacking his palm with a pointer stick. The students all sat with their heads lowered, none brave enough to meet Pak Ustad's fiery old eyes.

"I'll be explaining this plan to every one of your parents today, and we have an appointment to meet with the pastor and start work tomorrow. Please bring a set of work clothes to school with you so as to not damage your, uh, only remaining set of school uniforms." Pak Ustad cocked an eyebrow at Pak Abdullah as he mentioned the uniforms.

"Now go to your classes."

Iqbal found Syukran sulking on the porch after dinner.

"Syuk, I didn't want to believe it when people started saying you were involved in the church burning, but I overheard a policeman tell Dad that they have witnesses who can pin it down to a group of six guys who match the description of you and your group. I can't believe you would do such a thing!"

"Then don't believe it! You going to believe some cop's accusations over your own brother? Gee, thanks a lot, Bali!"

Iqbal ignored the remark. "But why? Whatever possessed you? What have those church people ever done to you?"

"I'm not saying I did it, because I didn't! It was probably Hafiz and his gang. But I don't know why you're so surprised. You know how those *kafir* are Christianizing our brothers, using their money to buy converts or corrupting them with hedonistic parties of alcohol and dog meat. You know from personal experience, don't you, Bali?"

Syukran had turned the tables, and it was Iqbal's turn to squirm a bit. "What are you talking about?"

Syukran's eyes narrowed. "I knew you lied to Mom and Dad that time you went to that Christian party. I followed you. I went inside. I saw you eating from that *haram* table, flirting with those Christian sluts. Did you try the alcohol, too? What did I miss?"

"Why you...I ought to smack you!" Bali's right hand tightened into a fist.

"Just try it!"

Iqbal took a deep breath, uncurled his fingers, and confessed. "Yes, I lied to Mom and Dad. Yes, I went to a party at my classmate's house, who happened to be a Christian. Yes, I saw they had food and drinks that aren't *halal* for Muslims. So what? I didn't eat or drink anything I shouldn't. I also didn't flirt with any girls. I just hung out with my friends and had a good time."

"Yeah, I bet you had a good time. You put yourself in that much temptation, you're going to fall."

"Well, how do we know our faith has any depth to it unless we're tempted and can pass the test?"

"Listen, bro, I don't blame you if you slipped and fell. It could happen to anyone. I blame the people who tempted you, those *kafir* who intentionally try to corrupt the youth of our nation with worldliness, then pull them out of Islam into everlasting damnation." Syukran punctuated this by kicking a gecko off the porch.

"Chill out! Christians are people just like us. They're not trying to corrupt us. They just want to be free to be themselves and get along with everyone."

"Fine! You be a get-along-with-everyone Muslim and enjoy your booze-and-babes parties! I'm choosing the path of the Prophet. I'm choosing to follow the 'real' Islam, Islam that has teeth in it. Someone in our family has to do it!"

Syukran stood up and strode into the house. Iqbal stared at his brother's back. *How did my brother ever get so mad at the world? It's got to be his friends. I better warn Dad that Syuk's hearing some bad stuff from somewhere. Maybe it's Hafiz. Dad will know what to do.*

Syukran wasn't the only one who didn't like the idea of helping rebuild the church. His mother agreed. As the family ate fried tofu, fried tempeh, kangkung leaves, and rice for dinner, Siti presented her arguments to her husband.

"I don't understand why Syukran has to help rebuild the church. He didn't burn it down. Make the boys who are responsible for the crime take the punishment. It's not fair to punish the innocent with the guilty."

Dad didn't seem to be in the mood for going over this yet again. "For the last week all you've been talking about is getting the police off our backs. Now that we've reached an agreement to keep them from pressing charges, you're still not satisfied? You want our son to protest his innocence from behind bars? I don't care if he was holding the match or just covering for his friends. My *pesantren* is responsible, my *silat* club was involved, and we will *all* work hard to remove this stain to our school's name! End of discussion!"

Syukran noticed Bali staring at him. *He knows I did it.*

He broke the silence with the calm reasoning of a saint: "It's OK, Mom. I guess I wouldn't be a good friend if all my 'brothers' have to suffer and I don't stand with them." Then he stood and lifted his chin toward his father just for a moment and stalked out of the room.

❧ Chapter 54 ❧

ASTOR DAVID HAD hoped to meet the *silat* club alone at the site of the church ruins on Tuesday afternoon; however, Pastor Susanna had heard about the meeting and decided to look the perpetrators in the eye for herself. At the sound of the *silat* club's arrival they both turned away from watching the construction crew patch up the mostly intact foundation, the debris and damaged walls having already been cleared away.

The boys filed into the gate and stood shoulder to shoulder before the two pastors, most with their hands clasped behind their backs like privates facing an angry sergeant.

Their leader introduced them. "Good afternoon. My name is Abdullah. These are my students from the *pesantren* just down the road a bit thataways." He pointed south. "All of us at the school feel terrible about the tragedy your church experienced. These particular students," he waved to the boys, "are determined to work hard for you every afternoon until this building is rebuilt. What happened was an evil thing. We want to do all we can to make it right."

Pastor David responded, "Thank you, Mr. Abdullah. Boys, my name is David, and I'm—"

Pastor Susanna interrupted him. "And I'm Pastor Susanna, the *senior* pastor of this church. Do you have any idea how much it's going to cost us to rebuild? Do you? Will these pitiful boys be bringing us money to buy supplies? Do they even know how to do construction work? This is all fine for you to soothe your own consciences, but are you really *helping* us here? That's debatable!

"Have you people *ever* helped us minorities here? No, never! Why does it take your people three years to give our church a building permit, then once we build, three months to burn our building down and make us start over? Do you know how many times your people have attacked, burned, vandalized, defaced, or stolen our church property? No, you don't. Do you care? Only if the police catch you!

"What kind of religion teaches violence against a house of worship? I don't know what kind of school you run, Pak Abdullah, but if I were you I'd spend less time teaching those juvenile delinquents Arabic and more time teaching them morals and ethics. I try to teach my people how to build a peaceful society, while you people are teaching them how to burn society down! It's no wonder this country can never move forward. May God have mercy on you!

"Well, do you have anything to say for yourselves?" Susanna took her first breath. "I thought not."

And with that, Pastor Susanna ran her eyes slowly and scornfully over the boys, gave a final "Harumph!" and stormed away.

Syukran could feel the anger pounding in his chest louder than the hammer-cracks of the construction crew. He could feel it in Hafiz to his left and Juki to his right as well. He looked at his father, standing silent before the witch's diatribe. *Why do you let her insult our religion like that? Why don't you defend Islam? Why don't you defend us?* Syukran's shame over his father was morphing into something dark inside him, though he wasn't quite aware of what.

Once Pastor Susanna was out of earshot, Pastor David attempted to diffuse the tension in the air. "I apologize. Our senior pastor was quite upset by this tragedy, as you can imagine, and still needs some time to cool off and see more clearly. Personally, I want to thank you, Pak Abdullah. I understand you're the one who risked your life to save one of our church members, Ibu Kris. You are an amazingly brave man, and it's my honor to work with you and your students. In this church I'm the youth pastor, so like you, I get to enjoy watching the younger generation grow and develop in hope that they'll make this nation a better place than the previous generation could."

Pastor David smiled warmly. "And I thank each of you young men for agreeing to help us rebuild! It looks like you're all pretty strong, so I don't think you'll have a problem with the workload. Perhaps it'll be an opportunity for you to learn some new skills that may help you with finding a construction job after you graduate from the *pesantren*. As you try new things here, feel free to ask me questions at any time. I happen to have some background in construction myself and will be happy to teach you all I know.

"Now, I'd like to take just a few minutes to get to know each one of you. How about if we sit down in a circle, and maybe each of you can tell me your name and a little about yourselves and your families?"

Syukran saw his dad smile back at Pastor David. Some of the boys relaxed their taut muscles a bit. Syukran sat down with the others but let a silent rage course through his being. *Build a church? I don't think so.*

❧ Chapter 55 ☙

PASTOR DAVID LOOKED delighted to see Sari in his Sunday school class for the first time in nearly a month. She didn't feel the same delight. There was a dark cloud over her.

After class they only had fifteen minutes to vacate the hotel meeting room they had rented temporarily, so David asked Sari if she'd sit with him in the lobby for a few minutes and catch up.

They settled themselves in some comfortable red-cushioned sofas with ornate carvings of pineapples and palm leaves in the dark amber teak frames. David ordered a Sprite for each of them from the bar.

"How's your mom recovering?"

Sari tried to smile. "Pretty good. She still isn't getting out of the house much, but she's in good spirits. Several of the neighbors have come over to visit her, which really makes her day. At least she can sit in the kiosk now, so we have some income again." She took a deep breath. "Our Muslim neighbors were amazingly kind to help us when we were in the hospital."

David looked at his feet. "Yeah, I knew we'd have to talk about this. Sari, I'm really sorry that no one from the church came to visit your mom in the hospital. The truth is…we were forbidden to come."

"By whom?" Sari's voice rose angrily. There was an awkward silence. She knew the answer to her own question without a doubt. *Pastor Susanna!* She wanted to explode.

"First when Pastor Susanna humiliated my mother in front of the whole congregation, I was already mad. When the fire happened, I think I partly blamed Pastor as well for always asking my mom to stay late and clean up. Now this! Maybe we don't belong here."

David leaned forward. "Sari, you've been through some incredibly tough circumstances! I wouldn't blame you if you walked away from our church. But I think we do need people like you here, and I hope you'll find it in your heart to forgive us and stay."

Sari's hands gripped the chair beneath her. She couldn't speak.

"You know I've told you before how my father was abusive to me and my sister when we were small. Forgiveness is a battle I fight every day. So does Pastor Susanna. Did you know this wasn't the first time her church has been burned down?"

"No, I didn't know that."

"The first time her husband became so mad at God he left the church. She stayed. Now they're divorced. They had only been married for less than two years at the time and hadn't yet gotten pregnant. That church burning cost her a husband and children. I think this one is stirring up some of that old trauma for her. You see, even pastors have to deal with forgiveness."

This new information tried to penetrate Sari's wounded heart. *Pastor Susanna has suffered too. Now she's passing it on to us.* She decided to think about forgiveness later.

"So, Pastor David, how are the repairs on the church building coming?"

"It's moving along. Thank God it's still dry season. If we can get the walls and roof up before the rains hit in October, I'll be happy. God willing, we'll be out of this hotel by Christmas! Rebuilding has allowed us to redesign things a bit too. For one, we're adding several windows and an extra door this time. This will be important if we ever have another emergency."

"Are you sure it's a good idea to have the *pesantren* boys help you build? Isn't that just giving them the opportunity to do more vandalism?"

"I don't think so. I think it's a good opportunity for us to build friend-ship across religions. You know how we invite our Muslim neighbors to our Christmas program every year, but no one comes?" Sari nodded, smiling wryly. "Right now we have a group of young Muslim men coming to our church every day of the week! I've enjoyed getting to know them. They're pretty much just like the young people in our Sunday school class. Maybe on the outside the issues they face look different, but it all comes back to the same heart issues: wanting someone to love them and someone to love, struggling to find their identity in this world, trying to figure out how God intersects with real life, learning how to forgive, hope and persevere; they're just like you and me.

"You know, I'm really thankful to God for this chance. I've been praying for a city that doesn't settle for 'tolerance' between religions, which in practice seems to me to be 'mutual ignoring.' God's standard is 'love your neighbor.' Our neighbors are Muslim, and we've yet to learn how to love them. Perhaps this church burning tragedy, and the rebuilding of it, is something God will redeem to bring—"

Just then Pastor Susanna walked by. When she saw Sari she stopped and threw an icy stare.

"You and your mother are to blame for all this! You're no longer welcome in this church. Now get out!"

❦ Chapter 56 ❧

THE STRUGGLE CONTINUED to rage in Iqbal's heart over how his religion could produce such horrific evils as church burnings and terrorism, and whether or not Christianity might have the answers to what he was missing in his Islamic experience. Since his father had encouraged him to seek out some more moderate Muslim thinkers, he spent his Saturday at a seminar titled "Mutual Understanding With Humility in Muslim-Christian Dialogue." The seminar was held at *Institut Agama Islam Negeri* (IAIN), one of a national chain of Muslim universities and the largest religious university in Banjarmasin. Nearly every one of the four hundred seats in the auditorium was filled, and a few people even watched from the balcony over the rear entrance.

The event was sponsored by the *Ushuluddin* department, where they taught comparative religions, and also by the FORLOG Interfaith Forum and a group called Peace Generation. Iqbal had never been to IAIN before or heard of such groups. He decided he'd stay after the event and try to find out more information about them. The Peace Generation members, who were all wearing green T-shirts with *Peace* written in English, Indonesian, and Arabic, seemed to have some members that looked like teenagers even younger than him. There were also people in the crowd that just looked Christian—whether it was the dark skin and curly hair of the more eastern Indonesian islands, or girls who were uncovered and wore skirts that came down just below the knees. Yet they seemed at home in this Muslim university event. This was truly mind-blowing for Iqbal.

But the main thing Iqbal would take home cemented in his memory was how the Muslim presenter explained the terms *Islam, Allah, tauhid*, and *kafir*—terms he'd known his whole life, but today their meaning had changed dramatically. He took notes and later wrote out the speaker's points as best he could remember, something like this:

The word *Islam* comes from the word for "submission." The central teaching of Islam is *tauhid*, or that there is no God but God, who is One. We show our submission to God by keeping Him as the only One we worship. He can have no rivals in our hearts.

Some people want to divide us by claiming that the Christian God is a rival to the Muslim God, whom we call Allah. The name *Allah* in Arabic comes from the words *al-Ilah*, meaning "the God," or the one and only God. Though Christians in Indonesia prefer to call God "Tuhan," my Arab Christian friends in the Middle East where I studied all used "Allah," just as we do. I believe in our dialogues we're all referring to the monotheistic Creator God of our common fathers, Adam and Ibrahim, God of the prophets and Holy Books, Master of the Day of Judgment, though we may understand some aspects of His nature or workings differently.

Then who or what is a true rival to God? Some would say that violating the *tauhid* is like our Dayak *kaharingan* neighbors in central Kalimantan, who worship idols made of wood, or worship the spirits in trees. Others argue that Christians *violate* tauhid, claiming they worship three gods. Those people are *kafir*, infidels, while we are the people of true *tauhid*. But I don't think we can get off the hook so easily.

Anything in our hearts that refuses to submit to God becomes His rival, becomes like an idol to us. What are those things in our hearts as Muslims that refuse to submit to God? Greed, corruption, lust, immorality, bitterness, hatred, violence—we all know that God commands us to shun these thoughts and actions. But whenever we keep these in our hearts, or act on them in destructive behavior toward others that God created, that part of our heart refuses to submit to God, and socially, culturally, intellectually we may be Muslim, but our hearts are rebellious, pursuing a rival to God; yes, our hearts are really *kafir*.

The more we submit ourselves to God, the more our thoughts and actions become mirror reflections of Him. He is *Ar-Rahman, Ar-Rahim*—the Most Merciful, Most Compassionate. To submit to this God requires us to grow in mercy and compassion toward others. One of the most famous sayings of the Prophet recorded in the Hadith is *"Hablumminallah hablumminannas"*—"Love God, love others." This is a high standard. The Prophet didn't say,

"Love your friends and hate your enemies," or "Love your enemies with a bomb." He didn't even say, "Live tolerantly, avoiding those who are different than you." But he said, "Love them."

Once the Prophet had a neighbor who was not a Muslim who often ridiculed and threw rocks at him when he went to do his daily prayers. One day the neighbor didn't come out to throw rocks, so the Prophet inquired of his family and found the man was sick. The Prophet went to visit him and wish him a speedy recovery. This neighbor's heart changed from the Prophet's enemy to become his friend.

Because the Prophet had no rivals in his heart, nothing that was not submitted to God, he was free to mirror God's attributes of mercy and compassion. This, in turn, overcame the hatred in the neighbor's heart, allowing him to experience God's love and submit himself to God. The story ends with the neighbor choosing to become a Muslim, and I believe he became a true Muslim because of the change of his heart. He had been a *kafir*, submitted to hatred and violence; he became a true Muslim, submitted to *Ar-Rahman, Ar-Rahim.*

Iqbal was beside himself with excitement when he showed his father what he had written that night. "Dad, for a while I was so afraid that Islam taught us to hate and kill, while Christianity taught us to forgive. But I was wrong. If it wasn't for meeting Sari in the hospital, I might never have discovered how much I've misunderstood my own faith. One of Allah's beautiful names is *Al-Ghaffar*, 'the Most Forgiving.' Now that I see what it means to truly surrender to God by mirroring His attributes, I'm content to be a Muslim."

Abdullah breathed an obvious sigh of relief.

"*Alhamdulillah!* May God continually reveal to you the straight way, son."

"Dad, there were other teenagers there, high school kids like me, who are part of a group called Peace Generation. They invited me to one of their meetings. Can I go check it out?"

"Is it a Christian group?" Abdullah shifted his feet carefully on the couch with a slight wince.

"No, it's a mixed group of Muslim and Christian students who are promoting peace through a curriculum produced by Pelangi Mizan. They showed me a couple of the books, and they're great! They take this curriculum into local junior high schools and teach about peace."

"Sounds fine to me, son." Abdullah smiled. "Actually, I've been working at the church construction site with a Christian pastor named David and find I'm really enjoying getting to know him, too."

"Wow, Dad, that's cool! And hey, one of the speakers mentioned a new candidate likely to run for president next year who is an award-winning peacemaker. His name is something Ramadani. Maybe he's the right guy to change things in this country! You know, this is the first election I get to vote in next year, and I'm already excited about it!" Iqbal pounded his right fist into his left palm.

"Hmm. I haven't heard of him. I'll start watching the newspaper for him. I hope you can talk to your brother sometime about what you're learning. But do it carefully. He may not take it well at first."

"OK, Dad. I'll look for a chance. I'm sure if Syuk hears things like what I heard today and stops listening to that rebel Hafiz, he'll come around.

"Hopefully I'll see Sari tomorrow. I can't wait to tell her about all this!"

❧ Chapter 57 ❦

'M NOT GOING to church today, and I'm glad.

Sari couldn't remember ever thinking that thought before. But besides Pastor Susanna's exiling her, she had another reason not to go—one of their neighbors had actually invited them to a wedding reception! For years she'd watched as the neighborhood men spent Saturday night securing a large tarp over a front yard or even the street and set up rented plastic tables and chairs. She'd watched the neighborhood women carry food cooked early Sunday morning to the wedding house to feed all the guests, usually double the number of invitations given, Sari heard. She'd been envious of how everyone dressed up beautifully and seemed to enjoy the party. Because she and her mom had been pointedly not invited.

But this time, not only had Ibu Noorminah invited them, but she'd asked them to help with the cooking too. Because her mom was still recovering from her burns, Ibu Noorminah gave her the easier task of just cooking tons of rice, while other women were cooking chicken soup, chicken in red sauce, pickled vegetables, or curried goat meat. Ibu Noorminah delivered a sack of rice to them on Saturday, along with a two-gallon thermos-like container that could hold enough rice to feed between fifty and one hundred people. Starting at 3:00 a.m., Sari's mom had her pan on the kerosene burner cooking the rice. When it was done, she'd dump it in the two-gallon thermos and refill her pan to cook some more. Her goal was to have the thermos filled by nine.

Sure enough, her diligence paid off, and by 9:00 a.m. Sari went off to find a neighbor guy to help her carry the rice to the wedding. She hoped she'd see Bali, but didn't. The bride's younger brother was standing around with no guests to greet yet, so he agreed to loan her his muscles.

After Sari had dropped off the rice, she and her mom got dressed for the wedding. Sari only had one dress that covered down to her ankles, a black shimmering satin-looking (though not real satin) gown with bare shoulders and an open back that showed her bra. She never knew what possessed her mother to buy such a dress for her. In Banjarmasin she always had to wear a jacket over the top. She chose a black-and-gold half-jacket that covered her shoulders and back but not her waist.

Kris went with a more conservative top-and-bottom green *batik* outfit. It also had long sleeves and a skirt to the ankles. This would be Kris's first public event since coming home from the hospital, and she looked excited to get out of the house. Her skin was healing wonderfully. You could hardly see the different shades of skin on her face or arms anymore. Sari figured it would do her mom's heart good to rejoin the world.

They walked down the alley to the beat of a hired *dangdut* singer with cranked-up speakers already entertaining the first few guests. After signing the guest book at the first table, they each picked up a plate of Banjar chicken soup and found some chairs to sit in as far from the throbbing sound system as possible. Only a few guests were this early. Mama Rizky came over to say hello, then moved on to talk with someone else. Kris was chattering on about how happy she was to get out and wondering who she'd see today, but Sari wasn't really listening. She had seen Syukran and several other neighbor boys bringing out boxes of bottled water and was looking everywhere to catch a glimpse of Bali.

Mama Shafa came over with her plate of goat meat and sat down.

"Where's Shafa? Is she here?"

"No, my husband is home and wanted to take Shafa to the mall. I wanted him to come with me to the wedding. Sometimes I don't understand that man. Why would he come to spend the weekend with me and then leave me alone like this? He didn't even offer to take me to the mall with him! He just said, 'I'm going to take Shafa to the mall today.' That's it. He didn't ask about my plans, or why I was dressing up. Sometimes I wonder if he even cares about me at all."

Sari could tell this conversation could go on for a while, and she wasn't terribly interested in Mama Shafa's romantic problems. For one, it was depressing. For two, she had a romantic problem of her own, like, where was Bali? She decided to get up and walk around to see if he was helping in the back with Syukran.

Sari headed for Ibu Noorminah's front yard. She checked around the side of the house but just saw some young guys carrying plates of food from the kitchen to the serving tables. She checked in the house. A canopied "throne" had been colorfully decorated in red and gold for the bride and groom to sit on, but they were still putting on their traditional outfits in a bedroom. The long living room looked kind of bare, with only a tiny handful of cakes on a knee-high table and an even tinier handful of grandmothers sitting there gossiping.

Sari exited Ibu Noorminah's, figuring Bali probably hadn't made it to the wedding yet. She happened to glance over toward Ibu Dina's house, wondering if Nina was sleeping at home again or not. Maybe she should stop in and ask. She headed that way.

Three steps later she froze in her tracks. Behind the jackfruit tree in Ibu Dina's yard she could see a guy talking to a girl. The girl was leaning against the tree with her back against it and looked suspiciously like Nina. Her skirt was criminally short. Surely Nina wouldn't dress like the other day here in the neighborhood, on a Sunday morning! The guy was leaning in close to her ear, as if whispering something he didn't want the rest of the world to hear, and looked more than suspiciously like Bali! Sari didn't know what to do. The conversation looked so private; she felt she shouldn't interrupt it. But why would Bali be having such an intimate conversation with any girl but her? They weren't dating of course, but still, she thought...

Syukran happened by at just that moment delivering another box of drinking water. He paused next to Sari and followed her gaze. Then he mumbled as though half to her, half to himself.

"I told my brother to stay away from that girl. She's almost as bad as you are! But he wouldn't listen to me. Guess my playboy brother has a weakness for *kafir* girls in the day and prostitutes in the night." Syukran strode away.

Sari stumbled through her tears toward her mother, grabbed her arm, and said, "Time to go." Kris stood, confused.

"We haven't congratulated the bride and groom!"

But Sari would have none of it, propelling her anxious mother past the reception table, down the alley, and back into the house, where Sari gently closed the front door then collapsed on the floor in a flood of tears.

"My goodness, Sari. What's wrong? What could have upset you so? Can you tell me?"

Sari was in no state to talk and continued weeping. Her mom sat quietly beside her and stroked her hair.

Finally Sari heard her mom use her most gentle voice. "Haven't I warned you many times about falling in love with a Muslim boy?"

That sent Sari into greater heaves of sobbing. The sounds of a breaking heart.

Chapter 58

A T THREE O'CLOCK Syukran slipped away from the wedding cleanup crew to join Hafiz, Udin, Juki, and Juki's extended family headed for Martapura. They managed to pack seventeen people into a yellow minivan, with Hafiz and Juki both hanging halfway out the side where there used to be a sliding door.

The trip took a little over an hour. Syukran remembered how in elementary school the entire *pesantren* would go there at least once a year to hear Guru Ijai, the charismatic spiritual leader of the Banjar people, for many years before his death. Today Juki's uncle was taking them to Guru Ijai's old mosque for a special Sunday afternoon sermon, but Syukran had never heard of the speaker before. He figured it was a good way to avoid his parents and brother, who understood him less and less every day.

The imam who spoke turned out to be a guest from Aceh Province in North Sumatra. He wore the long white robe and turban of an Arab; had the long, hooking Arab nose; dark, piercing eyes; and an unshaven face full of black stubble with a short black beard. He began his sermon with a long and impressive recitation of the Qur'an. Then he started telling stories. He told about his experiences of *jihad* in Maluku, a small group of Indonesian islands east of Borneo where Christians had vandalized mosques and attacked Muslim villages. He had been on the para-military team that had found the perpetrators of this heinous insult and brought God's judgment of fire on their homes and churches. The crowd cheered. He told about his experience burning the Danish flag in front of their embassy in Jakarta when their infidel government refused to prosecute the infidel journalist who had drawn a caricature of the Holy Prophet in a newspaper cartoon. The crowd booed. He exposed the sinister duplicity of the Americans who say they champion human rights then locked up our Muslim brothers in Guantanamo for years with no trial and subjected them to torture. The crowd booed louder now, feeding on each others' anger. He shared how he and his para-military team had responded to the American atrocities by sweeping the Central Java city of Solo for Americans, searching the hotels and warning them to leave town or die. The crowd cheered. Then he quoted a verse about fighting the infidels wherever you find them—fight them in the city, fight them in the country, fight them in the streets, fight them in their homes; this is the way to save the world from moral degradation and return the glory of Islam!

He shouted, *"Allah Akbar!"* "God is great!" The crowd joined in the praise, pumping their fists in the air and shouting *"Allah Akbar!"* over and over again for several minutes, not even noticing that the imam had already left the mosque.

After the meeting broke up, Juki's uncle brought the boys to meet one of the *pesantren* teachers. When he told the teacher how the boys' *pesantren* in Banjarmasin was forcing them to help build a church, the teacher scowled and made a very generous offer.

"Boys, how would you like to transfer to our school? I'm sure you'll find our facilities much better, our teachers experts in *syariah* law and interpretation of the *Hadith*. We'll even let you finish this first school year for free. How about it?"

The boys played with the idea all the way home. In one sense it was a chance to get into the system that could lead to a *pesantren* in Malaysia or to one of the major *jihad* organizations. On the other hand, none of them expected their parents to agree.

When the minivan pulled up in front of Juki's house, the four boys walked over to Hafiz's porch together and sat down. They had done their *Mahgrib sholat* at the mosque in Martapura, and Juki's uncle had treated them to deer meat satay at Gambut on the way home. It was now early evening, and a cool breeze drifted in off the river. Udin lit a cigarette and handed one to Hafiz.

Juki summarized the discussion so far: "Basically, none of our parents will agree. Hafiz's parents are only sending him to *Al-Mustaqiim* to 'reform' him since he got kicked out of PGRI 4. Udin's and my parents need us close to home to help them work after school. And Syukran's dad is a church-lover."

Udin laughed. "Yeah, a church-lover, black-Christian-pastor-hero-worshiper who knows how to fight but won't teach us because he cares more about the Christians than his own religion."

"I don't know why we even follow his *silat* teaching anymore, now that his true colors have been exposed," added Hafiz. "I'll bet he was never even in Afghanistan. You made up all those stories, didn't you, Syuk! Admit it; it's all a lie. If your dad ever went on *jihad* to Afghan then I'm Michael Jackson."

He looked challengingly at Syukran, who returned the glare but refused to respond.

"Come on, Syuk, admit it! You've been stringing us along with a pack of lies. If your dad really did all those things you said, swear it's true, swear on the Qur'an right now that it's true. Well?"

Still Syukran held back. But he could feel his breathing speed up and the tension in his jaw. They all stared deep into his eyes, as though trying to see the truth.

"Tell us the truth, Syuk," Udin prompted.

"Coward! Just like your father!" Hafiz spat on the ground.

Syukran finally exploded, leaping to his feet, fists clenched. "Shut up! My dad is what he is, and I'm not like him!"

"Prove it!" Hafiz challenged. "I saw you at the church burning. You just pretended to cough so you could avoid setting the fire. You got no guts. You're worse than your father!"

Syukran cocked his fist for a shot at Hafiz's face, his eyes blazing. Then slowly he dropped his hand to his side, and without a word he turned and walked away.

He wandered up Kelayan B toward the city, not knowing where to go. His thoughts slipped into a dark pit.

I can't go home. I hate it there. My family is completely self-absorbed. Bali only cares about his worldly pleasures. Dad only cares about Christians. And Mom only cares about herself. They couldn't care less about me.

I can't go to my friends. They think I'm a coward. How can I blame them? Why couldn't I light the fire? I should have told them what I painted on the door. No, they'd say I was lying again.

"Worse than my dad." Someday I'll make Hafiz eat those words. I am nothing like my dad! Those fools! But they're not the ones really at fault, are they?

No! I will not turn my back on my Muslim brothers like my father did. He shamed our family. This whole thing is all his fault. How could he do this to me? I hate him!

Syukran didn't know what to do. He needed someone to talk to, someone who would understand his pain. And then he realized that there was one person who would understand. He had to find him.

His gait changed from a lost wanderer to a man with a purpose and a destination.

He wondered why he hadn't seen the light sooner. His life *did* make sense. Everything was preparing him for this moment. And now that it was here, he was ready.

Yes, now he was ready.

❧ Chapter 59 ❧

Congressman Louis Staunton had just taken his first bite of his salami on rye when he noticed the portly figure of one of his aides running, actually *running*, toward him. He put down his sandwich on the marble tile around the reflecting pool that complements the Washington Monument. The leaves were just beginning to change color, and during the fall and spring Louis preferred to take his lunches outdoors. It gave him a chance to disengage from the details of governance and remember why he was here in the first place. The majesty of the Washington Monument towering over him was a mere echo of the greatness of vision George Washington and the other founding fathers left to us. *Be a visionary, not a manager,* Louis reminded himself daily.

"Congressman Staunton! Congressman Staunton!" William was huffing and puffing, waving what looked like a fax. He handed the paper to Louis and put his chubby hands on his knees, wheezing for air. As he bent at the waist, his thick, black-rimmed glasses slipped off his sweaty nose and onto the stone walkway. He picked them up and pushed them back on his nose and waited, like a puppy for a doggie treat.

"William, whatever this is, I'm sure it can wait till I'm back in the office! Why do you think I come out here for lunch? It's because I want to look at something besides faxes!"

"Sir, you gotta read this. It's from the CIA."

"I haven't sold any national secrets to the Russians *this* week. What can they want?" Louis joked.

"Please, sir. I can't calm down till I know you've read that fax and told me what I should do about it."

"Well, I guess I can't have my aides huffing and puffing around Washington all day, can I?" Louis remarked wryly. He took another bite of his sandwich, then looked at the fax.

"From John Harmon," he mumbled while chewing. "We used to play basketball together back in college. Uh-huh, uh-huh." He skimmed to the end. "OK, William. Got it. Thanks much." He held the fax out for William to take back. Then he took a swig of his Dr. Pepper.

"But sir, it says the Densus 88 in Indonesia discovered another terrorist training facility in Aceh and seized documents outlining their planned attacks on the president, the US embassy, on airplanes, even one about an attack on United States soil! Sir, you can't go over there! It's less than a month away! I don't want you to get blown up by a terrorist bomb! Think about your family! Think about my job!"

"William, take a deep breath and count to ten. I'm sure the CIA is on top of it. In my opinion, it's probably just another normal day in Indonesia. I'm not canceling the trip." He took another bite of his sandwich.

"But sir!"

"Tell you what. If the CIA sends you any faxes about a planned attack on a certain new presidential candidate or on a visiting US Congressman that we both know, you make sure I get that information as soon as—" Louis broke off his sentence to swallow.

"As soon as *possible*, sir?"

"No, as soon as *I enter the office*. Got it?"

"Yes, sir!" William almost saluted. *The brain of a Georgetown grad; the enthusiasm of a hyperactive kindergartner.*

"And one more thing. Not a sniff of this fax gets near my wife!" Louis smiled. "Now beat it."

❧ Chapter 60 ❧

Sari dreaded school on Monday.

Ever since the hospital Bali had saved seats for her in classes, talked with her at lunch, even passed her notes during class.

But after what she'd seen yesterday, how could she know if he really cared especially for her or if he saw her as just any other girl?

In first period she went straight to class and sat in the back corner next to Maya. When Bali entered, he looked confused but smiled and waved, then found another seat.

During the break she went straight to the bathroom and stayed inside till the bell rang.

At lunch Bali found her and sat down across from her. "Sari, is something wrong?"

Don't look in his eyes. You'll get sucked in. She looked away. "I'm fine."

"You don't look fine to me. Tell me what's going on." *His voice is so gentle and sweet. Don't listen to it! You'll get sucked in with his voice too!*

"I'm sorry. I told Ibu Tina I'd help her set up the science lab at lunch. Gotta go."

Sari abruptly left for the lab but had only gone just around the corner when she realized she couldn't lie to Bali and turned around. But when she reentered the lunch area, there he was sitting with a bunch of girls talking to Maya! *Out of sight for less than a minute, and he's off playing the field. Maybe Syukran was right. Maybe Bali is a playboy, and I just never saw it before.*

A tear trickled down Sari's cheek. After all that had happened this year, having her heart broken by the only boy she'd ever started to care about had to be the worst. *Why did I ever let my heart open up to a Muslim guy? I knew it was wrong. This pain... Well, I guess I deserve it.*

Sari told the school security guard at the gate that her mom had an emergency. The guard knew the story of her mom's near death, so he immediately let her go. No one else noticed her ditching class. She needed to be alone.

The tears blurred her vision as she weaved her motorbike through the traffic. The pain in her chest was so tight she could hardly breathe. She wanted to pray, but the words didn't come. Only one thought kept reverberating around her head.

Why, God? Why?

❧ Chapter 61 ☙

NOT KNOWING WHERE else to go, Sari drove home. Her mom wasn't there, which was just as well. Sari knew that just seeing her mom would probably set her bawling on the floor again. She lay back on her bed and thought about how nice it would be in heaven. No more tears. No more pain.

Sari lay there crying softly into her pillow for a while. *Why does life have to be so hard?* She thought of her mom's broken heart over her husband leaving her. *Maybe she felt just like me.* A deeper appreciation for her mom's pain brought momentary relief from her own.

She knew at a time like this her mom would probably read the Bible. She always told Sari that when she was hurting she'd read from David's psalms. Sari realized she'd left her Bible in her backpack at school; she'd been in such a hurry to leave.

Not a problem. She headed into her mother's room and found her larger black leather Bible on the nightstand. She opened it to the psalms. Skimming through a few of them, her gaze riveted on chapter 55.

> Open your ears, God, to my prayer;
> don't pretend you don't hear me knocking.
> Come close and whisper your answer.
> I really need you.
>
> My insides are turned inside out;
> specters of death have me down.
> I shake with fear,
> I shudder from head to foot.
> "Who will give me wings," I ask—
> "wings like a dove?"
> Get me out of here on dove wings;
> I want some peace and quiet.

I want a walk in the country,
I want a cabin in the woods.
I'm desperate for a change
from rage and stormy weather.

And this, my best friend, betrayed his best friends;
his life betrayed his word.
All my life I've been charmed by his speech,
never dreaming he'd turn on me.
His words, which were music to my ears,
turned to daggers in my heart.
Pile your troubles on GOD's shoulders—
he'll carry your load, he'll help you out.
He'll never let good people
topple into ruin.

And I trust in you.

Sari laid the Bible on the bed and started weeping again. Betrayal...like daggers in the heart. She found herself repeating her favorite part of the psalm: "Who will give me wings?...Wings like a dove?" *If only I could fly far, far away...*

The front door creaked open. Mom must be home. Sari hurriedly grabbed the Bible to put it back in its place, but in her rush accidentally knocked it off the bed onto the floor. As she bent to pick it up, something fell out. An envelope. It had her mother's name on the front center above an old address. The return address was a bank in Jakarta under the name "H. Gunawan." The envelope was yellowing, as though it were quite old. Most curious of all, it was sealed. Maybe her mother had just forgotten to open it. Sari slipped her pinkie finger in the unsealed edge of the envelope to rip it open just when her mother walked in.

"*Stop it!*" Kris screamed. She lunged for Sari and snatched the envelope from her hand, scaring Sari half to death. Kris hugged the envelope to her heart and angrily questioned her daughter.

"What are you doing in my bedroom? What are you doing with my Bible? Who told you that you could touch my letter?" Kris was shaking all over. Sari started crying again. She'd never seen her mom act like this in her whole life.

"I'm sorry, Mom. I'm sorry. I just thought you forgot to open it." Sari's hair hung down over her face, hiding the fear in her red, puffy eyes.

"Never, never touch this letter again. Do you hear me?" Sari nodded. She wanted to run away but was too terrified to move. Yet a curiosity about the letter nagged at her. Kris put the letter into the Bible and closed it, then put it inside a dresser drawer and closed that. Sari watched, unsure if she was allowed to ask her question or not. Finally she screwed up her courage and asked.

"Who is it from?"

Kris glared angrily at Sari. "It's from my husband, your father. After he abandoned us, this was the last thing I received from him. I've never opened it." Sari waited for more, but Kris stopped talking and tears formed in her eyes.

"What if he wrote something in there for me?"

"It's mine! Don't you ever touch it again. Now go to your room!"

Sari realized she was crying again. She stumbled past her mom into her bedroom and threw herself on her bed, sobbing uncontrollably. The last person who loved her in this world had turned against her. *If only I could fly far, far away . . .*

For several minutes Kris sat trembling on her bed, afraid of her own outburst of anger. *How dare my snoopy daughter open my letter? Hendri's last words are a secret, a precious secret that not even I know. I'll open it when I feel ready.*

She thought about moving it to a safer place, but after considering a few decided to leave it in the drawer for now. She took two aspirin, then lay down on the bed, still shaking.

Three hours later Kris woke up. It was already dark. She realized she hadn't made any dinner for Sari yet, so she headed for the kitchen. There were no dirty dishes or food laid out anywhere. Maybe Sari was still in her bedroom, where the evil mother had banished her. Kris felt terrible; that was no way to treat her daughter. She knocked on the bedroom door, then gently pushed it open and turned on the light.

Sari wasn't there.

She went through the house calling Sari's name, but there was no answer. Sari was gone.

Kris was suddenly struck by a horrible premonition. *Oh my God! What have I done?*

❧ Chapter 62 ❧

SAIFULLAH CHECKED HIS watch again. Fachmi was late. As he let his eyes wander watchfully around Soekarno-Hatta International Airport, he reflected on how the nation had named its airport after its founding fathers. If he and his comrades were successful overthrowing democracy and establishing *syariah* law in a brand new *Daulah Islam*, or Muslim nation, would the names of airports, streets, and monuments change? How about Bin Laden Airport, Noordin M. Top Toll road, or the Saifullah *Mujahidin* Academy? That had a nice ring to it.

He had flown to Jakarta that morning for a couple of very important meetings: the first with an Arab financier; the second with Fachmi, their "sleeper" inside the Bellagio. Both meetings were held at the airport, a place convenient for all and where no one would likely notice them.

Fachmi's smiling face finally appeared, apparently untroubled at his tardiness. The two men sat in the downstairs corner of what used to be a McDonalds. As Fachmi went to get his meal, Saifullah played with his already empty coffee cup and missed the old days. *Not only was the food better before; so was the target! How can you throw mud in the eye of the Americans by bombing an Indonesian-named place?*

Fachmi sat down with his fried chicken and Coke. He was a tall, thin fellow with neatly cropped hair, beige slacks, a lavender long-sleeve dress shirt, and an exceedingly friendly face. No one would ever suspect this man to be involved with JI. But he was.

Saifullah was team leader for the mission, and started first.

"Update me on the plan for delivering the 'wedding gift.'"

"Well, we've had some setbacks. I've been working at the 'Bell Tower' for almost three years now. At first I was in a cafe called Vegas. I had an ingenious plan for hiding it inside a TV speaker. It took me about three months to perfect it. Then all I'd have to do is wait for the right event, tell the boss one of the speakers was out, and replace it with mine. Right about that time, Vegas closed. Fortunately, the event organizer kept all our names on a list for extra staff at special events. That's how I found out about this one coming up and alerted our mutual friends."

"So what's the new plan?"

"Still working on it. I'm signed up for food catering. I can't get anyone new on this late but maybe could get a participant signed up. They'll be properly checked out though. So will the staff. I've looked at trying to get the gift under the food cart—too risky, could be discovered in the kitchen. I've looked at potted plants like we did at 'Mary's'—out of my sphere of authority." Fachmi paused.

"In other words, you got nothing."

Fachmi shrugged and grinned. *You better do your job, brother, or I'll wipe that smirk permanently off your face.*

"Could we get someone in one of the businesses near the ballroom?"

"There's a wedding boutique next door. You got a girlfriend who needs to try on a dress?"

"What else?"

"Restaurants, health clinic, chiropractor, massage, jewelry, clothing, karaoke. There's even a church up one floor on the opposite side of the building."

"Work on it! I'm almost ready to bring my 'bride' to town for the final 'wedding' preparations. Figure out a way to get her into that ballroom or close enough that they'll feel her presence."

"I'm on it. By the time you arrive, I'll have a plan."

"How are you doing on the wedding 'decorations'?"

"Some of the most important pieces are in hand. Others I know where to find. I'll have all the pieces ready for assembly a week before the wedding."

"Good. I'll see you at our old friend 'Amin's' house a few days before for the 'rehearsal dinner.' If you encounter any obstacles, pass the word on to Amin."

"Will do."

"Oh, and earlier today I bumped into my former 'teacher,' who wanted me to pass this book on to you."

Saifullah took out a large, hard-backed Arab-English dictionary and passed it to his friend, who put it straight into his laptop bag. The pages had been hollowed out on the inside, and in their place was about Rp.30,000,000 and another $12,000 in US $100 bills. *More than enough for this mission. May Allah bless the Saudis and all their oil!*

He left Fachmi to finish his fried artery-clogger and headed for the domestic terminal to catch his plane back to Banjarmasin.

He felt sure that the bride he'd found was ready to say, "I will."

❧ Chapter 63 ❧

THE FIRST THING Kris did was kneel down beside her bed and pray. *Oh God, I don't know why I have this feeling that Sari is thinking about suicide. It's so unlike her, but please, please send Your angels to keep her safe. Please forgive me and bring her back to me. She's so much more important than my stupid letter and my stupid pride. Please tell me what to do.*

Then she listened. After a few minutes, she knew what she had to do.

She threw on a jacket and walked as quickly as her still-healing feet would carry her to Pak Abdullah's house. She banged on the door. "Hello! Hello!"

Siti opened it. "Oh, it's you. What do you want? We're eating dinner."

"I'm sorry to bother you, Ibu Siti. I need to speak to Iqbal. It's very important."

Siti frowned for a moment considering this. Then she spun on her heels in retreat. A few seconds later, Iqbal appeared.

"Hi, Ibu Kris! Is something wrong?"

She motioned with her hand for him to come outside. He came out and closed the door behind him. "What's going on?"

"It's Sari. Yesterday she was already depressed." Kris decided not to mention why. "Then today I did a horrible thing. I yelled at her and scared her." She put her face in her hands, sniffing back the tears. "She took off and didn't tell me where. But I feel in my heart that something bad could happen to her. I can't go look for her. I don't have a motorbike and don't know how to drive if I did have one. I thought of you and Nina. You're her closest friends. Would you please look for her for me?"

"Sure 'Bu Kris. I'll go right now."

Iqbal turned around to tell his parents and grab the motorbike key, then raced over to Nina's house to see if she was home. Kris watched from her porch as Iqbal and Nina careened down the alley toward Kelayan B. Then she went back inside.

She kneeled by her bed, determined to pray until Sari returned.

Nina was more than happy to help search for Sari. While Iqbal drove she took out her cell phone and text messaged every mutual friend they knew.

As they headed up Kelayan B, Nina asked where they were going.

"I don't know. I thought I'd start at the church. Ibu Kris didn't say it, but I think she's afraid Sari might kill herself."

"That doesn't sound like Sari!" Nina protested.

"Yeah, I'm with you, but Ibu Kris looked pretty scared. Let's say if she were going to kill herself, where would she do it?"

"Gee, maybe jump off a bridge or a high building."

"Well, I guess that gives us a few places to start looking."

They screeched up to the gate around the church building project. It was locked. It was hard to see but looked like no one was inside.

"Sari! Sari, are you here?" No answer.

"Let's try the new bridge from Pekauman to Teluk Tiram." It was the closest bridge and arched high over the Martapura River, an excellent choice for a jumper with a death wish.

Three minutes later they were on the bridge, scanning both sides slowly. There were a handful of dating couples who had parked their motorbikes on the bridge for a romantic view. But no young woman standing alone.

Next they tried the bridges downtown, the Freedom Bridge and the bridge between Pasar Lama and Kampung Melayu. By this time Nina had text messaged everyone in Iqbal's phone as well. Message after message came back: "Haven't seen her."

"Should we go all the way to the north end of the city, the Kayutangi Ujung bridge?" Iqbal asked.

"Well, if she were going to jump off a bridge, why would she pick the one farthest away?"

"You're right. Oh God, how are we going to find her?"

"Maybe a tall building?"

"What kind of building could she get on the roof?"

"What about Duta Mall? She could jump off the second-story parking area?"

"It just doesn't sound like Sari to look for a crowd when she's upset. I think she'd want a quieter place."

They parked the motorbike on the side of the road, helpless, growing hopeless.

Nina removed her helmet and tossed her hair. "There's no way we're going to find her, Bali. All we can do is hope that she'll come home."

"You're probably right. But I can't stop looking. You want me to take you home, and I'll look some more by myself?"

"No. Maybe we could get a drink and think till something comes to us. I could really use a Fanta."

Iqbal's eyes burst open wide. "Fanta! I think I might know where Sari is! Come on!"

He revved the Kharisma's engine and headed back downtown.

Sari sat on the edge of the roof of Pasar Sudimampir, three stories above a fifteen-foot-wide concrete dock on the side of the Martapura River. Across the river she could see the Mitra Plaza's children's arcade her mom used to take her to when she was a toddler. Behind her were a few small snack and drink *warungs* on the roof, the last one having just closed. Two empty Fanta bottles lay beside her. She had come here just to be alone and think. But she could feel a darkness settling over her.

She watched the waves below her lap against the dock. They were hypnotizing. *What would happen to one of these bottles if I flung it into the river? Would it float all the way to the ocean? Would it wash ashore on some beautiful beach of a far distant land, a happy land?* "Who will give me wings?... Wings like a dove?" *If only I could fly far, far away...*

But there was no one to throw her as far as the river. She would only make it as far as the concrete below. Then, like a glass Fanta bottle, she'd be smashed into tiny little broken pieces. *Like my heart is right now.*

She'd come here because it was the last place where she'd ever felt truly, splendidly happy. The day she had a mommy and a "daddy" both holding her hands. If she had the power to choose her last moment on earth, this was the memory she wanted to take with her to heaven.

Darkness swirled around her, clouding her thoughts. A voice whispered that she *did* have the power to make it all go away. The whisper told her to stand up. She obeyed. She stretched out her hands like wings and stared at them. One perfectly formed, but never to wear the ring of true love. The other hideously deformed, never to be redeemed. She'd always hoped the left hand would win out in her life. But destiny had made her right-handed. Bali's bracelet would be the final witness to her tragic, deformed life.

The whispering was more urgent now. It was time to make it all go away.

Mom, I'll see you in heaven. Dad, I hope to finally meet you there, too. Bali...good-bye.

She let herself lean forward over the edge and fall.

Chapter 64

"THERE'S THE ACCESS ramp." Nina pointed ahead.

"But it's gated and locked. I guess she isn't here." Bali's shoulders slumped in defeat. "I was so sure. I guess you're right, Nina. This is hopeless." He turned the bike away to head for home.

"Wait, I think there are stairs to the top on the other side. Look over there." Around the other side of the building was another locked gate blocking stairway access. And parked in front of the gate was Sari's motorbike.

Bali screeched to a halt screaming, "Sari! Sari!" He shook the locked gate, and the chain fell off. It had only looked locked! They sprinted up the stairs to the roof shouting Sari's name.

As they burst onto the roof, they saw Sari on the opposite side, arms open wide and falling forward.

"*Nooo!*" Bali cried.

From out of nowhere a mighty gust of wind hit them head on, knocking them right off their feet. They grabbed on to each other to keep from blowing off the roof. A Fanta bottle flew into the metal railing next to them, sending shards of glass past them. Another bottle whistled by just over their heads. The roar of the wind was deafening.

As suddenly as it had come, the wind ceased. Iqbal and Nina scrambled up to look where Sari had just been standing.

She was lying on her back on the edge of the roof, unconscious.

As they ran toward her they crouched, anticipating another blast of wind, but none came. Finally they knelt beside her and called her name. Nina took her left hand and squeezed as her tears dripped on Sari's shoulder. Iqbal stroked her face and whispered her name in her ear, his tears wetting her hair.

After what seemed like eternity, Sari opened her eyes.

"Oh, Sari!" wailed Nina as she burst into tears, burying her head into Sari's chest.

Sari and Bali locked eyes. She could see his wet cheeks and reddened eyes. She mouthed the words, "You came..." He answered with a gentle kiss on the forehead. Sari felt the spirit of death lift right off of her and life flood in.

Finally, Sari sat up. She didn't have any words to say, but she felt in her heart that she was *loved*, and that was enough.

Bali wanted to know if it was all his fault. "Please, Sari, you've avoided me all day. Did I do something wrong? If this is all my fault, I'm so sorry."

"It's not your fault."

"Your mom said you were upset since yesterday. What happened?"

"I got upset when I saw you two talking behind the tree at Nina's house. Syukran said you, uh, you wanted Nina."

Both started protesting at once. "No, that's not true!" Bali motioned for Nina to go ahead.

"Bali was just asking me what you liked, because he wanted to buy you a gift. Then he told me I should stop going to the nightclubs 'cuz I'd never find a good husband that way, and I got mad and left."

"I'm sorry. The way you leaned into her it was like you shared a secret or something."

Bali explained, "The music was so loud we could hardly hear each other. Please believe me, Sari. There is no other girl for me but you."

"What about at school today? No sooner did I turn my back than you went straight to Maya and her gang."

"I went to Maya to ask her what was wrong with you, to find out if you'd told her you want to break up with me."

"Break up with you? I didn't know we were even dating."

"If it's OK with you, maybe we could." Bali smiled invitingly. Sari smiled back.

Nina interrupted their moment. "We should get you home. Your mom is worried sick about you."

Sari's smile dropped. "I don't know. I really hurt her."

"Listen, girl! You are so lucky to have a mom that loves you. She sent us to look for you. Remember when I didn't come home for a few days? My mom couldn't have cared less. She didn't send anyone to look for me. I've never seen a mom love their child like your mom loves you. I used to be so jealous of you when we were kids. Whatever happened between you, please go back to her and work it out."

Sari threw her arms around Nina, and they both cried. Sari stroked Nina's hair and whispered, "I've missed you."

Nina answered, "I've missed you, too."

When they separated, Sari asked, "Could I ask you guys to do a favor for me?"

"Anything," Bali answered.

Sari stood on the edge of the roof where she had given in to the darkness just moments ago, stretched out her hands, and closed her eyes once again.

It took them a minute to understand, but eventually she felt Nina take hold of her left hand, while Bali took hold of her right hand. Her deformed hand tingled with pleasure in the hand of a boy who accepted her the way she was.

Sari felt herself transported through space and time to the happiest day of her life once again. Except something had changed. That blissful memory yielded to today's, the new happiest day of her life.

❧ Chapter 65 ❧

SARI CALLED HER mom to tell her she was coming home. Then she gave her motorbike keys to Nina and climbed on the back of Bali's bike, wrapped her arms around his chest, and buried her face in his back. She couldn't think about the future; for now, she just needed to enjoy being *alive*.

Kris was on the porch and met them in the street. She threw her arms around her daughter, weeping. Sari cried too, hugging her mom tightly. Iqbal and Nina looked at each other, then quietly left mother and daughter alone.

Through the tears both were saying, "I'm sorry," over and over, then, "I love you," over and over. Eventually Sari pulled back, took her mother's hand, and led her into the house, where they sat on the living room floor.

Kris apologized. "I'm so, so sorry for how I acted earlier. I want you to know that you are far more important to me than that letter, or anything else in this world. Please forgive me for lashing out at you. It will never, never happen again."

"I know, Mom. I'm sorry I ran off like that. I just felt like the last person in the world who loved me had turned against me. But I know now that wasn't true. I know you love me."

"It was so wrong of me to make you feel that way. I was a fool to let a piece of paper come between us. If you want to read that letter, you go right ahead."

"Mom! It's your letter. I shouldn't have touched it. You read it when you're ready."

"Maybe I should. Maybe it's time I faced it. But I'm scared."

Sari took her mother's hand in hers. "You'll never be free from the fear until you know the truth."

"You're right. I think it's time to read it. And if you're willing, I'd really like you to be there with me when I do."

"Sure, Mom. I'd love to do that."

"But not tonight. No more talk of letters now. The only thing that matters to me tonight is having my daughter back again."

They embraced. That night they stayed up late, Sari recounting the whole story, Kris interrupting at times to give glory to God for His answer to her prayers.

Kris thanked God repeatedly before falling asleep. Her final thought before she drifted into dreamland was, *Tomorrow I'm going to open the letter.*

♛ Chapter 66 ♛

KRIS PACED BACK and forth in the living room waiting for Sari to get home from school. Her kiosk was closed. The letter lay on the kitchen table. She felt like she should dress up and put on makeup but chided herself for such foolishness. It was just a letter!

Finally Sari walked in the door. She kissed her mom and went to her bedroom to change. *What's taking her so long?* Kris thought, twisting her hair into a knot.

Sari headed for the kitchen table looking for a banana and saw the letter. Kris was right on her heels.

"Mom, are you sure you're ready for this?"

Nodding, Kris picked up the envelope. She grimaced. "Let's get this over with before I chicken out."

"OK." They both sat down.

Kris closed her eyes and took a deep breath. She felt like the volunteer standing ever so still with an apple on her head waiting for the knife-thrower to let it fly.

A little *snip-snip* with the scissors, and the letter was open.

One side had some numbers and bank information. Kris flipped it over to the other side. She knew she couldn't read it out loud, so they each held one side of the letter and read it to themselves.

Dear Kris,

This is the hardest thing I've ever had to do in my life. I have to admit that I made a terrible mistake and deeply hurt someone that I truly love.

I don't consider it a mistake to have fallen in love with you. You are an amazing woman, a woman I'd gladly spend the rest of my life with. Every minute with you was invigorating life to me.

But I deceived you, thinking if I told you that I was married you'd reject me. I deceived my wife, too, by not telling her about you until after I married you. My foolish insecurity greatly damaged both of you.

My wife gave me an ultimatum—choose you or her. I always thought the godly Muslim man could handle having two wives at once. Apparently I am not that man.

My first wife has a prior claim to me. She also is the mother of my three children. I see no other way but to choose her. I'm so very sorry.

I was ecstatic when I heard you were pregnant, as I really wanted to have children with you too. I'm putting aside some funds in a special account (look on the back of this letter) to help you raise our child. I hope that in spite of your understandable anger at me you will allow me to write to our child and tell him/ her how much I love him/her. Of course, that's your decision, and I'll respect it.

Please go on to live a full life. Fall in love with a more worthy man than I. Forget about me. Though I will never forget you.

Your husband,

Hendri

They turned over the letter. On the back was a bank account number in Kris's name and information on how to access it without a bank book, including a note from Hendri for the bank teller.

Only the ticking of the clock broke the silence. Sari looked at her mother and saw her smiling and crying at the same time.

"What a fool I was," Kris finally whispered. "All this time I struggled to make ends meet, cursing the man who abandoned us, not knowing he put money away for me to raise you. I'm afraid I've judged him too harshly. All I could see was my pain, and my fear of more pain. I'm so sorry, Sari. You have a very foolish mother."

"He said he wants to write me. Mom, can we contact him? I'd do anything to get a letter from my dad."

"I don't know. I never wanted to see him again. Now, I don't know how I'd find him."

"Could we start at the bank? Maybe they know."

"What if we do find him? Then what?"

"At least you can tell him about his daughter. Maybe he'll write me! Maybe he'll want to be a part of our lives in some way."

"And maybe he'll break our hearts again. Have you thought of that?"

"Mom, he already abandoned us. How much worse is it going to get? Please, can we at least try?"

"All right," Kris conceded. "I'll see if I can find him."

And just like that the great power of fear that the letter had held over her transformed into a fresh hope and a mysterious bank account.

❧ Chapter 67 ❧

SITI WAS WORRIED. For several days now her home had felt more like a funeral parlor. Syukran hardly spoke to them anymore, eating his meals in a brooding silence. Iqbal was hardly ever home. Siti had seen him a couple times outside Kris's house talking to that Christian girl. *Why isn't my husband dealing with this now before it's too late? The* arisan *ladies would certainly not approve of my son dating a Christian!* She wanted to talk to Iqbal, but he never seemed to sit still for long enough.

And then there was her husband. She was used to Abdullah being quiet and distant, but this was something else, a restlessness she'd never observed in him before. As though he were thinking of taking a new job, or a new…surely not! But the more time she spent making herself beautiful and cooking his favorite meals, the less he seemed to notice. *If he's interested in that Kris woman, I'll kill her first!*

The boys and Abdullah were off to school, so Siti was cleaning the house. She worked her way from the kitchen and living room to her bedroom, then the boys' bedroom. With hands on her hips she surveyed the mess: dirty clothes on the floor, beds unmade, Syukran's schoolbag hanging on the chair. Siti did a double take. *Why didn't Syukran take his bag to school? Did he forget? That wasn't like him.*

Then she saw the envelope on his pillow.

She waded through dirty jeans and underwear to snatch up the letter, hoping her son had a pretty good explanation if he were skipping school! She read it.

Dad and Mom,

Uncle Husein called me last night and said that he has a guest staying in his home, a teacher from a *pesantren* in Malaysia. He said the guy was open to giving me a scholarship to study there but wanted to meet me first. I took my savings to buy a ticket to

Jakarta, but Uncle Husein said he'll pay me back when he picks me up at the airport this morning. Sorry I didn't tell you about this, but I was afraid you'd say no, and I really want this scholarship. I promise I'll study hard and make you proud. Don't worry about me; you raised me well, and I'll be fine.

Wassalam,

Syukran

A smile broke through Siti's dark cloud. *Good for you, son! I should be mad at you for not telling us first, but a scholarship to study abroad! I'm so proud of you, son.*

Didn't one of the arisan *ladies have a cousin who worked as a maid in Malaysia? If I'm not mistaken, she sent home quite a bit of money to her family. Maybe Syukran can get a job there after he finishes school and help support us in our old age! Now, which one of the ladies was it? I have to find out.*

Alhamdulillah! This could be the answer to our financial needs that I've been praying for!

Her dreamy bubble burst with her next thought: *I'm not sure if Abdullah will be quite so pleased.*

Chapter 68

OCTOBER WELCOMED THE rainy season in style. For several days in a row the clouds piled up darker and thicker all morning. By noon the wind would start to pick up, and Kris could taste the moisture in the air. Then about one o'clock every afternoon the skies would pummel the earth with rain that stung the skin like bullets, bringing a refreshing chill to the air that was perfect for afternoon naps. In normal rain, people would cover themselves with a rain poncho and still go out on their motorbikes or take an umbrella and still drop by Kris's kiosk, but not in this deluge. Streets were flooded, as were many front yards and a few houses, just for a few hours. Then before sunset the rain would relent from its fury and, on at least one day, compensate everyone's suffering with a rainbow in the sky.

After the rain Kris would reopen her kiosk and wait for Sari to get home from school. Her daughter didn't finish school until 2:30 p.m., so she was often stuck there for hours waiting for the rain to abate, which seemed to suit her just fine. She always came home bubbling about Bali. Kris felt happy for her daughter to get some deserved attention after years of being overlooked but wondered where this romance could realistically end. Surely her daughter wouldn't marry someone from a different religion, would she?

The Monday *arisan* fell victim to the heavy rains. Kris was disappointed because she'd only been to one meeting since her accident and was hoping to get back into the rhythm of the neighborhood. But she also had plenty of other things to occupy her thoughts.

The primary source of both excitement and anxiety was her plan to meet her ex-husband again. It had taken her several days to track him down, but she had, and he sounded genuinely glad to talk to her. They'd spoken by phone twice, and she'd given him their home address so he could fulfill his promise in the letter to write to his daughter. Hendri had asked a hundred questions about Sari and wanted desperately to meet her, but Kris still wasn't sure he wouldn't get her daughter's hopes up and then dash them. So they compromised—he would pay to fly Kris to Jakarta to meet him, and if she then felt comfortable with him meeting Sari, on his next vacation he'd come visit them in Banjar.

Sari seemed thrilled to hear this and even took her mother shopping to buy some more "modern" outfits for her trip. Kris knew in her heart that this was a big risk, letting Hendri back into their lives, even opening the door just a crack. But she needed closure. Sari seemed to need to know who her father was. And Hendri? What did he need? She'd never once thought about it during the seventeen years they'd been separated.

Hendri booked Kris on Garuda Airlines, the most expensive of the domestic fliers, for a flight on Sunday afternoon, October 10. He also reserved a hotel room for her for three nights at the Ritz-Carlton. Kris would have been happy with a small guest house. She'd never imagined staying in a five-star hotel. Apparently Hendri had done well in the banking industry and was now a vice-president of something. She promised she'd call Sari when she got to the hotel and tell her all about it.

On Saturday afternoon, Iqbal brought over a small plastic bag and handed it to Kris.

"My mom said if it's not too much trouble, could you please take this to Syukran? It's his favorite Banjar snack, *dodol* from Kandangan. If you call him or Uncle Husein from the hotel, they'll probably be able to come pick it up there. The phone numbers are in the bag."

"Of course! I'd be happy to." Kris smiled graciously.

Sari nodded in agreement and grinned at Bali. Kris noticed this and gave them both some final instructions.

"While I'm gone, I trust you two to behave yourselves! Remember, talking only on the porch or at Bali's house, not inside this house. You got it?"

"Yes, Mom."

"Yes, 'Bu."

Kris trusted her daughter but knew from experience how easy it was to "fall" in love.

"I'm going over to say good-bye to Ibu Aaminah. Be back in a jiffy."

"OK, Mom." Sari sat down on the porch, and Iqbal sat beside her. Kris turned back to add something but stopped, since they looked lost in each other anyway.

Ibu Aaminah was fussing with her new bougainvillea, which was now waist high and about to outgrow its pot, chanting in a quiet voice one of the Prophet Muhammad's favorite prayers, which had become one of her favorites as well:

> *O Allah, place light in my heart*
> *Light in my sight*
> *Light in my hearing*
> *Light on my right and on my left*
> *Light above me, light below me.*
> *O Allah, who knows*
> *The innermost secrets of our hearts*
> *Lead me out of the darkness*
> *Into the Light.*

Praying this prayer for many years had led her into many interesting experiences, new perspectives, and unusual friendships. She wondered when Allah would next bless her with another gift of light.

She heard the gate creak and straightened up slowly, without complaining over the discomfort in her hip. Cheerfully she turned to welcome her visitor.

"Ibu Kris! How are you?"

"Fine, Ibu. And you?"

"I'm still moving around, thank God. Are you all ready for your trip tomorrow?"

"Yes, I just came by to say farewell to you tonight in case you're busy at a wedding or something tomorrow."

"How kind of you! Would you like to come in?" Ibu Aaminah waved her hand toward the front door.

"No, thank you. I can't stay too long. Still have some packing to do and dinner on the stove. I just wanted to thank you once again for all you've done for me. For many years, I think, I would have been glad to leave this neighborhood but didn't know where else to go. Now I feel like even being gone three days I'm going to miss it."

"Well, dear, I didn't do anything really. I just gave the others the chance to meet the real you. Once they began to see what I see, their perspectives changed." Ibu Aaminah patted Kris's shoulder affectionately.

"Ibu, I wanted to share something with you, if that's OK." Kris looked questioningly and received a nod. "This week I went back and read Siti Hajar's story again, preparing myself to meet my own 'Ibrahim.' Remember how the two sons, Ishmael and Ishak, separated and didn't get along? Well, I found out that there was one event that brought the two boys back together as family once again. It was at their father's funeral. They stood side by side to bury him."

"How interesting!"

"It made me think: the two wives could never get along, but the two sons found a meeting place. Each generation has a new choice."

Ibu Aaminah wondered aloud, "How will we ever get our generation to make that choice? Or is it too late for us? Do we have to wait for Sari's generation? What will it take to bring Ibrahim's two families back together once again?"

A brand new thought popped into Kris's mind and slipped out before she had time to catch herself. "Maybe someone has to die."

꧁ Chapter 69 ꧂

SARI WOKE UP at 5:10 a.m. with the images of her dream still vivid in her mind. She grabbed her journal just like her mother had taught her and wrote down her dream.

October 10

I saw Nina's family begging on the street. No one would give to them, their heads hung down with discouragement. Then the scene changed, and I was the beggar on an empty road, all alone. I saw dust rise up, and in the distance the glint of sun on gold. A golden chariot drove up to me with a glorious king driving it. Surely he would be generous to me! But when he stopped next to me, he held out his hand and asked, "What will you give me?" I emptied out my pockets and found I had nothing to give— but I drew close and kissed his feet with joy. He took my hand and pulled me up into the chariot and gave me a hug. With his arm around my shoulder we rode off together... I felt like I was adopted!

Sari puzzled over the dream for a while, wondering if the king in the dream was her long-lost father who was going to take her back again. Wouldn't that be amazing! She also wondered why she was a beggar. And what did the king mean, "What will you give me?" What could her father (if the king *were* her father) want from her?

She reminded herself to share the dream with her mom and went back to sleep.

Unfortunately, with the busy excitement of getting to the airport, Sari forgot all about it until her mom was already soaring away on the wings of Garuda, blessed by God with an afternoon free of rain for her journey.

Oh well. I'll just tell her when she gets back.

❦ Chapter 70 ❧

SAIFULLAH AND FACHMI were less than twenty miles from the Bellagio outside a luxurious mansion in Senayan owned by a certain Dr. Wally. Their attire betrayed their intent—black clothing from head to toe, including gloves and ski masks. Saifullah carried a 45-caliber FN Llama Max; Fachmi, a Smith and Wesson.

They slipped noiselessly through the tall pine trees looking for open windows with their mini-binoculars. Finally Fachmi got a clear view into the living room through a half-open curtain.

"Three kids watching TV. Profile says doc has three kids."

"See the parents?"

"Not yet."

"We've got to get them all together before anyone grabs a cell phone. Keep looking."

Fachmi kept focused on the living room, while Saifullah edged to the right for a look in the next window. He raised his own mini-binoculars and examined the kitchen. Mom was making coffee. Now if they could just find Dad. He headed back to Fachmi's position.

"Mom in kitchen to the right of the living room. Any sign of Dad?"

"Not yet."

"You're sure he's home?"

"Yeah, I followed him home from work. That's his Mercedes in the driveway. He's here all right. Probably on the Internet."

The easiest thing to do would be just to shoot them all. But that wasn't part of the plan. And for this mission to work, every single part of the plan had to fall into place. That meant getting the family all together.

"Let's get him downstairs. Make the call."

Fachmi took out a cell phone and was about to dial Dr. Wally's health emergency number, given only to his patients and the hospital where he worked, when Saifullah took another look through the binocs and hissed, "Hold it. He just walked through the living room. Looks like he's headed to the kitchen. Let's move."

They crossed the grass to the front door unafraid of being seen by the neighbors since the doctor's estate was surrounded by a ten-foot-high cement wall. Saifullah checked the door. Unlocked. This was going to be easier than he had anticipated.

"Get both parents into the living room. Go."

He eased the door open and, guns forward, they entered the front hallway and eased the door closed. Saifullah pointed down the hallway to the living room while he turned right, hoping for a shortcut to the kitchen. He entered a room for receiving guests. There were large oil paintings on the walls, and he felt the softness of the carpet beneath his feet but had no time to appreciate the doctor's wealth. There was a door on the far side of the room, conveniently situated to serve tea to the guests, he thought. He pushed the door open cautiously and stepped into the kitchen. Doc was sipping a cup of coffee at the bar. Mom was pouring a cup for herself.

"What the—?"

Saifullah pointed the gun at the doctor's head and ordered, "Do exactly as I say."

Mom turned around and dropped her cup with a clang onto the counter. Saifullah could sense a scream coming. He put his finger to his lips while touching the gun barrel gently behind her husband's ear. She held it in, at least for the moment.

He spoke softly but distinctly. "Good. Noise annoys me. If you choose to scream, my annoyed trigger finger might accidentally jerk. Then you'd have more than spilt coffee to clean up in here. Keep quiet, and you might keep me happy."

"What do you want?" Doctor Wally tried to sound strong, but Saifullah could see the trembling. *Probably sees blood every day of his life. Just not his own.*

"Right now all I want is for you to keep your hands where I can see them and to walk slowly into the living room. Can you do that without annoying me?"

They obediently headed for the living room. Fachmi had the three kids wide-eyed and quiet on the couch. Only the youngest, a little girl of about five, was whimpering softly.

"Each of you please sit on opposite ends of the couch with your children." The parents sat, their kids clinging to a leg or arm, parents trying their best to calm them.

Saifullah directed Fachmi: "Jojo, pause the movie. Thank you. Now, if you all can be quiet and cooperative and keep from annoying me, we will only be here for a few minutes, and then we'll let you get back to your movie. Nod your head if you will be cooperative." Everyone nodded.

"Good. My first cooperative task for you is to take out any cell phones in your pockets and place them on the coffee table." Doctor Wally went first, placing his cell phone on the table, and nodded for the others to follow suit. The two older children did the same. Mom, voice trembling, whispered that hers was by the sink. Fachmi brought it back and placed it beside the others.

"How about you, sweetie?" Saifullah addressed the whimperer. "Do you have a cell phone?" The girl shook her head no. "After this your parents will definitely buy you one, I promise."

He took all the phones but the doctor's and dropped them in a black cloth bag. "I'll be borrowing these for a week; then I'll give them back. I'll let the good doctor keep his phone for now in case I want to talk to him. Fair enough?" He stuffed the bag in his belt, then took the doctor's phone and explained, "But I'll leave it somewhere in the front yard for you to find later. Jojo, the telephone line." Fachmi disappeared for a few seconds then came back and lifted the telephone receiver, listening hopefully for silence. He smiled.

"Now to answer the astute doctor's earlier question, 'What do I want?' Actually, I'm not here to steal anything but to give you something." He pulled an odd-looking silver bracelet out of his pocket, so small it looked like a doll toy. Flipping it around casually in his fingers he squatted down before the youngest girl again. "I want to give you this special bracelet. Don't worry; it won't hurt you." He handed it to the mother. "Put it on her. Now. Before I get annoyed." The sharp edge in his voice sent chills down the mother's spine, and with shaking hands she slipped it over her daughter's slender wrist.

"Lock it." Mom clicked the latch, and the bracelet locked. A red light started to flash.

"Now, isn't that cool? All your friends will be jealous that their bracelets don't flash. But you may not get to see your friends for a few days. I would suggest you keep her home from the *Ar-Rahman* kindergarten for a few days. Your other kids are welcome to go to their schools. And you can feel free to continue your painting lessons and visit your salon in Kelapa Gading. And you, doc, I'd be very annoyed if you didn't continue your practice at the Bellagio and the Medistra Hospital. We don't want any of your sick patients to *die*, now do we?

"No, we're not going to take anything from you. We just have some new medical equipment that we'd like the good doctor here to test for us. These tests are rather risky; some would say controversial. But if they are successful we will make millions. Tomorrow the equipment will be delivered to your clinic in Bellagio. Please clean out one entire room in the morning to make room for our new equipment and standing room for up to four people. Tuesday afternoon a brilliant scientist and doctor from Singapore will arrive to train you in the testing procedure. Unfortunately, he couldn't get permission for these tests in his nation, so we're trying to be more accommodating. We'll be bringing in our own patients, so you don't have to worry about you or your patients being our guinea pigs. The testing will be finished by the end of the week, and we'll pack up our equipment and move out. On that day I will also remotely turn off the flashing red light on this bracelet, and it can be safely removed from your daughter's arm.

"Oh, you're wondering about the purpose of the bracelet? This is called an 'insurance bracelet.' If anything happens to this bracelet, someone in your family will be punished. If it is broken, if the latch is lifted and it is removed from her arm, if it travels outside the city limits of Jakarta, any of these things will transmit an electronic signal back to us, and we will know that Dr. Wally's family has decided not to be cooperative. This will annoy us. Your son's shattered knees may make it hard for him in his next soccer match. Your daughter may find it hard to play piano with no fingers. Or one of you will die. And don't think you can hide from us. Your cell phones have provided us with plenty of places to look for you, and if we look there and don't find you we might just be annoyed enough to kill your friends off till we do find you. And please don't go to the police. If we even sniff one undercover cop around your clinic we'll start finding more unpleasant ways to motivate you. Am I completely understood?"

Doctor Wally seemed resigned to his fate. "Yes."

"How about, 'Yes, I will fully cooperate.'"

"Yes, I will fully cooperate."

"Good. Now I feel better. Remember, this will all be over in a week, and you'll have your lives back to normal. Until then."

Saifullah and Fachmi turned and left the house, dropping Dr. Wally's cell phone in a bunch of gardenias, where he'd hear it the next time someone called. Instead of heading for the gate they took to the trees, climbed over the wall where they'd come in, put on gold helmets and gold jackets that said Corona Racing Team, and headed back to the safe house.

❧ Chapter 71 ❧

IF ONLY MIRRORS weren't so honest, Kris thought.

She'd picked out her favorite of the two new outfits Sari had made her buy. It was a beige woman's suit with a jacket and knee-length skirt and a white blouse that showed just a little more neckline than Kris was used to. She looked very professional. If only she looked as pretty.

She did her best with her makeup and hair, but she wasn't going to look twenty-three again no matter how hard she tried. Anyway, what was the point? This wasn't a date. It was an interview, and she was the interviewer not the interviewee. *He* was the one who had a point to prove, that he was sincere and stable enough to bring blessing into Sari's life and not a curse.

It was almost ten o'clock. Hendri had said to call his cell phone at ten to set their lunch plans. She didn't know how she'd be able to eat she was so nervous. Besides, the Ritz-Carlton's breakfast buffet was enough to last her for the whole day.

She played with her hair in the mirror until the long hand of the clock hit the twelve. Turning from the mirror, she picked up her cell phone and dialed Hendri's number.

He answered on the third ring. "Kristyana?"

"Yes, Hendri?"

"Thanks for calling. Everything all right at the hotel?"

"Oh, yes, it's fine! I can't believe you're paying for me to stay in such a fancy place."

"Don't worry about it. Our bank gets a corporate rate there. Kristyana, I'm dying to see you."

"I'm looking forward to this too."

"But something's come up. I hate to do this to you, but we had a robbery last night at one of our branches in Bandung, and the president wants me to go out there and deal with it. What with traffic being horrific there, I won't be home till late. I feel terrible about this! But my hands are tied."

Something about this situation sounds familiar. Hendri, don't do this to me all over again!

"Sure, I understand. How about tomorrow?"

"Definitely! I already informed my staff weeks ago that tomorrow I have to go to my chiropractic appointment from ten to twelve. Actually, I can probably get the doctor to get me in a bit early and get out of there by eleven. That would give us two hours together, including lunch. How about you meet me there? It's walking distance from your hotel, just down the street at Bellagio Mall. I'll call you when I get out of my chiropractic adjustment, and we can meet at a restaurant there. They've got everything: Chinese, Italian, American, Mexican, Japanese. Is that OK with you?"

"OK, sounds fine. I'll meet you there tomorrow then."

"Great. Sorry, but I really got to run. It's chaos here. See you tomorrow."

"See you."

Kris turned back to the mirror for comfort.

"What do you think? Is he the same old Hendri? Is he all charm and no follow-through? Don't let him break your heart again, girl! Or Sari's!" Her mirror image had nothing new to add to the conversation, so she stood up and walked to the window. The skyscrapers of Jakarta were a wonder to her. Banjarmasin had nothing like this!

"All dressed up and nowhere to go. Kris, don't stay here moping. Go out and have some fun. At least let the Jakarta men appreciate your new outfit!"

Now I'm talking to myself! I must be getting old.

The fact was, she wasn't particularly interested in spending her limited resources taxiing around to malls where she couldn't afford to buy anything. As long as she ate lunch at the hotel, Hendri would cover it. So, what to do, what to do?

Suddenly she remembered the *dodol* she was supposed to deliver to Syukran. At least she could take care of her good deed for the day. She opened the plastic bag and rummaged around for the paper with the phone numbers written on it.

She tried calling the first number, Syukran's, but a recording said it was unavailable. She tried the second number, and a friendly female voice answered.

"*Assalamu alaikum.*"

"*Wa alaikum assalam,*" Kris answered. "Is this the home of Pak Husein?"

"Yes, I'm his wife. How can I help you?"

"Hi, my name is Kris. I just arrived in Jakarta from Banjarmasin, and Pak Abdullah and Ibu Siti gave me some *dodol* from Kandangan to deliver to their son Syukran."

"Yes, Ibu Siti is my husband's sister. How can I help you?"

"Well, I'd like to bring the *dodol* to you, but don't know where you live."

"I thought you said the *dodol* was for Syukran."

"Yes, he's staying with you, isn't he?"

"No. We haven't seen Siti's son for nearly two years, since our last visit to Banjarmasin."

"Oh! Well, they told me he's been with you for a few days now."

"No, we haven't seen or heard from him."

"I'm so sorry to bother you! I'll call Ibu Siti and sort this out."

"No problem. Give them our regards."

"Yes, I will. Good-bye."

Kris hung up the phone confused. *Where was that boy?* She thought she'd better let his parents know. Maybe Syukran had already contacted them with his new location, but surely Iqbal would have told Sari to tell her.

She text messaged Sari, who was still in school, to ask Iqbal for his parents' phone number and text her back. Now she'd have to wait.

Maybe she could go downstairs to the salon and get a manicure! Would Hendri pay for that? Ditching her for some bank robbery in Bandung…Yes, he could pay for a manicure.

Later that afternoon, Sari sent her Ibu Siti's and Pak Abdullah's cell phone numbers. She decided on protocol over personality and dialed Ibu Siti.

"*Assalamu alaikum.*"

"*Wa alaikum assalam.* Ibu Siti? This is Kris."

"Yes. Did you meet Syukran?" *Sounds like Ibu Siti's been drinking lemonade with no sugar.*

"Well, that's what I'm calling about. Syukran's phone number isn't working, so I called Pak Husein. His wife told me that they haven't seen or heard from Syukran at all. He's certainly not staying with them. Have you heard from Syukran?"

"No, but that's impossible! Did you dial a wrong number?"

"No, they asked me to give their regards to you. What should I do with the *dodol*?"

"I don't know. Abdullah will be home soon. I'll ask him. Good-bye."

"Good-bye."

That was rather abrupt! Give the woman some grace, Kris. She's probably worried about where her son could be.

Nothing about this trip seemed to make sense.

❧ Chapter 72 ❧

ON MONDAY MORNING Dr. Wally kissed his wife and kids good-bye and went to work. They had decided to keep all three kids home from school for a couple days to see how things went. His wife held him close a few seconds longer than usual, wondering if she'd ever see him again. The bracelet's red light kept flashing a reminder to them all that they'd better be *cooperative*.

The first thing he did at his clinic was to announce to his staff that he'd ordered some new equipment and could they please clean out room number three so they could store the new stuff there? His answers to their queries about what the equipment was for were rather vague.

The equipment arrived at noon. Two men wearing light blue uniforms and ID badges stating they were employees of Dr. Wally's Clinic got out of a white van with the same name and logo on the side. The mall security guard called Dr. Wally to confirm. Dr. Wally answered that yes, he had ordered the new equipment and to have it sent straight up. The guard took the delivery crew around to a back door and unlocked it for them so as not to disturb the shoppers coming in the main entrance.

Saifullah parked the van as close to the door as possible and jumped out. As he blocked the back door open he examined its lock carefully. *Shouldn't be too hard to force tomorrow if we need to.* Meanwhile his young assistant opened the van's back doors for the guard to inspect. The guard took a peek in the back of the van, seemed satisfied, and left them to their work.

Saifullah's assistant had no idea what the supposedly high-tech equipment in the van was useful for; his boss had chosen not to explain it to him. Saifullah came around and grabbed one end of a heavy machine, looking at him to grab the other. They wrestled it out of the van and over to the elevator, then up to the third floor. Grunting and groaning, they managed to get it into the clinic, then into room three, where they set it down and paused to catch their breath. Dr. Wally said nothing, and neither did they.

Eight more trips, and they were done. Saifullah closed the door to room three and reminded Dr. Wally that tomorrow afternoon the esteemed doctor from Singapore would come in to assemble the equipment and start training Dr. Wally on how to use it. He recommended the doctor keep the room locked, and as they left the doctor compliantly acceded to his request.

Saifullah paused outside the front door of the clinic and lifted his chin slightly to the opposite side of the walkway, to the main events room. Then he bent down and tied his shoe slowly, giving his apprentice a chance to really look at the place where tomorrow he would make history.

Back at the safe house, Amin had an identical set of three of the medical equipment items. Like the ones delivered to Dr. Wally's, they didn't work. This was because they were merely Trojan horses to transport the more important equipment, the items they needed to assemble the bomb.

Amin hadn't been trained personally by the father of Indonesian bomb-making—Dr. Azhari—like Dulmatin, Nana (who assembled the bombs for the Marriott and Ritz-Carlton), and many others. But he had Noordin M. Top's bomb construction manual as a PDF file and had practiced with this particular bomb several times. It was his job to train the "bride" in how to assemble the bomb and detonate it.

From one of the machines he would remove a battery and clip the machine's electrical cables and electrical nodes; from another machine he would extract a timer and some hidden vials of sulfur and aluminum powder; from the third he would release a false bottom and pull down a container full of potassium chloride, six times as much as the other two chemicals, to mix with them into a black powder. Then all he needed to add was a layered firing device that would be attached to a cable with a simple, hand-held open/close switch. And this little beauty would fit in a small suitcase; in fact, there was a special one they used for practice.

The dummy equipment that Amin practiced on used sugar, salt, and powdered milk. No sense getting blown up during rehearsal.

As Saifullah pulled the van up to the safe house he gave some last-minute instructions to his young apprentice.

"Amin will teach you how to assemble the wedding gift. Practice it again and again until you can do it with your eyes closed. Don't stop practicing until Amin says you can stop.

"After that, go over the timetable with Amin until you can say it forward and backward without thinking. Tomorrow we leave nothing to chance. We will be perfect and glorious. We will bring the mighty to their knees.

"If you finish all that before bedtime, record a video for your family and for this nation, a message they will not forget. *Al-jihad sabiluna!*"

"*Al-jihad sabiluna!*"

❧ Chapter 73 ❦

AFTER NEARLY TWENTY-FOUR hours combined in their three flights, Louis Staunton and the two US Secret Service men assigned to him were grateful to hear the United Airlines pilot announce they were beginning their descent into Jakarta. The Secret Service men had taken turns sleeping, but Louis had never been able to nap on airplanes. He was exhausted and ready for a hot shower and a good night's sleep before tomorrow's event.

Louis hadn't wasted his plane time. He'd brought a two-inch thick pile of notes on the upcoming review of federal immigration laws. However, every time he'd started to take it out of his briefcase he'd ended up putting it back and returning to his notes on his Jakarta speech.

The speech was basically written two weeks ago, but he was still agonizing over a couple key issues in it. The first was whom to quote. He had a terrific quote from Imam Feisal of New York, a well-known American Muslim moderate who had written widely on how Islamic and Western values are not entirely incompatible, just needing people committed to bridge the gaps and make the relationship work. Feisal's Cordoba Institute, which had both Muslims and Christians on its board, was trying to establish a center for interfaith peacemaking at the site of the World Trade Center tragedy. Some Americans interpreted this as Muslim triumphalism, when in fact it was precisely the opposite; it was an effort to build a more peaceful world. Louis had attended an event during Ramadan this year where a Jewish synagogue had cooked the *iftar* meal and invited Imam Feisal and his followers to break the fast in their house of worship and discuss how to improve relationships between them. After hearing Feisal speak and getting to chat with him a few minutes after the event, Louis felt a great affection for the man. He hoped to be working with him more in the future.

On the other hand, maybe he should go with a quote from a local moderate Muslim leader. He'd downloaded three or four from the Wahid Institute website, a peace-promoting institution founded by the late former president Abdurrahman Wahid, more widely known by his nickname "Gus Dur." Yet he didn't want to come across as supporting any local political party, and the PKB party boasted a lot of Gus Dur's followers. Whom to quote was a conundrum. He hated holding up America as the model for the world—no one outside America believed it anyway—but he recognized the dangers of quoting well-known locals without understanding the cultural context through which his audience would filter the words.

Maybe a third alternative: quote a moderate Egyptian scholar? He started thumbing through his notes for the right quote.

Meanwhile, he still hadn't decided on whether to connect the long list of Indonesian bombings to the tragedy of 9/11 or not. Could the locals feel that was unfair, as there were no Indonesians involved in that heinous attack?

There were other concerns lying just under his consciousness, thoughts he refused to waste thinking time on but there nonetheless. *Was he a target? Was he a fool taking this risk? What happened to the six US Secret Service men the president had promised? Were two enough to protect him? And if everything went well, would Selena still be waiting for him when he came home? When he left, she didn't look too happy.*

Both Service men were awake now. Bill Rogers leaned forward to pull on his size eleven shoes. Bill was a big man, raised on rich Wisconsin milk and cheese. His blond hair had been trimmed so short since his college days that no one even noticed it was starting to disappear. Bill had the perfect physique for football—he was big, strong, lean, and fast. He made all-American his junior year playing tight end for University of Wisconsin. There was talk of a shot at the pros, but his senior year his quality of play inexplicably tapered off. That was the year President Ronald Reagan was shot and nearly killed. When Bill saw USSS agent Tim McCarthy take a bullet to save the president, he knew that's what he wanted to do with his life. He couldn't graduate soon enough, already applying to the Secret Service Academy before his transcripts were even in his hands.

Bill was just over fifty now, with plenty of wrinkles showing above and around his piercing blue eyes and a broken nose. His supervisor had informed him that this might end up being his last field assignment. He was facing a tough decision between requesting to stay on a few more years at a desk job or just retiring outright. Desk jobs held no appeal for him. The only reason he'd consider staying would be the camaraderie with the few old timers still around. His supervisor had tried pushing him toward teaching at the Academy, but he had no patience with the young recruits these days, including the one sitting next to him.

Dante Prince was the opposite of Bill Rogers in almost every way except his athleticism. Dante was a young African-American who grew up in East Los Angeles. He had received a good education at a private Catholic school and an even better education on the streets. Dante had joined the Service for the risk factor. But he wasn't a star pupil at the Academy and had already screwed up badly less than a year after being assigned to the New York office. Busting up a counterfeit money operation, someone got shot who wasn't supposed to get shot, and Dante was in the doghouse—which in this case meant getting stuck with babysitter Rogers on a boring Third-World jaunt to protect someone about as far from being president as you could get. He'd have happily told Rogers how much the whole thing sucked if he didn't need Rogers's evaluation to be positive enough to get him another shot at New York. For now, he was stuck listening to the old man's endless stories.

No sooner did Bill see Dante's eyes open than he started another one.

"You ever been to Indonesia?" Dante shook his head no. "I was here with Trailblazer in 2005. That's George W. Bush's code name by the way, Rookie. 'Blazer tried some local cuisine, something with peanut sauce, and was up all night with diarrhea. Eventually one of us had to go look for some Imodium; dang near impossible to find anything in this country. It's an organizational disaster.

"Yup, security for this event is gonna be a mess. Not like you got trained in at the Academy. This ain't no NSSE affair with magnetometers, K-9, and explosive detection units sweeping for bombs, countersnipers on rooftops. No siree. Most likely gonna be you, me, and a couple local cops. Events like this we rely on scanning faces, anticipating entry points, not on technology. You sure you're up for this, Rookie?"

"I've got you to teach me the finer points, don't I?" Prince's sarcasm was barely held in check.

"You better thank your lucky stars you do! If there's a terrorist or madman in the crowd, I'll spot him. Did I ever tell you that's how I got into the Service in the first place?"

Dante wanted to answer in the affirmative but bit his tongue and readied himself to hear it again.

"Nineteen eighty. Ronald Reagan, whose code name was Rawhide, was shot and nearly assassinated. *Rawhide*—what a great moniker! That guy was as tough as the cowboys he played on TV. That madman Hinckley fired six shots. One would have probably taken out the president if agent Tim McCarthy hadn't blocked its path. But the sixth shot bounced off the limo and entered Reagan's left armpit. When they pushed him into the limo he was vomiting blood, so they took him straight to George Washington University Hospital. He had an emergency operation to get out the bullet and drain the fluid in his lungs, but the quick actions of the USSS saved his life. As he was getting anesthetized before the operation, what do you think was on Reagan's mind? He told the team of doctors, 'I'm hoping that all of you are Republicans!'" Rogers guffawed loudly at this joke, one he never got tired of telling.

"You see, your job is to scan the crowd looking for Hinckley. Watch their eyes. Are they looking somewhere no one else is looking? Watch their neck muscles—tight or loose? Watch their hands—fidgeting? Reaching for something? Watch their movements—jerky? Carrying some extra weight under their clothes that restricts their movement even slightly? You getting all this, Rookie?"

It's not like I didn't go over this a million times at the Academy. Chill out, old man!

"Yes, sir."

"I was in Chicago when *Renegade* was making his acceptance speech. I spotted this one guy who kept looking toward the front, but not at Obama. Finally he fixed his eyes on something or someone and started pushing through the crowd. I moved to intercept. As he got closer to his goal I could see his eyes widening, see his chest breathing faster. 'This guy's gonna kill someone,' I thought. There's all kinds of big shots in the crowd, too, you know. I pulled my SIG but kept it down so the crowd wouldn't see. They're all chanting, 'Yes we can! Yes we can!' and I'm thinking they're just encouraging Hinckley here, see. Finally I reach him, and he hardly sees me coming. I tell him, 'Freeze,' and he turns toward me with a hand in his pocket. I'm thinking, 'What's he got in there? Derringer? Knife? Pepper spray?' I put the gun two feet from his chest and tell him to take his hand out of his pocket slowly, or I'll blow him away. The sweat is pouring off this guy like Michael Jordan after a playoff game. He takes his hand out, and I spin and cuff him. Then I check his pocket, and you know what I find?"

Dante shook his head.

"A love note. For Oprah. The guy's an Oprah stalker and figures *Renegade's* acceptance speech is his best chance to get to her. All he wanted to do was slip the note in her pocket, kiss her on the cheek, and walk away. What a whack job!"

Dante couldn't wait for the plane to land. "Cool story, sir."

"Oh, I got a million of 'em. When you've been in the Service as long as I have, you've seen everything, and I mean *everything*! Did I ever tell you about..."

Dante closed his eyes again and wished that this trip were already over.

☜ Chapter 74 ☞

ONDAY AFTERNOON WHEN Abdullah got home from checking on
the boys at the church construction site, Siti told him about Kris's
phone call. He hardly had a chance to respond when a motorbike horn
honked outside. Abdullah looked out the front window and could see the
bright orange color of the post office delivery bike. *Surely it's not for us*,
he thought. Abdullah couldn't remember the last time they'd received a
letter. He went outside to check just in case.

Sure enough, it was for them. And on the top left corner of the envelope was Syukran's name and no return address. Siti snatched it out of
her husband's hand before he even got back into the house and ripped it
open. She started reading it out loud but couldn't finish.

Assalamu alaikum Wr. Wb.

Dear Mom and Dad,

I'm sorry I had to lie to you, but it was the right thing to do.
I've been given an awesome opportunity to prove my love for
Islam. I want to restore the family honor. I want to finish what
Dad should have. I want to save my and Bali's generation from
Western corruption. I want to make you both proud.

This is something I have to do. It's *fardhu ain*—it's a sin for
me to *not* do it. I'm sorry you didn't get a chance to say good-
bye to me. Watch the TV, and you can say good-bye to me there.

I'll be waiting for you in heaven. Make sure you get there.

Wassalam,

Syukran

Siti collapsed on the green plastic chair they had on their front porch, shaking from head to toe. Abdullah read the letter through twice, pushing down his pain as a father, pushing down his fear, trying to think rationally what to do. He felt his throat restricting, his blood pounding in his temples. It was like the world had stopped spinning and was waiting for him to start it up again. But the only visible clue to his heart's suffering came out in a whisper. "My son! What have you done?"

Abdullah turned to enter the house. As he passed by, Siti grabbed his shirt, stopping him in his tracks. She tugged his shirt downward till he was bending over her, then suddenly she slapped him hard.

"This is all your fault!" Siti screamed. "You drove my son away. He's going to die, and it's all your fault! I hate you! I hate you!" Now she was standing, pounding him on his chest and screaming hysterically. Abdullah grabbed her elbows and pushed her in the house before the neighbors all showed up.

Iqbal abandoned his homework and came running out of his bedroom. "What's going on?" He stared at his mother thrashing about violently while Dad tried to keep her from hurting herself. Abdullah let go of Siti's arm long enough to throw the letter toward his son. He paid for it with fingernails drawing blood on his neck.

Iqbal read the letter and exploded. "That idiot! He's going to do something really stupid, isn't he? How could he do this?"

Abdullah looked to his son for help. "Bali, I need your help. There may be a way to save your brother, but I've got to go right now. Can you take care of Mom? Don't let her hurt herself, OK?"

Iqbal looked like he'd rather go with Abdullah but nodded and took over gripping Mom's elbows.

"Come on, Mom," he said in a soothing voice. "Let's sit down on the couch."

Abdullah grabbed the keys to the motorbike and headed back to the church.

White paint clung stubbornly to Hafiz's hands as he washed them under the hose after his afternoon's work. Pastor David had mentioned maybe five more days of work, and they'd be done. He couldn't wait. Spending every afternoon working in the hot sun was such a drag. Hopefully it wouldn't keep raining them out, putting off their freedom indefinitely. He was ready to move on to more exciting activities, like Syukran did.

Abdullah pulled up on the bike and called Hafiz over. He ambled toward his teacher, drying his hands on his shirt.

"Hafiz, this is extremely important. Do not lie to me. Do you know where Syukran is?"

Hafiz was taken aback. "In Jakarta, right? Where you sent him."

"What do you mean?"

"Don't worry, sir. I can keep a secret." Hafiz glanced around to make sure no one else could hear. Then he leaned in closer. "Syuk just text messaged me this afternoon. He told me the Malaysia scholarship and all that crazy stuff you were saying at school was just a cover for your secret JI cell and that you sent him on assignment to Jakarta to teach Uncle Sam a lesson in Muslim diplomacy. Told me to watch for him on TV!"

"Let me see your phone!" Hafiz turned over the cell phone, opened to Syukran's message. Abdullah memorized it. Hafiz hadn't been lying.

"You must be pretty proud of him! Hey, if you need recruits for more assignments, I can get them for you. You sure had me fooled with your 'Christian lover' tricks the other day. Now it all makes sense."

But Abdullah wasn't listening. He started the bike and zoomed away.

On the drive home he had time to think through his strategy. One thing was for sure: he couldn't go to the police. Not only would they shoot Syukran on sight, but if the boy had told anyone else that Abdullah was a JI cell leader, he'd be arrested, and his past would all come out. No one would believe that he was no longer that man.

No, the only way was to try to get to Syukran first. He had no clue when the "lesson" would be; he just had to get to Jakarta and hope to find Syukran before anything happened. It was the only way to save his son.

Abdullah paused on the side of Kelayan B street and called a travel agent he had known for years, who booked him a one-way ticket on the first flight in the morning for Jakarta. Then he swung a U-turn and went to pick it up. He didn't have the Rp.450,000 the agent asked for, so he gave him all the money in his wallet, about Rp.220,000, and his driver's license, promising to pay the rest when he returned. He had to use "the voice," saying that it was a matter of life or death, till the agent reluctantly gave in.

Back at home, Siti had considerately fallen asleep. Abdullah explained to Iqbal what he planned to do. Iqbal offered his dad all his savings, which only came to about Rp.200,000, and agreed to stay home the next day and take care of Mom. Then Abdullah packed a change of clothes in his backpack, had a bite of rice and tempeh with his son, prayed desperately to God during the *Mahgrib sholat*, went to borrow another Rp.1,000,000 from Pak Darsuni, prayed once again at *'Isha*, and tried to sleep.

As he lay there waiting to fall asleep, his dream of Mullah Omar came back to him. "Are you ready to die for Islam?" Then the *rat-a-tat* of the AK-47 sending Syukran to the hereafter.

No, Allah, it can't end this way. Don't let my son pay for my sins. I'm the one who deserves to die. Take me, but let him live.

❦ Chapter 75 ❦

Kris awoke Tuesday morning not with Hendri on her mind but another dream. God had spoken to her through dreams off and on since her childhood, but lately they seemed to be coming more frequently and more *loudly*, as though they were extra important.

She had forgotten to pack her journal, so she tried to memorize the dream by repeating it to herself out loud.

"Let's see. Sari was going to dance ballet in a theater, at night. I went to the theater, but there was a security guard who wouldn't let me in. I protested with tears, 'I have to see my daughter dance!' But he refused. *What does that mean?*

"Then the head of the ballet came to the door. I knew her and felt sure she'd know me and let me in. But she didn't let me in. She said something like, 'Nice to see you! I need you to do something very important. My baby is crying. Could you hold him please?' And she gave me her baby boy!

"What happened next? I remember I called to her, 'But I want to see *my* daughter dance!' as the ballet master disappeared back inside the door. I felt terribly disappointed, like crying, like the baby I was holding was crying. But this compassion welled up inside me, and I started singing to the baby softly, 'Ishmael, Ishmael,' and he stopped crying. Then I thought, 'I guess someone else will have to watch Sari dance.' What a curious dream! God, what does this mean?"

Kris pondered the dream all through her buffet breakfast downstairs and as she showered and dressed for her "interview." There was a vague sense in her spirit that it was important to her to show love to someone else's child today. Maybe a Muslim baby? She decided that if she saw a mother holding a crying baby today she'd offer to help.

The other outfit Sari had picked out for her consisted of black slacks and a deep purple top with a half-turtleneck collar and long sleeves. It had no buttons or zippers, and the elastic stretch hugged her body, accentuating her figure. *It shows my bulging waistline too well*, she thought.

While she dressed and did her makeup, she flipped on Metro TV to hear the news. As she was applying a glossy scarlet lipstick that Sari had lent her, she caught the word *Bellagio* and stopped for a moment to listen. Bellagio was where she was to meet Hendri.

"...*where American Congressman Louis Staunton and Indonesian presidential hopeful M. Rizki Ramadani will be speaking at an event titled 'Peace—the Way Forward.' The event kicks off at 10:00 a.m. and is sponsored by Mr. Ramadani's political party, SALAM. The relative newcomer to Indonesian politics has created a fervor among the youth through his visits to college campuses and use of the Internet to spread his views. Mr. Ramadani has discussed in general terms ideas such as appointing a cabinet of mixed ethnicities and religions, new laws for the protection of minorities, the establishment of a conflict negotiating team made up of moderate Muslim and Christian leaders, and has even offered himself as a mediator in the Palestine conflict. The former university professor has come under heavy fire from more radical groups such as Front Pembela Islam, or FPI, who have threatened to protest outside the Bellagio today. At this point Mr. Ramadani has not officially declared himself a candidate in the next presidential elections, but one of his staff has intimated that the announcement could come any day now.*

"The economy remains sluggish this quarter, with earnings reports from—"

Kris reached over and turned off the TV set. She had never heard of Ramadani or his party SALAM but found herself intrigued. *Maybe he's a kindred spirit. They said ten o'clock? Maybe I could get in to hear part of this event while Hendri gets his back adjustment. I hope I don't need a formal invitation! Well, the least I can do is try.*

It was still only 9:15. Too bad Sari was in school, or she'd call her and tell her about the dream. At least she could text message Sari to call her after school. She wrote a quick message, mostly to remind Sari how much she loved her. These two days apart from her daughter had been hard. How was she ever going to face it when Sari wanted to get married someday and she'd have to let her go?

Oh, Sari! When that day comes, I'll try to be brave and let you go.

❧ Chapter 76 ❧

EVERYTHING WENT AS planned at Dr. Wally's house. The doctor exited his home promptly at 8:30 a.m. as usual, with plenty of time for him to get through the morning traffic to his clinic at Bellagio and open his doors by 9:00 a.m. Except today his Mercedes had a slashed tire. He didn't notice it yet, but so did his wife's minivan. He also ran into a familiar-looking unwanted guest. One of the guys who had delivered the equipment yesterday was standing by his car.

"Good morning, doctor!" Saifullah grinned, and he wasn't just being polite. No, he was in a positively buoyant mood today. This was his day for *redemption*!

"My car has a flat tire."

"Yes, what a shame! And with your patients slated to arrive in less than an hour. Tell you what: why don't you call your receptionist Cynthia and ask her to reschedule all your appointments today, as you'll be coming in at noon and focusing on your training on the new equipment with our doctor from Singapore. Meanwhile, I'll make sure Cynthia can get in the door to make those calls if you'll kindly turn over your keys to the clinic. It'll give me a chance to start assembling the machines before you and our esteemed guest arrive." Saifullah held out his hand.

Dr. Wally hesitated just a moment, then with a sigh turned over his keys.

"Thank you. Have fun playing auto mechanic this morning, and we'll see you at noon, OK?"

Without a word Dr. Wally turned and went back into the house.

Don't be so grumpy, doc! You don't know it, but I'm probably saving your life.

Saifullah trotted into the trees, climbed over the wall, and jumped into the same van he'd used yesterday. Syukran was there waiting. His face looked a little pale.

"Hey, son, you need to go pee again?" Syukran shook his head no. "OK, then let's go."

Saifullah started the van and headed for Bellagio.

The security guard at the front door recognized Saifullah, Syukran, and the van as they pulled into the parking lot. Nearly thirty protesters had already gathered wearing Arab headgear and robes, holding signs like "Death to America," "Yankee Go Home," and "Ramadani Is a Traitor to Islam." Saifullah left Syukran in the van and waded through the crowd to the guard.

"Hey, you've got quite a mob forming here. I hope you have some backup if this gets ugly!"

"Yeah, normally there's just two of us on this shift, but we're trying to get a hold of the other two and have them come in."

"Look, sorry to bother you, but one of the machines we brought yesterday the doc says was malfunctioning and could we take it back and get a replacement? Where do you want us to load it into the van? Looks like a mess out front here."

"Yeah, right. I should call up to Dr. Wally to make sure..."

"Oh, the doc told me to tell you he's running a bit late today. His five-year-old, what's her name? Little Julia, yeah, she threw up just as he was leaving, and he said he had to check her out and change his pants. He gave me the keys to go ahead and open up for Cynthia and deal with the equipment crisis before he gets here." He showed the guard Dr. Wally's keychain.

"All right. I'll call Budi on the walkie-talkie and have him open the same door as yesterday for you. See if you can get your van through this crowd and around back."

"Thanks, and hope you make it through the day OK." *Now that would be luck!*

"Right."

As Saifullah pulled the van through the protestors, he reviewed for the hundredth time Syukran's task.

"We go up to the clinic. I'll tell Cynthia Dr. Wally is coming in at noon and that he said as soon as she's done rescheduling she can leave on break until noon. Next I take out a piece of the bogus equipment and carry it to the van. I'll wait there till I see the mission is accomplished. You go into room three and lock yourself in and build the bomb. When you finish, Cynthia should be gone, and the clinic will be yours. Hang out the sign that says, 'Closed till 12:00,' and keep the door locked. When Fachmi shows up, have the bomb in the case ready to deliver. Get as close as you can to the American before you detonate it. Got it?"

"Yeah, I got it."

"Don't screw up on me now! This is a time for strength, not weakness. You have the strength inside you to do this? If you don't, tell me now, and I'll put a bullet through your brain right here in the van and do the mission myself. Are you strong enough, Syukran?"

Syukran stuck out his chest and clenched his jaw. "Yes, I'm strong enough."

"Al-jihad sabiluna."

"Al-jihad sabiluna."

Saifullah parked the van near the back door and waited for Budi to show up. He could wait a few minutes, no problem. He'd waited a very, very long time for this day, and it was finally here.

Redemption.

❦ Chapter 77 ❦

THE EARLY FLIGHT to Jakarta was only slightly delayed, getting Abdullah out of Soekarno-Hatta airport by 8:00 a.m. He jumped in a taxi with no idea where to go, so he decided to start with the American embassy.

As the taxi cruised past rice fields a brilliant green with the recent rains, Abdullah leaned forward and tried pumping the driver for information.

"Excuse me, but do you know if there are any famous Americans coming to Jakarta right now? Maybe the president or vice-president? Another diplomat? Anything?"

"Hmmm. Let me think. There's usually some American bands playing here, especially in the summer. Why, just last week I think there was one, now what was their name . . . ?"

"Sorry, I don't need to know about last week. I need to know about today and tomorrow."

"Oh, yeah! I think there's a high school basketball team here today. I just read about it in the paper this morning."

"Americans? Where are they playing? What hotel are they in?"

"Hmmm. I can't remember where they're playing or where they're staying. Wait a minute! I think they're from Australia. Yeah, they're from Australia, not America. Sorry, can't think of any Americans . . ."

Abdullah sat back in his seat and put his hand over his mouth. *Ya Allah, give me a sign.*

They drove for about thirty minutes before exiting the freeway for the jammed-up city streets in morning rush hour. They got stuck at one particular intersection for several minutes as the stoplight was out and the lonely cop in the intersection seemed to be most concerned about not getting run over. The slow pace was killing Abdullah. And he didn't even know where to go!

He saw a teenage boy about three lanes over selling newspapers. Newspapers! The driver had mentioned reading about the Aussies in the paper—maybe he'd find the clue he needed.

He tapped the driver on the shoulder. "I need a newspaper!"

"But that guy's way over there. We'll never get there in this traffic!"

Abdullah pounded his fist on his knee. He looked out the other window. No newspaper sellers; just a kid with a box tied around his neck selling bottled water and cigarettes.

He rolled down the window and called the boy over. "Bring me that newspaper guy, and I'll pay you Rp.5,000!" The kid took off weaving through the cars and was back in seconds with the newspaper boy. Abdullah paid the kid, then saw they were near the front of the line, and the policeman was waving them through! He held out Rp.20,000 to the newspaper guy. "Give me one of each! Quick!"

The newspaper boy threw four different papers in the window as the taxi pulled away. Abdullah perused the headlines. When he looked at the *Jawa Pos*, his blood ran cold. There it was on the front page. A preview of today's meeting between a US congressman and the presidential hopeful M. Rizky Ramadani. He skimmed the article. "Ten o'clock a.m...at the Bellagio Mall."

He said it so loudly the taxi driver reflexively ducked his head. "*Subhanallah!* Go to the Bellagio Mall! You know where that is? Bellagio Mall? Go, go, go!"

"Yeah, I know where it is; it's in Kuningan. But that's the other way!" The driver pointed to the street to the left they'd just passed by.

"Just get there, and step on it!"

This cursed traffic! Would he be too late?

❦ Chapter 78 ❦

WHILE LOUIS STAUNTON was reading over his speech notes on the way to the peace event, the US Secret Service agents reviewed their docs on the Bellagio Mall for the umpteenth time as well. Diagrams showed the Bellagio to be almost horseshoe shaped, with a strip across the center like a rounded-top letter *A*. There was an open area in the center from floor to ceiling. All traffic was to enter the mall's front door. Two locked doors in the back were available for emergency exits if needed.

The event itself was to be held on the third floor at the top of the *A* shape in a ballroom called the Akhaya Room. The room could seat five hundred and was frequently used for weddings or banquets. There was a back entrance for the caterers, in this case all long-time employees of the mall. The participants in the event would all file through a single front door, where they were promised security help by the Jakarta police department.

Dante was grateful his partner was busy studying the layout and not telling stories. He'd called his girlfriend at six this morning—3:00 p.m. Los Angeles time—to catch her before she took off for the Staples Center. Yup, he had himself a Lakers cheerleader, and she was one fine woman. He couldn't wait to get rid of his current roommates and get back to Charlene.

Dante checked his SIG Sauer P229 .357 caliber pistol one last time. These standard-issue babies had a twelve-bullet magazine, weighed less than one kilogram in the holster, and were effective up to one hundred meters. Both agents were wearing Safariland™ soft body armor, and they'd made Staunton wear the bullet-proof vest too, just in case. Dante and Bill already had their curly wire earpieces in place and ready to switch on. The Motorola XTS® 5000 allowed them to talk openly, as the transmission was encrypted and couldn't be intercepted. Both wore Oakley® sunglasses to avoid glare or flashing lights, with the extra advantage of being able to hide where they were looking.

At 9:50 their rental car followed the police escort into the front circular driveway of the Bellagio. The crowd of protestors had grown to about sixty now, and the four security guards were having a devil of a time keeping them away from the shoppers and event participants, who were asked to walk down a roped-off sidewalk to the left of the front door. Protestors were roped off to the right, with a neutral zone in the middle.

The police disembarked first, three of them heading to deal with the demonstrators, the fourth waiting for Bill to join him and check out the interior while Dante stayed with Staunton in the car.

Dante's eyes were wide as he tried to read some of the few English-language protest signs through the closed window. "Sir, is America hated this much all over the world?"

Louis smiled. "America is hard to ignore. They're like the New York Yankees—you either love 'em or you hate 'em. And in many countries there are strong feelings on both sides. Hopefully the way we handle ourselves today will take a small step in the direction of people seeing the good side of America."

Dante hoped the protestors were satisfied with yelling insults and felt no need to express themselves with violence. A rioting mob of sixty was more than two USSS agents and a handful of local badges could handle.

Bill shook the hand of the cop named Rinto and walked past the protestors into the mall. *Rinto, how can I remember that? Let's see, "Rent-a-cop, Rinto-cop." OK, got it.*

Bill went through the Akhaya Room thoroughly with a handheld bomb detector. Nothing suspicious on the inside. Ready to focus on threats from the outside.

He pointed to the long table on the stage with three microphones on it. "Mr. Staunton will be sitting here. My partner and I will be on opposite sides of the table standing, watching the crowd and caterers. You'll have two policemen at the door checking participants, right? Where will your other two be?"

"I think they'll be needed out front helping with the protestors," Rinto replied in passable English.

"Anything happens, you take the participants out the front door, me and my partner take the congressman and Ramadani out the caterer's door, down to the ground floor, and out the back. You radio the squad car to meet us there. All clear?"

"All clear."

Bill switched on his earpiece. "Let's go, partner. It's showtime."

Dante turned to Louis Staunton. "Sir, they're ready."

Louis reached for the door handle. "Time to do our part for world peace."

❧ Chapter 79 ❧

A T 10:10 THE public relations director for SALAM gave a brief welcome speech, mentioning the names of the speakers and dignitaries
attending the event, then invited Louis Staunton and M. Rizky Ramadani to take their seats at the long table on the stage, as well as an attractive young woman wearing a head covering who turned out to be both
emcee and translator. Staunton took a seat and surveyed the crowd.

There were about two hundred, he guessed, already seated. The front
row of elegant white couches on plush red carpet contained a number of
government officials and diplomats, including the ambassadors of Jordan,
the Philippines, Denmark, Australia, and of course, the USA. He recognized Yenny Wahid, Gus Dur's daughter, there representing the Wahid
Institute. The emcee whispered to him that the distinguished-looking
Indonesian gentlemen in the front row were all cabinet ministers or their
representatives. There were a few people he thought he recognized from
their photos in the media. He'd definitely have to take some time after
the event to make new friends.

In the rows of white padded chairs there were also media people, university students, religious leaders of all types in their distinctive garb,
and who knows what other kinds of people. *Hopefully not any terrorists*,
he thought. People were still streaming in the door, being patted down
by two policemen. *Everyday people who hold the keys to our world's
future peace.*

Ramadani had privately informed Staunton that he was going to
declare his candidacy for president at this event. Staunton had asked him
to wait until after the Q & A time to avoid the event being sabotaged for
political reasons. As Ramadani started his opening remarks, Staunton
hoped he would honor that request.

Staunton took notice of his esteemed colleague's dignified way of
speaking, while radiating passion. As Ramadani spoke in Indonesian,
the young woman seated between them translated to English.

"...and as today is October 12, the anniversary of the first Bali Bomb, which has been followed by a devastating string of attacks these last several years, ruining our reputation as a hospitable, peace-loving nation, it is only fit and proper that we gather together and discuss a new way forward! Muslims and Christians need to recognize that it took both of our religions to get into this cycle of hatred and violence, and it will take both of us working together to get out. There is a way forward, and later I'll be sharing the specific steps I believe that we need to take. That way forward is called 'aggressive cooperation.' We Muslims need friends in the Christian world to move forward with us. That is why we invited one of the great American friends of Muslims, Congressman Louis Staunton, to join us here today. Congressman, thank you for your service to the world community and your service to us here in Indonesia today."

Ramadani started applauding Staunton, and the crowd joined in. Staunton nodded politely. *So far so good. I hope these people like my ideas. I have a feeling I'll really like Ramadani's.*

The emcee now introduced Louis Staunton's profile, reading from a paper in front of her. Then the floor was his.

Staunton turned on his table microphone and began to share his heart.

❧ Chapter 80 ❧

THE BOMB WAS completely assembled, hidden in the doctor's bag so kindly provided by Dr. Wally, covered over with a stethoscope, bandages, etc., in case anyone was looking. A tiny switch on the handle of the bag was in the "locked" position. A firm twist clockwise forty-five degrees, and the switch would be armed, ready to detonate.

It was 10:20 a.m. Syukran knew he'd been told to wait in the doctor's office, now empty since Cynthia had long since left. But there was one thing Syukran felt he had to do before he died. He needed to pray for his family.

Still wearing his uniform with the ID tag "Doctor-in-Training: Kevin Adrian," he exited the office, locking the door behind him, and headed past the line of people trying to get in the Akhaya Room, past the wedding dress shop, to the *musholla* on the opposite corner of the third floor.

He let the cold running water wash over his hands longer than usual as he did his *wudlu* for the last time. He washed his face, thinking how good it was to die in a state of purity, right after *sholat*. *And a bonus—I get to wash this dirty world clean of an American and a Muslim traitor.*

After his *sholat* he stayed on the carpet just a few seconds more to beseech Allah for his family to return to the true faith, have their sins forgiven, and meet him in heaven.

It was harder than he'd thought it would be to rise to his feet after his prayers. He would miss *sholat*. He would miss his friends. He would miss so many, many things about life.

Life on the other side is a thousand times better. You said you were strong. Now prove it! Get up! Go face death like a true soldier of Islam!

And then he was moving on trembling legs toward the *musholla* door.

Chapter 81

THE TAXI COULDN'T break through the wall of people to enter the Bellagio Mall parking lot. The protestors now numbered nearly two hundred. Abdullah wondered if Syukran had joined up with FPI or another one of the protest groups and was in the crowd. He jumped out on the street and scanned the faces as he raced to the front door and pushed his way to the front. No sign yet of his son.

"Where's the peace event?" he yelled to a stressed security guard.

The guard eyed him suspiciously, "Why?"

"I've got to find my son—family emergency!"

"Third floor, opposite side. Escalator that way."

Abdullah sprinted for the escalator. His feet still hurt, and he hadn't used his leg muscles in so long they weren't responding the way they should, but he pushed through the pain. He apologized to a large Chinese woman he accidentally bumped as he squeezed past her on the escalator.

Then he reached the third floor. He could see to his left a line of five people waiting to be frisked to enter a room with a sign posted outside: "Peace—the Way Forward." He'd made it! *All right, Syukran, where are you?*

He stood at the back of the line to get in and looked around the mall. There weren't too many shoppers, as it was a Tuesday morning, but there was more activity on the first two floors than on this one. A young couple was eyeing the wedding dresses in the window next door. A medical worker walked past them heading straight toward Abdullah, head down. *Something about his walk looks familiar.*

As the medic drew closer, Abdullah turned to face him and called out, "*Mas!*" The young man lifted his gaze just for a moment. Father and son stared at each other, stunned. Before his father could say anything, Syukran ducked his head and continued walking past.

Abdullah followed him to the health clinic. Syukran picked up his pace, whipping out his door key as he walked. Maybe he'd try to lock his father out? Syukran made it inside, but as he went to close the door Abdullah's foot and arm blocked the doorway. He thrust with his left shoulder, and the door opened. Abdullah swung the door closed behind him and faced his son, whose countenance transformed right before his eyes. Outside the clinic Syukran had looked like a boy whose hand was caught in the cookie jar. Now there was a defiant fire in his eyes, a boiling rage that looked ready for volcanic eruption.

"Dad, what are you doing here? You shouldn't be here!"

"I came to take you home, son."

"That's not going to happen. You better get out of this place before you get hurt."

"I don't want anyone to get hurt. That's why I came to stop you from whatever it is you're about to do. Come on. Let's go home."

Syukran's face and neck were turning red. He slammed his fist down on the receptionist's desk. "No, Dad! I'm not going anywhere. You are! Now get out of here! I have work to do."

Syukran moved toward the door to open it, but Abdullah stepped in his way, back against the door.

"I'm not leaving without you."

"Dad, we're not messing around! Get out of here before there is no way of escape!"

"Or what? You going to kill me like you're going to kill that American? Is that what I taught you, son?"

"No, Dad, that's *not* what you taught me! You taught me to stand by and do nothing as the West invades and destroys our world. You never taught me the real Islam. You never taught me *qishash*—our Muslim mission is *anna al-nafs bi al-nafs wa'al-ayna bi al-'ayn*. You taught me to run away from pain. Well, now it's my time to fight for Islam, and your time to face the pain."

The attack came so suddenly that Abdullah wasn't ready for it. Syukran's left hand darted toward his father's stomach in a feint, and when his father fell for it, crunching forward in anticipation of the blow, his jaw was exposed to Syukran's right jab. Pain shot up Abdullah's nose, filling his brain, and he knew his nose was broken.

Syukran leaned back as though relaxing, and for a moment Abdullah thought the fight might be over. But suddenly Syukran's right foot whipped up in a T-kick, his upper body leaning back and balancing on his left leg. The T-kick should have hammered Abdullah's chest right into the clinic door, but he had enough presence of mind to sidestep just in time, instinctively throwing his left arm up under Syukran's leg.

With his son off balance, Abdullah dropped to a squat and whipped his left leg around in a sweeping motion, taking out Syukran's back leg. The boy crashed to the hard tile floor on his back. He lay there holding his lower back in obvious pain.

"That's enough, son. Let's go home." Fresh drops of blood fell from Abdullah's nose on the white tile between his son's legs. As Abdullah extended his hand to Syukran, he had a flashback of teaching his one-year-old son to walk. *Surely we can get through this and start all over again.*

Syukran took his father's hand with his left and stood up slowly, hiding till the last second his vicious right-handed blow to his father's lower stomach. Abdullah grunted in surprise, the wind knocked out of him. As he bent over holding his midsection, Syukran held his father's head down with his left hand and brought his right knee up hard into his father's face once, twice, three times. Abdullah was gasping for air now. Syukran's fourth knee missed Abdullah's face and struck his injured right shoulder. A white flash of pain scorched through Abdullah's whole body in a silent scream. His body went limp in Syukran's arms, and he crumpled to the floor unconscious.

Tears were falling from Syukran's face, but he hadn't realized it until now. He heard himself throwing the words at his fallen father as though someone else were saying them: "Why won't you be the hero I need you to be?" *I hate you!* he thought, and kicked Abdullah's motionless body one last time in the stomach. *I hate myself for needing you. From now on, I'm my own hero.* He slapped the tears off of his cheeks and shook his head as though all his emotions could be flung off like water after a shower.

He stepped over his father's body purposefully, an Asian act of utter disdain, and picked up the doctor's bag. The clock said 10:35. *Fachmi should be here by now. I've probably killed my dad. Now it's my turn to die.*

Syukran stared at the clinic door, willing that knock to come quickly.

❦ Chapter 82 ❦

IKE MOST INDONESIANS, if an event started at ten o'clock, Kris usually left her house at ten o'clock. In this case, it was her hotel. She walked the short distance from the Ritz-Carlton to the Bellagio Mall excited to discover what adventure awaited her today.

There was so much on her mind. First the dream. She was still curious about what God was trying to tell her through it. Second, the peace event the TV had mentioned. She hoped she'd at least be able to glance inside before meeting Hendri. And that was number three—Hendri. How could she know what he was really like now when she'd already twice misjudged him? The first time was when she married him. Then she'd done it again when she'd judged him harshly instead of reading his letter. *Maybe I should have brought Sari. She's better at seeing through people's masks than I am.*

The protestors outside the front entrance to the mall surprised Kris, even scared her. *How could so many people not want peace? What do they want?*

She decided to skirt far around them so as to not get caught in any unexpected mob violence. This meant crossing the grass to the safe sidewalk roped off for mall visitors. She picked her way between the flowers carefully.

It was nearly 10:30 by the time she reached the mall entrance. It wasn't any bigger than Duta Mall in Banjar, but Kris was interested to see a different selection of shops.

The first floor turned out to be mostly restaurants. As she meandered through she imagined at which place she'd like to eat with Hendri. The Japanese place was well-lighted, and she'd never had Japanese food before. Maybe Japanese cuisine would be part of her adventure today!

As she headed up the escalator to the third floor she could see people lined up to enter a ballroom. *That's probably the peace event,* she thought excitedly. *Pak Ramadani and an American. I wonder what a real peacemaker looks like.*

❧ Chapter 83 ☙

THE CATERERS WAITED until most of the late arrivers were seated before bringing in boxes of bottled water and personal snack boxes of cakes for the participants. Each box contained three different kinds of cake and a small banana, with a paper napkin. First the speakers at the table on stage were served, then the dignitaries in the front two rows, and finally the rest of the audience.

Louis Staunton was rolling now. The young woman translating beside him was extremely animated, matching his enthusiasm, and the crowd seemed to be on the edge of their seats. He felt there was a sincere hunger in Indonesia for a breaking of the cycle of violent retaliation disguised as religious zeal. If people like Ramadani and these participants could only apply what he was sharing, they could change the paradigm of this young generation and make terrorism as popular as the bird flu.

"We have to see our enemies as though they were our extended family. When we blacks were being oppressed and denied our civil rights in America fifty years ago, there were whites and Jews and Asians who would sit with us on the streets and take a brutal beating, just like we did. They would stare into the jaws of ferocious police dogs, just like we did. They would go to jail for what they believed, just like we did. A white man named David Hartsough sat with my uncle in a segregated Virginia restaurant. Like my uncle, he was refused service for two days, harassed by the local whites day and night. The owners refused to serve them food. The protestors refused to leave. A raging white man jerked David out of his seat and put a knife to his chest, saying, 'You got one minute to get out of here, nigger lover, or I'm running this through your heart.' David calmly responded, 'Well, brother, you do what you feel you have to; and I'm going to try to love you all the same.' The man's hand started shaking, and the knife fell at David's feet. The man wiped a tear from his eye and walked away.

"David saw my black uncle as his brother. He also saw a violent, armed white man as his brother. He stood in the middle as a peacemaker, though it could have cost him his life."

When Fachmi handed the snack box to Rudy, the handsome university student in the third row center aisle, he slipped a small capsule into his hand. Rudy smiled almost imperceptibly, faked a cough, and popped it into his mouth. Fachmi continued on down the row, counting the seconds. The chemist had said under two minutes. He had to make sure he was passing boxes in the row right behind Rudy when the drug took effect.

Fachmi had recruited Rudy in an Internet chat room. Rudy seemed the adventurous type, a lover of pranks, and a true hater of America. Fachmi and Rudy worked up this little scheme to disrupt the peace event. Rudy's job was to collapse, drawing all the attention to himself. While the event stopped to take care of Rudy, Fachmi's job was to slip two more capsules to two other recruits in the audience. More chaos would occur. Then Fachmi would cry out that the water had been poisoned, and everyone who drank the water should get to the doctor as quickly as possible. Pandemonium would erupt, canceling the event, and hopefully scaring the pants off of any of the speakers who had already taken a drink. The chemist swore that within twenty minutes Rudy and the others would be back to normal, no side effects.

Fachmi had Rudy convinced the whole scheme was Rudy's idea. He also told him he'd recruit the other two participants without them knowing each other so none of them would accidentally give anything away. What Fachmi didn't tell Rudy was that there were no other recruits for this plan; just a kid across the hall carrying a bomb. A bomb guaranteed to annihilate anyone within a twenty-five-foot radius. Rudy was sitting a mere eighteen feet from the foot of the stage.

Just under two minutes later, Rudy stood up, grabbing his throat and gasping for breath. Then he passed out, falling dramatically onto the young woman sitting next to him, who screamed.

Fachmi was passing through the row behind. He quickly made his way toward Rudy and held up his wrist as though taking a pulse.

"Move back everyone. Give him some room!" People stood and moved their chairs away, everyone's eyes riveted on Rudy.

Dante spoke into his Motorola, "What the heck, Bill? What's going on?"

"Looks like a sick kid. Could be a distraction. Don't look at him, look at the others, watch for suspicious movements, someone taking advantage of the opportunity." He stepped closer to Staunton and watched for the attack. But none came.

Not today, Hinckley, not on my final field assignment.

Fachmi gently laid Rudy's hand back across his chest and stood up. "Don't move him. He's in bad shape." He started moving quickly toward the back, calling out, "I'm going to get Dr. Wally!" He told the policemen, "We gotta get Dr. Wally over here now!"

Fachmi heard the emcee trying to take charge as he walked brusquely out the door. "Please everyone return to your seats. We'll continue Mr. Staunton's speech as soon as the doctor has taken care of our regrettably sick participant. Please take your seats. Thank you."

Facmi was proud of Rudy's success in his mission. *Allah will reward him in heaven.*

❧ Chapter 84 ❧

CRIS WAS WAITING outside the Akhaya Room behind a grandmother waving her cane at a policeman when she heard a commotion inside. The policeman stopped frisking the grandmother and turned to watch. Kris wondered what was going on. Suddenly one of the staff-uniformed men rushed out the door, nearly knocking grandma over. Kris grabbed her arm to steady her.

"Are you all right, Ibu?"

"Yes, yes. Young man, stop touching me, and take me to my seat now!"

Grandmother looped her arm in the policeman's, so he obligingly walked with her inside to find a seat. With the other cop trying to keep people back from Rudy's body, Kris found herself suddenly all alone outside the doorway.

Her attention turned back to the running mall employee. She saw him knock on Dr. Wally's door. *Didn't I just walk past there and see a sign that they were closed till noon?* The door opened immediately, and there stood a young doctor with his stethoscope around his neck and a black bag in his right hand. It happened so fast; it was almost like he was waiting by the door. The two spoke for only a second or two, then the doctor started toward her, and the mall employee ran for the down escalator on the opposite side of the mall. *I wonder where he's going so fast. This just gets more and more curious.*

She watched the young doctor walking toward her, head held high, *almost like he is marching,* she thought. But when he got about five yards away from her, he froze. She stared at him, and he stared back. She realized first, *He recognizes me!* Then it hit her, for she recognized him too. *It's Syukran!*

The synapses in her brain suddenly bombarded her with electrical impulse connections: *Syukran, the serious religious one. Helping rebuild the church after the fire. Ran away from his parents. Here at a peace event posing as a doctor when he's obviously not one.*

He's involved in some kind of terrorist attack on this event!

252

Kris wanted to scream, but nothing came out. She wanted to run, but her legs had grown roots into the cement walkway. Syukran started walking toward her. She felt powerless to stop him.

But she had to try.

She blocked his path to the Akhaya Room door and started walking toward him. When they got nose-to-nose, they both stopped.

Syukran looked down at Kris like she were a bug about to be squashed. "Out of my way. I've killed you once. If you're not off this floor in thirty seconds, I'll kill you again."

The terror in Kris was lifted off by a strange peace, like a breath of air more powerful had just filled her lungs. Her dream rushed back at her, and she knew—this was her Ishmael.

She threw her arms around Syukran and hugged him.

He wasn't expecting that. "Let go of me, pig!"

"Your father told me in the hospital how much he loves you. Return to him."

"I killed my father."

"Then I will love you in his place. I love you, my son!" She squeezed him tighter.

"Stop it!" he screamed. His right hand held the doctor's bag, so he used his left hand to try to break her grip, but for some reason she felt strong enough to resist.

"I love you, my son!"

Every time she said it, her grip grew stronger, and his strength faded. Slowly she moved him backward, pushing him away from the door. He managed to get his left hand around from behind her shoulder to grab her face. He poked at her eyes, then tried to cover her mouth.

"Stop it! Stop it!"

"I love you, son!" The words were muffled now, covered by his hand. She realized he was crying.

Far behind Syukran a door opened, and a voice they both knew well shouted, "Syukran! No!"

Kris felt an eruption from deep within Syukran. He screamed like an animal, throwing her off him as if she were a rag doll. At the top of his lungs he yelled, "*Isy kariman au mut syahidan!*" She thought she glimpsed a policeman with a gun then a flash of light from Syukran's medical bag.

As Kris fell backward, her last thought was, *Sari! Someone else will have to watch you dance.*

The explosion shook the entire building. The third floor walkway Kris and Syukran had been standing on was blown violently in all directions. Pieces of the railing just two yards from them flew across the open courtyard, shattering windows on the far side. Great chunks of cement crashed to the second floor walkway, breaking through it, then on to the first floor below. The picture window exhibiting wedding dresses next door was blown inward by the blast. On the heels of the deafening roar of the bomb came the screams of hundreds of shoppers and peace participants. Pandemonium broke loose.

At the sound of the bomb Rogers and Prince had tackled Staunton onto the floor behind the table. When they realized he wasn't hurt and that the explosion had come from outside the room, they hauled him to his feet.

"Sir, we have to get you out of here. Now!"

Staunton reached back to grab M. Rizky Ramadani, frozen to his chair in a state of shock. "Let's go, my friend."

Dante took over, grabbing Ramadani by the arm and physically propelling him along behind Rogers and Staunton as Bill led the way through the caterers' access to the afore-planned emergency exit.

Abdullah had been knocked off his feet by the blast back through the open doorway into Dr. Wally's office. The front window had shattered, showering him with broken glass, but the important thing was, he wasn't dead. He tried to get to his feet. His whole body ached like a train wreck, but his adrenaline was through the roof.

Was that Kris? What was she doing here? He scanned the carnage briefly for his son's body, and Kris's, but knew it was useless. They'd been blown to smithereens.

He looked across the chasm of devastation toward the Akhaya Room. There was no walkway now, no way to get over there and check on the policeman he remembered seeing just before the blast. There was no sign of him anyway; undoubtedly he was dead. But it looked like the wall to the event room remained mostly intact. *It looks like Kris just saved a whole bunch of lives. Lives taken by the hand of my son.*

He buried his face in his hands and found they were covered with blood. *He's my son. Try as I might to escape my past, I can't. The blood is still on my hands.*

He started to painfully make his way around the opposite side of the mall toward the down escalator. Something was gnawing at the back of his head. Something he was supposed to know or do.

What was it his son had said before beating the snot out of him? "We're *not messing around...No way of escape.*"

Abdullah had a terrible feeling rip the lining right out of his stomach. He started running for the escalator. His training in bombing public facilities exploded across his mind.

What if Syukran had one or more partners? What if the attack wasn't over yet?

🦋 Chapter 85 🦋

SAIFULLAH HEARD THE explosion from the safety of the van and smiled. No musical orchestra could compete with the beauty of that sound. The sound of infidels filling hell.

The engine hummed, ready to jet out of there as soon as Fachmi showed up, confirming the mission was accomplished. He had left the van parked around back after he loaded the bogus equipment, and with security overwhelmed with the protestors out front, no one had noticed. Yes, his anonymous call to the FPI offices warning them about this anti-Islamic event had paid off handsomely.

Fachmi reached the van only seconds after the explosion. He jerked open the passenger door but didn't climb in.

"He failed! The kid blew himself up before he got in the door! The target is on the move!" Fachmi was wheezing from the run, his eyes wild with the ecstasy of *jihad* as he'd always imagined it.

Saifullah quickly ripped out their two pistols that had been taped under the seats. "They're most likely headed out one of the back exits. I'll take the one down there; you stay here. Make sure to peg both targets. If you see me running toward you, that means mission accomplished. Get behind the wheel and get us out of here."

He didn't wait for a response but took off running.

Within fifteen seconds he had taken up his place in the bushes of the garden behind the mall with a perfect view of the back door. He settled in, resting the barrel of his gun on a V-shaped branch. *They'll never even know where the shots came from.*

The training he'd picked up from Abdullah Sonata in using bombs as diversions to get the target moving through an unexpected and lower-security area—more convenient for snipers or assassins to take out the main target—was proving to have been well worth it. With a bit of luck he'd complete the mission and get away *alive* to receive the glory that would erase his shame forever.

He relaxed his finger just a hair off the trigger and breathed deeply.

Patience. Focus. Any second now you'll have the reward of all your hard work.

When Abdullah reached the front door, there were already dozens of panicked shoppers trampling one another to get out. The security guards had their hands full extracting the people safely. Abdullah rudely pushed his way through to the front, wondering if he would make it in time.

A shock awaited him outside the mall. There were over two hundred protestors now filling the parking lot, and they were clapping and cheering, shouting *"Allah Akbar!"* He felt like vomiting. The utter fools! *That used to be you, Abdullah. And your son.*

A second police cruiser had joined the first one, and there were several more cops handling the crowd now. He grabbed one of the policemen by the shirt.

"The bomb didn't kill the American. There could be more terrorists waiting for him at the back exits."

Maybe it was his bloody face, or maybe it was his desperate voice. For whatever reason, the cop believed him. He radioed to the others as he ran with Abdullah back toward the mall.

Abdullah shouted over the din of the crowd, "You can't go through. Go around! You go the long way; I'll go this way."

The policeman nodded, and they separated.

The agony in Abdullah's body was radiating from his nose to his toes, but the worst was his shoulder. As he ran he tried not to swing his right arm too much. He also tried to ignore the excruciating pain. Someone's life could still be at stake.

He burst around the corner of the mall into an empty garden. *What a perfect spot for a sniper!* He dropped behind some bushes and surveyed the layout. To his right he could see the back door about fifty yards away. *If I were a sniper, where would I be?*

He looked up and back to his left first. No high buildings near enough. No, if there is someone, he must be in the garden somewhere. *And if there is someone, he has a gun, and I don't.*

He made his way along the trees in the back of the garden, farthest from the mall. He knew he had to move quickly. Any second now the American could come out that door.

❦ Chapter 86 ❦

THE US SECRET Service agents had bundled Staunton and Ramadani successfully through the hallway into the catering kitchen when they ran into their first setback—someone, probably overzealous security, had locked the door connecting the kitchen to the emergency stairs.

"Geez!" yelled Dante. "How you supposed to escape in an emergency if you lock the emergency doors?"

"Stand back!" Bill commanded. He emptied a couple slugs from his SIG into the lock. Then he gave it a kick and busted the knob clean through to the other side. He reached into the hole and slid back the locking mechanism, then opened the door.

They raced for the stairs, aware that the crowd of attendees would probably be right on their heels.

Their second setback occurred just moments later. In Ramadani's hurry, he stumbled on the stairs. To catch his balance, his right arm shot out to grab Staunton. This slight bump in the back made Louis overstep one of the stairs, turning his ankle and ending up in a heap on the floor.

Bill felt Louis go down behind him. "Hey, what's going on?"

"Dang! Dang that hurts!" Louis was holding his ankle and writhing on the floor.

The other three gathered around him. "Can you walk, sir?" Dante asked the obvious.

"Dang! I've sprained my ankle before on the basketball court, but this feels worse. Let me try..."

Bill and Dante helped Louis stand on his left, and he gingerly tried to put weight on his right but started to fall. The agents caught him.

"Sir, we're going to have to carry you between us. Prince, you got him? Mr. Ramadani, stay close to us. Let's go."

Their speed was hampered considerably, and the sound of the rushing mob filled the stairwell above them. If they didn't get to the ground floor soon they could be bowled over by the hysterical horde descending upon them.

"Take the stairs in rhythm, Prince! Move, move, move!"

❧ Chapter 87 ❧

A SLIGHT RUSTLE IN the bushes not ten feet in front of Abdullah gave Saifullah's position away. Now that he knew where to look, he could see the outline of a man's body in a position that could only mean he was holding a gun.

The only weapon Abdullah had found while skirting the garden was a rake. He now brought it up like a rifle and crept up behind the terrorist like a cat after its prey. He firmly touched the top of the rake just to the left of Saifullah's spine and spoke with "the voice."

"Freeze! We got him, boys! Now lift that gun very slowly above your head, your other hand up, too."

Abdullah would have been furious at himself for being so focused on watching the door that he hadn't anticipated the possibility of someone coming up behind him. He could feel Saifullah's anger burning. But the assassin complied, raising his hands slowly, fingers around the butt of the gun, not on the trigger.

"Now throw your gun into the rose bushes on your right." Saifullah tossed the gun at the roses. As he did so, he glanced as far as he could see to both left and right without turning around. Abdullah knew what he was looking for and what he wouldn't find. *What if he calls my bluff?*

"Now let's move nice and slow out of these bushes toward the grass in front of you. Move!"

Saifullah stepped sideways out of the bushes. The small circle of the rake was still against his back. He headed for a narrow sand pathway, Abdullah right behind him.

Suddenly Saifullah ducked his head into a handstand, kicking up with his feet. He caught the rake, and it went flying out of Abdullah's hands. He completed the forward flip and came up with his back to Abdullah but with a handful of sand. As he spun to face the man he'd disarmed, he flung the sand at Abdullah's eyes.

Abdullah raised a hand to block the sand and stepped backward. The space between them gave each a chance to size up his opponent. Saifullah first saw the rake and snarled with anger. Then his eyes narrowed in hate. Both men were shocked to see a ghost from their past.

"It's *you*! Sutrisno, the coward, the defector! It will be a pleasure for me to settle the score against you today."

"I am no longer that man. Today it is I who have a score to settle, Syaafii! That was my son you blew up in there!"

Saifullah laughed. "Ha! He died a better man than you! And I am no longer Syaafii. I am Saifullah, the sword of God!"

"The police are on the way. You'd best run."

"Like you ran from us in Afghan? See this?" Saifullah pointed to a cigarette burn on his throat. "You gave me this! Every Indonesian in the camp received one, with the warning that the next Indonesian to run like a dog would mean Afghan swords stuck in those marks. All of us hated you and swore to get even. Oh, the glory when I tell all our brothers how I killed you!"

Saifullah took the arrogant position of a *silat* master, right hand opened and raised forward from his shoulder, left hand behind his back. Abdullah took the position he taught his students: right shoulder facing his opponent, right hand downward between bent knees, weight on his toes, left hand tucked up near his chin. He knew Saifullah was in better shape, much stronger, and would destroy him even if Abdullah was healthy, which he wasn't. His only hope was to drag the fight on long enough for the police to get there.

Saifullah brought his right hand down and back up face-high with a hop forward and a yell, "*Das!*" His left hand came out to jab at Abdullah's face, his right foot following with a kick to Abdullah's ribs. The school teacher successfully blocked the jab with his right arm swinging out, sending shock waves of pain up to his shoulder, and tried to sidestep the kick, but it grazed him. Saifullah continued rapidly with a sole kick that caught Abdullah full in the chest, knocking him backward. Only a friendly bush kept him from falling on his rear.

Saifullah smiled and curled two fingers, calling his opponent forward. *This is the man who killed my son!* Abdullah drank from the cup of vengeance for strength and charged.

Three feet before the jihadist, he spun into a back kick, aiming for the chin. Saifullah crossed his wrists to block it. Abdullah followed with a series of close kicks to the ribs—right, left, right, the first two blocked by downward swings of Saifullah's muscular arms. His third kick was blocked with a raised left knee. Off balance, Abdullah couldn't avoid

Saifullah's right-footed cobra kick. He crashed into a frangipane tree, breaking its tender branches, and crumpled to the ground.

Saifullah started to walk past his fallen foe to retrieve the pistol from the rose bushes. Abdullah pretended to be out cold and let him get past one outspread leg. Then a vicious scissor movement brought Saifullah down hard just short of the roses.

Abdullah felt the momentum turn. He rolled on top of Saifullah's back. But the powerful man succeeded in twisting sideways enough to get a jaw-shattering elbow to Abdullah's face.

"Aaaaah!" Abdullah screamed as his previously broken nose now felt like hamburger meat. The blood started flowing profusely again.

Both men staggered to their feet, but it was clear who would win this survival of the fittest.

"I don't have time for this!" Saifullah closed his eyes and took in a deep breath. Abdullah had seen this done before by the true *silat* masters and knew what was coming but could do nothing to stop it.

Suddenly the "sword of God" thrust his right foot and right palm forward in Abdullah's direction and released his *tenaga dalam*, his inner power, with a yell. "*Yaaaa!*"

Abdullah felt the invisible power hit him like a giant hammer. He flew eight feet backward through the air and landed with a thud against a tree, hitting his head and blacking out.

Saifullah scrambled through the rosebush thorns to find his gun. He returned to his hiding place ready to finish the job.

❧ Chapter 88 ❧

ORTUNATELY FOR LOUIS Staunton, the crowd caught up to his party just after they made it down the stairs to the first floor. Bill and Dante held Louis back against the wall until all the peace participants had raced past them. From the foot of the stairs, people ran wildly in every direction looking for an exit. A few preceded the Secret Servicemen to the back door, but when they found it locked they ran on after the others to the front entrance.

Once the crowd had cleared out, Rogers took aim at another lock. One shot was enough to break the catch between the double doors, and they were out.

The outside air hit them with a wave of tropical heat, but at least it was free of the dust kicked up by the falling debris in the mall. The glare of the sun caused Ramadani and Staunton to raise their hands and cover their eyes. It didn't bother the Oakley-wearing agents.

They exited the double doors onto a small street winding around the back of the mall, adjacent to a garden. Rogers and Prince scanned the horizon for threats, Staunton still hanging between them. Dante pointed to a body propped up against a tree in the garden.

"What the heck?"

Rogers decided the body wasn't a threat. He took charge. "Here's the plan. We can't take the congressman through those protestors and panicked people out front to the car, and we've lost our police escort. Prince, you get us some wheels and get back here ASAP. We'll sit you down here on the grass, sir, and have you out of here in no time."

They started lowering Staunton to the grass.

Come on, give me a clean shot at the American! Saifullah's finger was on the trigger. The American was now on the ground and harder to see.

Suddenly he heard shots fired at the other end of the garden, about seventy yards away, near the van, and heard someone scream. Rogers tackled the sitting Staunton just as Saifullah fired. The bullet whistled so close to Bill's head Saifullah thought he might have killed him.

Ramadani froze in absolute terror. Saifullah decided he made a better target under the circumstances and swiveled his pistol toward the Indonesian who would be president. He pulled the trigger.

But Saifullah wasn't as quick as Dante Prince. Dante knocked Ramadani to the ground just as Saifullah fired. The bullet penetrated Dante's right triceps and passed right out the front of his upper arm. He cried out in anguish but stayed on top of Ramadani.

Saifullah could see policemen coming from Fachmi's direction now. He had one last chance to bury as many bullets as he could into those infidels and then make a run for it. He stood up now, pistol cradled in both hands, and took two steps forward to get a better angle at the men lying helplessly on the ground.

Go to hell, infidels!

For the second time that day Saifullah neglected to watch his back. The "sword of God" never heard the "rock of Abdullah" crash down upon his head, crushing the right side of his skull.

Abdullah just stood there staring down at Saifullah's dead body. He painfully released his grip on the rock and noticed the blood on his hands. Once again, he was the guilty one, yet the one chosen to live.

Bill Rogers pulled his SIG and aimed it at Abdullah's head.

A policeman came running up. "No shoot!" he yelled in English, holding up his hand. Bill hesitated. Two policemen grabbed Abdullah and threw him to the ground and handcuffed him, while the first one protested something in Indonesian that Bill didn't understand. The other two didn't seem to listen.

Bill ran to check on his partner. Dante was bleeding badly but conscious. Clearly he'd saved Ramadani's life. Bill yelled, "Get an ambulance back here!"

"Don't worry, partner. We're going to get you to a doctor."

Dante closed his eyes and murmured, "I hope he's a Republican."

At that moment Bill Rogers decided he'd give his highest recommendation for Dante Prince.

❧ Chapter 89 ❧

THE NEXT FEW days were a blur for Abdullah. The pain meds he was on in the police hospital had him floating in and out of consciousness as doctors labored to repair his severely damaged face and shoulder and treat his superficial wounds. He vaguely remembered the police questioning him during his waking moments. He just told them the whole story as best as he could remember it. Fortunately he had the one policeman he'd spoken to on his side, and there was never serious talk of an arrest.

On the third day, in one of his moments of feeling moderately coherent, he asked the nurse for his cell phone. She retrieved it for him, but the battery was dead.

"I need to call my family. Please. They don't know whether I'm dead or alive."

"I'll see what I can do."

A few minutes later the nurse brought in her own cell phone. "You have permission to make one call, and the policeman outside the door wants to be in the room to hear it."

"OK, thanks."

He dialed Iqbal's cell phone number. His son should be home from school by now, he thought.

Iqbal answered, "Hello?"

"Iqbal, this is your father."

"Dad! What happened? Where are you?"

"Listen, I can't talk long, and I'll tell you the details later. Did you see the TV reports about a bomb at the Bellagio Mall in Jakarta?"

"Yeah, were you there?"

"Syukran was the bomber." He heard Iqbal's gasp, and a noise like Iqbal had stumbled into something.

"There's more. I tried to stop him. He knocked me out cold. When I woke up he was on his way with the bomb to kill the American congressman and all the participants of the peace event. I don't know how

265

this happened, but Ibu Kris, Sari's mom, appeared outside the event's door and stopped him. She was hugging him when he detonated the bomb. I saw them both—" He couldn't finish the sentence.

Iqbal could only squeak out, "My God!"

"I'll tell you the rest later. I'm in the hospital, but I'm OK. I'll get home as soon as I can."

"Dad! Tell me where you are. I'll borrow some money and come and get you!"

"Thanks, son, but no, I'm fine. I need you to stay home to take care of Mom and Sari. If Syukran's and Kris's names haven't been on the news yet, they will be anytime now. How's Sari?"

"She's totally panicky, Dad! She hasn't heard from her mom since a text message on Tuesday, and she's worried sick. She called the hotel, and they don't know where she is either."

"Maybe it's best you break the news to her before she hears it on TV. And try not to leave her alone too much. For Mom, try to keep her away from the news, and I'll tell her about it myself when I get home."

"OK, Dad. Hurry back."

"I will." Abdullah paused, but the words had been in his mind and heart for three days now and they needed to be said.

"I love you, son."

"Same to you, Dad."

That night while Iqbal went to "check on" Sari, Siti was left home alone. She had been increasingly worried about her husband and youngest son. Iqbal's cryptic message that Dad was in the hospital but OK and would be home soon seemed to be hiding something. She turned on the TV.

Metro TV was still covering the Bellagio Mall bombing in depth, interviewing as many eyewitnesses as possible, passing on information as the police investigation continued, and today they promised a "fresh development": the police had identified the bombers.

Up on the screen flashed four vertical rectangles, three with mug shots, the second box with a question mark. She leaned forward and listened intently.

"...named Fachmi was an employee of Bellagio Mall and was in the Akhaya Room serving snacks to the participants when a young man became suddenly ill. Fachmi offered to go get Dr. Wally, who has a clinic just across the courtyard from the peace event. Then Fachmi ran out the front exit and around to the back to watch for the American congressman, Louis Staunton, and presidential hopeful M. Rizky Ramadani. He was carrying a gun, ostensibly to assassinate one or both of these politicians. Fachmi was killed in a gun battle with police.

"The second accomplice we do not yet have a photo of but police suspect him to be a teenager rumored to be from Banjarmasin named Syukran. This young man was waiting in Dr. Wally's office disguised as a doctor-in-training. He carried the bomb in a black doctor's bag. He was supposed to burst into the peace event to help the sick participant, then detonate the bomb less than seven meters from the stage. For reasons as yet unknown he detonated the bomb outside the room. Police suspect that Officer Rinto, who was the only known casualty from the third floor, may have stopped Syukran from entering, and the boy may have panicked and set off the bomb.

"By the way, Dr. Wally's testimony is that a man matching the fourth bomber's description threatened him to not come to work until noon and stole the keys to his office. The man apparently attached an electronic device to Dr. Wally's daughter's arm as a threat to gain his compliance. The device was found to be harmless and removed, bringing great relief to Dr. Wally's family. Police are questioning him only as a witness at this point.

"A third suspected terrorist, the sick peace event participant, was an economics student at the University of Indonesia named Rudy. Police have not yet confirmed whether or not he was involved in the plot. When police returned to the Akhaya Room to investigate in the aftermath of the bomb, they found Rudy still lying on the floor, dead from a heart attack.

"The fourth team member is a well-known terrorist with Jemaah Islamiyah known as Syaafii, Santoso, Joko, Ali, or Saifullah. Police suspect him to be the leader of the attack. Syaafii was waiting by the other back door to the mall, the door from which Staunton and Ramadani eventually exited. He attempted to assassinate both leaders but was foiled by the quick reactions of the two US Secret Service agents and an unlikely hero, a school teacher named Abdullah."

Now two new images filled the TV screen—Dante and Abdullah in the hospital.

"In an unusual twist to the story, Abdullah is rumored to be the father of Syukran. He followed his son to Jakarta to try to stop him from the suicide bombing but was too late. Yet, he had the presence of mind to alert the police to a possible threat outside the mall, and he himself killed Syaafii during his shooting spree by bashing him on the head with a rock. He's currently recovering from his injuries in the Bhayangkara Hospital.

"Dante Prince has also been hospitalized for a bullet wound to his upper arm that he sustained while diving in front of presidential hopeful M. Rizky Ramadani. Police have stated unequivocally that had Agent Prince not acted so quickly and bravely, one of Indonesia's brightest new political figures would most likely be dead.

"By this one act of selfless heroism, the young African-American has done far more to help the recently strained Indonesia-America relations than all the politicians put together.

"We have here with us Police Officer Hadi Sutiyoso to explain more about the actual bomb itself..."

Siti didn't really pay much attention to the reporter. All she heard was "...a teenager from Banjarmasin named Syukran...Abdullah...father of Syukran...try to stop him from the suicide bombing, but was too late." She stared at the images on TV in total shock. Her entire body felt numb. Inside her a voice was screaming, *It isn't true! It can't be true!* For an hour and twenty minutes she sat as though in a trance, her mind fighting those images desperately with her mantra. *It isn't true! It can't be true!*

Then a new thought, a doubt, found a chink in her armor. *But what if it were true?*

Slowly Siti stood up and turned off the TV, images already changed to those of local politicians visiting beautiful Java rice fields. Like a zombie she glided into her bedroom, started taking clothes out of her wardrobe, and laying them on her bed.

❧ Chapter 90 ❧

THE NEXT DAY Syukran's name was in bold print on the front page of the *Banjarmasin Post*. By the end of the day everyone who had ever known Syukran was avidly discussing whether or not the Syukran they knew from Kelayan was the suicide-bombing terrorist.

The *B-Post* covered various reactions to the bombing and failed assassination attempt. The president and several religious leaders vehemently condemned the attack as anti-Islamic behavior. Other hard-liners praised the courage of "a young man who was willing to die for his Islamic convictions." The *B-Post*'s article almost treated Syukran as a hero, since he was the first person from Banjarmasin to become a famous terrorist.

In Kelayan reactions were also mixed. The neighborhood of Gang Hanyar was visibly shaken. People went about their business almost in a daze, unable to comprehend the horror brought about by one of *their* kids from *their* street. Many had known Syukran since elementary school. They remembered a quiet boy who loved soccer, had once caught a four-foot-long monitor lizard with his bare hands, who was more faithful to pray in the *musholla* than most kids. No one in their wildest dreams could have imagined him a terrorist. Many a tear was shed by the mothers and fathers in Gang Hanyar. And many took extra time to ask their children probing questions, to make sure their kids would never fall for the sneaky tactics of terrorist recruiters.

At Simpang Gerilya, Hafiz and the gang went over the *B-Post* article with a fine-toothed comb for anything that could shake their belief that the bomber was *their* Syukran, one and the same. They all felt the tragic sense of losing their friend yet couldn't be more proud that one of their own had made the big time. Hafiz took back every disparaging comment he'd ever made to Syukran. Their old friend began the transition to legend in the boys' mind.

Pastor David overheard the boys talking about Syukran's heroics as they finished their last day of painting the inside walls of the church. He shook hands with each one and thanked them at the end of the day. Then he went inside the empty building, knelt where the old altar used to be, and wept.

Pak Darsuni caught Iqbal walking home from Sari's. "I'm so sorry to hear about your brother. It was your brother, wasn't it?"

Iqbal nodded.

"Just a friendly warning: when the press finds out who Syukran was, they'll be all over this place like peanut sauce on satay. You might want to think about moving your mom somewhere, keeping the door locked, whatever."

"Thanks, Pak."

Iqbal considered the advice. *Maybe that's why Mom didn't sleep at home last night. Maybe she's avoiding the reporters.* Then he thought about Sari. When the media figured out Kris's involvement in the story, she could be hounded by journalists and TV cameras too!

Dad told me to take care of Sari. I got to think of something.

After six days the doctors pronounced Abdullah ready to go home. The police investigation was also complete, and they concluded that the school teacher should be considered a national hero.

The morning he was set to check out of the hospital Abdullah was surprised when the nurse handed him a brand new suit to put on. But he was even more surprised at who he found in the waiting room. M. Rizky Ramadani was there with a slew of TV cameras. Ramadani gave a short speech on how Abdullah was a champion of all those who loved peace. Then he solemnly proffered a plaque titled "Peace Champion" engraved with Abdullah's name, along with an envelope filled with cash as a peace award from SALAM. Various diplomats who had also been saved from the bomb, including the American ambassador, applauded enthusiastically and gratefully pumped Abdullah's hand. The head of Densus 88 even came. He saluted Abdullah, then embraced him gingerly. He offered round-the-clock protection from any jihadist revenge attacks. Abdullah thanked him but mumbled that he'd seen enough violence for one lifetime and was ready when it was his time to die. The TV cameras soaked up everything. A reporter tried to ask Abdullah to tell the story, but he just smiled and said that the real hero was a woman named Kris who stopped the bomber when he had failed.

Apparently this was new information for the reporter, who followed up with, "And do you know where we can find this Kris now?"

"She wrapped her arms around the bomber and moved him away from the door of the peace event. Her body was blown to tiny little pieces. She was a Christian woman who paid the ultimate sacrifice for our Muslim madness.

"Thank you all for coming. If you don't mind, I'd really like to go home."

Ramadani himself escorted Abdullah to a limousine with a giant SALAM painted on the side and sent him off to the airport with a complimentary ticket back to Banjarmasin.

That night as Abdullah was flying back home the TV crew was frantically searching for more pieces to the bombing puzzle. Somehow the police had never mentioned to them that a woman—a Christian woman at that—had saved the day! They had to know the whole story. The whole world had to hear this story. There could be presidential awards forthcoming, and they were determined to be the first to break the news.

Even if it meant tracking the story back to its roots in Banjarmasin.

❧ Chapter 91 ❧

THE HOUSE WAS dark. Selena hadn't met him at the airport. Maybe she wasn't planning to meet him at home either. Louis fumbled with his keys and dropped them on the welcome mat. Jet lag from nearly four days of a problematic journey home, or anticipation of coming home to no one?

The door creaked open. "Selena?" he called. No answer. All the lights downstairs were off. He hung his coat in the hall closet, looked up at the long flight of stairs ahead of him, and decided the suitcase could make its way up in the morning.

He trudged up the stairs gingerly, favoring his still painful right ankle, gently pushed open his bedroom door, and flipped on the lights. His wife was sitting on the edge of the bed facing the door, wearing her green and white pajamas. Her red eyes stared holes through him, and suddenly he was afraid, more afraid than he was of facing terrorists in Jakarta. He was afraid of what his wife was about to say, or do.

"Selena…" Louis took a hesitant limp toward her, then another. Still she stared at him. A tear trickled down her cheek. He kept moving closer until they were close enough to touch. Now her head was tilted back, still meeting his gaze, her face seeming to ask the question, "Why?"

Finally she broke her silence with a raspy voice, "What if they killed you? What would I do?"

Louis decided to sit next to Selena on the bed. She didn't continue, so he did. "When I heard the gunshots and Bill tackled me, all I could think about was you." He wanted to reach for her but wasn't sure she would still have him. So he waited.

Selena's tears were falling faster now, but there were no sobs or sniffles. She seemed to have come to a decision, and all Louis could do was wait for her to say it.

"I…I never stopped praying for you. Good thing, huh?" She reached for his hand.

Louis swallowed hard. "Yeah, honey, you probably saved my life. Again. I'm sorry."

Selena leaned into his face, almost like she would kiss him. "You're not doing this to me again, Louis. I've made up my mind...Next time, you're taking me with you."

Louis was stunned. He felt his breath return, colors return, music return—everything that he was counting as loss if Selena left him, suddenly it belonged to him once again. He pulled her head to his chest, and she yielded to him. "I'd love that, honey."

After a few moments, she broke free. "Take a shower. You're not sleeping in my bed smelling like that!" She pushed him off the bed. "We've got a lunch tomorrow with a leader of a mosque just ten minutes from here. Imagine that! I had no idea we had one so close! I found his letter in your pile of hate mail and noticed the address and opened it, and it's a good thing I did since he's probably the only person in a hundred-mile radius who *doesn't* hate you. So I want to meet him and try to figure out why."

Louis grinned as he stumbled toward the shower. *Looks like peacemaking has survived to live another day.*

❧ Chapter 92 ☙

IQBAL PICKED HIS father up from the airport with the motorbike. He almost didn't recognize his father with his expensive new suit (a gift from the American ambassador), designer backpack (from the Filipino ambassador), and bandages still covering Abdullah's nose.

They didn't get home until *Mahgrib*. When they walked in the door they could smell the sweet fragrance of coconut milk. They found Sari in the kitchen washing dishes and three plates of *Ketupat Kandangan* on the table.

Iqbal was incredulous. He stared at the compressed rice chunks, jackfruit, and haruan fish in the coconut milk base. "Did you cook this?"

"No, I bought it. I just thought you'd be hungry when you got home, Pak Abdullah."

"Thank you, Sari." Abdullah sat down. The other two joined him at the table. Iqbal thought it odd that his father said nothing about his mother's absence, but he had more important thoughts on his mind anyway. Sari and Iqbal exchanged a knowing glance.

"Dad, I know you're tired, but Sari said she couldn't wait till tomorrow to hear about her mom. Can you please tell her the story tonight?"

Abdullah looked at Sari, her brown eyes big and round and moist already.

"Let's eat. Then we'll talk."

They ate their dinner in silence.

After Sari had cleared the plates away and returned to the table, Abdullah shared the whole story with her, at least all he knew of it. When he got to the part where the bomb exploded, his voice choked.

"I could see them across the courtyard. I shouted to them. And then...my son detonated the bomb. He and your mother...they both..." He put his hands on his bowed head, unable to finish the sentence. "I was so close. I could have stopped it...I'll never forgive myself." A wail rose in his throat, and he had to turn away to push it back down. Sari cried softly behind him. When he got his composure back he turned, and she motioned for him to finish.

"At first I didn't mention your mom to the police and media, hoping to keep you out of the spotlight. But then I thought, the deed your mother did, the sacrifice she made, deserves to be known. There are a great many people who owe their lives to your mother's courage. She was...the most amazing woman I've ever known."

Sari smiled through the tears. She pulled her hair back off her face and wiped her eyes with a tissue Iqbal had provided. He prompted her.

"Tell my dad about what you know."

Sari collected herself, then fixed her eyes on a dirty corner of the green linoleum floor and began.

"The night before the bomb, Mom called me. She told me how my dad had postponed their meeting till lunch on Tuesday at the Bellagio. She was still nervous, she said. Would he just get our hopes up and then dash them again? She said she'd be wearing the purple top I picked out for her and complained that it made her look fat." Sari paused and sniffed before continuing.

"She never mentioned anything about a peace event or seeing Syukran. Tuesday morning she sent a text message that she'd had an interesting dream she wanted to share with me, and I was in it. She wrote that she loved me—" Sari's voice broke—"and she was proud of the...woman I was becoming—" another pause—"and that she missed me." The tears came faster now. Iqbal moved closer to her and put his hand comfortingly on her upper arm. Sari dropped her head forward, and her face disappeared behind her hair.

The men sat quietly, waiting for Sari to finish crying. When she looked up, Abdullah met her eyes. Her pain was all his fault.

"Sari, it's because of my sins, and my son's, that your mother died. I'm so very, very sorry. There's no way we could ever pay that debt we owe you. But I do have an offer—"

"No, please, Pak. You don't owe me anything. You saved my mother's life! I'm the one who owes you! It sounds like Mom died knowing what she was doing."

"Nevertheless, my offer stands. I'd be happy to take you as an adopted daughter. I don't want you to feel like you are all alone. We'd love to be your family."

Iqbal seemed surprised at his dad's idea and jumped in with his own counter-offer. "Dad, you don't need to. I don't want Sari as an adopted sister. I want to marry her!" He turned to Sari, "How about it? Will you marry me?"

Sari looked overwhelmed. She just stared back and forth from one to the other. Both hoped for a positive response, but her face showed no emotion.

Finally she said, "You're both wonderfully kind. I need some time to think about it. One thing is for sure: I don't want to accept either of your offers just because I'm a pitied orphan."

She stood up abruptly.

"I promise I'll think about it. I really should go now. Good night."

Sari headed for the door. Iqbal followed to walk her home, but on the doorstep she put her hand gently on his chest.

"Bali, not tonight. I need to be alone."

She gave him just the hint of a smile, then turned and walked home.

Iqbal could tell his dad was exhausted and needed to sleep. He, on the other hand, found all sorts of new thoughts and emotions colliding inside him and needed someone to talk to. Abdullah laid back on the couch while his son paced and talked.

"Dad, I'm sorry I interrupted you. I'm sorry I didn't ask you first about marrying Sari. It just came out! I didn't plan it; it just tumbled out of my mouth before I could think about it.

"But I do want to marry her! I'm sure, so sure, that she's the one for me, Dad. Please, you have to agree!

"Besides, where is she going to go? She can't afford to take care of herself. I can get a job after school and take care of both of us. I know this is right. I can feel it in my heart. Dad, why don't you say something?"

Abdullah's eyes were closed, but he responded clearly, "What if she doesn't want to marry a Muslim?"

"Then I'll become a Christian!" Iqbal answered without thinking. "Whatever it takes; I'll do it."

"Son, I mean what if she wants to marry a *real* Christian, not a Muslim who pretends he's a Christian but knows nothing about it?"

"I can learn. That's not the point. Dad, I can't imagine a single day in my future without Sari in it. If I can't marry her, it'll kill me, Dad!"

"What if she doesn't want you?"

"Dad, don't even say that! I can't imagine that—it would be like that bomb all over again but exploding inside my heart. If she says no, that kind of pain...I don't even want to imagine that. She has to say yes!"

Iqbal paced some more, trying to shake off the shadow of impending doom if Sari said no. Finally he sat down by his father's feet and asked, "Why does love hurt so much?"

Dad's voice was barely audible, like the whisper of a ghost. "I don't know, son. I still don't know how to love."

They sat together in silence for a while. Iqbal was still wide-awake, thinking. He thought his father was asleep and was about to head for bed himself when Abdullah spoke in a hushed tone.

"Son, Pak Darsuni sent me a text message as I got off the plane today. Your mom wrote a message to his wife, asking him to pass it on to us. Mom's gone home to her family in Java. She doesn't want to come back to Banjar ever again."

Iqbal blinked twice and stared at his father, still speaking with his eyes closed.

"Let's give her a little time to mourn the death of her son. Eventually I'll go find her."

"OK, Dad." Iqbal stood to go to bed but figured there'd be no sleep for him tonight. There was too much to think about.

❧ Chapter 93 ❧

HE SUN HAD been up for a while, but still Sari lay in bed staring at the ceiling. It was her fourth day staying home from school, and she promised herself she'd go back tomorrow. She couldn't imagine facing everyone. She didn't want their pity. But she knew her mom would have wanted her to get on with her life, and that meant finishing high school with good enough grades to get a scholarship to a good university.

She also promised herself to reopen the kiosk in front of her house tomorrow. Money was starting to get tight. She'd have to be more careful about spending now. Maybe she could catch a ride to school with Bali and save the cost of fuel for the motorbike.

She had been thinking a lot about Pak Abdullah's offer and Bali's offer. It was awfully kind of Pak Abdullah to offer to take her in, but she already had a home. Maybe it was enough to be able to relate to him like a surrogate father. Besides, living under the same roof with Bali wouldn't be easy if he wanted to date her.

Now, Bali's proposal—she didn't know what to do with that. The battle raged in the pit of her stomach and in her temples just behind her eyes. She knew she had feelings for Bali, but would those feelings lead her down a path that would destroy her life, just like her mother's?

Whenever romantic thoughts knocked, the door was answered by a simple fact—they were different religions. Her mom had taught her to never even think such a thought. Yet Mom had liked Bali. And who else did she have in this world?

She finally stretched and forced herself to get out of bed and get busy. She cleaned the house during the morning, cooked herself some tempeh and rice for lunch, and lay down again for a rest during the heat of the early afternoon. She was just nodding off when she heard a motorbike horn honk outside and a man yell, "Pos!"

Sari ran outside, hoping against hope that her mother had sent her a letter before she died. But her hopes were dashed when she saw another bank envelope addressed to her. *It's probably something about that account my dad set up for Mom.*

She signed for it and took it inside to open it. Inside was a blue bank book and a typed letter from her birth father, Hendri.

Dearest Sari,

It is with tremendous sadness that I write this letter to you, a letter promised years ago yet only now fulfilled in the most tragic of circumstances. I join you in mourning the death of your mother. I regret that I didn't get to see her before she died. Life is full of *if onlys*—another one of mine is, "If only I could have seen you grow up, at least from a distance." This is still my heart's desire.

I've discussed with my wife the idea of having you move in here with us. Our kids are grown now, with only the youngest, a college student, still living at home. But my wife objects, so for now I must do my best to be your long-lost father from a distance. If you don't mind, I'd love to write to you and perhaps have lunch with you if I have business in Banjarmasin. Unfortunately, that is all I can offer you at the present. If you choose to reject it, I'll understand. I'm sure it's not easy to forgive a father who abandoned you. I'm so sorry.

On a happier note, your mother may have told you about the bank account I had established for you when you were born. The interest accumulated in that account has now grown to a tidy sum. I spoke to the bank president about your mother's death, and he agreed that we should transfer the account to your name and issue you a bank book right away. All you need to do is take the book to your Banjarmasin branch and have them witness as you sign your name in it. Then you can withdraw the money as you need.

After the news broke that it was your mother who saved so many lives, including some important dignitaries, I also took the liberty of contacting Pak M. Rizky Ramadani about your situation. He agreed to (1) not harass you with TV cameras, and (2) have his staff at SALAM contact all the survivors of the peace event about making a donation to your account as a thank you to your mother for saving their lives. By the time you receive this I expect some new donations will already be coming in.

I know this money means nothing in comparison to losing your beloved mother, but I hope it will allow you to pursue your dreams.

Please don't hesitate to write or call me if there's anything I can do to help you.

Affectionately your father,

Hendri

She opened the blue book and gasped at the balance typed inside. She slammed the book closed, then opened it again, more slowly, to see if it had been a trick of her mind. The number was the same. This would pay for college, for a wedding, for…for the pursuit of her dreams.

Sari had lots of dreams, but she'd never taken most of them seriously. Maybe it was time she did.

She took her bank book into her bedroom and put it in a drawer where she wouldn't lose it. Then she flopped back on her bed and stared up at the ceiling. Her mind was spinning. Then like a bumblebee landing on a flower it landed on one particular dream.

A golden chariot…a majestic king…asked, "What will you give me?" I emptied out my pockets and found I had nothing to give…He took my hand and pulled me up into the chariot and gave me a hug. We rode off together…Adopted!

It's not Hendri. It's not even Pak Abdullah. It's God. He's going to parent me now. And I can trust Him to take care of all of my needs.

She lay with hands raised and sang a song of praise to God. As she sang, she felt a tiny ray of light break through her dark clouds of sadness. She still had God watching over her.

Death had been beaten once at the church fire, beaten twice on the Sudimampir roof; finally death had succeeded in taking Sari's mother from her.

But strangely enough, Sari felt just as alive without her mother as with her. In fact, Sari was *glad* to be alive. It had been the hardest three months of her life. She'd been knocked down again and again, but she wasn't knocked out. Death had not beaten Sari—she felt more ready than ever to *live*.

280

When Bali found Sari that afternoon, he got straight to the point. "So, have you thought about, you know, marrying me?"

"Yeah, I've been thinking about it. I still have some questions."

"Like what? Tell me!"

"One of them you can't answer. And the other one, you can't answer either."

Iqbal scuffed Sari's porch with his foot, the content of those mysterious questions driving him crazy. He decided to change tactics.

"You know, Pak Darsuni said we should watch out for the press. I was thinking, maybe we should move somewhere else temporarily."

"Where?"

"I don't know. Neither of us has any helpful relatives around. Neither of us has money for a hotel or anything. But maybe someone in your church would take us in."

"I doubt it. The pastor didn't like my mom being friends with Muslims. How do you think they'll feel about me considering marrying one?"

"What if I became a Christian? I'd be happy to do that for you, if it meant you'd marry me."

"Marriage isn't a good reason to leave your religion, Bali, and you know it."

He was stumped. *What will it take to convince this girl?*

But he wasn't about to give up. "Maybe we could elope and move in with some school friends for a week or two till we find our own place." He looked hopefully at her.

"Can I tell you about a dream I had recently?" Sari asked.

"Sure."

She told him the King-beggar dream. As she finished, a tear rolled down her cheek.

"I had that dream the night before my mom left, and I never got to tell her."

He took her hand. Her right hand. "What do you think it means?"

"I think it means God sees my situation, and He's going to adopt me. He's going to be my parent and take care of me."

"Sari, please, I need to know. Are you saying you want to make this journey with just God? You don't want to do it with me?"

"Why do you want to marry me?"

"Because I love you. I can't imagine a single day of my future without you in it. If you say no I'll die. Please say yes!"

"If my mom and your mom were still here and both disagreed with this marriage, would you still want to do it?"

"Yes. Absolutely. If it took us years to convince them I'd still try with all my might. I don't care what the obstacles are: family, finances, religion. All that matters is that we're together."

Sari mulled over Iqbal's responses in her mind, then she grinned at him.

"Maybe it would help me to talk to your dad. Can I come over tonight?"

"Of course! Come now if you like; he's just resting!"

"I'll see you after dinner." Then she paused, "Do you have any food in your house?"

"Don't worry about us! I cook a mean fried rice and egg."

She laughed. "I'll have to try it sometime."

"I'll save you some. Please come over tonight." He stepped off the porch and started to walk away, then turned back.

"And remember that I love you!"

❧ Chapter 94 ❦

THE FRIED RICE wasn't bad. A little too much oil, and it needed some shallots or something more for flavor than just chili paste on the side. But Sari figured Bali was acceptable raw material for a woman to work with.

Pak Abdullah still looked exhausted, as though he needed a month of sleep to catch up before he'd even be functional again. Sari thought, *It's almost as if the life has been sucked right out of him.*

She needed him though. He was about to become the voice in her life that her mom had provided all these years. The voice of the elder's wisdom from experience. The voice of a parent's love.

She tilted her head coquettishly at Bali and batted her eyes.

"You know what I'd like?"

"What?" Bali had already bitten the hook and was being reeled in.

She had to think of something not too expensive and not too close by. "I'd really like some *rambutan.*"

The light dawned on Bali. "You're just trying to get rid of me, aren't you?" Sari smiled innocently. "Well, if it's *rambutan* you want, it's *rambutan* you're gonna get." He grabbed his motorbike keys and took off hunting for the distinctive hairy fruit so prevalent in Borneo.

As soon as they heard the door close behind him, Sari started.

"Bapak, I need to ask you some things. These issues are really, really important to me, and I need you to be brutally honest, even if it hurts me. It's better to know the truth now than to make a huge mistake because I based my decision on a lie, don't you think?"

"What is it, Sari?"

"Tell me the truth. Is Bali doing this because he feels sorry for me or feels guilty about his brother killing my mom, or is it because he really loves me? And if he thinks he loves me, what do *you* think? Does he really love me?"

Abdullah swished the tea in his cup and answered carefully. "Bali is not doing this out of pity or guilt. He's always been somewhat impulsive, so I pushed him last night to try to answer this question for myself. And the conclusion I came to is that I believe he really does care for you.

"Having said that, it takes more than love to make a good marriage. You two have a lot of obstacles to talk through, and I hope Bali doesn't ignore the challenges because he's so caught up in the feeling of being in love. Do you understand what I'm saying?"

"Yes, Pak. Like the challenge of religion. How do you feel personally about the idea of your son marrying a Christian?"

"There was a time in my life when I would have killed my own brother if he'd married a Christian. But I'm not that man anymore.

"When I look at people like your mother, a truly good woman, I long for my son to have a wife like that. So personally, I don't have a problem with it.

"The bigger problem comes in what you would have to face. If one of you leaves your religion, you'll be ostracized by your own community. And if you did it with a selfish motive, you'd be betraying yourself.

"Then there's the problem of raising the kids. It's not easy in a multi-religious home. But if you are committed to working through all the difficulties together... Well, it would take two extraordinary people to succeed."

Sari found that to be a very reasoned answer, along the lines of what she herself was thinking.

"Bali offered to become a Christian if that would help me decide to marry him. I told him that was a bad idea. I want you to know I don't agree with people changing their religion to get a spouse, as though religion were merely a tool to get what you want."

"Good girl! You are wise beyond your years."

"And I definitely don't want to leave my faith! But I know it's almost impossible to get a wedding performed with the bride and groom from different religions, isn't it?"

"Yes, in Banjar it's almost impossible. Maybe in Jakarta with all the celebrities who marry across religion it's more common."

"Well, if we had to choose between a Christian or Muslim wedding ceremony, I'm the one who should yield. I have no family here anyway. But if I did that it would be a statement of my respect for my husband's religion only, not a reflection of the faith in my heart; I want you to understand that. I don't want to deceive you in any way. But honestly, I'm still not sure if it's the right thing to do."

The door opened, and Iqbal returned with a handful of bright red *rambutan*. He sat down at the table and started popping open the thick skin with his thumbs to get the sweet white meat out for his beloved.

"So, what did I miss?"

Sari and Pak Abdullah exchanged a smile. Sari summarized.

"Your dad thinks that you really do love me."

"Duh! I could have told you that!"

Sari laughed. "I know. You did. And I believe it. But..." Her forehead wrinkled, and the corners of her mouth dropped.

Bali's forehead wrinkled too. "But what?"

"I just don't know, Bali. It's not like we could get married now anyway. We still have one semester of high school left. Can we take that time to, you know, be sure this is the right thing to do?"

Bali was obviously disappointed but knew Sari was right. "Sure, we'll take all the time we need." He turned to his father. "Dad, what did you tell Sari while I was gone?"

"I told her marrying across religions is difficult, but if that's your choice I will support you. The important thing is that you two know what you're getting into and are committed to go through it together.

"Why don't you both take time to pray? Allah will lead you on the straight way."

❧ Chapter 95 ❧

BY THE END of the second week the story of the bombing had been broadcast around the world. The most voracious audience, however, was Banjarmasin. The *Banjarmasin Post* ran detailed updates on the front page every day, and every day they sold out before noon. Apparently the Banjar people were far more fascinated with this suicide bombing than any previous bombings since both the bomber and the courageous people who stopped the assassination were from Banjar.

The Monday morning edition of the paper added fresh details taken from interviews with locals who claimed to have seen Saifullah and suspected he was recruiting jihadists, also from an unnamed *pesantren* teacher who had connected for the reporter his missing student Syukran with the *silat* group previously suspected in the Pekauman church arson case, all this leading to the revealing of Kelayan as the likely origins of the tale. The newspaper promised to track down and interview surviving family members in the upcoming issues.

Ibu Aaminah's brow furrowed as she read this news. She had felt utterly incredulous reading about her neighbors Abdullah, Syukran, and Kris the last couple of days, not the least because of Kris's last words to her: *"Maybe someone has to die."* The last thing these poor families needed were reporters hounding them or chatty neighbors gossiping about them to the press. She decided the *arisan* meeting was the best place to address her concerns.

That afternoon at Mama Shafa's house the living room was abuzz with updates, corrections, and speculations when Ibu Aaminah arrived. She decided to break with tradition and discuss this hot issue first, before reading the *Yasin* prayer. She called the meeting to order.

"Assalamu alaikum Warahmatullahi Wabarakatuh."

Everyone answered in unison, *"Wa alaikum assalam."*

"Good afternoon, ladies. I'm confident that the same topic is on all our minds today, the tragic story of our own neighbor, Ibu Siti's son, who was involved in the Bellagio bombing in Jakarta; and the heroic efforts of our own *arisan* member Ibu Kris, who managed to stop an assassination attempt at the cost of her own life. Though the details are still sketchy we can be sure that the people mentioned in the news are indeed our neighbors."

Whispering broke out around the room, a combination of shock and the gossipers' desire for more juicy details.

Ibu Aaminah continued, "Please, everyone. The *B-Post* today mentioned that reporters will be hunting down further information about the surviving family members. I learned already that Ibu Siti has left the neighborhood, most likely to escape the reporters so that she can mourn her son in peace. I'm sure all our hearts go out to her, a mother who has just lost her son, and to Pak Abdullah and Iqbal, and even more to the orphaned Sari, who is now alone in the world. These dear ones are in great pain of loss. They need our support and comfort through these dark days. What they do *not* need are reporters hassling them or neighbors gossiping about them. Therefore, I plead with you, beware of any stranger entering this neighborhood and asking questions, even if they claim not to be a reporter, because journalists are often deceitful and not to be trusted. Do not answer any questions about these two families; don't even point out their houses. I suggest you direct any strangers to speak directly to Pak RT and let our neighborhood chief decide best how to handle them. I've already spoken to Pak RT, and he's willing to deal with the press. Are you all willing to protect the hurting ones in our midst in this way?"

Several ladies nodded. A couple were wiping moist eyes from Ibu Aaminah's comments about a mother losing her son. She felt confident that most would honor her request.

"Ibu Kris was a member of our *arisan* for only a few weeks. When I first invited her, I remember that some of you were unsure whether it was a good idea—after all, she was not from the same religion as the rest of us. But the fact is, one of Indonesia's most popular Muslim leaders, M. Rizky Ramadani, is still alive and running for president today because this Christian woman gave her life to save his.

"I'd like to remind us all to look beyond the surface of people to see the treasure inside their hearts. When I teach at the street kids' school, I have to remind myself of this every day. The kids are dirty, stinky, and don't look smart on the outside. But what treasures they are on the inside! They have the potential to change their lives and the lives of many around them. So do we all.

"Ibu Kris was just a mother and homemaker, like many of us here. But there was the potential for greatness inside her. This potential also exists inside you. When the opportunity presents itself to you, do not shrink back to do something great."

The women sat still and silent, as though shifting their sitting positions could destroy the mood. Ibu Aaminah reached for a *Yasin* booklet and held it up.

"Today as we read the *Yasin*, a prayer we commonly recite for our own dead family members, let us recite it for Ibu Kris, that her soul would be received by a merciful God."

The women's heads were mostly bowed with the solemnity of the moment. Ibu Aaminah was touched that many of those who had opposed Kris's involvement in the *arisan* at the beginning were now nodding their heads, ready to pray for her soul. *Even we old ones can change*, she thought. And how does it happen? She couldn't shake Kris's words from her mind: *Someone has to die. Someone has to die.*

"Before Ibu Hajjah leads us in the *Yasin*, let me remind you all to talk to your children and grandchildren about these things so we never have to lose another one of our children like we lost Syukran. I'd like to read a quote from one of my favorite poems of Goenawan Mohamad."

She reached in her purse and pulled out a white three-by-five card and read:

> *Tomorrow one of us may betray us and plan Doomsday*
> *once more...*
> *But we still have our children, generations of thousands...*
> *Therefore let us speak...*
> *Before it is too late.*

❧ Chapter 96 ❧

A CLASS LEADERS' MEETING kept Sari late at school that afternoon, but she didn't mind. She still wasn't used to going home to an empty house, though she was trying to make the best of it. She kept telling herself, "This is real," and, "Life from now on is whatever I make of it."

Sari's classmates had warned her about the *B-Post*'s promise to find her. The last thing she wanted to go home and deal with were nosy reporters poking into her life or front-page photos titled "Pity the Poor Orphan Girl." She decided to change clothes and head over to Pak Abdullah's to ask for his advice about what to do.

When she opened her front door she nearly stepped on a white, square envelope. *Someone must have slipped it under my door. If it's from a reporter it's going straight to the trash!*

She took it to her bedroom, sat on her bed, and ripped it open. It was a sympathy card! She opened it and saw Pastor David's signature and the signatures of her few church youth group friends. *How sweet!*

Sari smiled and began reading Pastor David's atrocious handwriting.

Dear Sari,

All of us here join you in mourning your mother's death. In spite of Pastor Susanna's unfortunate outbursts, many of us love you and are still here for you. If there's anything you need, you just let me know.

From the news it sounds like your mother did not die in vain. It is my fervent prayer that I and the youth under my care die such noble deaths, deaths like a seed that falls into the ground and brings forth new life.

I found a verse from the Bible that I hope will encourage you. Keep trusting in what you cannot see.

Love from all the youth group,

289

Pastor David

The Messiah….tore down the wall we used to keep each other at a distance…. Then he started over. Instead of continuing with two groups of people separated by centuries of animosity and suspicion, he created a new kind of human being, a fresh start for everybody. Christ brought us together through his death on the Cross. The Cross got us to embrace, and that was the end of the hostility. Christ came and preached peace.

—EPHESIANS 2:14–17

Sari read the verse over three times. *What a curious verse to choose!* She had expected maybe a comforting verse about heaven or something. *God, are you trying to speak to me? Maybe about me and Bali?*

She puzzled over the verse as she changed clothes. It was nearly six when she went to the fridge looking for some dinner. She decided to eat the breakfast leftovers of fried rice. At first she dug her spoon into the cold rice in the container and took a bite. Then she chided herself for not embracing *life* and took it to the kitchen to warm up on the kerosene burner. It tasted much better hot, and she finished it all, washing it down with a glass of iced tea. Six twenty. She'd have to wait till after *Mahgrib* prayers to go over to Bali's house.

She moved to the living room to work on her homework and was just opening her calculus book when she heard the knock on her door. *Who would come at* Mahgrib? *What if it's a reporter! Maybe I should pretend I'm not home.*

She didn't answer the door right away but moved to the curtain and tried to peek outside at the visitor. Kicking herself for forgetting to turn on the porch light, she realized with frustration that she couldn't tell who was there. The knock came again. Sari felt panic rising up inside her. *What if it's the person who painted the threat on my door?* She started praying and realized her hands were trembling.

"Sari, I know you're in there. Open up! It's me, Nina!"

Relief flooded over Sari, and she jerked the door open, pulled Nina inside, and embraced her.

"What's up with you?" Nina asked. She was wearing jeans and a T-shirt, Sari noticed. *A good sign.*

"Sorry, Nina. I was just scared that you might be someone else, and when I saw it was you I felt so relieved!"

"Who did you think it was?"

"Maybe a reporter, or...a stranger."

"That does it! Pak Abdullah was right. You're coming to my house tonight."

"You talked to Pak Abdullah?"

"Actually, he was waiting outside his house when Mom came home tonight and suggested you might need to sleep somewhere else for a few days to avoid the reporters. He said he'd love to take you in, but since you and Bali are, you know, it probably wasn't a good idea. Mom promised him she'd call me. So she did, and here I am."

"But don't you, uh, have to work tonight?"

"I can take a night off for my best friend, can't I?" Nina smiled and hugged Sari. Sari felt all her fear melt away. She breathed a prayer. *Thank you, God!*

Books in her backpack. A change of clothes and a toothbrush. She was on her way to a safe night at Nina's.

Several hours later the girls were side by side on wicker mats on the hard wooden living room floor. Sari knew that Nina usually slept in the only bedroom with her mom and sister, but there wasn't room for four on the floor in the tiny room, so the two older girls took the living room. There was no furniture to move out of the way anyway. Nina's house was tiny, simple, and convenient for sleepovers.

But one of them wasn't sleepy. Maybe it was the new life-rhythm Nina followed now; she was wide-awake at midnight and talking Sari's ear off. A couple times Sari started to doze off but caught herself. She knew this was a precious chance to hear her friend's heart. So she kept pinching herself to stay awake.

"So, I heard Bali proposed to you. Did you say yes?"

Sari's jaw dropped. *How could Nina possibly know?*

"Where did you hear that?"

"Everybody's talking about it! So what did you decide? Is it a yes or a no?"

Sari smiled sadly. "I'm not sure."

"What's not to be sure about? I think you guys are absolutely perfect for each other!"

"Thanks. I'm just not sure if it's right to marry someone from a different religion."

"Oh, yeah." Nina's face dropped. "I guess one of you has to change religions."

"I don't think that's a good solution. If we did, it wouldn't be real; just for show. And if we're going to marry, we should marry as our real selves. Don't you think that's better?"

"I guess so. But I'd change religions in a heartbeat to marry a guy like Bali."

"Nina, don't say that!"

"I'm sorry, I know he's yours, I didn't mean..."

"No, I mean, don't say you'd throw away your religion so cheaply."

"My religion? What religion? I haven't done *sholat* since kindergarten. I don't even remember the words anymore. I'm a prostitute. What religion would take someone like me?"

"I know God still loves you, Nina. Jesus loved everyone, including prostitutes. Isn't Jesus one of your Muslim prophets, too?"

"Maybe," Nina shrugged, her face wrinkling up in discomfort. Then she said quietly, "I don't know how Allah could love me when I can't even love me. I hate myself." She wiped her hand over her face. "Sari, I hate my job. I hate my life. You remember that night we found you on the Sudimampir roof? If we hadn't made it there in time to see that wind save you from falling, I might have jumped right after you."

Sari didn't want to probe too much but knew this might be her only chance. She spoke gently. "I thought you said you liked how men look at you now."

"Yeah, for a while I did. I still like how they look at me on the street or in the nightclub. But once we get into the hotel room it's different. I don't like it anymore. They treat me like raw meat. They rip my expensive clothes like a plastic meat wrapping. Then they sink their teeth, and other things, into my flesh like they're starving animals. And when they're done they throw the rest of me—my heart, my soul—into the garbage.

"At the end of the night I pull myself out of the garbage; check my body for cuts and bruises; tell my mind, heart, and soul to shut up and go buy a new outfit; and take two sleeping pills. If I don't fall asleep within thirty minutes, I'm afraid of what I might do.

"Then I wake up at 3:00 p.m., and by the time I've showered and eaten and shopped, I feel under control again. The guys at the mall are really nice to me. I see all these other women walking on the arms of their lovers. And I tell myself, 'One day the right guy will come along. I better look my best, or he'll pass me over for someone else.' Back to the nightclub I go.

"But on the days when I can't shut my brain down, I have doubts. Voices whisper to me. Voices like, '*What if my clothes and body are really all I have to offer? What if being a prostitute is the only job fit for me because I could never be a good wife? What if it's too late—that no decent man would ever take me now?*'"

Nina pulled her sarong up under her chin, then lowered her head as though talking into it. "And then I want to kill myself."

Sari didn't quite know what to say. She held out her hand and felt around the mat next to her for Nina's, then found it and held it. They were quiet for a long time.

Finally Sari spoke. "Do you know what I see in you?"

"What?" It sounded more like a statement than a question.

"I see a girl who has sacrificed all her life to love others. Remember that time we got in trouble for cheating in Pak Tatang's class and you tried to take all the blame and get me off the hook? And all the times you cleaned the house and cooked so your mom could look for work? Also how you helped her look for alms even though you hated it? And all the neighbors you've washed dishes for at their weddings or other events? I don't think any husband could ask for more than a wife who makes sacrifices to love him. I think you'll be a great catch for some lucky man, because you *do* know how to love. I think you'll be a great wife and a great mom. You certainly make a great friend!"

"I don't know…" Nina started to reject Sari's words, but maybe she didn't completely want to. She squeezed Sari's hand. "I'm glad you're my friend, Sari."

"So am I. I might be dead today if it wasn't for you."

"And I might be dead tomorrow if it wasn't for you."

❧ Chapter 97 ❧

STORM CLOUDS WERE building in the afternoon sky when the *Al-Mustaqiim Pesantren* finished their MTQ Qur'anic recitation preparation. Hafiz had barely missed being the South Banjar representative last year and in spite of lost practice time from rebuilding the church was determined to be the *qari* for the under-twenty-one age group in Til-awah Qur'an. Kiki, who preferred not to recite things out loud, was practicing his calligraphy to enter the Khatil Qur'an competition. Juki and Udin were still working on Tahfizh Qur'an, which only recited shorter sections of the Holy Book. The boys were all enthusiastic students. Yet the excitement of *jihad* still called out to them.

As they exited Pak Ustad's classroom, the first drops of rain were beginning to fall. Hafiz watched Kiki run for his bicycle, more of a vigorous waddle than a run, really, and head straight home. Kiki's parents had told him that once the church rebuilding was done he wasn't allowed to hang out with his gang anymore. Fani's parents didn't care who he hung out with, but after watching his older idols doing manual labor at the church day after day, Hafiz knew Fani had decided to ditch them for some guys his own age who liked to play street soccer and tear the legs off of frogs. The gang was now half its previous size. Hafiz, Juki, and Udin took their bikes over to a nearby *warung* and ordered some hot tea, sitting on a bench under a tarpaulin roof to wait for the rain to pass.

All of them had read the articles about the bombing in the *B-Post* every single day. Today's article had guessed that the Kris who had stopped the assassination attempt may have been the very same woman burned in a church fire in Pekauman, a fire for which the police had never found the culprit or culprits. Kris had been on the boys' minds all day during school. They needed to talk.

"Guys, I keep thinking about our brother, Syukran," Hafiz started.

"Yeah, what?"

"He gets sent on this great mission, right? He's going to teach Uncle Sam a lesson, that's what he told me. But then what happens? He doesn't teach anybody squat! All he does is blow up a couple unimportant people and disrupt shopping at the mall. And you know why nobody's learning their lesson from this? Because of that meddling *kafir* pig, Kris! She screwed up everything for our brother."

"What are you saying, 'Fiz?"

"I'll tell you what I'm saying. I'm saying she knew about the bombing. I don't know how she knew, but she knew. She was there at the right moment to stop it. Think about it. Why would she do that?"

"I don't get it."

Apparently Hafiz would have to lay it out plain and simple for Juki. "I'll tell you why. Revenge. We burn down her church and hurt her. What does she do? She follows Syukran around and figures out what he wants to do and then messes it all up. She was getting him back! Our boy could have been the most hated name in America, and she steals all his glory!"

"You really think so? She did it for revenge?" Juki didn't sound convinced.

"Yeah," Udin chimed in. "I see it. She probably hid outside the room where the American was. Then when Syukran came along, she tackled him, laughed at him, and set off the bomb herself."

"What a perfect revenge! Syukran dies unable to fulfill his destiny or hurt her for what she did." Hafiz felt a bitter taste creep into his mouth and tried to drown it with another drink of the sweet, hot tea. "And we can't even get her back for our brother. She's dead."

"I guess there's nothing we can do to avenge him then," Udin decided.

They were quiet for a minute. The rain continued to pitter-patter on the *warung*'s tarpaulin roof. In spite of an increasingly darkening sky, slowly the light dawned.

"Doesn't she have a daughter?"

Once again silence prevailed as each allowed his pain of losing Syukran and the frustration of thwarted goals to mix with his hatred for Kris and Christians in general. Finally, Hafiz spoke.

"It's been just over two weeks. We'll honor our brother Syukran's death with mourning for forty days. After that we'll make our plans and watch for the perfect moment. Kris's daughter will pay."

❧ Chapter 98 ❧

AFTER DEALING WITH reporters trying to force open his locked door and trying to take photos through the windows, Abdullah packed a bag and moved in with Pak Ustad Hasan Amman for a few days. He asked Iqbal to also move into a classmate's home. Abdullah heard that Sari had been sleeping at Ibu Dina's, and he knew Iqbal was checking on her daily.

At his own home Abdullah had stopped reading the newspaper or watching TV. Every description, every photo or TV image, brought flashbacks of him standing there helplessly, watching his son blow himself and Kris into the hereafter, and he couldn't stop it. He wondered how long it would be before he could be free from those memories. Judging by his memories of Afghanistan that still haunted his dreams, it could be a very, very long time.

But Pak Ustad's wife kept the TV on practically twenty-four hours a day. Thus it happened that Abdullah came face-to-face with his son for one last time.

Pak Ustad called him to the living room.

"Pak Abdullah! Come in here! The news says they're going to show a video made by the bomber before the bombing. It could be your son! Come here!"

Abdullah left the dining room table where he'd been trying to finish his *Three Cups of Tea* book and wandered toward the living room. He felt an oppressive dread settle over his shoulders like an iron cape. Pak Ustad was sitting on the couch. Abdullah chose to stand behind him, hands on the couch's back, where no one would see the reaction on his face.

The reporter began: "Behind me to my left is the 'safe house' discovered by the police on Monday. They arrested a man named Amin, a.k.a. Purwanto, and his wife for harboring terrorists. Police believe this may be the last stopping place of Syukran before he bombed the Bellagio Mall. Earlier today they released a copy of this video that they found inside the house. Although other parts of the video are classified until the investigation has been completed, we have been given permission from the police to show you just a short clip."

The video showed a young man sitting on a white plastic chair with a bare wall behind him. The young man was wearing a white formal Muslim shirt with Arabic writing down along the front buttons and a white skullcap on his head. Abdullah knew without a doubt it was his son Syukran. The boy seemed antsy, eager to get something off his chest. He rocked back and forth as he talked to the camera intensely.

"My father was a *mujahidin* in Afghanistan. He killed many Americans. He fought valiantly for the cause of our beloved Islam.

"But when he came home, something happened to him. He became depressed. He started drinking alcohol. When I was a young child, sometimes he wouldn't talk to me for days. He never played with me. It was almost like he left his heart in Afghanistan. From my dad I learned that once you've had a taste of the glory of *jihad* ordinary life becomes meaningless.

"My mom tried to comfort me. She told me that my dad was a hero and someday I'd be just like him. And here I am. I'm just like my dad. Except my dad's heart died the day he left the *mujahidin* and tried to live an ordinary life. I won't make that mistake. I'm not coming home. I want to *mati syahid*, to die as a martyr.

"Maybe somehow by seeing the way that I die, my father can find the courage to live again."

Abdullah swallowed to release the tightening in his throat.

Syukran continued rocking back and forth as he spoke to the camera. "I hope my family will be proud of me, but more importantly I hope my sacrifice draws the attention of Allah to our noble cause to rid the world of those evil influences that lead our *umat* astray. May Allah bless me to strike my blow deep into the heart of evil. And when I pass on to my reward, may many others rise up to take my place.

"*Allahu Akbar! Al-jihad sabiluna! Isy kariman au mut syahidan!*"

As Syukran raised his fist over his head, Abdullah turned away, then silently slipped out to his guest bedroom, where he eased the door closed and slumped onto the bed.

How did I fail my son so miserably? Have I really been dead since Afghan? Do I really have to see my own son die in order to gain the courage I need to live?

Abdullah had no more tears to cry. He'd cried enough. He'd seen enough. Syukran was right. It was time for him to start living again.

He lay back on his bed, hands crossed on his chest. Tonight would be his last night of mourning. When he woke up tomorrow, he was going to do something new, but what? Something that made him feel alive.

Before he fell asleep he whispered a heart-prayer: *Ya Allah, I've had enough nightmares for one life. Please, have mercy on me, and give me a new dream, a dream about living.*

And Allah answered. That night in Pak Ustad's home Abdullah had a dream that changed the entire direction of his life.

❧ Epilogue ☙

"IT'S SO PEACEFUL tonight. I wish every night were like this." Sari lay on her back next to Bali on the Sudimampir roof looking up at the stars. A soft breeze off the river wafted over her, giving her skin goose bumps.

Bali was quiet, so Sari continued. "You know, it's been exactly one month since I lost my mom. Some mornings I still wake up expecting to find her in the kitchen making breakfast."

"My house feels strange, too, without Mom and Syuk. And at the end of the school year I'll be losing Dad."

"You mean he took the job with Pak Ramadani?"

"Yeah, he just told me last night he'd accepted it. 'Religious Reconciliation Crisis Team'—sure beats that boring old *pesantren*. But he said he'll wait till I graduate before moving to Jakarta. Though I'm not sure if he's more worried about taking care of me or taking care of you!"

"So far I'm doing fine on my own," Sari answered. Sari still hadn't told Bali about the bank account. That was a secret she'd save for her wedding night, if it ever came. "After all we've been through, surely the worst is past."

"I hope so, for your sake. But if anything bad were to happen to you, Dad says he would feel responsible." Bali paused, then added hopefully, "At least until your wedding day."

Sari took Bali's hand and rolled on her elbow to face him. "You know I care about you, Bali. But can we really get married?" She sighed. "My mom used to tell me about how Muslims and Christians both come from the same family of Abraham. Maybe we're destined to be brother and sister."

Bali's shoulders hunched, and he shook his hair like he were flinging such a thought out of his mind. Sari looked sadly into his eyes.

"I'm sorry. I don't know what to do. I wish Mom were here. Maybe she'd have a dream to guide me."

"Maybe it's time you were guided by your own dreams."

They both lay quietly brooding. The sound of a *klotok* rumbled softly by from the river below. Something Bali said was stirring Sari's subconscious. Finally a deep memory resurfaced. *Now it made so much more sense.*

"Bali, did I ever tell you about a dream I had when I was twelve? About dancing?"

"No, tell me."

"I had just started learning worship dance at the church. One night I dreamed I was dancing in a big, empty ballroom with my Christian friends, and then I saw on the other side of the room a line of Banjar girls wearing their traditional *batik* clothes and head coverings, doing a traditional Banjar dance. First we would dance, then stop, and they would dance, then stop. We took turns like this a couple times. But in the dream something came over me, and I danced away from my group and started dancing a weaving line between the Banjar girls. When I came to the last one I took her hand and led her to the middle of the floor, and we danced our own dances but did it together. The others just watched at first, but eventually they all came and joined us in the middle. It was then that I noticed the skylight above us. The sun was shining so brightly on that circle in the middle of the floor where we were dancing. I looked back to where we had been, and from where I stood now it looked much darker than I remembered it. I looked back up into the light, and I felt the pleasure of God wash over me. You know, even now, whenever I dance, I often close my eyes for a moment and remember that feeling of God's pleasure. It helps me to forget everything around me and just dance for Him.

"I've never told anyone this dream except my mom. It's a very sacred thing to me, because I think it speaks to my identity and my future. I don't exactly understand how it's going to work out yet, but I want to give it to you as a trust. Whether we marry or not, will you help me fulfill my dreams?"

Bali stared at her for several seconds. When he finally smiled, it was unlike any smile Sari had ever seen. No bravado, no insecure searching for her approval. This smile looked... Well, she couldn't put her finger on it. Maybe something like *forever.*

"Your dreams are now my dreams, Sari, whatever happens."

At that moment, Sari felt that her days of dancing in the darkness were past, and she was dancing into a brand-new, marvelous light.

About the Author

Jim Baton lives in the world's largest Muslim nation, building bridges between Muslims and Christians who both desire peace.

Contact the Author

www.jimbaton.com